A LIGHT IN ZION

Books by Brock and Bodie Thoene

THE ZION COVENANT

Vienna Prelude
Prague Counterpoint
Munich Signature
Jerusalem Interlude
Danzig Passage
Warsaw Requiem

THE ZION CHRONICLES

The Gates of Zion
A Daughter of Zion
The Return to Zion
A Light in Zion
The Key to Zion

THE SHILOH LEGACY

In My Father's House
A Thousand Shall Fall
Say to This Mountain

SAGA OF THE SIERRAS

The Man From Shadow Ridge
Riders of the Silver Rim
Gold Rush Prodigal
Sequoia Scout
Cannons of the Comstock
The Year of the Grizzly
Shooting Star

NON-FICTION

Writer to Writer

THE ZION CHRONICLES/BOOK FOUR

BODIE THOENE

A LIGHT IN ZION

BETHANY HOUSE PUBLISHERS
MINNEAPOLIS, MINNESOTA 55438

A Light in Zion
Copyright © 1988
Bodie Thoene

With the exception of recognized historical figures, the
characters in this novel are fictional and any resemblance
to actual persons, living or dead, is purely coincidental.

Cover illustration by Dan Thornberg,
Bethany House Publishers staff artist.

Published by Bethany House Publishers
A Ministry of Bethany Fellowship International
11300 Hampshire Avenue South
Minneapolis, Minnesota 55438

Printed in the United States of America by
Bethany Press International
Minneapolis, Minnesota 55438

Library of Congress Cataloging-in-Publication Data

Thoene, Bodie, 1951–
    A light in Zion / Bodie Thoene.
        p. cm. — (The Zion chronicles ; bk. 4)
    Sequel to: The return to Zion.

    1. Israel—History—1948–1949—Fiction.
I. Title. II. Series: Thoene, Bodie, 1951–   Zion
chronicles ; bk. 4.
PS3570.H46L5   1988
813'.54—dc19   88–4578
ISBN 0-87123-990-6 (pbk.)   CIP
ISBN 0-7642-2110-8 (mass market)

For my only
Only One . . .

For Zion's sake I will not keep silent,
for Jerusalem's sake I will not remain quiet,
till her righteousness shines out like the dawn,
her salvation like a blazing torch.

—Isaiah 62:1

BODIE THOENE (Tay-nee) began her writing career as a teen journalist for her local newspaper. Eventually her byline appeared in prestigous periodicals such as *U.S. News and World Report*, *The American West*, and *The Saturday Evening Post*. After leaving an established career as a writer and researcher for John Wayne, she began work on her first historical fiction series, THE ZION CHRONICLES. From the beginning her husband, BROCK, has been deeply involved in the development of each book. His degrees in history and education have added a vital dimension to the accuracy, authenticity, and plot structure of the Zion books. The Thoenes' unusual but very effective writing collaboration has also produced three other major historical fiction series with Bethany House Publishers.

Acknowledgment

This acknowledgment is long overdue, since without Chuck Roberson THE ZION CHRONICLES would not be. As Hollywood's finest stunt man and Second Unit Director, Chuck took this budding young writer under his wing and shared his life and experience with me. What I know about writing action scenes I learned from him. I cannot count the doors he opened for me. I cannot measure the depth of love and respect I have for my dear amigo. God has always loved Chuck's big heart. It is one of the joys of my life that I am privileged to know him and call him friend.

> "You can count 'em all on one hand—
> count me in . . ."

Contents

Prologue

Nathan pulled his new cloak tightly around his shoulders to guard against the frigid wind that had blown in from the sea. The fabric flapped loosely on his gangly frame as he sat alone on the rocky outcropping that overlooked the gorge. He imagined that he looked like a vulture gazing down on the scene unfolding on the narrow, twisted ribbon of road below him.

He was only fifteen years old—not yet a man, but all the responsibilities of manhood had been thrust upon him as he cared for the tiny flock of sheep alone. For days, Nathan and his father had grazed the flock on the new grass of this mountain slope while a tide of Jewish pilgrims surged through the pass toward Jerusalem and the feast of Passover. Nathan's father had estimated that more than a million people had entered the gates of the Holy City in the last week alone. And when the human flood had diminished to a trickle, the sheep had been divided and the yearling lambs driven into the city to be sold for the feast. For two days and nights, Nathan had kept a solitary vigil, tending the ewes that remained. His family had gone up to the Holy City where they, too, would celebrate the feast.

The Psalms of the Great Hallel had been sung tonight; the meal of remembrance had been eaten. Yet Nathan had remembered God's mighty deeds in hungry solitude beneath the stars. As the firstborn of the family, tradition dictated that he could not partake of the first meal of Passover. He had spent the night fasting and praying out of respect for the firstborn of Egypt who had fallen on the very first Passover so long before.

Behind him, a ewe stirred inside the stone walls of the sheepfold. She bleated forlornly, grieving for her missing lamb. Nathan shuddered, then looked eastward to where the full moon rose slowly behind the white towers of Jerusalem. The city glistened in the light like a snow-capped peak. *The gates are shut. The feast is over, and my family sleeps. They do not know what morning will bring.*

Across the deep gorge, the peak of Nebi Samuel glowed with silver iridescence. On that very mountain, Nathan knew, the ancient prophet Samuel had sat in judgment upon the nation of Israel. *Had the eyes of Samuel looked out across the ages and seen this night among his visions?*

Above Nathan, countless stars shone, a reminder of God's promise to Abraham that his people would be as many as the stars in the heavens and the sands on the seashore. Abraham had believed, and tonight nearly two million of his descendants celebrated Passover behind the locked gates of Jerusalem. They had gathered in one place from the far corners of the world, packed together like fish in a net. Below him, Nathan watched, horrified. He could see the net being drawn in; a terrible roar like the sea itself moved up the gorge to encircle the Holy City. An endless line of Roman torches flickered on the road, illuminating the pass. The tramp of the soldiers was a brutal echo that assaulted the hills and shattered the mystical silence of the most holy night of the year. And Nathan was helpless. He could not run ahead to warn the people in the city. The pass was blocked. He could not run away to the sea, for Roman torches stretched unrelenting, far to the west. In the morning, Nathan's father and mother and little brothers and sister would wake to the sound of the shofar blowing its message of freedom. But when they opened their eyes, they would see that, in fact, they were trapped, pressed in on all sides by a wall of Roman flesh and Roman swords and Roman rage. Then they would die. Of that Nathan was certain—as certain as old Samuel had been when he sat upon his mountain and cried out against the sins of Israel. Tonight, it was easy for Nathan to prophesy.

Nathan tore his eyes away from the spectacle below him, and gazed upward into the heavens. The stars grew fainter and fainter as the glare of the moon overpowered them. "Shall we be as the stars?" Nathan said aloud, startled by the sound of his own voice competing with the tramp of the Legions of Titus. "Do you remember, O Eternal One, what you have promised? Are we not to be as numerous as the lights in the heavens?"

The moon rose higher, obscuring all but a few of the more brilliant stars. All the others, it seemed to Nathan, had fallen flaming into the gorge below, impaled upon the points of the Roman lances.

Strangely numb with resignation at what was certain to come upon Jerusalem, Nathan was not surprised or afraid for himself. His father had repeated the prophecies of the one called Yeshua from the time Nathan was a small boy. *I was only a child myself,* his father had said, *but I remember it as clearly as yesterday. Our Lord Yeshua raised His eyes—such sad eyes—to the great buildings of the Temple and said that not one stone would be left upon another. Imagine, Nathan! To think that something so beautiful will one day be torn to the ground! And then He said that when we saw the armies come and surround the Holy City, we should run quickly to the hills and hide! We must not even go back for a coat, eh? But we must not be afraid, Nathan, though the foundations of the earth itself be shaken. For when all is finished, our Messiah himself will return and rebuild this Holy City in true righteousness, and even the wolf will sleep beside our lambs.*

Nathan touched the fringe of his cloak; he remembered his mother's eyes when she had presented it to him only two days before. Although he was unable to share in their Seder meal, she had wanted him to have something special to wear for his lonely watch. The thought of her gentle face brought a lump to his throat. If his family was to die, he wished only that he might die with them.

He stood slowly and brushed away the dirt from his cloak. Turning toward the east, he noted the first distant campfires of the Legions as they encircled the city.

"And so the day Yeshua spoke of has finally come," he said. "If it is to be as he said, we are to be slaughtered like lambs and the Great Temple destroyed. Then it must also be true that He will return someday and bring us home to a nation once again." He raised his voice to heaven. "I believe this, O God! You will not forget this place! Though your Temple lies in the dust, you will not forget!"

With the fierceness of a warrior, Nathan unsheathed his knife and turned his back on the Roman horde below him. Carefully, he picked his way over the rock-ribbed slope to an outcropping of limestone where he had often found shelter with his father against the rain. The glow of the moon seeped into the shelter and illuminated the smooth walls as Nathan began to chip away at the stone with the blade of his knife.

Though the Temple lie in the dust and our bones as well: though the sacred light of the menorah be put out and the light of our lives extinguished, you will remember your people. The world will see our light once again and know that once and forever this is your people and your nation and your light.

As a small column of Roman torches broke from the main body of troops to wind upward toward Nathan's cold and desolate camp, the boy hacked at the soft stone, carving a message that would stand, though the stars were falling into the sea . . .

PART 1

The Thunderbolt
The Eve of Passover, 1948

"They thought that the thunderbolt
dwelt in the sky,
But their thunderbolt struck
from the ground. . ."

Ibn al Khatib

1   David's Return

David slept fitfully on a sagging twin bed while Ellie dozed in a small rocking chair taken from the parlor of the Red House on the beach. Great ocean swells slammed against the sea wall of Tel Aviv. Like distant artillery, the sound of the waves was a prologue to the battle that would soon rage in the hills.

The room was dark, but a thin ribbon of light shone beneath the door, and harried voices floated up the stairway. On the events of this night, the fate of all of Jewish Jerusalem hinged. Perhaps the fate of a Jewish nation. Yet, for all that, Ellie could hear only the sound of David's ragged breath, his sleep interrupted by restless dreams. To her it was the sweetest sound on earth; he was *alive*! That blessed relief was the only fact her heart could hear tonight.

"Michael!" David cried out. He was dreaming—a nightmare Ellie could only imagine. *Flaming engines and twisted metal. The blood of Michael in a congealed pool at his feet. The woman. Montgomery.* Ellie shuddered once and squeezed her eyes tight against the memory of the woman's limp and bloody body being lowered from the plane onto the damp ground just two hours ago. The faceless rag doll bore no resemblance to the friend Ellie remembered from school. *Angela St. Martain.* They said she was a servant of the Mufti. That she was responsible for the death of Michael and others as well; that the plane lay in pieces because of her. *But David is alive! Oh, God, thank you! Take care of him, Lord. Help him forget.*

Voices from the room below drifted up. A telephone rang, and footsteps rushed across the floor. Ellie could not make out the words, but in the tone, she heard worry, excitement and urgency. The battle David had fought against time and the weather and the vile woman who worked for the cause of the Jihad was over. Smuggled guns in the hands of the Haganah defenders would now decide the fate of Jerusalem and her Jewish inhabitants.

Ellie heard the voice of Ben-Gurion booming over the others. "Moshe Sachar will be stranded up there if they don't do their job in Ramle!"

The old man sounded furious, and Ellie guessed that things were not going well for the men who fought to open the road to Jerusalem.

David moaned, then sighed softly. "Hassida!" His voice was a hoarse whisper. "Mama, this is Hassida . . ."

"David?" Ellie stroked his forehead. "David, darling. You're safe. This is Ellie, hon."

"Ellie?" he asked in a sleepy voice.

"Uh-huh. You're dreaming, David. Go back to sleep," she soothed like a mother comforting a child.

He sighed again and squeezed her hand, murmuring her name through a thick fog of exhaustion.

Only David would sleep through this night. Luke Thomas was somewhere in the rocky fields outside of Ramle, preparing to fight a pitched battle against the Jihad Moquades. If he could draw them away from the tiny village of Kastel long enough, Moshe could sneak in and capture this strategic position. And Ehud, no doubt, prowled among the campfires of three hundred Jewish truck drivers who were to drive the food convoy up the Arab-held pass of Bab el Wad to a starving Jewish Jerusalem. Tonight marked a crisis point: either a turning of the tide of hopes for a Jewish nation, or premature death for the embryo state.

"Michael!" David cried. "Scarecrow!" In the depths of his dreams, David lived again the death of his friend.

"Oh, David!" Ellie whispered, her own voice etched with grief. "You're safe. It's Ellie, David. I'm right here."

He clung fiercely to her hand. "Was I on time?" he asked.

"Yes. You were on time. You were wonderful." She did not know if he was asleep or awake, but her words seemed to satisfy him and he relaxed and murmured her name gently.

"Ellie."

For ten minutes, Ellie stayed beside him, listening to the frantic activity downstairs. She was exhausted herself, yet unable to sleep. She still had on the khaki slacks and shirt that she had worn through the day and into this terrible night as she waited for David's plane and prayed he would make it back alive. The cuffs of her sleeves were damp from the bath water; an hour

earlier she and Ehud had bathed a filthy and nearly unconscious David. His clothes and boots were splattered with blood;
Ehud had carried them downstairs to burn in the incinerator.
Fresh clothing had been gathered from several men who now
worked at the Tel Aviv headquarters of the Jewish Agency. Ben-
Gurion himself had rounded up a heavy, hand-knit wool sweater
and tiptoed to David's side to lay it on the foot of the cot.

David was quiet now, and Ellie rose stiffly, aware that her
cramped muscles craved a warm bath. Hesitant to leave him,
she stood over him for another minute until she was certain he
would not wake or call out to her.

Closing the door to the bathroom behind her, she switched
on the light and was sickened by the murky water still in the
white porcelain tub. It was a reddish-brown color, the shade of
diluted blood. Closing her eyes for a moment, Ellie reached
down and pulled the plug, breathing a sigh of relief as the water
gurgled away. Visions of the canvas tarp over Michael's body
returned. What nightmare had David lived through? How many
more bad dreams would become reality before this was all finished?

Wearily she scrubbed the tub, then turned the tap on. She
sat back on her heels and watched as steaming hot water
gushed from the faucet; steam rose around her to fog the mirror
and cling to the pale green walls of the bathroom. Slowly she
undressed, letting her clothes fall to the slick tiled floor. She was
chilled, and the steam warmed her. Her head ached, and as she
sank down into the water, she let her head fall back, soaking
her long curly hair.

"Relax," she muttered to herself, her voice drowned out by
the stream of water. "You were almost a widow before you had
a chance to be a wife." She closed her eyes and felt the hot
liquid lap at her chin. "Forget what's happening out there. Forget the war. You deserve a little vacation. After all, your honeymoon was wrecked by a terrorist bomb, and your husband
almost murdered."

The tense muscles in her shoulders began to loosen, and
Ellie slid deeper into the tub. She opened one eye and reached
her foot out to turn the faucet off with her toes. For now, she
decided, she would not think about Luke fighting in Ramle, or
Moshe in Kastel. She would not imagine the hungry faces of
Rachel, Uncle Howard, Yacov, and Grandfather as they waited

and prayed for Ehud's food convoy to struggle through the pass to Jerusalem. At this moment she would try to forget everything except the fact that her husband was alive and near enough to touch. He might be dead to the world, but he would open his eyes sooner or later. Just for now, she decided, she would pretend that she was in Paris, or London, or even Santa Monica. Any place but Tel Aviv in the middle of a war. She reached for the shampoo and lathered her hair. *David is in there, Ellie,* she thought. *He's sleeping, but he'll wake up. There is nothing you can do to help everyone else. That is up to God. Think about David for now. He's going to need you to help him forget.*

She slipped back into the water, rinsing the soap from her hair. White suds drifted in the tub like bubble bath; Ellie dipped her fingertips into the foam and stroked her skin as the tension disappeared.

Then a soft knock sounded at the door.

"Who is it?" Ellie called.

A sleepy, confused voice returned, "Who is it?"

"David?"

"Where am I? Is this the bathroom?" David sounded like a lost child.

"I'm in the tub, hon," Ellie called. "Out in a minute."

There was a long silence on the other side of the door; then David's imploring voice asked, "Well, can I come in? I can't find the light switch, and it's dark."

Ellie smiled slightly. *That's your husband out there,* she reminded herself. "Sure," she called brightly.

The door opened just a crack and David's face poked in. He blinked against the light, then waved his hand to clear away the steam. He spotted Ellie, then blinked again as if to clear his mind of what was surely only a dream. "Is that you?" he whispered.

"Last time I looked," she answered. "Feeling a bit more awake? Come on in and close the door. You're letting the cold air in."

He rubbed his hand over his face and squeezed through the crack in the door. He held up baggy blue pajama bottoms with his left hand, and shut the door behind him with his right. He stood awkwardly, staring into her face. "I thought I was dreaming," he said quietly at last. "I was having a nightmare." He looked confused. "Michael. Angela and the plane." He searched Ellie's eyes. "Was it a nightmare?"

She shook her head slowly. "No. But it's over now. You're alive."

David stared at the beads of moisture that ran down the mirror. "Scarecrow," he said dully.

Ellie did not move or speak, but a feeling of profound loss engulfed her. What was the use of pretending? This was not Paris or even Santa Monica. It was Tel Aviv, and right now, at this moment, people they knew and loved were dying in a war. "David?"

His tortured gaze swept over her and tears welled up in his eyes. "Oh, Ellie!" he cried, falling to his knees and wrapping his arms around her as bathwater overflowed and spilled onto the floor. He pulled her tightly against himself and buried his face in the nape of her neck. "Oh, Ellie, I thought I'd never see you again! I thought—" His voice caught in a web of emotion.

Ellie stroked his hair, oblivious to the fact that he was now nearly as wet as she. "I know, David," she shivered. "I know, love." She felt the tightness of his back as he fought to control tears that raged within him. "Let it out, hon. Go ahead and cry. It's just me. It's just Ellie."

His breath escaped as if he had been punched hard in the solar plexus. Tears followed, entangled in great, heaving sobs.

"I thought I'd never see you again," he wept. "Not ever again."

Then she cried, too, because she realized that until this was over, there would be no pretending. *This is Palestine and we're in the middle of it. Until it's settled, one way or the other, people are going to die, and there can be no pretending.*

Ram Kadar gazed out the car window at the row of empty trucks waiting on the airfield near Damascus. For the first time since he had known her, Isabel Montgomery had failed to deliver what she had promised. After two hours of waiting for a plane that had never arrived, Kadar was sure she was dead, certain that only death would cause her to fail. The Jewish aircraft was in flames on the ground at Golan, unless—

Haj Amin nodded slowly as a tall Syrian officer spoke to him in the headlights of Kadar's vehicle. The Mufti's face was expressionless in spite of the bitter disappointments the night had

21

brought. He stepped from the light and the officer followed, extending his hand palm up for the reward his news would bring.

Kadar opened the car window a crack to hear the quiet words exchanged between the Mufti and the Syrian.

"And you are certain the aircraft did not crash?"

"It did not crash in Syria, at any rate. Our agent in Nazareth reports he heard a roaring overhead about two hours ago, and when he looked up there was a plane flying low, dangerously low over the valley. But there has been no word of a downed airplane. No explosion. I can only assume it passed over Nazareth and perhaps landed safely."

Haj Amin pondered the words again. "If that is so, then the Jews will have what they want by now." He looked toward the empty trucks. "And Kadar will return empty-handed to Palestine and his command."

"But you must not forget the ship, Haj Amin. The *Trina*. The Arab League has promised you the entire contents of the arms ship."

"Empty promises!" Haj Amin raised his chin angrily at the thought of the betrayal of the Arab League. "I cannot believe any longer that they will send us these vital supplies of ammunition and weapons. No! They wish for us to fail in Palestine so that they might step in and take over when we have already done the work. They will carve up Palestine among themselves—Transjordan, Egypt, Syria, Iraq. They have no vision of an independent Arab state in Palestine."

The Mufti paused and glared at the Syrian. "You do not take me for such a fool as to believe that! No, your government wishes me out of the way. That is why they fired on the Jewish plane as my agent Isabel Montgomery brought it here. That is why they will promise me weapons from the arms ship and then they will take it all for themselves, down to the last bullet. I can trust no one. Except those I pay well enough." He shoved an envelope into the hand of the Syrian soldier. "Now," he said, "you will give me the list of the ship's ports of call. Sailing times and cargo manifest."

The Syrian glanced back over his shoulder, then passed a sheaf of papers to Haj Amin. "There it is. Everything you required. I have kept my bargain, and now you must keep yours."

"Of course. Of course. We shall not forget the service you have done for us. Or the price you asked." The Mufti nodded slightly. The interview was at an end.

Kadar sat back and stared impatiently ahead as the Syrian officer strode away. Haj Amin walked deliberately to the car and tapped on the window. "You heard?" he asked Kadar.

"All of it. The plane is not destroyed, then? That means the Jews will attack. If they have weapons, they will attack."

"There can be no doubt of this. Unless the British find the plane and capture the American flyer first. What is his name, Montgomery's American?"

"Michael Cohen. And one Captain David Meyer. Meyer seems to be in charge of the American operations."

"Montgomery has served us well. Names. Places. The illegal Jewish cargo. All of this will be of great interest to the British government. We shall contact them through channels. Whatever the Jews hope to gain by this cargo, we shall snatch from them."

"But if the English pick up Meyer and Cohen, will they not also arrest Montgomery?"

The Mufti appraised him coldly. "You and I both know that she cannot be alive now. The Jews knew who she was the moment she directed the plane toward Damascus. They have by now killed her, Kadar. We now have one more martyr to the Jihad. And you have lost your lover."

Kadar knew he was right and, strangely, he felt no emotion. Montgomery was dead. The Jews had their guns now and their bullets. Haj Amin was out of favor with the different factions of the Arab coalition. "What shall be done?"

"Return to Palestine. There will be attacks, surely, this very night. When we hear where, we shall radio ahead at the checkpoints so that you may have the information. Go then, and take command." He extended the handful of papers to Kadar. "And remember, this is our salvation."

Kadar squinted, but could not read the writing in the dark. "What is it?"

"A ship called the *Trina*. Its cargo is bound for Lebanon, then Damascus; and then it is promised to us. I cannot believe this promise, so I desire that you send one whom I trust to board the ship in Yugoslavia before it sails, and change its destination for arrival in Palestine. What is meant for us we will take."

"But will the English not confiscate a cargo of weapons from us as well as from the Jews?"

"They will not know its true cargo, Kadar. That is made certain. But it is enough for our nation to equip our army. Six thousand rifles. Not for an army of Syrians or Egyptians, but an army for Palestine and for the House of Husseini." His voice was steady, but his eyes betrayed a rage and a desperation that Kadar had rarely seen in his cold-blooded leader.

"As you wish, Haj Amin."

"And as for Gerhardt." His eyes narrowed. "We have heard rumors that he styles himself a general, that perhaps there are even whispers of disloyalty to us." He paused, and his words spat out the venom of his desire. "Finish him, Kadar. Use him and then finish him. There will be no place in our government for disloyalty. Finish him."

2 Holy War

As the women of her family gathered around her, giggling and whispering, Sarai Tafara gazed at her own reflection in the dim mirror before her. They removed the ornate wedding veil glistening with scales of gold coins, exhibiting the wealth of her family. It was fitting, for they were cousins of the great Haj Amin Husseini, and her brother Yassar had lately become a captain in the army of the Jihad.

Although she had only turned fifteen in the winter of the year, Sarai had begun to wonder if she would ever be married. The price her father had established for her hand in marriage was 600 English pounds. This was a *mohar* only a rich aged merchant could afford, and Sarai had cried herself to sleep many nights as she thought of life with a paunch-bellied old man who bought her as a wife. But Allah had smiled on her. She raised her hands and laughed aloud at the sound of gold bracelets clinking together.

"Your brother Yassar has done well for you, Sarai," whispered her older sister. "Your bridegroom is very handsome, indeed! And *young*!"

Sarai hugged her sister. "And I am the last of our father's

daughters to wed. Though I did not believe it would ever be so!"

"And you are the most beautiful," said her mother softly, with tears in her eyes. "I only regret that the wedding could not have taken place in Jerusalem. To be wed *here* of all dusty villages in Palestine—Deir Yassin!"

"Oh, Mother!" cried the girl happily, "it does not matter. Since my bridegroom must remain in hiding, it is fitting that he have a bride to keep him company."

The women in the room giggled and Sarai blushed as her mother responded, "Yes! And no doubt there will be grandchildren soon to visit me, my daughter." She dabbed at her eyes. "Still, it would have been good for a cousin of Haj Amin to wed in Jerusalem."

Sarai's sister tugged on the hem of her long gown. "Now, Mother," she said, "everyone wishes to hang the bridegroom of my sister. The Americans wish to find him because it was their automobile used in the bombing. The Jews would kill him because he helped blow up the Jewish Agency building. And the English would like to catch him to demonstrate how fair and just they are here in Palestine." More laughter of agreement filled the room. "Unless Basil would spend his wedding night in Central Prison or at the end of a Jewish rope, it was best that Sarai sacrifice and have the wedding in a safe place. Deir Yassin is as good as any place to be wed."

"I suppose so," the mother agreed reluctantly. "After all, he did earn the money for the *mohar* by sacrificing his job with the American Consulate and nearly losing his life in the deed."

Sarai frowned. "Yes. He might have been killed himself driving the vehicle. He *is* a great hero, my mother. And I shall do my best to make him a wise and loving wife." She glanced at her sister again. "You think he is handsome?" she asked in a little-girl voice.

"Very handsome. And also very nervous. He trembles like an olive branch in a wind storm!"

Sarai sat down, a pout suddenly on her face. "I wish that Yassar could have been here among us to celebrate my marriage. After all, it was he who arranged it! It was he who brought Basil into the service of our cousin, the Mufti. And then he spoke to Father. . . ." She looked as though she might cry.

"Now, daughter," her mother admonished, "Yassar is in Kastel tonight, guarding the pass and supping late with the headmen of the villages. He does his duty for the Jihad, and you know he could not take time away."

Her sister interrupted. "Besides, Sarai, when your bridegroom takes you into his little home tonight, you will not care any longer who is near!"

"Consider all your dear brother has done for you already!" scolded her mother.

"He has found you a young and handsome husband!" added her sister with excitement in her voice. "Tonight, we must leave you to return to Jerusalem for the old men our father has chosen for us." She winked at the three other sisters who huddled around Sarai. They all chimed in with agreement.

"Allah has blessed you!" Her mother raised her hands high over the head of the young bride.

"Yes," the girl agreed. "What do I care if I was wed in the dust of Deir Yassin? My new husband is young and handsome and wellfavored by Haj Amin. My brother is a trusted captain." She smiled broadly in the candlelight. "Though Yassar, my beloved brother, could not be here to celebrate my joy tonight, I shall one day offer him another joy." She rose and stole to the curtain. Peering out, she glimpsed Basil, the nervous bridegroom, waiting for his bride.

"Praise be to Allah for this gift!" she whispered, her heart filled with love for the man she had just met and just married. "Our children shall be beautiful, Mother! And tonight I shall speak to my bridegroom. Together we shall make a vow to Allah that our firstborn son shall bear the name of my honored brother . . . *Yassar!*"

———

The days had passed peacefully in Kastel since the destruction of the last Jewish food convoy. Tonight Fredrich Gerhardt and Yassar Tafara supped at the table of the village muhqtar, Ibrahim el Mashay, and shared the bounty of their plunder with the leaders of five Arab villages that defended the road to Jerusalem.

Gerhardt patted his stomach appreciatively as choice chunks of lamb were served up on a bed of steaming *falafal*. Platters of vegetables, fruits, and fresh pita bread were set before the men, who ate with the satisfaction of knowing that every morsel had been intended for Jewish tables in Jerusalem.

Only the lamb had been taken from an Arab flock for this occasion.

"You have done well, Commander Gerhardt." El Mashay wiped his lips on the hem of his keffiyeh. "In the absence of Kadar, you have stopped every Jewish convoy that has dared to pass below our humble fortress of Kastel."

Gerhardt smiled slightly and nodded. Kastel was far from being the fortress its muhqtar pretended. It was, in fact, a pitiful collection of stone houses and ruins perched atop the most strategic point of the pass of Bab el Wad. Yes, Gerhardt had done miraculously well in destroying the Jews that had attempted to slip by him and the ragged rabble of Arab peasants he commanded. Filthy and ignorant, the Arab Irregulars were nothing more than fanatical farmers who had rallied to the cry of *Jihad! Holy War!* Yes, Gerhardt had done well.

He was gracious in his reply. "Your men have fought bravely on behalf of the Mufti and the cause of Palestine. It has been my honor to command them."

"Yes!" a fierce, black-eyed man named Kajuki exclaimed. "While Kadar and the Mufti sup in Damascus, we are left here to defend against the Zionists! This Husseini and his brood!" He spat with disdain.

At the last comment, Yassar drew himself up, and all eyes fell on the young, angry face. "You insult my cousin!" he said with a returned vehemence.

"Your cousin lives on the blood of the peasants!" Kajuki's words were now measured and controlled. "Who are the true patriots? The men who offer their own blood on the battlefield, instead of the blood of others! I give you Fredrich Gerhardt! A true patriot of the Jihad!"

Yassar's puffy eyes narrowed as he contemplated the man in surly silence. "And who are you?" he said disdainfully, tossing his bread onto his plate. "You! Muhqtar of Deir Mahsir! Headman of nothing! A village of shepherds. Stone huts and hovels! Who are you to speak against the House of Husseini?"

"Gentlemen . . ." began el Mashay, holding up his hands for peace. "Allah will not be pleased for us to argue as we celebrate such great victory against the Jews! Look! They starve in the city while we share their abundance among ourselves and our brothers!"

Gerhardt said nothing, but smiled inwardly at the bitter dissatisfaction of Kajuki against the Mufti. He reached to dip another piece of bread into the common bowl. From the corner of his eye, he could see Yassar as his thick lips turned downward in a scowl. Yassar himself was regarded at a cautious distance by all who were not of the Husseini clan. Perhaps the Mufti, Haj Amin Husseini, had great plans for this ugly young peasant. Only a fool did not respect and fear the power of Haj Amin and his family.

Kajuki, the Muhqtar of Deir Mahsir, seemed to have no such fear. "And who are you?" he demanded of Yassar. "You are nothing! A puppet of your mother's cousin! By what right do you sit and sup among the headmen of these villages? Parasite!"

Yassar's fingers closed slowly around the curved knife in his belt. "You will regret your words, Kajuki." His voice was a hoarse whisper.

"Look at him!" mocked Kajuki. "He does not have a beard, and yet he threatens me! I, who fought the Turks and the English before he was weaned from his mother's breast! You are no threat, Yassar Tafara. You are but a dog beneath the table of your cousin. You wait for his crumbs and go at his command! We of the pass Bab el Wad are men who fight when the call comes! We fight because it is the will of Allah and his prophet— not because Haj Amin requests it!"

"Then *this* is the will of Allah! To kill traitors who rage against the one he sent to deliver Palestine!" Yassar drew his knife and sprang to his feet, knocking a samovar of coffee to the floor. "Fight, you coward!"

Guests at the table scrambled back as Kajuki drew his blade and rose to the challenge of Yassar Tafara. Gerhardt watched coolly as the two men moved to the door of the muhqtar's house and out onto the moonlit street of Kastel. It mattered little to Gerhardt who won this fight, although he favored the dark-skinned, battle-scarred Muhqtar of Deir Mahsir over the scrawny cousin of Haj Amin. It was enough that, tonight, dissatisfaction had been expressed over the cowardly absence of the Mufti. It was enough that Gerhardt was recognized as the true leader of those who fought to hold the pass against Jewish relief.

As the women of the household removed the dishes to warm in the ovens, the guests of the headman of Kastel gathered in a wide circle in the dusty street. A yellowed moon rose slowly in the east over Jerusalem, illuminating the desolate mountains.

Yassar and Kajuki faced off. Their skin seemed already gray and dead to Gerhardt. This meal of the muhqtar's was becoming more enjoyable than Gerhardt had ever suspected.

"Allah Akbar!" shouted Yassar, his face intense with passion.

Kajuki laughed and replied in a low-threatening voice, "Allah Akbar. God is great. Prepare to meet him, you servant of Shetan!" With that, he gathered his robes and tossed them over his arm as a shield against the blade of Yassar Tafara's knife. He waved his own knife, and the steel glinted in the moonlight like the eager eyes of the on-lookers. "Come to your death, you son of seven fathers!" Kajuki growled and began to circle slowly around Yassar, who lunged toward him with a scream.

Kajuki stepped easily to the side and twirled around to face the young man with the fierceness of a caged animal. "Come to your death, you child of Husseini cowards and dogs!" Kajuki heckled.

Yassar cried out in fury. His body trembled in the torrent of emotion that surged through him. "Swine!" he cried, lunging at the still-circling Kajuki, who dodged his thrust and tripped him. Yassar stumbled and fell to the ground as the men around him raised a cheer.

Kajuki bowed slightly and laughed at the fallen youth, obviously an unworthy adversary. "Pretend I am but a lowly Jew, Yassar," he jeered. "One who speaks the truth about your family of Palestinian parasites!"

Yassar's face contorted, and Kajuki laughed more loudly. "See how the little locust roars!" As Yassar jumped to his feet, Kajuki took his stance again—the stance of a man who had killed many challengers in similar fights. *No doubt all of them were more worthy than this foolish youth,* thought Gerhardt.

As Yassar crouched and jabbed the knife at Kajuki, the headman said softly, "I think I shall not kill you entirely, for what glory is there for a warrior to butcher a sheep? No. I shall cut off your lips as my trophy—thick lips that speak foolish words. And in removing them, perhaps it will improve your face as well, eh?" Kajuki waved the knife slowly before Yassar's eyes. "Shall I kill him?" Kajuki asked the spectators. "Or only maim him?"

The men chuckled nervously, certain that Kajuki's question was serious. None dared answer. Who would dare recommend the death of a cousin of Haj Amin Husseini? Even though Kajuki was certain to win the fight, he would most likely have to spend the rest of his days looking over his shoulder for the Mufti's assassins. But then, Kajuki was always rash in his words and actions.

Gerhardt smiled. "Yes. Kill him," he said.

Yassar gasped and shot him a quick, yet foolishly-spent glance. In that moment, Kajuki kicked out at Yassar's wrist, sending the knife flying to the ground a dozen paces away. With a shout, Kajuki rammed into him, sending him sprawling and breathless into the dust of Kastel. The headman leaped easily onto the chest of his dazed opponent and pinned him hard against the ground. Kajuki's knees pressed against Yassar's wrists. He held his knife high in the moonlight and his smile faded into an expression of disdain for the ease with which Yassar had fallen. "Husseini spawn," he snarled with the acid of true hatred. Then he spit into Yassar's terrified face.

"Kill him," said Gerhardt coolly as Kajuki hesitated. "I can find a more worthy apprentice. Kill him!"

Kajuki's eyes narrowed. The upheld knife wavered a moment, then, from the rock quarry near the village, the sound of gunfire was heard. Voices, excited and angry, seemed to swarm toward them.

"The Jews!" echoed outraged voices. "The Jews have attacked Ramle! The Jews have attacked Deir Mahsir!"

Kajuki jumped up from the prostrate form of Yassar. "Deir Mahsir! My village!" he cried. Then he began to run with the other headmen toward the stone quarry.

"The Jews! An army of Jews has come to take the road!" the voices cried. "We must hurry! The Jews have attacked Deir Mahsir and Ramle! They are many!" A warning burst of gunfire split the night, and then another followed and another as breathless messengers from the villages to the west entered Kastel. "*Allah Akbar! Nashamdi! Nashamdi!* Let those who are ready go!"

The small battle in front of the muhqtar's house was forgotten as all the men of the village rushed to get their rifles. Yassar dusted himself off and retrieved his knife. The Jews were attacking the villages in the west. There was no time to spill the blood of Arab against Arab.

"Allah Akbar," muttered Yassar as he rubbed the back of his head and adjusted his keffiyeh. "I am ready. *Nashamdi.*"

Only moments passed before five hundred men of the Jihad gathered in the moonlit street. Women and children clustered in tight knots and spoke in hushed tones about the meaning of the Jewish assault in the west. Had the British armed the Jews? Or turned their heads as weapons were brought out from dusty corners? Where had this army of Zionists come from? Others whispered about the Mufti and his great captain, Kadar, who had gone to Damascus to procure more arms and money for the Jihad of Palestine. When would Kadar return? And who would defend Kastel while these men hurried to Ramle to fight?

Horses stamped and snorted, as impatient as their masters to ride to Ramle.

Grim-faced, the village muhqtars strode through the crowd to hurry away to the defense of their own villages. Gerhardt raised his hands for silence. While Kadar was gone, he alone was the commander of the forces of Bab el Wad.

"What shall we do?" a voice cried from the edge of the soldiers. "If we go to fight in Ramle, perhaps the Jews will come here!"

"Who will protect our women?" shouted another.

Gerhardt surveyed the soldiers and the clusters of frightened women who clung to ragged children. "The Jews will not come here in force; not if we hold them in the west." He gestured broadly at the fortifications of the village. "Soldiers of the Jihad! Do not fear the Jewish dogs! Women! Go into your homes and gather food to last until tomorrow. Take your children into the mosque and you will be safe there until we return with word of victory." Like shadows, women hurried away to obey the words of Gerhardt.

Gerhardt gazed up at the black pinnacle of the village minaret. High atop the tower, a British-made machine gun was secured behind sandbags. Its sights pointed toward the eastern approach to the village. One man could hold an army at bay from this deadly vantage point.

"It is my machine gun," said a tall Jihad Moquade named Hamed Safed. The warrior's eyes were proud and fierce. "I have fought Turks and Jews and even the English. I am alive, but many of them are dead. Together, my gun and I defy any Jews to come."

"We may need your gun in Ramle," Gerhardt said.

"This is my village and my gun! Let the men of Ramle find their own machine gun."

The men of Kastel murmured agreement. "You can hold the

eastern approach to the village?" Gerhardt asked, certain already of Hamed's answer.

The village muhqtar, el Mashay, coughed and stepped forward. "Take who you like, but do not take the gun of Hamed." His voice was apologetic.

Gerhardt raised his chin in thought. He knew full well that he was bargaining for soldiers to take to Ramle. The more skilled his men were in battle tonight, the more acclaimed he would be when the battle was ended. "The Jews will not come to Kastel tonight. This is a waste."

"These bullets," Hamed gestured angrily toward the tower. "I have purchased them myself. I have twelve children here. Let the men of Deir Mahsir and Ramle fight for their villages. This is the gun of Hamed Safed; I will kill the Jews that pass on the road below Kastel, or dare to enter my village. These are not the bullets to defend Ramle."

Gerhardt considered his words. He despised this clannish peasant mentality. He despised the man who stood defiantly before him now. "If the machine gun is to remain in Kastel, then I shall need to take with me the best of our forces to Ramle."

There was no argument. These warriors lusted for the cry of *Jihad*! and the smell of gunpowder in their nostrils. No one else in the village had so many children to defend as Hamed. Let him stay and nurse that gun of his. The Jews would not dare come to Kastel anyway. Hamed shouldered his way through the group and climbed the minaret without waiting for further discussion. Gerhardt had not won the use of the machine gun, but now he could demand the obedience of the villagers of Kastel.

"Men between the ages of eighteen and fifty, you will come with me to Ramle. The others among you, step forward!" Nearly two hundred old men and young boys passed through the crowd to stand before Gerhardt. The eyes of the young were filled with disappointment. The old had seen many battles before and were not so eager to run to another, especially not in Ramle. They did not believe the Jews would come so far, and besides, only an army of thousands could capture these heights, even from a mere two hundred men. Of course, the gun of Hamed could scrape any trace of Zionist scum from the eastern approach. And the quarry caught the Jews in the west like trapped birds. One warning shot from a sentry and the village would be mobilized in seconds. In the meantime, they could sleep and leave Ramle to the younger men who had a taste for such things.

Gerhardt pointed at three men who had proved themselves capable in the slaughter of the Jewish convoys. "You three stay here. I give you command of the defense of Kastel. No doubt you will be well rested tomorrow." He glanced up at the gun. "And Hamed will have all his bullets still. We will keep the Jews busy. If a raiding party should come to Kastel, they have no hope." He directed his words to the three hundred who were to follow him. "And now! For the glory of Allah and his prophet! *Jihad!*"

Their voices rose as one as they shook their rifles in the air. "*Jihad!*" The high-pitched war cry of the women accompanied them from the village as they chanted and raged against the Zionists who threatened their western borders. "*Jihad! Jihad!*" The cry echoed in the mountain pass while three hundred swarmed down the path to where captured Jewish transports waited to spirit them into battle.

Gerhardt, fierce and brave, led them as he had a dozen times in the last weeks. He had promised them victory over the Jewish convoys, and loot heaped to the ceilings of their meager shacks. And he had made good on his promises. He was always first to leap screaming from the ravines by the roadside. Jewish trucks had been blown up at the touch of his expert hand on the plunger. Here was a man they could trust, a man to follow against the Jews. In their packs they carried food from the captured convoys. On their feet they wore the boots of the fallen enemies of Haj Amin. It was always as Gerhardt had promised.

In the village, their arms laden with captured bounty, the women and children made their way to the mosque. The impatient young men of the village clustered among themselves to speculate on the events of the night, secretly praying that the Jews would dare to violate the fortress of Kastel. The old among them settled back and covered themselves against the cold until they dozed and dreamed of other battles. Trucks below rumbled away toward Ramle, and the chant of "*Jihad!*" still echoed from the mountains.

3 Kastel

A good meal, served up by some of the best chefs in Tel Aviv, had not erased the surly anger on the faces of Ehud Schiff's kidnapped truck drivers. They stood in little knots, or sat in silence beside the campfires that dotted the grounds of Kfar Bilu, a former British Army camp where the massive convoy was being loaded for the mad dash to Jerusalem.

Three hundred civilian trucks and vans had been commandeered for this mission. Huge dump trucks, trucks from a shoe factory, a dairy, a kosher butcher shop; hay wagons and open trucks from the nearby kibbutzim all mingled together, rolling into line to be loaded by stevedores shanghaied from the docks of Tel Aviv.

Ehud had long since stopped trying to be civil to these unwilling draftees into the Haganah. He prowled up and down the long line of trucks and carefully removed the bulbs from the headlights of each vehicle, lest a panicky flick of a switch along the road point out the location of the convoy to Arab snipers.

"Hey, you!" shouted an angry driver as Ehud labored over the headlights of a van that advertised a local baby-food company. "What are you doing to my truck?" The fellow was short and squat, with the build of a professional wrestler. His fists were clenched as he broke from a small group of men and strode to where Ehud knelt in the mud at the front of the van.

Ehud did not look up, but continued to remove the bulb of the right headlight. "What does it look like I'm doing?" he said in a low, unthreatening voice.

The driver stood glowering over Ehud. "First you point a gun at me, steal my truck, keep me here against my will! And now you will tell me please why you are stealing my lights?"

"You can have them back when we reach Jerusalem, nu?" Ehud's voice was patronizing, as though he were promising a child that he might have a lollipop after dinner.

"I don't want them after we reach Jerusalem!" shouted the driver, with a small group of equally belligerent men clustered around.

"Leave his headlights alone," demanded a spectator as a dozen or so mumbled sullenly and looked on.

Ehud proceeded with his mission, feeling the bulb loosen in its socket. "Now, fellows, there is no place for lights on a night like this. Suppose this gentleman accidentally touched his light switch and some nasty Jihad Moquade saw it. Eh? One tiny blink and you are all dead men." Ehud stopped and drew a finger solemnly across his throat.

"You think I would be fool enough. . . ?" The man bellowed.

Ehud shrugged and looked him over. "I don't know how much of a fool you are, but it takes some kind of a messhugener to drive a baby-food truck to Jerusalem in the middle of a war!"

A ripple of nervous laughter floated through the group of drivers. "You!" blustered the man. "You force me to come here! You take all of us by gunpoint right off the streets of Tel Aviv and tell us we are going to Jerusalem! What do you expect?"

"If you think our fellows are frightening," Ehud roared, standing up, "wait until you see the Mufti's men! Oy! You better pray the moon stays behind the clouds tonight, my friend. At least until we make it up Bab el Wad, nu? By the time this night is over, you'll wish never to see light again. You'll wish you could shut off your noisy engines and push these trucks in silence past the Arabs."

The group that had clustered around the enraged driver fell back and hung their heads as they contemplated the truth of Ehud's words. "Well, I will tell you this!" exclaimed the driver, too angry to back down. "You're nothing but a *gonif*! A thief! And you are taking my headlights over my dead body!"

Ehud gestured toward the heavens in exasperation. "If I don't take them over your *live* body, I can almost guarantee someone else will take them the way you suggest, nu? What's the problem? You'll get them back!"

"Over my dead body!" repeated the man, clenching and unclenching fists the size of small hams.

Ehud sighed and shrugged, rubbing a hand over his now cleanshaven face. "God, are you listening to this? Eh? Moshe you send to Kastel. Luke fights at Ramle. And you leave me here with these stiff-necked people of yours!" Ehud shook his head in disgust and kicked at a rock near the toe of his boot.

The driver took another menacing step toward Ehud, who stooped and picked up the stone. "Are you going to leave my headlights in my truck, or what?" shouted the driver.

Ehud clucked his tongue. "If you insist." He knelt and began to replace the headlight bulb securely in its socket.

"So! That's more like it! You can't bully Morris Schulte around anymore."

"I can see that," Ehud said in resignation. He stood and went to the left headlight; then, very deliberately, he lifted the stone and slammed it into the glass. He smiled slightly as the driver began to sputter and broken glass tinkled onto the ground.

"Wha—?!" The driver lunged toward Ehud, who stepped easily to one side and clutched the man by the tendons in back of his neck.

"Yes!" said Ehud in a determined voice. "You leave me here with these stiff-necked people! Ha!" He booted the man in the rear, then dragged him a few paces toward the other headlight, still intact. "So! You want the bulb on the truck, eh?" he shouted as the man struggled against Ehud's iron grip. "So! It shall remain in the truck!" Ehud slammed the driver's head full force into the glass of the headlight with a loud crunch. The driver moaned and crumpled into the shattered glass that lay in front of his bumper. Hands on his hips, Ehud stared down at the man. "Yes! Stiff-necked and *hard-headed*!" He rubbed his hands together and narrowed his eyes as he looked into the astounded faces of the now docile observers. "Now," he said, "I need a few volunteers to help me gather the rest of the headlights. Nu?"

————

Stone fences, like broken strings of beads, crisscrossed the arid landscape around the shabby Arab village of Ramle. Wisps of fog covered the ground and drifted through the silver branches of ancient, gnarled olive trees. Captain Luke Thomas knelt on the damp earth as a young woman desperately cranked the generator of the shortwave radio. Luke tapped his fingers impatiently on his thigh while the radio operator fiddled with the dial.

"Moses, this is Caleb. Come in, Moses!"

The whine of the radio was accompanied by the fierce crack of gunfire and Arab battle cries.

"Moses! This is Caleb! Caleb calling! Come in, please!"

Two dozen weary, smoke-smudged Haganah soldiers clustered twenty feet away. They sipped on coffee and talked in disconsolate monotones as Harney and Smiley tore apart the firing mechanism of one of a stack of rifles.

". . . and then they came at us! The horses! Like something out of *Arabian Nights*. We waited. We wanted to be certain of our targets so we wouldn't waste ammunition. I had a fellow in my sights! But when I pulled the trigger, nothing! A little click. Like stepping on a twig, but that is all!"

"They sent us out with defective weapons. Four died in my squad before we could pull back!"

"Moses! This is Caleb!" The radio operator's voice reflected the frustration of the young men and women under Luke's command. So far, only these two dozen out of forty had returned to throw their rifles to the ground in disgust and tell stories of narrow escapes and the deaths of comrades whose weapons had also misfired in the face of Arab counterattacks in the fields of Ramle. These few had been the last to receive the precious arms from the crates David Meyer had risked his life for only a few hours earlier.

The radio crackled and a distant voice responded. "Caleb, this is Moses. Come in, please."

Luke took the receiver from the relieved young operator. "Moses, this is Caleb. We've had a bit of hard luck with forty rifles. Lost nearly half of Aleph Platoon. Over."

A short pause accompanied the popping radio; then a deep voice answered, "Was that four–oh, Caleb? Over."

"Correct. Twenty-four made it back." There was an edge of bitterness to Luke's voice. For soldiers to die in battle was one thing; to face an enemy and fall because of a defective weapon seemed like the most tragic kind of waste. Most of those under his command were little more than inexperienced boys and girls, fresh off the kibbutz. And these were the best of the Haganah defenders. "Resistance is fierce. Repeat, *fierce*. Harney and Smiley experienced in ordnance examining the problem." Luke glanced to where Harney labored over the rifles while Smiley held a light aloft.

"Ha! Look 'ere!" Harney said triumphantly. "It's the firin' pin, Smiley!"

Smiley leaned in for a closer look. "Why, so it is! We'll 'ave your guns back t' y' in no time, gents." Then he nodded to the female members of the troops. "An' ladies. Nothin' but a bit of work with a file, eh, 'arney?"

The voice on the radio demanded, "Is the situation under control, Caleb? Over."

Luke rubbed a hand across his lips, searching for the words with which he could phrase his concerns. "Right, Moses. Situation being handled here." He studied the faces of the soldiers who sat in dejected silence now as Harney scraped at the firing pins with a file. He was sure that these few had been among the last to receive their weapons. Was Moshe's command, now marching to Kastel, also carrying weapons that refused to fire? "I am concerned that Staff Group may run into the same situation. Have you heard any word from Staff command? Over."

A longer pause crackled over the receiver; then a concerned voice replied. "Negative, Caleb. No word as yet. We'll try to contact Staff Group. Over."

"Right, Moses. Situation can be corrected by filing defective firing pins. Sergeant Hamilton with Staff Group should be able to take care of it. Over." Luke did not add his thought that Ham could correct the problem as long as they were not in the middle of a battle against the defenders who surely held Kastel.

"We will pass the word along, Caleb. Over."

"Right. Shalom and out." Luke held the receiver a moment, also aware that Moshe and his troops were under strict radio silence. There could be no contact until Moshe radioed back to headquarters that Kastel had been taken, or that the Arab defense was too strong for the untrained men he now led up the steep path to the Arab stronghold that guarded the pass of Bab el Wad. If the rifles were indeed defective, there would most likely be no warning until it was too late.

One young woman in khaki pants and thick sweater sat facing away from the small, unhappy group of soldiers. Luke recognized her as the girl who had written a letter to her lover by the light of the campfire a few hours before. Her head was in her hands and she stared at the ground. The sound of mortar fire echoed among the olive trees, making her flinch with each blast. Her dark hair was tucked under a stocking cap, her face childlike in its expression of grief. *She is too young for this,* Luke thought as he studied her. *What kind of a war have we gotten into, old man?* he asked himself. *Here you are, commanding troops of girls and boys right off the kibbutz. And these are the best the Zionists have to offer.*

"All right," he sighed and stood to his full height. "Let's not sit about like lumps. What's your name, soldier?" he asked the girl.

She looked at him in bewilderment. "Me?"

"Yes, you."

"Johanna Liebermann."

"Where are you from?"

"Kibbutz Kfar Etzion."

"And did they teach you how to take down a rifle at your kibbutz?"

Gunfire and shrieks a quarter of a mile to the front punctuated his question.

The girl's brown eyes darted toward the sound of the battle. She nodded and lowered her gaze again. "Yes."

Luke picked up one of the defective weapons and slid back the bolt. He inserted his finger into the chamber, then pulled it out, touching the blackened tip of his forefinger with his thumb. "These weapons have not been properly cleaned." He handed the girl a rifle. "You," he instructed, pointing at six other downcast soldiers, "make yourselves useful. The packing grease is not even off these."

"Right, Cap'n," Harney chimed in. "The whole lot of 'em is coated with grease. It's a miracle any of 'em is firin'."

From the sound of the battle, Luke could tell that the majority of the smuggled Haganah weapons were doing what they were meant to do. It was not expected that they would, in fact, capture the five Arab villages that lined the west end of the highway. Grease-coated and defective firing pins notwithstanding, the hope for these forces was that they simply engage the Arabs in battle; they were to distract the enemy long enough for Kastel to be stormed and captured by Moshe and his small company of shopkeepers.

Luke dared not hope for more than that. *Maybe Moshe can hold Kastel until the Jerusalem convoy gets through.* Fergus Dugan and Ham were the best of soldiers, and they had gone with Moshe to take charge of his otherwise inexperienced troops. There were also a few among the Haganah who had seen battle as members of the British Army in Africa during the war. They would man the machine guns. On this plan, and these few, Operation Naschon—named after the first Hebrew to step into the Red Sea as the waters parted—would succeed or fail.

Moshe pulled up the collar of his borrowed seaman's coat and tucked his head against the drizzle that beaded in his hair and trickled down the back of his neck. The night was black and rainy, yet Moshe was grateful for the thick clouds that shielded him and his men from the bright light of the full Passover moon. Carefully they picked their way up the muddy trail toward Kastel, the tiny Arab village where soldiers of the Mufti kept watch over the pass of Bab el Wad and the road to Jerusalem.

From this rocky promontory, every attack on Jewish food convoys had been launched, and the noose of the siege against Jewish Jerusalem had been tightened. The rusting metal skeletons of Jewish trucks that littered the road bore mute testimony to the success of the Arab Irregulars who stood watch from this desolate outpost.

Kastel. He who controls Kastel controls the road to Jerusalem. The Romans had been the first to fortify the 2,500-foot peak on their way to destroy the Holy City nearly twenty centuries before. The Crusaders had built the castle that had given the village its name, *Kastel.* Turks had followed and held the pass below in a grip of terror. And now, it seemed to Moshe, almost two thousand years of history had come full circle. The Roman Empire was no more. The Crusaders were dust inside their rusted armor. The Turks had fled before the armies of the British Empire, and now the British themselves were preparing to exit, while one hundred fifty Jews climbed through the mud and the rain to capture Kastel.

Each of the men under Moshe's command carried a brandnew rifle slung over his shoulder, courtesy of David Meyer's courageous flight into Palestine. Still, Moshe knew, his men were illequipped at best. Though rifle cartridges had arrived with the weapons, no cartridge belts had come with them. So the men had stuffed bullets into socks and tied them to their belts, carrying ammunition into battle like a small boy's bag of marbles. There were no uniforms—at least, none that matched. Trousers and jackets from a dozen different armies clothed the men who stumbled up the rocky slope with Moshe. A few lucky men wore boots, but more often than not, the thick mud sucked at the soles of street shoes made for taxi drivers and cooks and postal clerks and refugees. These men had walked out of their houses this morning, never dreaming that the night would take them to Kastel.

Behind him, Moshe heard a loud thump as a man stumbled and fell in the darkness. Not a word or a curse was muttered as the fellow scrambled to pick himself out of the mud. No one had even so much as whispered on the long trek to the top. In the far distance, Moshe imagined that he could hear the sounds of the battle now taking place at Ramle in the west. It was Moshe's hope that the Arabs would not learn about the action in Kastel until it was all over.

Groves of fig trees dotted the slopes as the small band neared the village, and wisps of clouds drifted through the pale branches like ghostly reminders of the ancient men who had also fought and died to win this stony ground. The drizzle became a fine mist against their tense faces, and the clouds began to break. Footsteps slowed. A man stifled a cough; suddenly all became aware that beyond the grove and above the floating mist was Kastel, now illuminated by the full moon. Perhaps an Arab sentry stood atop a hewn stone in the village rock quarry and stared down at the layer of pale vapor that lapped the tops of the fig trees. Perhaps he was listening for the sound of a snapping twig or a man's voice to emerge from beneath the blanket of fog below him.

Moshe glanced upward through the branches at the thin gray veil. Through an opening in the clouds, he caught a glimpse of the moon, shining like an ancient searchlight on the slopes just beyond where he stood. Another twenty-five feet in elevation and he and his troops would become easy targets for even one lone Arab sentry.

Moshe raised a hand, and the signal to halt was passed quickly back down the line from one man to another. Utter silence fell on the land, and Moshe listened as he imagined the enemy was listening now. A slight breeze rustled the new leaves and pushed the clouds over the face of the moon once again. Then just as suddenly they parted, and a beam of pure light shone down on Moshe.

Fergus Dugan, the small-boned Scotsman who had deserted the British forces with Luke Thomas, tapped Moshe lightly on the shoulder. Moshe turned to look at the gray face of the man who had rescued him and Ehud Schiff from a death sentence.

Drops of sweat clung to the little man's forehead; or was it only mist? Fergus tapped his wristwatch and pointed up toward the moon with his thumb to indicate that very soon the wind would blow away their cloud cover altogether, and they would be exposed—whether here or twenty-five feet nearer their objective. He pointed to himself, then nodded toward the edge of the grove and dropped down to move stealthily onward, while the one hundred forty-nine waited behind.

Moshe dropped to one knee and removed his rifle from his shoulder; as if of one mind, he heard the men of his command follow suit. Minutes passed slowly as Fergus disappeared into the light. Moshe stared at the slate-colored curtain that surrounded them as a full ten minutes inched by. Restless tension rippled through the men as they waited for the return of the Scotsman. And the waiting suddenly seemed to be the most difficult part of their mission. Hearts beat faster and breath rose in steamy spirals as each man searched for some movement beyond the gray curtain that surrounded them. Small doubts shot through the shadows, finding certain targets in the minds of Moshe's men. Waiting gave them a moment to think for the first time since they had left Tel Aviv.

What if we fail? What if Kastel is not taken and the convoy is blown up and looted by the Arabs like the others? One hundred thousand hungry men, women and children wait in Jerusalem. Their lives are in the hands of these few—in my hands. How many Arabs wait in Kastel? Where is the Scottish soldier who has gone to spy? Why is he not back? Is he dead? Does the enemy know we are here? Am I to meet my end here beneath the fig trees tonight? Where is the Scotsman?

As for Moshe, doubts assailed him like machine-gun fire. Every thought and prayer was directed toward the one he knew waited for him in Jerusalem. At this moment, the solitary life of Rachel seemed more important to him than one hundred, or even one hundred thousand. He pictured her with little Tikvah in her arms, standing at the window and gazing up at the unpitying face of the moon. He turned his eyes upward to where the same bright glow filtered through the fog. *God, let her hear my heart at this moment. If I am to die, then let her hear that in my mind not even the moon shines as brightly as her love for me. Tell her, God. Tell her I love her more than life.*

Rachel and the baby had suddenly become every hungry

Jewish woman and child who waited in long lines for meager rations in Old Jerusalem. Had he never met Rachel, Moshe knew, he would still be crouched here in the dark and cold, preparing to fight and die for besieged Jerusalem. But his love for Rachel had given this battle a new sense of desperation and had rekindled in his own heart a more urgent hope that at the end of all battles there might be found true peace for Jerusalem. And for the first time it seemed to matter that he, Moshe Sachar, might survive to see it happen.

Where is Fergus? Why has he not returned? Unexpectedly, a breeze penetrated the fog around them, breaking it into glistening streamers that swirled above their heads like smoke and drifted through the treetops, leaving them clearly visible in the moonlight. Exposed and vulnerable, here and there a gasp of despair was breathed along the line of soldiers. A few paces beyond where they knelt, and much nearer than they expected, the fig grove stopped abruptly. A stony incline led to the rim of the rock quarry, a crater littered with broken stone and huge blocks that had been hewn months before, then left to bleach in the sun while the Holy Jihad against the Jews had begun. Every Arab stone mason in Kastel had thrown down his chisel and picked up his gun at the first rallying cry of the Mufti, Haj Amin Husseini. These blocks of stone, once intended for the walls of a new home or shop building, would now be used as markers for the dead.

Across the quarry, Moshe could see the forms of two Arab sentries. They stood on opposite sides of the quarry's edge, and their long striped robes seemed to glow in the light. Faces were dark and obscure beneath the checkered keffiyehs they wore on their heads. One of the sentries stood half turned away from where Moshe and his men waited. He gazed toward the east and the outskirts of Jerusalem. The other man, a mere fifty yards away, perched on a massive block of stone and stared directly at the grove of fig trees. *No one move,* Moshe prayed silently. *Not a muscle. Do not flinch or blink your eyes or scratch your nose.*

The Arab cocked his head slightly to one side, as if to question the existence of tree stumps that he had never noticed before. He shifted his weight and stepped forward to the extreme edge of his stone perch and shielded his eyes against the glare of the moonlight to get a better view.

Moshe felt sweat trickle down his neck. His breath came in short, quiet panting; he felt a sudden urge to bolt and run back into the deep shadows of the center of the grove. *Do not move! He is not certain of what he sees. You are only the stump of a fig tree. But where is the Scotsman? Where is Fergus?*

The sentry turned to look at his companion, who still stood leaning on the butt of his rifle in serene boredom as he stared at the distant lights of the city. The nearest sentry shifted his weight uneasily as if he were hesitant to raise an alarm over what must certainly be only tree stumps. Moshe saw him rub a hand across his chin in thought for a long moment; then he glanced once again toward his inattentive comrade. Moshe's heart went cold at what the sentry did next. Slowly, deliberately, the sentry checked the bolt on his rifle. Then, contemplating the orchard opposite him, he raised the rifle to his shoulder. *God!* Moshe's soul cried out as the Arab swept his gun across the trees. *He is bluffing! No one move! He would not shoot and wake up the entire village for nothing. And he is not certain!* As the barrel of the gun pointed directly toward him, Moshe felt almost choked with an instinct to run. *Stand firm! He cannot be sure and will not want to look like a fool. Do not move!* And yet . . . Across the chasm that separated them, Moshe heard the distinct sound of the rifle bolt as a bullet slid into the chamber. The sentry stood poised, carefully taking his aim. *Shoot if you will. We will not break and run!*

Suddenly, from behind the sentry, Moshe saw the head of a man raise up from below the edge of a stone block. *Fergus!* The little Scot had crept up silently behind the sentry and now reached slowly toward the Arab's sandaled foot. The sentry adjusted the butt of his rifle a bit more securely against his shoulder. *He is going to shoot! He does not want the recoil to knock him down.* He laid his cheek against the stock and took clear aim. *Fergus! Now!* Slowly, Fergus crept forward on the stone. His right hand reached out only inches from the ankle of the sentry. The sentry raised his head from the gunsight one last time to gaze at his target in the moonlight. *Fergus! Quickly!* Yes, he would shoot.

As his finger slowly squeezed the trigger, Fergus lunged forward, gripping the man's ankles and pulling his legs out from under him. He gave a muffled cry as he spread his hands out to catch himself. He fell face first against the hard stone block beneath him as his rifle clattered to the ground. Even across the quarry, Moshe heard the crack of the sentry's chin. He crumpled like a rag doll, and Fergus grabbed the fallen weapon. With a quick glance toward the other sentry, Fergus dragged his prey over the edge of the stone and disappeared. At that instant, Moshe motioned for the men to silently drop to their bellies in the mud while the one remaining sentry still stared toward the east, oblivious to the drama just enacted behind him. It seemed a miracle to Moshe that the noise had not alerted him, so loud had it been in the stillness. Moments passed, and Fergus, now dressed in the unconscious sentry's keffiyeh and robes, sprang up to the stone block. He raised his weapon briefly, then leaped down and strolled quickly around the lip of the quarry toward the second Arab guard. With the carefree stride of a young boy out to explore, Fergus clambered over the stones that littered the rim of the pit.

Even as Fergus jumped from one stone to another, the second Arab did not turn his eyes away from Jerusalem. Moshe watched in amazement as Fergus approached within a few feet of the man, then raised his weapon and walked forward. At last he shoved the barrel of his rifle beneath the chin of the fellow, who cried out loudly with a cracked voice, "Allah Akbar! God is great!" Then he fell to his knees before Fergus and threw his own rifle to the ground. The little Scot in the billowing robes held the point of his gun at the Arab's head. He spoke to him in hushed tones as the Arab wrung his hands and wept with fear. Moshe could not make out the words from across the quarry, but at last Fergus raised his hand and motioned for them to move forward. Moshe imagined that he saw the glint of a smile on Fergus's face.

Almost as one, a sigh of relief rose up from the mud beneath the fig grove. Still on edge, alert for an ambush, the men of the Haganah moved quickly forward around the edge of the rock quarry. It would be foolish to scramble down the sides of the pit to reach the other side. If there were indeed a force of Jihad Moquades waiting over the rise, the Haganah would be trapped like ducks on a pond. So they took the long way around, their guns cocked and ready to fire at the first cry of "Allah Akbar" that might scream down from the tiny village above them.

Fergus tore the keffiyeh from his head as Moshe reached his side. Others crowded around the little man and his captive.

"Good work," Moshe said quietly. "And just in time. Where is the fellow that owns these robes? Dead?"

"Not dead." Fergus scratched frantically. "But a bit more comfortable than I am, I'll warrant. He's lying over there naked and bound, but all his fleas have taken up the attack!" He pushed the rifle into the hands of Moshe and took off the robe, flinging it into the pit with a fury. "And this old fellow didn't hear a thing. Deaf as a post. And can't understand a word of English either. Can you speak to him, Moshe?"

Moshe lowered the barrel of the weapon from the old Arab who sat shaking before them. "He's harmless enough," Moshe muttered. "How old was the other fellow?"

"A boy. Maybe fifteen. Maybe. Not more than that, certainly."

Moshe raised his face toward the moon for an instant; then, with a relieved sigh, he glanced at the men of his command, who were already taking up positions in the quarry of Kastel. This strategic location had been left in the hands of a young boy and an old man. It had been captured without bloodshed. Perhaps the simplistic plan of Operation Naschon was miraculously working as hoped. Four men, led by the British Sergeant Hamilton, kicked in the door of the quarry office, then waved and brandished a machine gun out the window. Fergus gave them a thumbs-up signal, then said quietly, "Easy. Almost too easy. Could they have been so foolish as t' leave this place unprotected? Ask the old man where the Arab soldiers have gone."

Moshe looked down at the toothless old Arab. "We will not hurt you," he said in quiet Arabic.

The old man cupped his hand around his ear and said loudly, "I am but an old man. Deaf as these stones. I beg you do not harm us. We are only stone cutters, my grandson and I. They have left us here. What have you done with my grandson?"

Moshe leaned forward and spoke loudly and distinctly into the old Arab's ear. "He will not be hurt if you tell us the truth."

"The truth! By Allah and the Prophet, I will speak only the truth! Only do not harm the boy! You must not kill him!" The words came in a rush. "His father and brothers have all gone to fight against the attack at Ramle! We beg you for your protection!"

This was a request that Moshe would honor. It was understood among the Bedouin tribes that protection asked for would be granted. Moshe nodded curtly, then glanced up at Fergus and

46

smiled. "The old man is, indeed, nearly deaf. We might have fired off a round and he wouldn't have noticed. If anything is going to beat the Arabs, it is foolishness like this. They are not an army; they are a rabble. Everyone runs off to fight the Jews and leaves an old man and a boy—"

"Well? What did he say?" Fergus demanded impatiently.

"Kastel is ours for the taking," Moshe replied, watching as two of his men pulled the naked Arab boy to his feet, then prodded him to where his grandfather knelt. "Old men and young boys. They have left them here to guard Kastel," Moshe said in wonder at the foolishness of their enemies. "The others have gone to fight at Ramle."

Blood was oozing from the lower lip of the Arab boy. He was humiliated, angry and afraid. His wrists were tied securely behind his back and his own blood-stained cloth belt gagged him. Fergus gingerly retrieved the boy's robes. He tossed them to a young Jewish soldier who held the boy firmly by the elbow. "Everyone always wants to know what a Scotsman wears beneath his kilt," quipped Fergus. "We've no need t' worry about the Arabs. This lad carried with him an army of fleas! Let the lad wear his robes, but keep his hands tied. If he can't scratch at will, that is torture enough! If there's anything t' tell, he'll talk!"

A ripple of laughter passed through the men, and the boy struggled against his bonds in fury as Fergus cuffed him lightly on the head.

"He is old enough to fire a carbine," Moshe appraised the skinny, fiercely defiant boy. "Had you been a second or two later, Fergus, I no doubt would have been as dead as a tree stump."

"Aye. The lad had a bead on you, that is certain."

"Yes. It's boys this age who burned the Commercial District and raped the young Jewish girls at Damascus Gate. They are not brave, but they are fierce. And too foolish to realize that they are not immortal. Youth! Passion and hot-headedness. Tonight I would say that these are the things we will fight against in Kastel." Moshe moved very close to the boy until his eyes locked with his. In Arabic he said, "You and your comrades were angry at being left behind tonight, weren't you?"

The boy lifted his chin and sneered from behind the gag. His black eyes hardened with hatred for the Jews and narrowed to slits. If it had not been for the cloth that gagged him, Moshe

47

was certain the boy would have spit in his face and braved death simply for the chance to insult this Jewish commander who stood before him. Moshe shook his head and smiled at his own foolishness. It had been easy so far. Too easy. Arab boys knew how to use a gun from the time they could talk. When Jewish children went to Torah school, the Arabs of Palestine thrust rifles into the hands of their youth and taught them marksmanship as a prerequisite to manhood. Hatred of the Jews, recklessness, and knowledge of a weapon could make a fifteen-year-old as formidable as an experienced Jihad Moquade. *Perhaps,* Moshe thought as the boy raged and lashed out, *Kastel is not as defenseless as I thought.* "Are there any others, old man?" Moshe asked the Arab. The boy shouted unintelligibly behind the gag.

"More like us. Young and old."

"How many?"

"Fifty, perhaps. Only boys and old men." The Arab did not look at his grandson. "Not more than fifty. You will have no difficulty. They will not want to die."

The boy lunged toward Moshe, who shoved him hard, sending him to the ground in a raging heap. Moshe shook his head again at the old man's words. "Yes. I can see they will not want to fight us," Moshe said sarcastically. "Your leader Haj Amin accepts the blood of children as martyrs of the Jihad just as readily as he accepts the blood of men." Then Moshe looked at the panting boy. "And you, boy. You have told me more than the words of your grandfather."

"What did they say?" Fergus questioned.

"I think they were placed here simply to warn the others. Maybe to draw us into the quarry pit. The old man says there are fifty. They are most likely boys like this one. No doubt they are all mad with the fever of the Jihad. And wanting to prove their manhood by spilling the blood of Jews."

"Then the taking of Kastel may not be as simple as all that."

Moshe frowned for a moment, then pressed his fingertips together. "Take your men to the west end of the village. There is a rise in the one road through the place. Set up a machine gun there. I am going around to the east side of the village. The long way around, through the fig groves." Moshe glanced at his watch. "Give me twenty minutes, then let loose with a round or two. These are boys, remember. Like this one. Not one of them will want to miss the party. Keep them busy on the west end for a few minutes and we'll move in from the east."

"Remember your promise!" the old Arab shouted. "You must not harm us!"

"Mind if I keep the old fellow on our end of things?" Fergus asked. "He sounds eager enough to lay down his arms and persuade others to do the same."

"Right. I'll take the boy. He might come in useful as well." Then Moshe said in menacing Arabic, "And we'll shoot the little Arab if he gives us any trouble." To emphasize his words, Moshe shoved his gun barrel beneath the boy's chin. For the first time since his capture, the boy flinched and cowered in silence.

"That's more like it," Fergus chuckled. "If I kept the lad I'd be likely to turn him over my knee and give him a beating with a stout stick!"

4   Tomorrow's News

Ellie laid her cheek against David's broad back and listened to the steady beat of his heart. He slept peacefully at last, as she stroked his hair and dozed fitfully beside him on the narrow bed. She had lost all track of time. The night seemed endless in its uncertain darkness. The faces of those she loved came to her one by one: old Miriam, chiding her as she packed for her journey on the *Ave Maria*; Moshe, his hands outstretched to a small refugee boy; Rachel, her eyes tender yet hesitant as she gazed at Moshe; Yacov, his face alive with the understanding that his sister had survived the terrible years of war, and had come home. Rabbi Lebowitz and Uncle Howard talked quietly in Ellie's distant memory of more peaceful days in Jerusalem.

It was not so long ago, Ellie reminded herself. *If I had known, would I have stayed? Would I have risked losing David if I had seen this night?* She sighed and turned over, certain of the answer. She and David were committed now. Not only to a dream, but to those who dreamed the dream. In the morning, David would open his eyes and be ready to fight again. And she would stay beside him. Tonight, she could not know the future, but she was filled with the conviction that what they did here was right. It was meant to be. She remembered the words Miriam had underlined in her tiny Bible: *Neither life nor death can separate us from the love of God.* On this, the darkest night, the longest night of her life, she felt that even now she must believe that promise.

Ellie snuggled closer against David, wanting to lose herself in him. "Not even death, David," she whispered. He did not hear her. A merciful sleep had shut him out from the reality of this uncertain night. How many lay awake tonight, wondering if the morning would ever come? For some, Ellie knew, it would not.

For the hundredth time, she recited the names of those whose lives were bound up with hers. *You see everything,* she prayed. *Even when a sparrow falls. Will you remember them?* Only stillness answered her. But she believed that the secret longings of her heart were heard. After all, hadn't David come safely back to her?

But what if he hadn't come home? Would you still believe? That was a question she could not contemplate. Vague shadows of doubt whispered to her from the corners of the room. Visions of the broken body of Michael Cohen lay before her. *Was he not worth more than a sparrow?* If morning ever came, she knew that was a question she would have to look at. For the sake of David.

For almost ten minutes, she lay next to David in the utter stillness of the Red House. *Stillness. Where are the voices? Where is the noise of the men downstairs?* The lights burned brightly outside the door, but the frantic activity of only an hour before was now replaced by a heavy, foreboding silence.

Against her will, fears shouted at Ellie. She sat up and swung her legs over the edge of the bed. Groping for her clothes, she dressed hurriedly in khakis and a heavy blue turtleneck sweater. She stopped and listened, but the only sound she could hear was David's breathing. Her feet were cold against the bare wood floor as she stood before the bureau, rummaging through the top drawer for a pair of socks. Thoughts of Luke and Moshe filled her mind; shouts of *Jihad* and Arab bullets. *Why is everyone so quiet? Has something happened?* Pulling a pair of socks onto her feet, she did not bother to find her shoes. David stirred slightly as she slipped out the door and tiptoed down the stairs to the open door of Ben-Gurion's cluttered study. She peeked into the empty room. A still-smoldering cigarette butt lay in an ashtray on the Old Man's desk, and cups of coffee sat on lamp tables and on the floor beside vacant chairs.

"Hello?" Ellie called from the hallway. No one answered, and she had the strange feeling that she and David had been left suddenly and unexplainably alone in the house. "Hello?" she called again tentatively. "Is anyone here?"

She imagined midnight raids and British soldiers swarming over the house in search of the leaders of the attack on Ramle. But why wouldn't they have awakened her and David? She padded quietly down the narrow, dark hallway to the tiny kitchen. Gingerly, she pushed open the door and peered in. A kettle of water simmered on the stove, but the normally pleasant face of Paula Ben-Gurion was not there. Ellie instantly dismissed the thought that they might have all wandered off to bed. They would not sleep until they knew the outcome of the battle for Bab el Wad.

Puzzled, Ellie fixed herself a cup of tea and stood at the window to stare out at the white line that marked the breakers crashing against the seawall. She glanced at the round face of a clock that hung on the wall above a small wooden table. *Nearly two-thirty. Four or five hours and it will all be over. Or it will still be just beginning.* She sat down at the table and sipped her tea.

Moments passed as Ellie rested her chin in her hand and listened to the droning of the wind as it swept around the corner of the house. *Was that a voice?* she asked herself, as a soft insistent counterpoint reached her ears. *Are they outside on the beach?* Again she looked out at the white sandy beach of Tel Aviv. It was desolate and windswept. The moon cast its light behind the clouds. There was no human silhouette along the shoreline. She closed her eyes for a minute, straining her ears for a snatch of conversation.

"Moshe . . ." The name was clear. Then an angry, impatient voice said loudly, ". . . what do you mean . . . can't . . ."

Ellie slapped her forehead and breathed a sigh of relief. "The basement!" she exclaimed, feeling foolish that she had not thought to look down the narrow stairs to the tiny basement bathroom. Still carrying her cup of tea, she hurried to the small door in the hallway and opened it a crack. The voice of David Ben-Gurion boomed up at her.

"Then we must send someone up to tell him! Before it's too late!"

"This is Moses calling Staff Group. Moses calling Staff!" another voice called urgently in the background. "Come in, Staff."

Ellie clearly heard the crackle of the radio as she made her way carefully down the steep steps to the basement. The dimly lit room was packed with a dozen members of the Jewish Agency staff. Ellie recognized most of the men. They had been familiar figures lately around the Tel Aviv beach house. All of them looked up in unison at the sound of her footsteps. She looked directly at the worried face of Bobby Milkin, who did not smile back at her. Something was terribly wrong, indeed.

The drama between the radio operator and the silent receiver continued as the boyish, curly-haired young radio man begged and coaxed for a reply, to no avail. Ben-Gurion looked more disheveled than usual. His eyes were swollen with exhaustion and worry.

"Keep trying," the Old Man instructed.

"This is Moses, calling Staff . . ."

Staff Group was the designation for the men who accompanied Moshe to Kastel; that much Ellie knew. Her face reflected her concern, and as the others in the group stood in silent knots, Bobby motioned to her. An unlit cigar dangled from his lower lip, his face mirroring the look of an irritated thug.

As she made her way toward Ben-Gurion, he looked at her as though he had never seen her before. Dread and curiosity made her want to shout questions at him, but the room was charged with an intensity that demanded silence.

"How's David?" Bobby asked brusquely, staring over the top of her head at the radio that was hidden behind a toilet in a minuscule bathroom.

"Sleeping. Okay, I guess. It must have been terrible . . . Michael and everything." Ellie replied in a whisper.

"Yeah." Bobby's tone was surly and preoccupied.

"Staff Group . . . this is Moses!"

Ellie touched the rough-looking flyer's arm. "Bobby? That's Moshe's men in Kastel they're calling, isn't it?"

He nodded. "Yeah. We sent him up there with defective rifles."

"Not the ones David brought?" Ellie felt sick.

Bobby nodded grimly. "Something about the firing pins. We lost a few out in Ramle before that English captain—Thomas, ain't it? Before he could put his finger on it. Nothin' to it. No big deal, except, who had time to check the rifles out?" He shook his head in disgust.

"How *many*?"

"Forty out of those at Ramle. Just forty. But sixteen out of those are . . ." He drew his finger across his throat. "Not real good odds, if you know what I mean. We ain't sure how many of them rifles went up to Kastel. But even one is too many."

Ellie nodded bleakly and shuddered at the thought of Moshe trying to fight with weapons that were no better than children's toys. "They can't reach him?"

"Moshe's on radio silence until the action is under way. Chances are, they ain't even got their radio on."

"Staff Group, come in please. . . ."

The Old Man turned away from the radio, his lips a grim line. "Milkin! How long would it take you to get up there?"

Bobby worked his cigar thoughtfully. "Twenty minutes, maybe. But what am I supposed to do when I get there?"

"Make a couple of low passes overhead," offered a middle-aged dark-skinned man Ellie did not recognize.

"Maybe they'll get the message and turn on their radio, eh?" said a younger man.

"The point is we've got to make some effort to warn them."

"Yeah, well, I guess that's the point all right." Bobby pulled his cap on. "I guess you guys will want me to keep my radio on, huh? Give you a play-by-play." He shouldered his way through the tight group of men and climbed up the stairs, muttering, "What a way to run a war!"

Ellie watched him disappear. She could not help but wonder at the strange mixture of humanity that had come together in this makeshift Tel Aviv headquarters of the Jewish Agency. *Refugees, malcontents, merchants, scholars, and—American thugs*. She smiled in spite of the heaviness of the moment. There was scarcely a professional soldier in the whole lot. If indeed, there was to be a Jewish homeland, it would be a supreme example of God's might—and His sense of humor.

Ben-Gurion looked at her and motioned to her to follow him as he climbed the stairs heavily. Unwilling to leave the radio, the others remained in the basement to keep silent vigil.

His face was a mask of exhaustion as he plopped down in his desk chair, but his voice was animated and interested. "So. How is David?"

"Sleeping."

"And why aren't you sleeping? Paula went to bed hours ago."

"I wanted to know; it was too quiet down here."

"You should go to bed, Ellie. There is nothing for you and David to do about all this—not tonight, anyway."

"But I wanted to know."

"You can't wait for the morning news?"

"I *write* the morning news!"

Ben-Gurion almost smiled. He appraised her from beneath raised eyebrows. "And so you do. Well, I have a bit of tomorrow's news for you. What is it you call such things? A scoop? Yes." He opened a drawer and pulled out a folded slip of paper, laying it on the desk blotter in front of him. A red stain marred the edge of the paper, and Ellie was filled with a strange fear as she contemplated it.

"I don't know if I'm up to writing tonight." She did not want to know what the contents of the note said, and yet, she could not tear her eyes away from the red stain against the white paper.

"We are fighting on many fronts, Ellie." The Old Man dismissed her hesitance with a wave of his hand. "We must sink a freighter—a ship filled with tons of weapons for the Mufti." He picked up the slip of paper. "Ehud found this in David's pocket—a very expensive little item. Back in December the Arabs led us—what do you Americans say?—on a 'wild goose chase' for this cargo. Already we know that four Jewish intelligence men have been murdered for it. But now it is ours. The name of this second ship. The cargo manifest. Date and time of sailing and, of course, destination."

"Why are you telling me this?" Ellie said miserably, already certain of the reason why the Old Man had taken her into his confidence.

"Because you are a very influential woman. Your words have a certain power, especially now. Especially with a certain young flyer, yes? Tomorrow, he will wake up and realize he has lost a friend, a brother. He may even want to pack up and go home. You may want the same thing. I wouldn't blame you. But I tell you tonight, we need you. And we need him."

"For what?" Ellie nodded miserably at the folded note. "For tomorrow's headline?"

He looked steadily at her. "Yes."

"So soon?"

"The presses cannot wait on this one. If not tomorrow, then a few days from now the story will have a different ending. The world will read that millions of rounds of ammunition and thousands of weapons have arrived for the soldiers of Haj Amin's Jihad." He paused and studied her expression. "And if that happens, tonight will make little difference in the long run. We will lose. Do you understand this?"

"Why David?"

"He is here. I suppose we could send Bobby Milkin." He shrugged, indicating that the thought of it was distasteful. "But I think David is the man. What do you say?"

"What do you want me to say?"

"That you'll help us. That you will help him."

Ellie sat quietly for what seemed like a long time. She studied her hands, folded in her lap, and she thought again about Michael. Tomorrow was too near. "I won't be apart from him again," she said, emotion cracking her voice. "If he has to go, I want to go with him. There are women fighting in Ramle right now. This time I won't wait on the sidelines while you send him off. I'm going with him."

The Old Man did not seem surprised. "So. You are the journalist. I did not expect less." He slipped the paper back into his desk drawer. "That is why I told you first. Now. You should sleep. You cannot change tonight's story. Someone else is writing that. Regardless of how things go for us tonight in Bab el Wad, you will have a job to do in the morning, yes?"

Ellie stumbled back upstairs to bed. Lying down next to David in her clothes, she pressed herself tightly against him.

"This time, David," she whispered, "not even death."

5 Goliath

The whir of wings rose up from deep shadows in the fig groves as wild birds awakened and fled from the footsteps of Moshe's men. The light and shadow of the night dappled the slopes below Kastel and tricked the eyes and minds of the soldiers. *Is that a rock? A tree stump ahead? Or a man? Was the old Arab lying? Are these ravines fortified with seasoned Arab fighters who lie in wait for us?*

The minutes passed too quickly, and by the time Fergus's first burst of gunfire sounded, the seventy men under Moshe's command had traveled only halfway around to the far end of the village.

The rocky remains of an ancient Crusader wall loomed above them, and Moshe heard the cries of the Arab defenders as they ran back toward the rattle of gunfire at the west end of the village. The report of rifle fire answered the Haganah machine gun, and soon the night was filled with the undulating war cry of the ancient Bedouin. Like the wings of the birds, it whirred and swirled into the air.

"Yehudah! Yehudah! Nashamdi! Allah Akbar! Allah Akbar!"

As he and his men struggled up a ravine, Moshe was certain that the voices were many more than either he or Fergus had anticipated from the words of the old man. Whether they were voices of young boys and old men was hard to tell.

"Nashamdi! Aiiiiyeeee!" shrieked a voice thirty feet above where they crept.

"Allah Akbar! Aiiiiyeee! For the glory of Allah and his prophet!"

Again, machine-gun fire punctuated shouts and cries of "Death to the Jews!" As Moshe and the seventy clambered through the trees toward the stone huts perched on the ledge of rock, Moshe caught sight of the exultant face of their young Arab captive. Though he was still gagged, his eyes were wild with excitement. His head covering had fallen off as he was pushed along by his captors; yet even at fifteen, with curly black hair falling into his eyes, he had the look of the *feladeen*—peas-ant warrior; child and man.

Moshe took the lead now, dodging from tree to tree. Arab shouts disintegrated into wails as some defenders were cut down by the hail of bullets. The heavy, gasping breathing of his own men accompanied the sound of bodies scrambling up over the rocky terrain toward the pitiful shack that marked the eastern extreme of Kastel's boundaries.

Moshe turned his eyes upward to the distant, darkened win-dows of the houses that looked out on the hillside where they made their assault. *Do black eyes stare out at us, gazing down gunsights?* There was no movement at the windows. No silhou-ette of a soldier standing guard on the ridge above them. In-credibly, there seemed to be no one watching the east end of the village for assault.

Like a jagged black scar, a narrow ravine gouged the ex-posed slope ahead and wound upward toward the village pla-teau. Moshe dropped to his belly and crawled from the cover of the fig groves into the mud at the bottom of the gully. The hollow thump of canteens echoed behind him as his men fol-lowed, careful not to rise up from the shadows into the moon-light. A human serpent, they slithered through the slime and garbage toward a rocky limestone outcropping that glowed as white as new snow. At its base, Moshe knew, was yet another shadowed pathway beneath the overhang. From there, they could wind their way around the boulders and enter the village.

Brambles grew in thick patches along the crumbling walls of the ravine. More than once, Moshe felt the sharp pain of tiny bayonets pierce his clothing and his flesh as he scrambled on-ward. Nature itself had fortified Kastel, growing barbed wire in the desolate soil and heaving stone barricades onto the hill-sides. The new grass of spring would soon arrive, but that, too, would give way to the thorns and searing summer sun that would heat the boulders until they were too hot to touch with the bare hand. And when every other plant had withered and died, the thorns would remain. These vicious barbs, they said, were woven into a crown for Yeshua on Passover Eve so long ago. Now they wove around Kastel and tormented those who had come to capture the fortress.

Behind Moshe, a soldier slipped on a stone and fell into a small patch of thorns. He cried out, then muffled his cry to a painful panting as he lay in the mud and plucked needles from his hand and arm. Others slid carefully past him, muttering oaths as the branches tugged at their clothing as well. Two men prodded the Arab captive along at the point of their bayonets. His hands still bound, the young warrior was a mass of bleeding wounds from the thorns. His muffled moans went unheeded by his captors as they pressed on.

Twenty feet ahead, the ravine rose to the face of the out-cropping. A thin corridor of light, a mere three feet in width, cut across their path. For one moment as they crossed, Moshe and his men would be vulnerable in the light. He searched franti-cally for a way around this obstacle, which seemed even more threatening than thorns. Behind him the soldiers slowed, then stopped, each uncertain and anxious about this one moment of delay. If Arab guns were trained anywhere on this exposed slope, it would surely be there, where light cracked the darkness of their shelter. Moshe looked up toward the silent houses that crouched above them. Behind him, a man tugged his boot and whispered.

"I'll go first."

Before Moshe could answer, the fellow scrambled past him and leaped over the beam of light like a deer jumping a fence. No rattle of gunfire met his crossing. From the west end of Kas-tel, Moshe could hear the continuing shrieks of frenzied Jihad Moquades as they faced Jewish guns with fierce determination. *How many are they?* Moshe crouched and fixed his eyes on the safe haven of darkness across the bright gulf. He held his breath and ducked his head instinctively for the instant of passage. Man after man followed him, and still they were not met by Arab resistance. *Had the old Arab told the truth?*

Only a thin ribbon of darkness wrapped around the bottom of the promontory. Moshe and his men brushed against the rug-ged wall as they inched their way around the point of the rock face. Ahead of them stretched a boulder-strewn field and then the village of Kastel.

Moshe surveyed the field and then whispered back: "Scatter and take shelter in the boulders."

He hesitated a moment, then sprang from the shadows, dart-ing toward a large car-sized stone half-buried in the hillside. The thump of boots and the clatter of equipment told Moshe that his men were right behind him. Then, suddenly, a burst of machine-gun fire echoed on the slope and a man to Moshe's right screamed and fell wounded in the bright moonlight.

"We have been spotted!" shouted a frantic voice in Hebrew.

The rattle of gunstocks against hard stone was heard as Haganah men scurried for cover. Above them in the village, the machine gun was heard again and again. Dust and chips of stone flew across the ground as bullets probed for Jews with deadly accuracy. Two more men cried out and then fell silent to the ground. Moshe hugged the boulder, conscious that light and shadow could spell the difference between death and life. He heard the agonized voice of the wounded soldier call weakly for help.

"In the name of God—please! My legs! My legs!" He writhed in pain on the most exposed face of the slope. No doubt he was in full view of the gunner. Below the man and to the left, a voice whispered hoarsely from behind a small boulder, "I am coming, Aram." Then a dark shape ventured cautiously out toward the wounded soldier.

Instantly, a hail of bullets slammed into the ground around the rescuer, and with a cry, he fell back into the shadows.

"Please help me!" cried the wounded man. Moshe put his hand to his head as a feeling of sick helplessness swept over him. He leaned his cheek against the stone and turned his eyes toward the clearly visible village. *If the moonlight works against us, then it will surely work against them as well.* He strained to see the position of the weapon that held them at bay with such deadly ease.

Was it any wonder this place had been the fortress for every conquering nation that had come to Palestine? *He who controls Kastel controls the road to Jerusalem.* Near where the village mosque stood, a minaret pointed skyward like a black sword. From the platform where the muezzin called the faithful to prayer, a burst of gunfire erupted. Gravel sprayed up less than three feet from where Moshe huddled. *If I can see him, then he can see me. Or at least the shadow where I am hiding.*

They were trapped—seventy men held at bay by one lone man at a machine gun. The thought of it seemed absurd. It was no wonder the Arabs had not bothered to post sentries every few yards along the wall. There was no need. In the meantime, the finest of the Haganah spilled their blood in Ramle, and a convoy of three hundred trucks waited for the word that meant victory: *We have taken Kastel!*

"For the love of God, help me!" came the feeble cry.

"Somebody help him!" an angry Jewish voice shouted.

A chilling laugh echoed down from the tower. "Yes, Yehudah! Help him!" It was not the voice of a child, thought Moshe. The old Arab had lied. At that instant, fire spurted from the barrel of the machine gun, illuminating the Jihad Moquade who pulled the trigger. Bullets sprayed the wounded Jew, who screamed and convulsed once, then lay silent.

Moshe groaned audibly as others in the group gasped and cursed or quietly prayed the Shema: *"Hear, O Israel . . ."*

The body of their comrade lay like a stone, an ever-widening pool of dark liquid beneath him.

One machine gun could hold a thousand. There was no advance and no retreat. *Our brothers fight at Ramle. Three hundred trucks are waiting. Will we fail because of one gun?* Three had been cut down in an instant. Shoemakers and scholars, the men under his command were not soldiers. Nor was he.

"Moshe!" a voice cried from behind a boulder opposite the ravine. "What should we do?"

The minaret towered above them—a Goliath, sinister and threatening in the moonlight. Beads of sweat formed on Moshe's brow. *Was not David a shepherd? Courage!*

"Moshe!" cried yet another voice.

"He is above us," Moshe whispered. "On the platform of the minaret." His words were passed from one stone to another as he waited and thought and prayed.

"Yes. *Yes*, Moshe. But what shall we do?" whispered an urgent and frightened voice.

Three fell in an instant. Your legs will be shot away. Moshe knew what he must do. "When I run," he whispered, hoping his words were not carried to the ears of the sniper, "you must all fire at once at the minaret."

Silence met his words for a moment, then a buzzing of voices as the plan was passed from one man to another. The clack of rifle bolts followed. *Three fell in an instant. Sixty-seven remained.* Moshe braced his back against the boulder, certain that the sniper searched the hillside for any sign of movement. He held his rifle up, tight against his chest, and prepared to fire. His hands felt clammy, and for a moment he saw the image of

Rachel. Dying would be easy were he not leaving her behind. Perhaps the gunsights of Goliath were trained on this position. *An instant and it will be settled.* He held his breath, then exhaled a prayer. With a shout, he leaped into the open, and fired at the black pinnacle as he ran. Broken stone tore at his trousers as bullets pursued him. Behind him, clerks and merchants and taxi drivers rose up from the shadows and aimed with questionable accuracy at the fire and light that burst out from the platform of the minaret. A deafening roar enveloped Moshe. He felt no pain, only his own movement as he hurled himself through the air and into the shadow of another boulder. Three other Haganah men huddled, trembling, behind it.

Gasping for breath, Moshe touched his legs where the sting of gravel was fresh. *I am alive! No major damage.* His heart pounded until he could barely hear his own words. "Did we get him?" he asked.

His words were answered by the angry rattle of the machine gun, battering at the boulder where he had taken shelter.

"You will have to do better than that, Jewish dogs!" a taunting cry echoed down from the minaret.

Moshe looked into the disappointed face of a young Haganah soldier next to him. The fellow shrugged. "I couldn't get my gun to fire."

"Neither could I," said another young man through chattering teeth.

Moshe propped himself against the boulder and took the rifle from the nearest soldier. He checked the bolt, then squeezed the trigger. A dull click answered him as the gun did not fire. Harsh and angry whispers hissed across the slope; someone called to Moshe, "Are you still among the living, Moshe?"

"Yes. So is our friend up there, unfortunately."

The voice lowered. "The guns, Moshe! Not more than half of them fired."

"I know." Moshe wondered if Fergus was having the same trouble.

"So what do we do?" the voice called.

Moshe frowned and bit his lip. The odds were becoming slimmer. If half the weapons misfired, those who carried them were as good as unarmed. He turned to the fellows who shared his shelter. "Which one of you is the best shot, eh?"

The youngest shrugged uncomfortably. "I did pretty well in marksmanship when we trained at the kibbutz."

"Good." Moshe handed his own rifle to the young man. "This works. Use it well for me, will you?"

"Moshe!" A voice demanded some direction to an increasingly hopeless situation.

"We try it again," Moshe said in a hushed voice. This time he was answered by the sound of only half the rifle bolts. Moshe looked steadily at the man who now held his rifle. "He will be aiming only at me. Until I go down he won't even notice you. Don't be afraid to aim," he instructed matter-of-factly.

Moshe crouched like a sprinter in the lee of the stone. He breathed in several deep breaths, giving himself a moment to conquer the fear that tried to pin him behind the rock. "Ready?"

Once again he sprang into the moonlight, a vulnerable jackrabbit, dodging the thunder of a hunter's gun. Machine gun bullets sliced the ground a fraction of an inch behind him and gravity threatened to hold him back and draw him into the fire. Around him, thirty rifles fired, their ammunition wasted as it slapped against the stone of the tower or zipped through the air. Then one lone rifle report echoed, piercing the even cadence of the deadly weapon in the minaret.

There was no scream from the tower, but a moment of silence as Moshe reached the cover of the large boulder. Then the machine gun fired wildly into the air as a single bullet found its mark. A limp and silent shadow lurched from the tower and toppled down onto the roof of the mosque with a loud crash.

"Move out!" shouted Moshe, jumping to his feet. "There will be others now!" Without waiting to see who followed him, he sprinted toward the body of the dead Jewish soldier and snatched up his rifle. As he sped up the terraced hillside, he fired the weapon with relief. Leaping over low stone fences, he clambered up and over the last barrier and onto the village plateau.

"Quick!" Moshe said to the two men who followed most closely behind. "Take the minaret!" They hunched over to dodge from one silent, brooding house to another toward the tower. Even as they ran, they could hear cries of *"Ya Allah!"* and *"Jihad!"* coming from the west to face this eastern assault.

Crippled by the useless rifles, Moshe's troops spread out to take cover behind fences and houses. Two men with one working weapon between them, the soldiers of the Haganah cursed the defective weapons, cursed the moonlight, cursed Kastel that had taken them from their lives of relative peace. Jihad Mo-quades swarmed across the road near the minaret, holding back the Haganah from this strategic position. The old Arab had asked Moshe for protection, when he knew this tiny group of Jews had little chance against the seasoned Arab Irregulars who led in the defense of Kastel.

They had been surprised by this eastern assault—that much was in Moshe's favor. Fergus still held the west end of the village and the quarry. But if his weapons were also defective, their force could not win in the face of such fierce fighting. A solid line of Irregulars crept toward the minaret. Four more Haganah soldiers joined forces with the two who zigzagged toward the black pinnacle, and together they succeeded in breaking down the door.

"*Jihad! Allah Akbar!*" Screams and bullets pursued them as they dashed to the top of the platform.

Bullets pinged and slapped the stone fence where the Haganah radio operator crouched with the radio pack on his back. Moshe slid past him, then tapped him on the shoulder.

"Take it off." Moshe tugged at the radio. "This may take a while and we don't want any holes in the radio, eh?"

A look of blank horror crossed the boy's face, and Moshe could see he was not more than eighteen. He shook his head and slipped the pack from his back. "What do I do?"

"Have you got a rifle?"

The boy held it up. "It won't shoot."

"Stay here," Moshe said quietly; then he moved cautiously to where the young Arab prisoner quaked at the end of a gun barrel which was also defective.

Moshe grabbed the prisoner by the back of the neck and shoved the point of his gun beneath his chin. "Look here," Moshe hissed. "Three of our fellows are dead because you did not tell us about the sniper. Any more surprises and *you* are dead. Yes?"

The young soldier nodded vigorously. Fear returned to his eyes and he looked nervously around.

"All right," Moshe said. "That is clear. I am going to ungag you, and you will tell your friends that they are surrounded! That it is hopeless! Do you understand me?"

The Arab boy nodded again.

"Good. One wrong word and you are also dead. You have my word on that."

Shoving the prisoner before him, Moshe moved cautiously around the corner of the small stone house. He could hear the footsteps of his men as they took up positions on either side of the dirt road. Flashes of fire marked the approach of Arab defenders as they moved up slowly through the village.

Moshe ripped the gag from the mouth of the Arab boy and pressed the gun more tightly against his neck. "Now!" Moshe ordered. "Tell your friends. *Now! We have taken the minaret!"

Moshe held the boy in a hammerlock and pulled the gag from his mouth. The young Arab warrior coughed and spit, trying to find his voice again. "Comrades!" he cried. "Comrades! Do not shoot! Throw down your weapons! They are many, and they have captured the minaret!"

As if to punctuate his words, a sudden rattle of machine-gun fire burst from the minaret, exploding onto the street in front of the approaching Jihad Moquades.

"Allah Akbar!" a cry arose from the deepest shadows of the village.

"Tell them to throw down their weapons or they will be butchered!" Moshe warned with frightening fierceness.

The young Arab cried out, "Throw down your weapons! They are too many for us to fight against, comrades! *Inch Allah!* It is the will of Allah! They will give us their protection if we will surrender!"

A defiant Arab bullet answered, slamming into the rock wall near Moshe's head. An angry voice called out, "Die like dogs, Yehudah! We will fight like men!" A round of sporadic firing began and was answered by the machine gun with an intensity that momentarily silenced the voices of the Arabs.

Moshe grasped his young captive tighter. "We can end this contest without further death. Or you can be the first to die. It is up to you!"

"Tell me what I must do!" The youth cried, cowering in fear. "Tell me!"

"Talk!"

"Lay down your weapons!" he begged his comrades. "They will surely kill all of us if we do not obey!"

Another round of Arab gunfire answered, sending dust and

gravel spurting into the moonlight.

"*Allah Akbar!*" came the defiant shout. "Death to Jews!"

The words echoed distantly from the deep gorge of Bab el Wad. *Death . . . Death . . . to Jews . . . to Jews!*

How many times in the last months had this cry sapped the life of the Jewish convoys struggling up the pass? *But tonight there are only a few voices to scream those words*, thought Moshe as the echo died away.

"*Allah Akbar! Jihad!*"

Moshe drew his breath and raised his rifle into the air. He fired three times; from the west end of the village, the machine gun of Fergus replied, then answered in kind by the gun in the captured tower.

The hills echoed with the sound of gunfire as though some other army also battled on the slopes below. "Hear, O Israel!" shouted Moshe. "The Lord our God is one Lord!" Again, he fired three times. From the distant peak of Nebi Samuel, his own voice replied. Once again he repeated the words and three of his men joined him in the chant. Then cooks, schoolteachers, fishermen and carpenters shouted and fired their weapons. From the west, the troops of Fergus Dugan added their voices to the fearsome cry: *THE LORD OUR GOD IS ONE LORD! ONE LORD! ONE LORD!*

Another volley was fired into the air and answered by voices as of a thousand troops gathered in the quarry to the west. Echoes loomed up from the gorge, rising louder and louder, and repeated by the stony hillsides in booming confirmation.

THE LORD OUR GOD . . . GOD . . . GOD . . . IS ONE . . . ONE . . . ONE!

The phrase refracted like light in a prism, breaking against the stones and multiplying into a thousand and then ten thousand who had come to take the village of Kastel! With a deafening roar, the mountains cried out: *HEAR, O ISRAEL . . . HEAR, O ISRAEL . . . HEAR, O ISRAEL . . . THE LORD OUR GOD . . . OUR GOD . . . IS ONE LORD . . . ONE LORD . . . ONE LORD!*

The air itself seemed to reverberate with the strength of the voices. *A thousand? Ten thousand? How many Jews had come to ravage Kastel? There were surely not enough bullets to kill them all! How many?* Moshe's captive went limp with fear and fell to the ground. The cry of the thousands continued for a full minute more and then, at last, one by one the echoes fell silent.

No cry of *Allah Akbar* dared reply. The street of Kastel was totally engulfed in stillness.

Moshe nudged the young captive. "Get up," he said quietly.

"Do not kill me! I beg you! I did not know you were so many!" he whimpered.

"Raise your arms over your head," Moshe instructed, by now himself uncertain that the hills weren't covered by thousands of Haganah men who had secretly followed.

The Arab obeyed. "Do not shoot me!"

"Now walk, boy. To the center of the street. Stand below the minaret for your friends to see."

"Do not shoot!" the boy shouted, walking slowly into the open.

Kastel was quiet now, except for the barking of a dog and a thin, high wail that drifted out from the windows of the mosque. The boy walked into the shadow of the minaret and stopped.

"Into the light!" Moshe shouted.

The captive looked over his shoulder in fear, then stepped into the light. His arms were high over his head and his eyes darted from shadow to shadow where his comrades lurked. Moshe could see him tremble and lick his lips.

"Tell them!" Moshe demanded. "Tell them!"

"My friends," the young Arab called haltingly, "they are thousands! *Thousands!* Everywhere on the hills. At first we did not see them, but surely they will destroy us all if we do not throw down our weapons. For the sake of our mothers and the little children! We have had dealings with the Jews before, and they have promised they will not harm us if we surrender! Come out, or we are all dead!"

A long still moment passed, and then the clatter of rifles sounded against the ground.

"Do not shoot! Do not shoot!" Dark shapes emerged into the light. Fifty, seventy-five, one hundred, then two hundred men. First the old walked hesitantly to the center of the street; then the young men and boys followed. Heads were bowed and arms raised in surrender.

Moshe turned to the youth with the radio. "Get Moses on the radio," he said in quiet urgency. Then he called to the captives, "All of you! Stand there in the center of the street! Beneath the minaret. Do as you are told and you will not be harmed!"

Behind him, the radio man cranked the generator fiercely

and called repeatedly, trying to raise headquarters in Tel Aviv. "Moses! Come in, Moses! This is Staff Group. Come in, Moses!" A dim crackle replied as the frightened young man played desperately with the tuning knob. He cursed, then called to Moshe, "I can't raise them! Not anybody! I don't know if it's the radio or what, but, Moshe, I can't raise them at all!"

Moshe and twenty others stepped out from their cover and cautiously moved in toward their captives. Glancing at the high-set windows of the mosque, Moshe shouted to two men at his right. "The women and children are in there. Let's herd these fellows into the mosque! Gather their rifles! Collect the ammunition!"

"Moses! This is Staff Group! Come in, Moses! We're at the Red Sea! Moses! Need further instruction!"

The empty hum of the radio served as background to the shouts of members of the Haganah as they moved in from the quarry, driving unarmed Jihad Moquades before them.

The youth cranked furiously at the generator. "It's not our radio, Moshe. It didn't take any bullets, and I was careful. There's something else. Something wrong with Moses." His voice was urgent as he repeated his call again and again. "Moses! This is Staff Group. . . ."

6   Naschon Waits

It was still dark when the sound of fists pounded heavily on the bedroom door. David groaned and mumbled unintelligibly, then rolled over.

"Captain Meyer!" An urgent voice called from the hallway. "You must get up! Quickly!"

Disoriented from the night of broken sleep, Ellie sat up groggily and blinked in the darkness. She was uncertain that she wasn't dreaming.

"Captain Meyer! Please! You must wake up! The English have found the plane! They are sending a patrol here! Please!" The doorknob rattled.

Ellie sprang from the bed and flipped the light switch in one move. She stood swaying in confusion for a moment. "Yes. I'm up," she called weakly.

"Please hurry!" There was an edge of panic to the voice that Ellie recognized as Sam Hamish, an aide with the Agency.

"David!" Ellie cried as he lay still on the bed. "David, wake up!"

"Not yet," he moaned, covering his head with a pillow.

Ellie jerked open the door. "Help me," she said as Sam charged into the room. "I can't wake him."

Two other burly, coarse-featured men in damp trench coats followed him, crowding past Ellie.

"Get up, Captain Meyer," Sam said sternly.

David did not reply, even when Sam shook him. Ellie wrung her hands. "He's had no sleep for several days. A while ago he was awake, but very disoriented. I don't think he can—"

Sam pointed and instantly one of the two large men scooped up David and threw him over his shoulder like a sack of potatoes.

David groaned and protested with a feeble wave of his hand.

"Sorry," Sam said, but his tone was not apologetic.

"There's no time," insisted the man carrying David. "They'll meet us on the front step if we don't get him out of here now."

"What's happened?" Ellie was filled with a sense of dread as she followed the men downstairs.

"The British aren't willing to commit their troops to breaking up the battle in Ramle, thank God," Sam explained over his shoulder. "They still haven't found out about the food convoy, either. But they're out for blood all the same. They found the plane. Apparently that Arab agent with David and Michael tipped off somebody in Damascus that David was flying it. The Arabs tipped off the British. Suddenly we Jews have weapons and the British have put two and two together. Micah picked up the British transmission on the short-wave. They're coming here." He jerked his thumb toward David. "For him."

Ellie nodded bleakly as they reached the front door. With his hand on the knob, Sam froze as the screech of brakes announced the arrival of the small British detachment that had come to storm the Red House.

Ellie's face blanched. "What do we do?"

After only a moment's hesitation, Sam whirled and hurried

back toward the door to the basement. As they rushed past Ben-Gurion's study, Ellie caught a glimpse of the Old Man dressed in a striped bathrobe as he sat grimly at his desk. Gone were the maps and charts that had cluttered his desk only a short time ago.

As they clattered down the narrow stairway, the fierce sound of knocking chased them into the darkness. Without switching on the light, Sam helped one of the men move the toilet out of the tiny bathroom.

The pounding sounded again, this time answered by the weary voice of Ben-Gurion. "Coming! Yes. What is it? Coming, I say."

Sam slid back a panel of wall, revealing the radio room, a space about four by six feet in size. "Get in." He stepped aside for Ellie to enter the tiny cubicle.

"Coming!" The Old Man snapped as he shuffled slowly toward the front door.

"No lights, I'm afraid. It shines through the cracks." David was carefully deposited on the floor. He blinked as though he believed that this, too, was only a dream. Then, unconcerned, he closed his eyes and slept instantly again.

"How long?" Ellie asked as Sam tugged on the wall panel.

"You'll know when they're gone," he said, his face disappearing as the panel slid into place.

"Coming! Coming! Patience, if you please!"

Ellie heard the clank of the toilet as it was replaced, then the sound of the three men as they hurried back up the stairs.

The blackness that surrounded them was oppressive and absolute. Ellie slid to the floor beside David, who slept soundly, oblivious to any danger. It seemed that only moments passed before she heard footsteps and angry voices above them.

"By what right do you presume to trespass on Agency property?"

"By order of the British Mandatory Government . . . There is a bit of a fray going on near Ramle. Don't tell me you haven't heard about it. Don't tell me the Jewish Agency might not have a bit to do with it."

"What the Irgun or the Stern Gang does has never been Agency business. Why aren't you out there right now if it is your goal to intercede in hostile action? We are the political arm of Zionism, not—"

"Spare me the lecture. We won't waste any more British blood keeping Jews and Arabs from killing one another. But we may well arrest and detain criminals—and hang them. As well as those who harbor them. Quentin, Ferand—search the house. Tear it apart if you have to. He's here. And a few others may spill out of the cracks before the night is over."

Ellie's heart pounded in her ears, a counterpoint to the heavy boots that stamped on the stairs and receded down the hallway. The crash of china caused her to wince. A teacup had fallen to the floor, she guessed. She hoped that the soldiers would not notice how many cups lay scattered around the cabinet near the kitchen sink. It had been a busy night at the Red House. *Surely they know.* Ellie felt a heap of books and papers piled to her right; the maps and plans that had cluttered Ben-Gurion's desk. She and David were in important company at any rate. She touched his head, grateful that exhaustion had drugged him so heavily.

"Down here, Major! The basement!" The light clicked on, shining through the slim cracks in the partition.

Ellie closed her eyes, much preferring the obscurity of the blackness. Angry footsteps tromped down the steps into the basement. Ellie prayed that David would not finally wake up behind the bars of a British prison.

"They could have slipped out the window. Thompson! Go 'round and check for footprints, will you?"

"The wire said the fellow's wife was staying here as well, Major. If he survived." The clatter of falling crates drowned out the words. ". . . and the blood in the cockpit. Bullet holes. Someone is dead, that's for certain."

"But somebody landed the plane intact. Guns and bullets are proof of that. The Arabs were pretty clear about it; we'll have at least one more hanging in Palestine before we're gone."

David moaned softly, trying to find a comfortable position on the hard, cold floor. To Ellie, the rustle of his movement sounded as loud as a shout. She held her breath and slipped her fingers gently over his mouth.

"Try the little side room there."

The door to the bathroom thumped open and Ellie heard the breath of the Englishman whose form now blocked the light. "The W.C. We won't find a Jew hiding in here unless he's in the water tank." The soldier jiggled the handle of the toilet and for an instant Ellie feared that he would hear the loud thumping of her heart. "Curious," said the soldier. "No water."

"What's that?" The voice of the major approached the doorway.

"No water," repeated the soldier. "In the latrine. See?" He jiggled the handle again. "No water."

"Curious." Through the paper thin wall panel, Ellie listened as the two men removed the lid from the tank. The beam of a flashlight, in search of hidden documents, scanned the inside of the empty tank.

Ellie wanted to cover herself with darkness and melt into the walls of their tiny hiding place. She tucked her chin, afraid to raise her eyes to the fraction of light that seemed to probe the wall. Neither of the pursuers spoke for a moment; then, in a very quiet voice, edged with disappointment, the major said, "I thought you were onto something for a second there, Hibbs. Yes. Quite. Ah, well, we're not likely to find treasure in a Jewish latrine. Alert the others, though. Have them search the tanks of the other W.C.'s in the house. No telling what these fellows might have hidden away."

"It is curious, nevertheless." The clank of the handle sounded again.

God! Make them go away. Go away! Ellie prayed in silent desperation.

"And a bit inconvenient."

"Sooner or later they'll slip up. At least we're not trying to referee out in Ramle, eh?"

"We'll get them when they straggle in from the orange groves. They'll have a time explaining new Czech rifles and cartridges, now won't they?"

"No doubt we'll find a few deserters among them as well. Aye. There are a few who will never show their faces in England again."

"Or America."

Ellie bit her lip at the words of the men who sought David's life and the lives of Luke and Moshe as well. *To never go home again!*

After a glimmer of light flashed one last time around the bathroom, the men withdrew. Their retreating footsteps allowed Ellie to exhale slowly.

The basement light was switched off. "It isn't over yet," said the major distinctly. "We'll haul in the nets in the morning, Hibbs. Never fear."

The roar of three hundred engines was almost deafening as the trucks of the Jerusalem convoy jockeyed for position in the line. The small, light trucks were at the front, and the heavier, more cumbersome vehicles brought up the rear. Each truck was fitted with a chain so that it could be towed in the event of trouble. Like a winding parade of circus elephants, nose to tail, they trumpeted and complained while their handlers cursed and argued chaos into order.

Ehud stood in the center of it all, clipboard in hand, shouting orders and oaths, threatening, cajoling, and blustering.

Without headlights or taillights, the baby-food truck rumbled past. The angry driver shook his fist at Ehud and shouted over the din, "You momzer! And you are worried about a little light bulb? Eh? Messhugener! The Arabs will hear us coming all the way to Jerusalem! In Damascus they will hear us roar! In Cairo! When we get to Jerusalem . . ." The sentence was an unfinished threat; Ehud waved him on as if he were brushing a fly from his face.

"So, God," he mumbled, "you don't give me enough to do without a crazy baby-food salesman wanting to kill me over a light bulb? Oy!" Then he shouted back to no one in particular, "Yes! Let the Mufti hear us coming! And may his nerves be turned to creamed carrots when he hears such a noise! So he'll think you are a Sherman tank!" His voice grew soft again. "You think he would be afraid of a baby-food truck?"

As a dump truck filled with boxes of matzo bread pulled in front of a florist's van crammed with powdered milk, Ehud slapped his forehead in frustration. "Idiot! Did your mother not teach you the difference between big and little? Dump trucks to the rear! To the rear of the line, you schlemiel! Oy! God! Did Moses have such trouble getting out of Egypt? No wonder they all wanted to go back to slavery! *To the rear!* Dump trucks *to the rear!*"

Half a dozen men clustered around him shouting questions and complaints. "Ehud! The hay truck has slammed into the fender of my truck. Such a dent! The fender is dangling to the ground nearly and the driver refuses to pay!"

"Does your truck still run?"

"Why, yes, but—"

"Will the bumper drag on the road?"

"Undoubtedly! A hazard to the convoy."

Without looking at the driver, Ehud motioned for a pair of young, strong Haganah guards. "This fellow needs help. Go quickly and tear the bumper off his truck off, eh?"

"But, but—" The protest was never finished as the guards took the driver by each elbow and whisked him away.

At such a display, two others who had been shouting angry accusations became abruptly silent and faded away, seeking safe haven in similarly damaged vehicles. Between two trucks, a bevy of Haganah men and two Haganah women approached, dragging a shame-faced, bitter young man by the collar of his torn coat. All of them were talking at once as they threw the fellow at Ehud's feet and waved a greasy distributor cap beneath Ehud's nose.

"We caught him!"

"Beneath the hood of his truck!"

"He ripped this out and was going to hide it!"

"He is a coward!"

"A coward!"

The uneasy criminal squirmed and rose to his knees. "I didn't ask to come along on this little trip, and you can't make me do it! There are laws!"

Ehud looked first at the distributor cap and then at the man kneeling before him. "Laws, eh?" he growled. "Are you English or something?"

"Of course not!" snapped the criminal.

"Are you an Arab?"

"No!" he spat. "Ask anyone who knows me. My name is Herbert Gold. My parents were from Hamburg."

"You are German, then?"

"I am Jewish! I am as Jewish as you are, and I say there are laws! You can't kidnap a man and confiscate his truck and make him go where he does not want to go. There are laws."

Ehud drew himself up to his full height. He appraised Herbert Gold through narrowed, angry eyes. Then he stooped and grabbed the man by the front of his shirt, pulling him up until only his toes touched the ground.

"There are laws, eh, Herbert Gold?" he growled. "If you are

73

a Jew you should know there are no laws left in the world for a Jew to take shelter in. That is why you are in Palestine and not in Hamburg, eh? Lucky you, Herbert Gold; you were not in Hamburg when Hitler made the laws, nu? So you are alive when braver men than you are no longer alive. And others are maybe going to die. Tonight the law says we need your truck, although we'd be better off without you dragging along. I should remake your face if I were not so busy. . . ." Ehud held him aloft a minute, debating the benefits of removing the man's teeth in one blow. Then he let him fall to the ground in a heap.

"You cannot threaten me—" The fellow drew back and attempted to stand, but a Haganah soldier shoved him back to the ground.

Ehud looked at the engine part for a moment, then scratched his chin. "It can be fixed easily enough, eh?"

"I can do it," volunteered a fair-haired young girl who looked to be no more than eighteen. "I'm in the motor pool on the kibbutz. Yes, I can fix it."

"The motor pool. Can you also drive a truck?"

"Yes. Often I have done it at home."

"Then, the truck of Herbert Gold is now yours, eh?"

"You can't do this!" shouted Gold.

"And you, Gold!" Ehud continued over the top of his protests. "We need a fellow to ride as rear guard, eh? Tie him up. Let him ride in the last truck. The open dump truck. He can ride on the top of the cargo. Canned sardines."

"The English will throw you into jail for this!" Gold's eyes were wide with fear.

"No doubt," Ehud sniffed. "They would like very much to hang me also. But maybe the Arabs will catch us first in Bab el Wad, eh, Gold? You must keep a sharp watch along the road and shout very loudly if you see the Arabs coming for us from behind. If you live, just think how proud you will be to tell your grandchildren that you were the rear guard on the convoy that saved Jerusalem. That you were the last man into the city, eh? And if you are killed we will erect a monument. Shaped like a distributor cap. And we will bury whatever pieces of you that we find in sardine cans." Ehud nodded curtly, satisfied with the judgment. "Take him," he instructed the grim-faced Haganah guards. As Gold was dragged, kicking and screaming to the rear of the convoy, Ehud sighed. "The wisdom of Solomon, eh, God?"

Wild-eyed and panting, a messenger from the radio truck ran to Ehud.

"We have been looking for you everywhere! Everywhere!"

"I have been right here."

"Captain Ehud! You must come right now to the radio truck!"

Ehud lowered the clipboard and briefly surveyed the line of vehicles before him. "The radio truck," he mumbled, hoping that the news was good. He grimaced and strode ahead of the messenger, cutting through small knots of men and women, Haganah soldiers, waiting for their assignments.

"Where shall I go?"

"Who do we ride with?"

"Captain Ehud . . . Captain . . . Ehud!"

Ehud raised his voice. "One soldier every other truck!" He waved his clipboard. "One soldier every other truck, if you please."

Forty trucks down the line, the squawk of the radio emanated from beneath a canvas tarp.

Ehud lifted the tarp and climbed into the back of the truck. A lantern burned brightly, hissing beside the harried radio operator. The light reflected on the lenses of his spectacles and beads of perspiration glistened on his forehead.

"Bad news, Ehud. I was listening. Waiting for the signal, like you said, and I heard from Moses. The British are raiding the Red House."

"Oy gevalt!" Ehud put his hand to his head. "What did they say?"

"Just that. The English found the plane. They were raiding the Jewish Agency, looking for the leaders of the attack on Ramle."

"Were we mentioned? By the Englishmen, I mean?"

"No word. Only the Red House."

"That wrecked plane is not more than a few kilometers from here. If they found that . . ." His forehead creased in a frown. "Did they give us any instruction?"

"Only that they were being raided. Then we were cut off."

Ehud raised his eyes to heaven. "God? What now, eh? Oh, such a night! You would think the drivers were half Muslim. If the Arabs don't kill them, or the English, they will kill each other, starting with me."

The receiver crackled and a distant voice called, "Naschon . . . Naschon . . . this is Raven. This is Raven calling Naschon; come in, will ya?"

Ehud recognized the voice of Bobby Milkin.

"Yes, Raven. This is Naschon. Over."

"That's great. I thought by now you guys was in the clink and the governor was suppin' on Jewish sardines. They got the Red House, Naschon. Did you hear? Over."

Impatient with the chatter, Ehud snatched up the microphone. "So this is all the news you have for us, Raven? Where is Staff Group? What has happened at Ramle? Three thousand tons of food and three hundred angry drivers and all you can give us is old news? Over."

"Keep your shirt on, buddy. I'm topside; it's blacker than Himmler's heart down there, and you're expecting a play-by-play radio broadcast like the Yankees playin' the Red Sox! Keep your shirt on, will y'? Over."

"Shirt on? Red socks?" Ehud sputtered in frustration. "So you think I care what you're wearing? Where is Staff Group? What is happening in Ramle? *Is the road open?* Save the rest for your tailor, Raven! A little news, if you please! Over." Ehud stared at the radio man in disbelief. "The world is falling apart and he wants to talk about socks."

"Naschon, this is Raven." The voice was flat and toneless. "Uh, look, pal. I'm just gonna take a little spin over the situation, see. I'll get back to ya in a minute. Stand by, okay?"

"Okay? What is this *okay*?"

"Uh, Naschon, this is Raven. Take a load off, buddy. I'll get back to y'in a minute. Got it? Over."

Ehud grimaced. "Oy gevalt! Over."

7 Raven's Flight

Moshe knelt beside the radio and called the headquarters code name again and again into the microphone. "This is Staff Group at the edge of the Red Sea. Moses. Come in, Moses." Nearly fifteen minutes of effort had not brought a reply from the Red House in Tel Aviv. Nearly five hundred Arab men, women and children were crammed into the mosque of Kastel. Haganah men now armed with Arab weapons held various strategic points on the hillsides around the village. The road was open, and yet precious minutes passed as Moshe attempted to raise the silent headquarters that could relay the news on to the waiting convoy.

Fergus sauntered from the mosque to the low stone wall where the radio rested. "Have y' raised them yet?"

Moshe shook his head and called into the radio once again, "Moses, come in. This is Staff Group . . ."

Fergus surveyed the high ground of the little fortress. "Well, it can't be interference from any mountains, lads. Look there. If the clouds would lift, we could see all the way to Tel Aviv, and to the east is Jerusalem. They've shut down on their end. Something is amiss in Tel Aviv, and that's plain."

"We'll need to get word to the convoy, Fergus." Moshe wiped sweat from his brow.

"Aye. An' we'll need to get rid of these faulty rifles as well, eh? I've got Ham working on it now. He is quite the fellow with ordnance. But had these Arab beggars known how ill-equipped we were, they'd have held us till doomsday."

"Fergus, if *we* had known, we never would have gotten this far ourselves."

"These Arabs have every conceivable kind of weapon among them. But we'll need rifles of our own, or when their ammunition is spent, *we'll* be spent."

"More rifles and ammunition. And reinforcements as well will be needed to hold Kastel."

"Aye, if we're t' hold this rock and guard the prisoners, too."

Beside them, the radio operator persisted in his call: "Moses, this is Staff Group."

Moshe pursed his lips in thought. "If there was some way to get word to the convoy, we could have them bring our supplies this far. We could meet them at the foot of the path and be refitted before morning."

"Moses! Come in, please . . ."

"It's twenty miles back to the departure point of Naschon. Twenty miles is a long way to jog, even if it is downhill, old boy. The Greeks did it on the road to Marathon, but have you looked at our troops lately? Nearly all of them were wheezin' before we got up the hill."

"Come in, please! Staff Group calling . . ."

Suddenly a human voice growled from the radio receiver. "Yeah, Staff Group! Uh, this is Raven, Staff Group. I gotcha loud and clear." The sputter of a Piper engine accompanied Bobby Milkin's New York twang. Moshe and Fergus glanced up as the tiny plane passed across the moon like a witch on a broom.

"It's that disagreeable American!" Fergus said happily as Moshe snatched the microphone from the startled radio man.

"Raven! You are a welcome sight! Over."

"Yeah, well, lots of fellas back at the ranch is waitin' t' hear from you jokers. Moses fell down the rabbit hole a while ago. Complete blackout. Big Bad Wolves come knockin' at the door, if you guys read me. Over."

"Raven . . ." The plane passed directly overhead and the roar of the engine drowned out Moshe's exultant words. Bobby dipped the wings in salute, then circled over the gorge. "Raven, we'll need more rifles. We've had some bad luck here with nearly half—"

"Yeah," Bobby interrupted. "I see you guys figured out them rifles was junk, huh? Yeah. I figured if I could raise you, you wouldn't need to hear what I come t' tell you. Over."

"Nearly seventy-five of the weapons misfired during the attack. We'll need reinforcements. Additional ammunition and weapons. Can you reach Naschon before they leave?"

"Roger. As a matter of fact, since Moses shut down, Naschon sent me along t' get a bird's-eye view of the situation, y'know. I'll let 'em know what you guys need. And by the way, them rifles ain't nuthin' t' fix. Have some of your guys file down the firin' pins. They'll be good as new."

"Raven, they *are* new. Tell Naschon we'll meet up with them by the Red Sea. Over."

"Yeah. You bet. This is some kind of ball game, ain't it?" Bobby circled slowly overhead.

Moshe grinned with profound relief at the words of Bobby Milkin. "You bet," he said in the closest thing to an American accent he could manage.

"Now you're readin' me. I'm headin' back to the nest now, pals. And on the way I'll let Naschon know you got the Red Sea wide open and dry. Over."

"Okay, Raven. Out."

Bobby chuckled into the receiver. "Oy gevalt! This is Raven, out."

Chin in hand, Ehud drummed his fingers impatiently on top of the shortwave. He did not hear the approach of the Piper over the rumble of truck engines, but he muttered quiet oaths at the tardy American flyer who had told him to wait only one minute. A full fifteen minutes had passed in silence. Still there was no word from Tel Aviv, and with the batteries of the convoy radio nearly spent after an entire night of use, Ehud would not be able to raise anyone further than a few miles away.

"Hey, Naschon!" Bobby called. "Naschon, this is Raven! The Yankees beat the Red Sox!"

Ehud rolled his eyes in disgust. "So. He's back, this American *nebish*. He tells me one minute and it is fifteen, and he's still talking socks. See what he wants, eh? Maybe you will make some sense," he said to the radio operator.

Bobby's voice was impatient, "Hey, Naschon! This is Raven. You guys still parked down there?"

"Raven, this is Naschon. We have been waiting. Still no word from Moses."

"Yeah? Well, Staff Group is sitting pretty, boys! And have I got news for you! The Red Sea is parted! Repeat! *The Red Sea is parted!*"

Ehud raised his hands to the cheeks of the startled radio man and planted a kiss on top of his balding head. "Now, this is news! Raven! The Red Sea is parted?" He repeated the code words to move toward Jerusalem, almost not daring to believe them.

"That's what the man said, Naschon. Get a move on. And while you're at it, boys, those fellas up there are needin' a few more crates of rifles and ammo if you got it, okay?"

Ehud cleared his throat. "OKAY!" he boomed loudly. "So! You tell that crazy Moshe he can have what we got, which isn't much, but what we have he can have, nu?"

"So tell him yourself. I'm low on fuel, pal. Headin' back to the nest to see what's happened to Moses. So you're burnin' daylight already, pal. Jerusalem by breakfast, okay? Over."

"Oy! Okay, already. Out." Ehud set the microphone down and clapped his hands together joyfully. He jumped from the back of the radio truck and called to the drivers waiting outside, "Okay! Okay! So we're roasting the daytime already! The Red Sea is parted! Jerusalem by breakfast!"

"They said they would get everyone in the morning," Ellie said breathlessly as the wall panel slid back, revealing the faces of Ben-Gurion and Bobby Milkin beside Sam.

The Old Man nodded curtly and extended his hand to help Ellie to her feet. "Yes. And they may catch some, but Jerusalem will have food by then."

"The convoy?" Ellie asked eagerly.

"Well on its way. Moshe has taken Kastel. We cannot hope that he will hold it for more than a few hours, but it is ours at this moment at any rate."

"I seen 'em down there." Bobby stooped to hoist David up. "Come on there, Sleepin' Beauty." He slipped David's arm around his neck and guided him out of the radio room. "Boy, somebody slipped this guy a mickey. Battle fatigue, huh? In a big way. He ain't flyin' nowheres, Boss. He'll end up in the drink for sure."

"I'm okay," David replied through a haze. "Okay."

"Sure, buddy." Bobby patted him patronizingly on the chest. "After a couple days in bed."

"You *saw* Moshe?" Ellie was hungry for information.

"Not him exactly, but I saw *us*. Our guys got them blanket heads corralled. No mistakin' it. We got Kastel."

"And Staff Group is no doubt trying to reach us on the shortwave right now," said the Old Man impatiently as the radio operator stepped out of the shadows and squeezed into the tiny room. "David *will* fly." His tone was matter-of-fact and he looked at his wristwatch. "In three hours, to be exact. As for you, young lady, if you're going I suggest you pack. And quickly. Samuel, we'll need coffee." He squinted irritably at David. "Lots of it. Very strong." He turned away from them and they were dismissed as the Old Man fixed his attention on the whine of the radio.

Staff Group. Come in, Staff Group, this is . . .

In the bedroom, Ellie stuffed her few belongings into a tattered duffel bag as David slept soundly with his mouth open. She pressed her lips tightly together in anger at the Old Man's seeming unconcern for David's exhaustion.

Sam nudged the door open and slipped in quietly. He carried a tray with a pot of coffee and two cups. "I know what you're thinking, and I'll tell you—the Old Man hasn't slept for at least two days. Only three hours the night before that. I guess he figures if he can do it—" Kindly brown eyes sparkled behind round wire-rimmed glasses. *He has the bearing of a librarian,* thought Ellie as he poured the coffee. She did not reply, but shoved a sweater into the bag with such force that there was no doubt about what she was feeling.

Sam continued softly. "Nobody is going to sleep around here for a while I guess. I think that's the real reason they moved the Agency from Jerusalem to Tel Aviv. . ."

"I don't follow." Ellie's voice was less than friendly.

"Well, there's no place else in the whole Yishuv where you can get all the coffee you need." He sat down on the edge of the bed and propped up David's head. "Come on, fella. Open your eyes now." He waved a steaming cup under David's nose.

"Ah no." David resisted.

"Come on now. Wake up. Uncle Sammy doesn't want to burn your lips off." Sam smiled up at Ellie as David opened his eyes. "I was sort of the resident den-mother in the service. Nursed a lot of guys back from some pretty nasty drunks."

"I'm not drunk." David sounded angry. "I'm tired and . . . *tired*!"

"In your case, it's close to the same thing, pal. Wake up."

"Els, tell this joker I just got to sleep."

Sam forced the cup to David's lips. "She told me. And you've got to get out of here, or the Mandatory Government is going to put you to sleep permanently."

81

"Wake up, Tinman," Ellie sighed wearily. "It's no use. You set the plane down in the wrong part of Oz. We've got to get out of here."

David struggled to sit up and shook his head as Sam looked curiously at Ellie. Something in what she said had pulled the exhausted flyer back to reality.

"A little private code," she shrugged.

David took the cup from Sam. "They got the Scarecrow." His eyes clouded and he sipped the hot brew, and he looked at Ellie questioningly. "Didn't they?"

She nodded, certain that it would take many questions before David finally believed that Michael was gone. "There was a note in your pocket. Remember?"

"From Avriel," he nodded and took another sip as it all came back to him. "In Prague. He told me one of our guys had been killed, and for a minute I almost got it . . . I almost had it figured out, you know. I saw *her*—Angela—and I almost put it together. If only I had followed through, Michael might be alive."

"David," Ellie said gently, pulling him away from the events that led to the death of Michael. "The note. It was all about that Arab arms ship. Remember? David, they want us to go find it. To Yugoslavia. Today. The Old Man says there's no time. We've got to go."

"Besides that," Sam said, topping off David's coffee cup, "the English are pretty sore about that cargo you brought in. I'm afraid that you're not exactly the most popular man in Palestine—although you might be voted most sought after."

David grunted and smiled sarcastically. "I can imagine. So. How's it going out there?"

"So far so good. We're holding our own. The convoy is on the move, but it won't mean much if the Arabs get their hands on the Mufti's cargo ship." Sam handed a full cup to Ellie.

"Yeah." David nursed his coffee thoughtfully. "I'm going to need a couple more pots of this, you know." Then, "Where to?"

"Ragusa, Yugoslavia, the ship's last stop before sailing for Beirut."

"You hear that, Els? Yugoslavia. Some honeymoon, huh?"

One abrupt knock and the reek of cigar smoke announced the entrance of Bobby Milkin. "Hi ya, Tinman. Feelin' more lively?" His grim expression did not change and his voice held no cheer as he plopped down beside David on the bed. A halo of green haze encircled his head.

"Well, I was doing okay until the cigar came in."

"Turkish. A mixture of stink weed and cow dung." Bobby took the cigar from his mouth and eyed it appreciatively. "Can't get real Cuban stogies over here. So we take what we can get." He grunted and shoved the cigar back into his mouth.

"Even at three-thirty in the morning?" Ellie's stomach revolted at the smell.

"We also take it *when* we can get it." Bobby's words were matter-of-fact.

"Put it out for now and we'll bring you a box of the real thing from Italy, after our business is finished in Yugoslavia," Ellie bargained.

"Nothin' doin'." Bobby studied the cigar a moment. "'Cause unless we can do somethin' quick, you ain't goin' to Italy or Yugoslavia. Or maybe not anyplace except maybe a British jail."

Sam leaned forward. "What are you talking about?" he demanded, suddenly angry at the nonchalant way Bobby reeled off such news.

"I'm talkin' about the Limeys. All over the place out there." Bobby blew a cloud of smoke into the air. "On just about every corner. They're waitin'—for the Tinman, I guess. You guys are the brains of this outfit. You want to tell us how you plan on gettin' him an' Ellie out of here?"

"The back way!" Ellie said eagerly as Sam leaped to his feet and gingerly pulled the curtains back to peer out into the darkened street. "The beach!"

Bobby shook his head slowly. "Nah. You wouldn't wanna do that. Quite a few of them out there on the beach too. Maybe they're plannin' on havin' a clambake, but I don't think so."

"How many on the beach?" Sam demanded as David wearily rested his head in his hand.

"I counted ten." Bobby's voice suddenly became deadly serious. "An' I'll tell ya, none of 'em was buildin' fires or crackin' clams, neither." He looked sternly at David. "Stay here, Tinman. Stay in that little hole of a radio room for a day if you have to, but don't let nobody talk you into goin' nowhere tonight."

"What will happen if they catch him?" Ellie's voice trembled.

"You'll be a young widow, that's what," Bobby offered.

"Shut up, Milkin," David threatened.

"They'll hang 'im, that's what," Bobby finished.

"I said, shut up!" David was angry. He rose and towered above Bobby.

"Hey, look"—Bobby spread his hands in a gesture of innocence— "I'm just tellin' the truth. What do you want me to say? Everything is gonna be hunky-dory? It ain't so, Tinman. You got yourself in over your head. The Arabs hate you. The British will hang you. The United States won't claim you. So what have you got left, huh? If I was you I wouldn't so much as poke my nose outta this place, or you're gonna get it shot off. Like Cohen."

David grabbed Bobby by his shirt front and snatched the cigar out of his mouth. "You talk too much, Milkin. I ought to ram this down your throat." He threw the cigar down on the floor and stamped it out.

"David!" Ellie shouted. "Stop it! He's just trying to help!"

David held Bobby threateningly for a moment, then let go and sank back onto the bed.

Milkin brushed the ashes from his shirt front and stared down at the squashed cigar. "Now look what you done. Mrs. B.G. ain't gonna like it. You got cigar all over her rug."

"Yeah. Sorry." David cradled his head in his hands, too weary to think. He would go or stay. He would do whatever he was told, only he didn't want to be reminded of Michael Cohen.

Conscious that his mention of Michael had opened a wound, Milkin sat silently for a long moment as Sam continued to stare out the window. "Sorry, Tinman. I know what good buddies you two was—I mean, just take care of yourself, will ya?"

David did not answer, but picked up the stump of Bobby's stogie and handed it to him. "Yeah. You too." Then he looked toward Sam. "So now what?"

Brushing aside the seeming impossibility of the situation, Sam directed his stern gaze at Bobby. Ellie thought again how much like a librarian the man looked. "So," Sam said, "they've got half the British army out tonight. Bobby, what happens when you go out there?"

Bobby shrugged. "I don't know. Probably they're gonna pounce like ducks on a June bug."

Sam lifted his chin and glared down his nose. "All right. Suppose you be a June bug and we'll see."

Moments later, lighting a fresh cigar, Bobby stepped out onto the chill damp street in front of the Red House. On nearly every corner shadows stirred as Bobby moved quickly toward the Agency car.

"Halt!"

Bobby continued to walk with deliberate intent.

"Halt in the name of His Majesty!"

"Halt, I say! Or we shall be forced to shoot!"

Bobby froze with his hand on the car door as soldiers swarmed toward him.

Sam observed the drama, smiling as Bobby leered and spat and argued with the offending British soldiers. "This will be no trick at all," Sam muttered as Bobby fetched a flight bag from the back seat of the vehicle and returned to the house. "It's all in the timing. Just the timing."

8 Waiting

Forty of the strongest men followed Moshe down the steep incline that led to the road of Bab el Wad. Every other man carried a confiscated Arab weapon and ten rounds of ammunition in the event of a surprise encounter with a stray band of Jihad Moquades. The rest had been left for the defense of Kastel. Empty backpacks waited to be crammed full of ammunition and supplies from the convoy in less than an hour.

As they descended back through the layer of clouds, into the dark mists of the pass, a short swarthy man in a black beret fell in behind Moshe.

"If we are ambushed before the convoy comes, then it is the end of us, you know," said the grim voice of Frenchman Emile Dumas.

Moshe glanced over his shoulder and nodded curtly. Emile was one of the few men among them with experience. He had fought in the Resistance during the war and bore the scars of the Gestapo on his body and in his mind. Moshe had grown weary of Emile's constant pessimism. He saw a trap laid around every bend; death and defeat over every rise. And yet he was a strong and capable fighter.

"Of course," Moshe agreed. "And if we do not carry back every bullet and gun we can lay our hands on, the Arabs will come back to Kastel anyway. And we will run out of ammunition and our guns will jam and Kastel will fall to them."

"We should have brought away more to defend ourselves."

"There is no point in carrying ammunition down the mountain and then back up again. Fergus and Sergeant Hamilton will need every bullet if we do not make it back."

Emile grunted with disdain at Moshe's reasoning. "And what will become of us?"

"Let us hope that we will meet the convoy on the road, Emile. And that they will have weapons for us and ammunition and perhaps even a few men to spare. But if we are attacked by Arabs, then we will hope that two hundred rounds of ammunition and twenty rifles among forty men will be enough to get us to safety."

"It isn't enough."

"Then if we are attacked and we are all killed, you will be right, eh? It will not have been enough." Moshe did not wait for Emile's sarcastic reply. "But at least Kastel will not have lost more than two hundred rounds of ammunition." His tone was patronizing.

"Only us pack mules." Emile slowed and dropped back in the line, not giving Moshe any further opportunity to discuss the logic of the decision to leave ammunition in Kastel.

There was a distinct possibility that Emile Dumas, with his finely honed sense of doom, was accurate. But every empty pocket and pack going down the mountain would be filled to the brim on the trek back to the top. Not one bullet more than was essential would be carried away from the village above them. Moshe and Fergus knew that it was only a matter of time—perhaps hours—until the men of the Jihad would rally to the cry of *Kastel*! The Jewish attack on Ramle would be known for what it was, a ruse; then the battle would begin in earnest. Their one hope was to hold out until they were joined by other bands of Haganah who were now busy drawing the enemy into the game. Kastel was theirs for now. How long it remained in Jewish hands would be determined by men and supplies. By tomorrow, minutes might be counted in rounds of ammunition. And if the convoy did not reach them, then more than this small detachment of men would die. Without the convoy, Jerusalem and the homeland itself would begin its slow descent into the open grave of world opinion.

The Jews of Jerusalem are starving. There must be no more bloodshed. End this misbegotten nightmare of Jewish homeland before still more die. Palestine for the Arabs! Palestine for the government of Transjordan! Give it all to Haj Amin Husseini!

Tonight, this moment, was everything. And yet, for Moshe there was more at stake than a nation. Against his will, the face of Rachel rose up in his mind. She reached up to touch his cheek, and her eyes were full of unspoken emotion. *I must not think of her now. I must not wonder if she is safe or if she knows that I am still alive. Not now, please, God. Guns and bullets. The convoy and Kastel. But my own Rachel is in Jerusalem.* Weeks and days had become a blur since he had been torn from her. How long had it been since he had caressed her? How long since she had whispered his name and brushed his lips with hers? *Don't let me think about it. Not now, please, God. But can a nation mean anything to me if I must live my life without her? God, who counts the sparrows, you have made her the homeland of my heart; remember our love. If I could only live to see her face again. But no, not now! Steel yourself against life. Guns and bullets. Kastel. The road to Jerusalem . . .*

"There," a hoarse voice whispered beside him. "The road to Jerusalem."

They stood on a high bank twenty feet above the road. It was only half paved, rutted and scarred by repeated explosions of mines and grenades. The ravines along the narrow artery were a virtual graveyard, littered with the ravaged, broken hulks of convoy vehicles that had been halted and destroyed here at the foot of Kastel. Streamers of fog glided among the skeletons of vanquished trucks, and for an instant, Moshe imagined the screams of Arab warriors as they scrambled down this bank and charged from the cover of the boulder-strewn gorge. Then Jewish blood had watered the ground and cries for mercy had gone unheeded. Moshe had seen this spot from the air, but only now could he know firsthand the extent of the devastation.

The moon shone brightly from behind the clouds for a minute; it was long enough. Scattered among the twisted iron of the vehicles lay nearly sixty blackened, bullet-riddled bodies. The Jihad Moquades had not taken time to bury Jewish dead. A gallon of gasoline and a match had been the only ceremony for the Jews who had fallen in the Pass of Bab el Wad.

"It is the smell of Jewish flesh!" said Emile Dumas bitterly as they moved down the bank. "Our own people! These Arabs are Nazis who have held this pass! They are no better than the Gestapo! No better than the S.S.!"

No one else spoke. The barbarity of what lay before them that one moment in the moonlight was too great. Had the enemy left their victims as a mute warning of what would come to all the Jews of Palestine? Moshe pressed his fingertips against his eyelids as if to shut out the sight of the horrors scattered on the rocky ground. *The S.S. Sonderkomandos. Yes, this is like their work. God, are they here among us still? Did our men survive in Europe to come here and die like this, hacked to pieces for the sport of torture?*

Moshe turned a slow circle. Vultures had continued the work, and then the human scavengers had descended from the villages. The doors of vehicles hung crazily on their hinges. Seats and steering wheels had been removed and engines stripped. Everything of any value, however small, had been carried away. Only Jewish bodies had been left behind to fall into dust beside the skeletons of their trucks. Only human life was held without value, it seemed, in Palestine.

Moshe's eyes were drawn to the body of a man who lay beside the open door of his truck. Hand outstretched, he seemed to be reaching for something. *Reaching. Like me. Reaching for an answer.* A hollow fear filled Moshe as though he were seeing into the future, seeing himself lying there on the ground. He blinked and swallowed, but his mouth was as dry as the gravel beneath his feet.

"Come," he said in a quiet voice. "We will wait farther up the road."

"We should bury them," someone said in a childlike whisper. "We are the first of their own people to find them." The voice cracked. "Left like this. We should bury them."

"Oh yes!" Emile offered bitterly. "So that they will be resurrected. And then we should take time to say Kaddish over them too. There are six million more just like them. You think it will make any difference, eh? Except the Arabs will come and kill us with shovels and prayer books in our hands!"

"It will make a difference to their wives. Their children. We cannot leave them here like this."

Emile spat. "And how will you tell which leg belongs to which body. Which head, eh?"

Behind him, Moshe heard a man groan and retch. "We have no time for this," Moshe warned Emile sternly.

"I will tell you what would better serve our dead!" Emile shouted. "We should kill the Arabs! *Nazis!* Every one of them. If you want to do something, go back and get the people from the mosque of Kastel and we will mingle the blood of their women and children with these! Bring them here and—"

Moshe stepped in front of the raving Frenchman, grabbing his shirt front and knocking his beret to the ground. Trembling with anger at his words, Moshe held him for a moment, then said loud enough for all to hear: "Yes, Emile. Butcher the villagers of Kastel. Mingle their blood with that of our fallen. And then what will we be, eh, Emile? *What?*" He shoved Emile, and the Frenchman fell into the dirt a few feet from a charred body. "*Would you make us Nazis also?*"

Seconds passed in heavy silence as Emile blinked up at Moshe with fury and hatred.

At last Moshe turned away and said quietly, "Come, fellows. We will not wait here." He walked through the men, who stood with their heads bowed in anger and helplessness at what they had seen. One by one they followed Moshe, who hiked a hundred yards to a clearing at the roadside before he stopped. Large boulders were everywhere. The men slumped wearily against them to wait for the rumble of the convoy. Emile came last, finding shelter near a stone that was a distance away from the others.

———

Exhausted, covered with grime from the long night's journey, Kadar arrived at the bustling headquarters of the Arab fighters in Ramle. Runners left and entered the small stone hut with an air of exultant urgency.

"We have routed them from the field of Hasmid! From the orchard of Ismail Kordeh! The Jews turn and run from us everywhere along the line of attack!"

Unnoticed at first, Kadar stepped from the automobile and stood before the entrance to the building. Kajuki, the Muhqtar of Deir Mahsir, strode from the dimly lit headquarters.

"Salaam, Kajuki," Kadar said as the man passed him without seeing.

With a start, Kajuki turned to Kadar. His face was exuberant but weary. Kadar saw his sweat-drenched horse tied to a post.

"Kadar! Ha! Returned from the side of our Grand Mufti who cowers in Damascus!" he said sarcastically.

"A busy night?" Kadar ignored the blustering muhqtar's impudence.

"Busy! Ha! You are too late! Too late for the glory. You can see that we have driven them back. They retreat in droves, the nearer the rays of the sun come to us. And this was done without Damascus. Without the Mufti. Without the Husseini puppets like you!"

"Then who has done this great thing?" Kadar's voice was a monotone. He knew the answer before it was spoken.

"There is none other who could have done this but he who has led us to victory against the Jewish convoys in the pass!"

"Gerhardt." Kadar's eyes focused on the door. "Gerhardt." He shook his head. "And what of Kastel?"

"Kastel?" Kajuki scoffed. "What of it?"

Kadar's face hardened. He stood erect and pushed past Kajuki and two Arab villagers who stood as guards at the entrance. They recognized him and smiled broad, gap-toothed smiles.

"Salaam, Commander Kadar! Allah be praised; tonight he has given us a great victory over the Jews!"

Kadar ignored them and threw the door wide. Gerhardt stood over a table covered with maps. He leaned on his hands and looked up sharply at the intrusion.

"Well, if it is not the great right arm of our near-sovereign, the Mufti! How is the life of luxury in Damascus? You will note, Kadar, that tonight we have won the first of many great victories against the Zionists." He cleared his throat and smiled with malice. "And Ram Kadar was nowhere to be found. How are affairs in Damascus?"

Kadar did not answer. His black eyes burned at the stupidity of the man before him. The muscle in his jaw twitched as he fought to control his rage. "The cargo of weapons we expected did not arrive in Damascus. Instead they came here. To Palestine. To Tel Aviv. To the hands of our enemies."

"A small concern. We have defeated them regardless."

"Have we?"

"As daylight approaches they turn and run. Kajuki's men killed sixteen when these precious rifles you speak of misfired."

Kadar stared hard at Gerhardt. Shadows deepened the scars on his pock-marked face. "And what of Kastel?" Kadar's voice was cold now and hard.

Gerhardt shrugged. "What of it? The Jews attacked us here in the west. Kastel is at the eastern end of Bab el Wad. The attack was here to the west."

"You did not answer my question. What of Kastel? Who defends Kastel?"

Gerhardt sniffed defensively. "Who cares about Kastel? We have stopped the Jews *here*! Here in the west we have stopped them! And without your cargo! Without you! And yes! Without Haj Amin Husseini!"

"Fool! You have left Kastel wide open! You came here with your men—"

"The attack was here! Not Kastel!"

"You left the most important fortress in the pass and—"

"There are men enough to hold it! And the machine gun of Hamed. You seek to discredit me! You are jealous that I, Fredrich Gerhardt, have led these men to victory while you were content to sleep in the luxury of—"

"You! You are nothing more than a butcher. Trained by butchers. You know nothing of—" Kadar stopped midsentence, his thought struck down by a distant rumble. Gerhardt's eyes narrowed with thought at the sound; as the lantern flickered the two men did not move or dare to breathe. "What is that?"

Gerhardt did not speak; then he dismissed the noise as a verification of all he had been saying. "Jewish trucks. No doubt carrying Jewish solders back from their defeat."

Kadar's brow furrowed. The rumble grew louder for a moment and then began to fade in the distance. "Trucks?" Kadar stood like a stag, sniffing the air for danger. Suddenly he whirled around and ran from the room, leaving Gerhardt staring after him with disdain.

"You will not steal this victory from me!" Gerhardt shouted as Kadar leaped into his car and sped away toward the highway. "The battle of Ramle is mine!"

———

Kadar cursed Gerhardt again as he pulled to a rise above

the highway to Jerusalem. Below him, Arab peasants, guns slung over their shoulders, straggled home after their victorious battle against the Zionists. The tramp of feet, the braying of donkeys, an occasional car crammed full of weary Jihad Moquades was all the highway yielded. There were no vehicles on this stretch of road that would create the drumming roar Kadar had heard.

"What happened to the Jews?" he shouted to a passing soldier.

The man continued to walk, raising his hands palm up. "Vanished. Like demons into the countryside."

"Where are the trucks?"

"Trucks?"

"Were they not carried back to Tel Aviv in trucks?"

Again the man raised his hands, this time to say he had seen no Jewish transports carry the Zionists away to safety. "They were frightened cowards. They will not come against us again."

Kadar raised his head and sniffed the wind. The acrid scent of gunpowder told him that the peasant was no prophet. The Jews had merely left this battlefield for another. He scanned the black fields of the Valley of Sorec beyond. There was no sign of Jewish movement. Not a light or a sound from the rocky hills to the south of Ramle. Where had they gone? And if Kastel had been their goal, how had they passed this point unseen?

Two fighters branched off from the irregular column and headed south across the field.

"You there! Where are you going?" shouted Kadar. They did not hear him, so he called to yet another warrior. "Where are they going?"

"Home. To Hulda."

"*Hulda*." Kadar's face whitened with sudden understanding. To the south lay Hulda, a tiny Arab village of no more than a hundred. Just beyond it lay another road, an ancient road that twisted and wove a rutted trail through the valley. He had not heard the roar of engines as close as this highway. No! The Jews had passed them entirely on the almost forgotten road beyond Hulda.

As the billowing robes of the Hulda villagers disappeared in the darkness, a frantic, terrified voice echoed back.

"They have come! They have come!" It was a wail of helplessness from a child sent to run three miles through the darkness in search of help.

A clamor arose in the ranks of the men as the two villagers carried the child back to the side of the highway. Kadar scurried down the short slope to find his answer confirmed in the panting breathless words of a ten-year-old boy.

"Many trucks. Many Jews! All with guns! They came by us like a giant serpent. I thought I was dreaming. There was screaming and a mighty roar like the dragon of Amtar! They did not stop. Everything was dark but the roar shook the earth. Mother sent me away into the fields to hide! I do not know if they have killed her!"

Kadar rose slowly. The crescent medallion glistened against his chest in the eerie glow of the headlights. "They will not stop to kill your mother, boy," he said, but there was no comfort in his voice. It carried in its tone a much heavier foreboding. "They have gone around us."

The form of Yassar Tafara stepped into the light. "Yes," he said angrily. "While Gerhardt kept us here, the Jews have gone to Kastel." His robes were covered with blood. "We captured a Zionist woman. She lived long enough to tell us. The Jews have gone to Kastel."

"The trucks?" Kadar did not look at the deep red stains on the fabric of Yassar's clothes.

"She died before we could learn more." Yassar pulled a crumpled letter from his pocket and passed it to Kadar. "But we have found this letter. Written in Hebrew. To her lover, she said. I told her if it was of any use to us, we would perhaps send it on to him." He smiled, and for an instant Kadar felt as though he were looking into the crazed eyes of Gerhardt. He opened the letter, not daring to ask how the young woman had died. It was evident that Yassar had somehow enjoyed his task of extracting information from her bit by bit.

Silently, Kadar skimmed the delicately penned letters. His hand trembled at the words of the unknown Jewess: . . . *my first time in battle, and I wonder if I can take the life of another human . . . Perhaps it will not come to that. If we can only draw the Arab Irregulars into the fight, then the convoy can slip past on the old road. We are under the command of a very fair British captain . . . Kastel is to be taken by the fellow Moshe Sachar from Hebrew University. Three hundred trucks carry the food for Jerusalem . . .*

Kadar's face was expressionless, but his thoughts were in turmoil. *Moshe Sachar!* It was a name he knew well, a face that rose up in his dreams to torment him. Kadar lowered the letter without reading the words that spoke of love and fear and longing. He crumpled the paper and threw it into the mud. The crowd around him had grown, and he heard his name whispered in reverence from one soldier to another. Raising his eyes he said grimly, "Our victory is defeat, bitter in our stomachs, unless we can catch this Jewish convoy in the Pass of Bab el Wad." A murmur of determined approval rippled through the ranks. "Three hundred trucks will not move quickly up the mountain! Come, Jihad Moquades! Victory may yet be ours!"

9 Captured!

From the window of the darkened bedroom, David and Ellie watched as Sam and Bobby stepped out onto the street. The Old Man followed with Mrs. Ben-Gurion, and the two stout bodyguards brought up the rear. The front door was locked, leaving David and Ellie alone in the house.

As Bobby moved toward the car, restless movement was evident in every shadow. "Halt!" echoed the hollow voice of a British soldier. "In the name of His Majesty!"

The Old Man looked up with impatient irritation as a dozen uniformed men converged on them. Sam and the bodyguards set down the hastily packed luggage. Ellie recognized her own suitcase among them.

Backs ramrod straight, the soldiers clustered about the Old Man. Hands gestured apologetically and flashlights glared into the faces of those in the entourage. David almost laughed out loud as Milkin grimaced threateningly at the light while his face was compared to that of a photograph in an officer's hand. A few minutes passed before the party was allowed into the Agency vehicle. As they drove away, the soldiers again took up their positions.

"Well, the Old Man leaving didn't make them want to go

home and go to bed," David whispered. He glanced at his watch. "Nearly four o'clock. Sam said we should give them at least half an hour."

"Will that be long enough?" Ellie asked anxiously.

"I don't know. It's five minutes to Fanny's house. Then they have to change into the uniforms and get back." He glanced into the street as an official-looking vehicle pulled away from the curb and slowly followed after the Agency car. "I guess it depends on whether they can get in and out of Fanny's without being seen." He sounded worried. "I don't know, Els. I don't." Preoccupied, David stared at the empty corner on the street. Would half an hour be long enough?

"Sam said it's all in the timing." Ellie held tightly to David's hand, noting that his palm was as icy as her own.

"Look," David said. "Just remember. Keep walking. No matter what happens, keep going. Don't stop. Don't look back and *don't* run. These guys are trigger-happy. They'll shoot if you run."

Ellie nodded bleakly, longing for the safety of the dark little radio room, but certain now that they could not really be safe anywhere in Palestine. "They said they'd get everyone in the morning." Her words were barely audible. "Did they mean us, too?"

"If Sam and Bobby don't get back." David leaned back and exhaled. "And God help us if Bobby opens his mouth. They'll know." He stared blankly into the gloomy corner of the room, then squeezed her hand and turned to her. "I'm sorry I got you into this."

Ellie leaned her head on his shoulder. "I think I am the one who got *you* into this," she said. Then, after a moment, "We're doing the right thing, you know. But sometimes that's not much comfort when we've been through so much already."

David nodded, his thoughts returning to Michael. "I suppose, Els. I suppose you're right. Sometimes doing the right thing seems so futile." He turned and searched the darkness for her eyes. Touching her face he said quietly, "Funny. I never felt like this in the war, you know? Up there against the Germans I never felt . . . so alone. I mean the whole country was behind me and the rest of the guys. We were fighting the Nazis. It was so clear-cut. Now we're fighting the Nazis again, but it isn't so clear. I mean, look at this." He gestured toward the window. "I was flying with some great guys from the RAF. Now I got the

English wanting to hunt me down and hang me." He laughed bitterly. "Why isn't it clear anymore to the world, Ellie? Why?"

Ellie pondered his words for a long time, then sighed, "I guess everyone wants to forget. Especially me. It's only been one *night* since I watched you crash land that plane full of ammunition and thought I'd lost you forever. One night is not enough time, David. I want to forget, too—to get on with living."

"So do I. But we can't. Not until this is over." He kissed her forehead. "Yeah, we're doing the right thing. But I wish there was somebody else to do it. I'm afraid . . ." He swallowed hard. "Doing the right thing could get us killed." He wrapped his arms around her and held her tightly against himself. "This is not a game. And Ellie, if anything ever happened to you—"

"You can't think about that, David. It won't change anything. Maybe the world has closed its eyes to all this, but God hasn't, has He? Don't you think He knows what's happening, David? To us? To Palestine? Ben-Gurion told me that it's all written in the Bible. In the scrolls. In Isaiah. God knew all about the heartache of His people and told about the return to this land. Every morning I walk by Ben-Gurion's study and he's sitting at that messy desk of his reading Isaiah. He says it keeps him believing in miracles. No matter how this all comes about, there *will* be a nation of Israel. No matter who fights against it, it is happening like the scrolls said. We're doing the right thing, David. And no matter what happens, we are part of the miracle!" She snuggled against him. "God is paying attention. We aren't alone."

"Yeah." He stroked her hair gently. "I just guess I would have done it a little differently, myself. Brought it about a little easier."

"I think the Lord would have too, David. It's just that the world has not exactly been cooperative, if you know what I mean."

———

They passed the thirty minutes in silence, holding on to each other as if this might be their last embrace. When at last David spotted two uniformed men strolling casually toward the empty opposite corner of the street, he kissed Ellie lightly. "It's time," he whispered.

She clung fiercely to him a moment longer. "I love you, David."

Kissing her lightly, he whispered, "And I love you." Then he took her by the hand and led her down the stairs toward the front door. "Remember. Don't speak. Don't stop. Just keep walking. No matter how badly you want to run, just keep walking."

She nodded and he turned the door handle and stepped from the shelter of the house. The cold salt air stung Ellie's cheeks, and she was suddenly aware that this was not a dream. Startled, she drew in her breath sharply and looked up at the shadows where she knew men watched them. She looked down quickly, remembering the fear she had felt as a child walking home after dark. Past gloomy houses and dark hedges, beyond the bright halo of every streetlight, the shadows of fairy-tale goblins had lurked. *Don't run, Ellie,* she told herself as David took her by the arm. *Remember when you were ten. Mrs. Coulter's juniper bushes on 10th Street. You didn't run, even though trolls lived there. Courage, Ellie.* The shadows on the street corners seemed to move toward them, black and menacing. Ellie did not dare look back at the eyes that studied their pace and calculated the seconds until they would pass into the center of the human vise waiting to take them captive. Her breath was heavy with fear. David squeezed her arm as her footsteps quickened. *Think about home. Your own front door. Hot chocolate and cookies to calm your fears. Do not run, Ellie.* The step of heavy boots fell in just behind them and to the right. Then a silhouette of an officer in an overcoat stepped into the light ahead of them. Soon another and another rushed forward. *Do not run!*

"Halt!" a voice called harshly.

"In the name of His Majesty's—"

Keep walking. Do not look back. Walk! Just ahead is safety! Do not run! Sam and Bobby. Are they here? Are they among the uniforms and voices?

"Halt!"

"Stop where you are or we will shoot!" *The click of the slide on a pistol. Do not run. . .*

"Stop, I say! You cannot escape!" Voices louder and harsher were accompanied by running footsteps.

Two dark figures rushed toward them, guns drawn and bodies tense. David pulled Ellie's arm hard. Beams of spotlights pinned them to the street, locked them in the sight of the soldiers who had waited all night in the cold for this moment.

Like a nightmare, Ellie's shoes felt as though they were

weighted down, dragging her into the net of the English soldiers.

"Halt! There is no use!"

How were they ever to find Sam and Bobby? A dozen men, then a dozen more pursued them. Ellie tried to see their faces, but everything was dark confusion and shouting voices. A shot was fired into the air. Ellie stumbled and slipped on the wet cobblestones. As she cried out, David grabbed her arm and dragged her after him; at that instant they slammed headlong into a hard, muscled body and tumbled onto the street.

"Get them!" The lights pierced the darkness, blinding them as hands reached out to grasp their coats and wrestle them to their feet.

"Well, lads, it's him all right!" A triumphant beam shone directly on David's face. "It's David Meyer all right!" The voice was distinctly British; the tone victorious.

"I knew they was in there! Felt it in me bones!"

"An' this must be the late Mrs. Meyer, eh?" A rough hand pulled her into the beam. Her hair tumbled down her face. Her eyes were wild, searching for some familiar face among the crowd of pursuers.

"David?" she cried, her voice thick with panic when there was no sign of Bobby or Sam.

His eyes met hers in weary defeat. Half an hour had not been long enough.

"David Meyer. American war ace. That'll do y' no good now. It's off to Acre Prison for both of you!"

"I demand an explanation!" David snapped defiantly.

"Aye. You'll get that, and more. Justice is swift here in Palestine. And you know what the penalty is for gun-running!"

"David?" Ellie cried again.

He tried to reach out to touch her, but his hand was slapped back.

"I'll get the van!" someone called from the edge of the group.

Only moments passed before the armored vehicle pulled around the corner, flooding the scene with a colorless light. David was shoved roughly against it, then made to stand spread-eagle while he was searched.

"Search her, too!" came the command. "After all, she's part

of this!" The voice behind the unrelenting flashlight was cruel and bitter.

"Cap'n." The order was obeyed and Ellie was held tightly against the cold steel of the vehicle while a large, brutish soldier ran his hands over her body. He coughed once, and it was only then that Ellie smelled the reek of cheap cigars on the soldier's breath. *Stink weed and cow dung! Bobby Milkin!* She nearly collapsed with relief and involuntarily cried out as he slapped his hands beneath her arms as though he was checking for weapons. He grabbed her by the back of her coat collar and held her fast. She was his prisoner.

"All right! Into the van with y'!" The light motioned toward the open doors of the van, and for a moment, the light out of her eyes, Ellie recognized the face of the small studious man who looked so much like a librarian. *Sam!*

Others stepped forward. "I'll run them in if you like, Cap'n."

Sam's accent was flawless. "No thank you. The rest of you stay and keep an eye on that building. There may be others." He herded David and Ellie into the vehicle with Bobby. The light, and the attention, still shone directly onto the face of the beautiful and disheveled redhead who climbed awkwardly into the van. Not once did Sam's flashlight beam leave her face, and never did the soldiers question the captain's insignia he wore.

The doors slammed shut, and the vehicle sped away with a roar. Bobby and Sam shared the barred compartment, locked inside with David and Ellie. No one spoke as Sam leaned forward to the window that separated the driver from the compartment.

"I say!" he shouted through the wire. "Stop this thing a moment and let me up front with you."

The driver nodded and pulled to the side of the road along a section of beach. He left the motor idling as he stepped out and came around to the back of the van. The doors opened wide and his glance was met by a blinding light.

"There's a good fellow," Sam said with gratitude. "Riding in the rear always makes one's stomach a bit upset, what?" Then the cylinder of the flashlight rose up and came down full force on the head of the driver. The man groaned and crumpled to the ground; an instant later, David, Ellie and Bobby scrambled onto the road over his prone body.

"Boy, am I glad to see you," David breathed, extending his

hands. Only now did Ellie see they were handcuffed together.

"I couldn't see your faces behind the light," Ellie said, almost giddy with relief.

Sam studied David's handcuffs briefly. "Sorry. I haven't got a key to those things. It will have to wait till we get you to the airport."

"No time to shoot the bull." Bobby slapped a cold cigar into his mouth and dragged the soldier to the sand on the side of the road. He pulled out a small flask and poured some of its contents over the unconscious Englishman; then he downed a hefty portion himself. "A little Who-Hit-John, as we call the stuff back home." He planted a cigar in the mouth of the man. "I never met a Limey who could hold his liquor."

Ellie's gasp caused everyone to glance up. Far down the road, the unmistakable headlights of an automobile approached.

"Get in!" David cried, shoving her back into the van and clambering after.

His jaw set grimly, Sam watched as the vehicle slowed to a crawl. The soldier moaned feebly and his eyelids fluttered. Bobby hit him again with the flask on the top of the head. Then the lights of the car caught them and Sam saw the insignia of the Palestine Police on the side.

"Let me do the talking," Sam warned Bobby in a low voice.

A concerned police officer unrolled his window as the car blocked the path of the van. "Any trouble here, officer?" he asked, stepping out into the cold night air. The roar of the surf echoed behind him.

Bobby towered over the unconscious driver and sized up the policeman. He would not be too difficult to take down. He was a dark, slightly built Arab Palestinian. His face was angular and his eyes suspicious.

"Nothing we can't handle," Sam assured him, his accent flawless.

"What's that?" demanded the officer; a larger policeman climbed from the passenger side of the vehicle.

"Is the fellow dead?" asked the big officer. His question was directed at Bobby, who stuck out his lower lip and shook his head.

"Quite inebriated, though," Sam said cheerfully. "And nearly was killed. The chap stumbled out in front of us just as we rounded the curve, you see. We nearly hit him, poor fellow. He fell and smashed his head, but seems to be all right."

The smaller police officer raised his chin slightly as if to question the story. He stepped forward to examine the prostrate driver. "Hmmm. Yes. Drunk I suppose." He sniffed unpleasantly. Then he gently patted the cheek of the driver. "Come on there, fellow, wake up, will you?"

The driver moaned and then opened his eyes reluctantly. "My head!" he whispered.

A cold ripple of fear passed through Sam and Bobby as the policeman knelt beside the driver. "A bit too much, eh, fellow?"

"No . . . no . . . my head!" The driver ran his fingers through his hair in confusion. "They . . . they asked me to open the door and then something hit me . . . something." He blinked up toward Sam as though trying to remember.

"Come on, old chap!" Sam rushed forward and clasped the driver beneath the arms, pulling him up to his feet with Bobby's help.

"Something hit me . . ." The driver's knees buckled slightly.

"A bit of Who-Hit-John, as the Americans say," Sam interjected. "We can take care of him, officer."

The two policemen stepped back as Bobby helped the driver into the cab of the van. "Perhaps you should take him to a hospital? For check, eh?" said the large officer.

"Right. There's a good fellow." Sam hoped the edge in his voice would not betray them.

"I opened the door and . . ." The driver tried to reconstruct the event.

As Bobby climbed in after him, he continued to mutter. The headlights of the police car shone into the cab as Sam hopped in behind the wheel and shifted into gear.

"I would stay away from the alcohol, fellow," called the small policeman with a smile and a wave.

"No!" said the driver, wedged between Sam and Bobby. "I have not had a drop." He sniffed his jacket as Sam backed the van and then pulled slowly around the police car. "Not a drop . . . something . . ." His face filled with realization. "No . . . *somebody* hit me!" He stared at Bobby a long moment; then with a shout, he struck out just as the van cleared the police car. "Who are you?" he screamed, struggling against Bobby's strength.

"Help me!" he shouted and the van swerved as he knocked Sam hard in the ribs.

David and Ellie stared horrified at the scene through the bars, and David called encouragement to Bobby. "Hold 'im! Clobber 'im!"

Bobby did not reply, but grabbed the driver beneath the chin in a grip that cut off the man's air supply. With a strangled cry, the driver passed out, relaxing at last in Bobby's grasp as Sam turned up a side street that headed toward the outskirts of Tel Aviv and the tiny landing strip of the Jewish Agency.

10 Dark Before Dawn

Moshe glanced at his watch. It was nearly four-thirty; only a matter of an hour before the sky in the east would pale. Daylight would bring new dangers.

Where is the convoy? Have they been stopped beyond Ramle? Ehud, the others—do they also lie by the side of the road in pieces? Moshe raised his eyes for a moment, wishing for the gray fog to dissipate, wishing to see clearly. *God? You who see when even the sparrow falls also must see us as well. And yet we do not always hear you answer. Six million prayers, and you were silent. Six million graves; here, sixty more beside this road, and still no word from you. So we are left like a nation of Jobs to wonder why and how there can be such injustice in the hearts of men. We die reaching for an answer, and you are silent.*

Moshe studied the brooding shadows of his men. They stared into the early-morning blackness, lost in their own thoughts of mortality. He did not know all their stories, but he knew that each one had suffered enough that had their loss and grief been spread throughout the lives of a hundred men, it still would be too much to bear. And yet they bore it. Some, like Emile, had died inside. Others simply raised their eyes to heaven and questioned the silence. Still others raised their fists and shouted, *Never again!* And some simply wept, never questioning or raging—only grieving.

The world had lost millions of innocent men, women, and children—not only Jews, but Christians who helped Jews, and the old, and the handicapped, and those deemed "useless" to society. And it had lost its *innocence* as well. Gone was the hope that the hearts of men were basically true and seeking after peace and goodwill. Gone was the belief that men might love their neighbors as themselves; that they might reach out to those in need. How had it come to this? Why was it still happening now? Had the world not seen the ovens of Auschwitz opened? And yet, a mere three years later, the road to Jerusalem was closed and littered with Jewish dead, and the Holy City went hungry.

The Nazis killed us and called us Christ killers, God. And yet their act itself denies Him. It is they who turn away from you. Surely you see those who die reaching . . .

Moshe sighed and laid his head back against the cold stone. Thoughts and questions were tangled with prayers. He was grateful that God was not threatened by his doubts and fears. *And now it seems that the only hope we have left is you, God. No hope in the world. Only in you. Will you be silent now? Now that we can no longer trust in any nation or man? Or will you answer?*

Moshe's gaze strayed upward into the fading night. "Yeshua." He breathed the single word. *Are you truly silent, or do you answer in ways we do not hear? You, too, died under the sword of injustice. God has spoken in the silence: He sent Messiah. Yet so few hear; so few listen. Yeshua, Chosen One, do not be silent now.*

A tear stung Moshe's eye; he exhaled a long breath, heavy with weariness. His thoughts turned to Rachel, and only one prayer now seemed to matter. *Rachel and I are small, God, compared to six million and sixty. Every woman who died was as precious in your sight as she is in mine. Every child you loved like Tikvah, and every man like me. I will tell you now . . . I long to live and spend a lifetime with them. But I will say, like Job, that even if you slay me, yet will I trust you. Even if you seem silent . . . even if I do not hear . . . because there is nowhere else for me to put my hope.*

———

The long dark chain of the Naschon Convoy moved forward

into the gorge by yards and inches. The lead vehicles rushed ahead, only to be slowed by the craters in the road. The more cumbersome trucks lurched and roared impatiently, crawling forward a few seconds, then grinding to a halt that jarred the entire line. A hundred times in an hour the chain reaction was repeated until backs and necks ached with the jerking progress.

Ehud perched on top of a small armored car. Like a sheep dog yapping at the heels of the flock, it sped the length of the convoy, then back down the row to the lumbering dump truck filled with cases of sardines and crowned with the wretched form of Herbert Gold.

The great walls of the gorge loomed above them, melting into the mists and clouds. There was no turning back once they entered the narrow canyon. There could be no return to the safety of Tel Aviv. The three hundred would either reach Jerusalem or fall to the side like those who had tried and failed before.

"Tighten up that line!" Ehud shouted to the driver of a complaining flatbed loaded over the cab with a stack of crates and crisscrossed with a dozen ropes.

"The engine is overheating!" returned the driver. Ehud could not make out his face in the dark, but his voice trembled with fear.

"So what did you expect? A luxury cruise?" Again and again Ehud heard the same complaint. The engines of the overloaded trucks hissed and groaned with the effort of hauling up the steep, rutted grade. As here and there trucks coughed and stalled, the convoy roared and stopped, gears grinding up and down the line. The road twisted and bumped along the tortuous route. Every mile was an agony. As the drivers squinted through mud-spattered windshields into the blackness ahead, the Haganah guards scanned the steep slopes that tumbled down to the very edge of the road. But there was no sign of the keffiyeh-clad warriors, no cry of *Jihad* to descend upon them.

The thunder of the trucks rattled the rocks loose as they rolled upward along the clefts and ridges of the gorge. The shouts of the drivers were smothered beneath the deafening roar of the motors. Occasionally an engine would backfire like the report of a rifle, sending drivers and guards alike ducking for cover beneath the dashboards. Curses and prayers mingled as minute by minute nerves became more raw and tempers flared with impatience at the snail-like progress of the convoy.

There were still a hard four miles from Kastel when Schulte's baby-food truck, a third of the way down the procession, coughed and moaned and died. Behind him two hundred trucks sputtered and slowed to a dreaded stop. Two more trucks stalled where they idled, their radiators hissing a venomous protest as the first third of the line continued ahead.

Ehud wheeled the armored car around at the sound of horns that accompanied the roar of engines.

"What now, God?" he muttered, darting back down the line, slowing the still mobile vehicles as he went. Never mind the lack of headlights: surely every Arab from Bab el Wad to Damascus heard the ruckus of blaring horns that resounded from the face of the cliffs. "So put a Jew behind the wheel and he'll blow the hooter. But here! Oy vey! So they think they are in America New York?"

He swore loudly as he came upon the baby-food truck with the hood raised. A dozen other drivers gathered around in the inky blackness, shouting directions as Schulte cranked the engine again and again.

"Someone get a light!" a voice shouted over the din.

"No!" shouted Ehud, bounding from his car. "So you want Arab snipers should blow your heads off!" He shook his hands in the air and the engine turned over reluctantly, then died again. "You're holding up the whole line!" Schulte glared at Ehud menacingly, then cranked the engine again. "Enough, already! Hook it to the cable on the next truck!" he ordered, slapping two drivers sharply on their backs. They ran fifty yards ahead to where the next truck had stopped, then directed it back down the slope toward the baby-food truck.

———

Herbert Gold, still bound hand and foot in the last truck, spotted a dim glow behind them to the west. At first he thought he was seeing the distant city lights of Tel Aviv reflected against the clouds. He squirmed uncomfortably on his perch of sardine crates. Gazing back at the lights, he longed for the safety of Tel Aviv engines, but he cursed the delay and cursed Ehud Schiff anyway. Somehow the oaths seemed to soothe his helpless frustration. More oaths followed, directed at the Jewish Agency and the Haganah guards with their guns. He glanced up and the glow of lights seemed brighter and more distinct. He shifted his weight and squinted, thinking that perhaps the glow had moved closer to them. He blinked hard, hoping that this was only his imagination. Then he closed his eyes and counted to three. When he opened them again, there was only darkness behind them, and he breathed a sigh of relief. He relaxed for a moment, then gasped as the ominous glow suddenly reappeared around a bend about two miles behind them.

He felt his mouth go dry and he tried to work free from the coarse ropes that bound him. "Help me!" he cried, but his words were drowned out by the thrumming engines. "They're coming! Dear God! It's the Arabs! The Arabs!" He shouted at the top of his lungs. "Somebody hear me! Somebody! Hurry! They are coming!" He sweated and wept, hysterical with fear and the knowledge that no one but he in the entire convoy could see around the rocky promontory to the approaching lights. "Oh, God!" cried Herbert, writhing on the crates of sardines. "Please, somebody hear me!" He threw his head back and screamed until his face reddened with the force. "It's the Jihad!" The words were lost in the wind.

Without the use of a light, the effort to hook the disabled truck to the towing cable went slowly. When at last the cable went taut and the baby-food truck crept forward, a cheer rose up and the men scrambled quickly back toward their vehicles. The convoy inched forward again for a minute and a half, and then the cable snapped and Schulte's truck rolled backwards, smashing the radiator of the vehicle behind him. More shouts erupted as the drivers jumped from their cabs and waved their arms in anger at the ineptness of the men who had connected the cable. Ehud backed up, furious at the further delay. As he climbed from the armored car and looked back down the row of two hundred trucks stalled behind Schulte, he saw the lights. They swept over the colorless limestone cliffs and bore down on the convoy with an almost unearthly speed. How many? Fifty, perhaps? Not trucks loaded with heavy tons of food, but weighted only by cargos of men. He felt his face grow pale in an instant; then he whirled and shouted to the drivers who hung out their windows: "Push these trucks out of the way! Out of the way! The Arabs! The Jihad Moquades are behind us!"

"You cannot abandon my truck!" shrieked Schulte. "I will not leave my truck!"

"Then stay and die, fool!" Ehud waved the large flatbed behind him on, jarring the crippled vehicle as it slammed into the bumper.

"My truck!" Schulte was blubbering as he opened the door and jumped onto the dirt of the road. "God will strike you dead for this, Ehud Schiff!" he wailed as the baby-food truck rolled to the bank at the roadside and over a small embankment to rest crookedly on its lightless left fender.

"God may strike me dead, Schulte." Ehud clutched the distraught man by his shirt front and dragged him toward the armored car. "Or the Arabs may beat Him to it, nu?"

Dirt and gravel flew as Ehud sped down the line, shouting a warning to the crews of the other vehicles. Schulte bellowed and swore, crying that his life was over, while Ehud shouted that he should shut up or be left to the Jihad Moquades like the baby-food truck.

Three minutes later, when he reached the dump truck at the end of the line, the lights of the Arab pursuers were plainly visible and closing fast. Herbert Gold was still shouting, "It's the Jihad! They know! We'll all be killed! God! This is the end!" His voice had been shrieked to a hoarse whisper.

"So," Ehud said sarcastically, as he spun the car around and raced back toward the front of the convoy, "our rear guard has done his duty."

As Sam rattled over the back roads toward the airstrip, Bobby gleefully gagged and bound the driver.

"Blindfold him," Sam instructed, cutting through an orange orchard.

"Gimme your tie."

The driver moaned once as Bobby secured a blindfold over the man's eyes.

"Well," Sam glanced down at him, "he's not going anywhere. Maybe we should figure out a way to plug his ears, too, so he won't hear anything," Sam joked as he glanced at the totally incapacitated Englishman slumped on the floorboard.

Bobby seriously considered his suggestion, pursing his lips

and furrowing his brow in thought. "Yeah. Yeah. Kinda hard, though."

"What will we do with him?"

"Easiest thing would be just t' kill him," Bobby replied.

At those words, the driver began to kick furiously against his bonds. Behind his gag he yelled and shouted unintelligibly.

"That got a response," Sam said dryly as their captive continued to squirm and fight.

Bobby patted the terrified man reassuringly. "Just checkin' t' see if your hearin' was okay, pal. Calm down, or you could hurt yourself." He was well aware of the fear the soldier must be feeling. Two British soldiers had been kidnapped and hanged by Jewish terrorists in reprisal for a hanging that had occurred three weeks before. "We ain't gonna kill you—not yet, we ain't . . . not unless you get rough, okay?"

At that, the man lay perfectly still and silent, although he was still as rigid and tense as a coiled spring.

"We could just dump him here in the grove. It would take him a day or two to roll out and by then—"

The man nodded his head excitedly and made an attempt to express his approval of the plan through the gag.

"I dunno. He seems to like that idea too much." Bobby lit a cigar. "We oughta come up with something a little more horrible for the guy that was going to haul David and Ellie off to the hangman. Besides, maybe we oughta keep him under wraps longer than just a couple days. You think? He saw our faces, after all."

"And smelled your cigar," Sam added, a twinkle in his eye. The prisoner was white with fear, and Sam found himself rather enjoying their cat-and-mouse game. "So what do you suggest?"

"We could strap a parachute on him and drop him out over the Negev." The prisoner began to kick and shout again. "He don't like that idea, neither. Calm down, pal; we ain't done anything to you yet."

"He's a lot of bother, isn't he?" The man lay still again at Sam's words.

"Yeah. And he's likely to be until the Limeys pull outta here in May. Almost six weeks. What are we gonna do with him for six weeks?" Bobby contemplated the problem as he searched the soldier's pockets for the key to David's handcuffs. "Ha!" He pulled the small silver key out and slipped it into his jacket pocket; then he patted his prisoner on the head. "Good boy. Hey! You wanna go home?"

Vigorous nodding and enthusiastic grunting replied.

"Right. We'll just shove him into a packing crate and ship him back t' London airmail, then."

A violent negative response followed Bobby's words.

"Not even with airholes?" Sam asked.

"Nyah! Nyah! Hewif!" shouted the man.

"Well, I can't understand a word he's saying. Guess we'll just have to figure out the problem ourselves. Ain't nothin' gonna please this guy unless we drop him off at the barracks pretty as you please and hand over the keys t' this van."

"Nyah! Nyah! Hewif hyu hyuiot!"

"There he goes, getting profane again. Maybe we ought to kill 'm. No, wait a minute," said Bobby, snapping his stubby fingers. "Where's the first-aid kit in this buggy?"

"Under the seat. Why?"

"Just give me a minute," replied Bobby, rummaging through the small tin case. "Ha! Just what I thought. Morphine!"

The driver jumped once at the prick of the needle, then subsided with a small groan.

"Rock-a-bye, baby," Bobby said.

———————

Ben-Gurion paced anxiously beside the makeshift hangar and glared impatiently as they arrived. They did not mention the captive British driver, but left him bound on the floor of the van while they set David and Ellie free and unlocked David's handcuffs.

"Passover will be here and gone by the time we get to Jerusalem," said the Old Man. "Three hundred trucks in a convoy move faster than us. Is everyone all right?" He glanced at Ellie. "Ah yes. Good. Any difficulty?"

"Well, we . . ."

"I thought not. Good you arrived safe and sound. Now, David, you know what you are to do. You must take action within forty-eight hours. Since this is the week of Passover, the Arabs will not expect such a bold action."

David almost said *bold and hopeless*, but thought better of it. "Yes. I couldn't imagine anyone would expect it."

"Then we are agreed." He rose briefly on his toes and turned his attentions to Bobby. "Are you ready to fly to Jerusalem, Milkin? I want to arrive before the convoy. Give a boost to morale. There will be food on the Jerusalem tables for Passover tonight and I want to eat my Seder in Jerusalem, if you please."

Bobby looked at Sam. "You'll take care of this other matter, I guess?"

Sam nodded and extended his hand to the Old Man. "Enjoy your Seder."

"I intend to. If we ever get to Jerusalem." He glared at Bobby, who then hurried to open the hangar doors and push out the little plane with the help of David and Sam. Mrs. Ben-Gurion sat inside the cockpit where she had slept quietly for the last forty minutes. She opened her eyes and blinked, then closed them and slept again.

Ellie placed a hand briefly on the Old Man's arm. "Will you see my Uncle Howard?" Her voice was hopeful.

"If the time allows. Is there something you want me to tell him?"

She nodded. "That I'm fine. With David. That I'm praying for them all and . . . tell him I love him, will you?"

"Of course. Yes, I will tell him those things. Now, God go with you. You carry our hopes, and I know this is a heavy burden for you both. But be strong and of good courage, eh? Shalom." He climbed into the little plane, and within moments Bobby taxied down the bumpy field and lifted off into the dark sky.

David and Sam pushed the silver Stinson out beyond the hangar doors as Bobby circled and soared above them. Ellie looked up at the belly of the little plane and longed to be going with them, back to Jerusalem and the pleasant house of Uncle Howard in Rehavia. But then, it was no longer the house it had been when she had first come to Palestine nearly a year before. So much had happened . . . so much. She shook her head clear of the memories. Now she was going to Yugoslavia with David.

"So what do we do with wonder boy over there in the van?" David asked Sam.

"Milkin thought we ought to shove him out over the Negev."

Ellie gasped at his words. "No! I won't be part of that, and neither will David! That poor man didn't do anything but just drive us away in a police van!"

"Hey, I was just joking, Ellie," Sam soothed. "The guy is a bit of a problem, all right. But if we let him go, I'll be a wanted man as soon as he hits the nearest military base. If he gets free anywhere in Palestine, you can bet he'll make his way back and tell them you're flying. A red-haired woman and an American pilot are hard to mistake. Not many are hopping around the Mediterranean, if you know what I'm saying."

David nervously zipped and unzipped his flight jacket. He was still almost too tired to think or plan clearly. "And what are we supposed to sink this ship with? Spit wads?"

"I'll get in touch with our men in Belgrade. Surely they can make up a package for you to take with you. Then all you have to do is spot the ship and drop your gift."

"Believe me," David said with bitterness in his voice, "nothing would make me happier right now." His words were laden with fresh thoughts of Michael.

"What do we do with *him*?" Ellie nodded toward the van and the captive English driver.

"Put these on him." David dangled the handcuffs out to Sam. "It wouldn't hurt to carry him along a few hours. We can let him off in Yugoslavia and see if he can figure out where he is." A faint smile crossed his lips for a fleeting instant, but his eyes remained dull and weary.

"Okay." Sam scribbled their route and destinations down as David dictated the information and times of arrival.

Ellie studied his face and wondered again if all this was not simply too much too soon. She rose slowly and, ducking under the wing of the plane, opened the door of the cockpit. Six thermos jugs of coffee were nestled in a large basket packed with food. *They know what they're asking of him.* Ellie's camera equipment and two small suitcases were crammed in the back, and the inside of the cockpit was saturated with delicious aromas from the basket. A small white envelope peeked out from beneath one of the jugs. Ellie plucked it out and opened it carefully, squinting in the dim light to read. *When you think you cannot go on, remember it is Passover. Eat well the bread of haste, and remember Moses and the children of Israel did not sleep while Pharaoh pursued them, either. The chariots of war pursue us still in the belly of a ship in the sea. May God assist you just as He closed the seas over our enemies so long ago. Be strong and of good courage. B.G.*

Ellie read the note again and again, then pressed it to her

heart. And somehow she found comfort in the thought that Moses had not slept, either.

11   Convoy

The very ground beneath Moshe seemed to vibrate with the distant drone of the convoy. The air hummed, then groaned and roared with one defiant voice.

At the first sign of the approach, the others rushed to the top of the embankment to search the road below for the trucks. Moshe climbed up more slowly as Emile shouted down.

"Yes! I see them! I see their headlights! Maybe two miles, maybe less."

A hearty cheer arose from the ranks as the men congratulated themselves for being a part of such a night as this.

Moshe scrambled up to where his men stood staring off to the west. Tiny, shimmering pairs of headlights traced the treacherous curves in the road. "Mazel Tov, Jews!" he said, smiling as a rush of pride flowed through him.

"This morning in Jerusalem!" cried another, and a round of backslapping commenced.

The lights moved up the pass quickly as Moshe watched and laughed with his companions. Then his smile faded as he counted the lights and guessed at the speed. "Too fast," he said with alarm. "They are moving too fast." The men around him fell silent and turned to look again.

"And not enough of them," Emile said bitterly. "They are not ours."

"Ehud would have removed the headlights," Moshe concluded, and they were all certain then of what was coming.

The thunder of the dark convoy still rolled up the pass, breaking off chunks of road as it came.

"What shall we do?" asked a tall, muscled young man in a bewildered voice. "I have no gun."

"They will reach the rear of the convoy certainly before it reaches us," Moshe warned as the din grew louder. "We must hold the Arabs here until the convoy passes." Even as he spoke, the first fire leaped from the barrels of Arab guns. The delayed sound of the reports resounded over the engine noise.

Emile studied Moshe with reproach as the others cried out at the clear sight of the attack. Explosions just behind the dump truck illuminated the Jewish procession clearly. "Twenty rifles. Ten rounds each. Against fifty truckloads of Jihad Moquades."

"From the look of it, Emile, Fergus and the others will need every bullet we left in Kastel. And as for us, we will hold them until we cannot hold them any longer."

"And then?"

"Get out any way you can. Back to Kastel or with the convoy. Pair up. Two men to a rifle. Take cover as you can. When the last of our trucks gets by, get out quickly."

"But I have no gun," the large young man repeated.

Moshe knew the fellow had been chosen for his strength and size, not for his ability as a soldier. "You," he said quietly. "Philip, isn't it?"

He nodded bleakly. "Philip Peres. Natanya."

"You look like a strong man. Stay with me. Maybe the soldiers in the convoy will toss us a crate or two of weapons and we may yet have something to carry up the mountain."

Emile stared at the battle below them, then turned on his heel and stalked away without another word.

Moshe led Philip to a rocky outcropping that overlooked the road. It was, he was certain, a favorite position of attack for some of the Arabs who now pursued the Jewish trucks. Unslinging his rifle, he loaded the clip of ten bullets. The convoy swerved and jerked on through the hail of bullets. Now and then the distinct sound of a shout or a scream was clearly heard as minutes crawled by and the fighting progressed toward them.

Philip's angular face was tense with worry. Every new explosion caused him to jump and gasp. "If only I had a grenade," he said, his eyes dancing in the light of a flaming truck that veered off the road and exploded at the bottom of a deep ravine. "If I had a hand grenade, the Arabs would not get past me!" His voice was a cry for revenge.

"Our men will make it!" Moshe shouted over the noise. "They will make it this far! If the Arabs cannot take this stretch of road, our trucks will make it!"

Suddenly, the lead truck in the convoy loomed around a corner. A small overloaded vehicle zoomed past at top speed. An armored bus followed, scraping the side of the canyon as it came around the corner on two wheels.

"They don't even know we're here!" Philip's voice was nearly drowned out by the smaller vehicles that ripped by. There was no chance that they would stop to drop off supplies when the enemy battered against them from the rear. Every other truck carried a Haganah guard, and Moshe could make out the barrels of their rifles as they sat ready to shoot anything that moved on the hillside. He wanted to shout to his own patrol that they must also stay under cover from the Jewish convoy as well. "They'll shoot at anyone who moves up here in these rocks," he called to Philip as the dust rose thick from the wheels of a dozen more trucks. Even as he spoke, two men nearest the road darted out to flag down a large transport.

From three separate cabs, fire burst toward them and they fell to the ground. "No!" shouted Philip. "God!" he screamed over and over as the Jews lay unnoticed while their own men raced by.

"Stay down!" Moshe shouted. "Keep your cover!" But he was certain none of his troops could hear him, and their eyes turned from their two dead comrades to a half-dozen small armored Bren-gun carriers that nipped at the flanks of the convoy. Arab fire was answered by the crack of Jewish rifles. And from beneath the canvas of a huge truck, the rattle of a machine gun pounded to spark against the metal of an Arab carrier. Volleys of exploding ammunition whined off in all directions as the burning vehicle swerved wildly and overturned. A second Arab carrier tilted up on two wheels, then slid on its side until it tumbled over a precipice, bursting into a cascade of fire and light.

A cheer rose up from Moshe's men, and they were then spotted by their own comrades in the cabs of Jewish trucks. But they did not stop for them or even slow their panicked pace.

From their own positions, the Jihad Moquades saw them as well and directed their fire toward the boulders. Gravel sprayed up, as suddenly a secondary attack focused on them.

Philip ducked and covered his head with his hands. "Why don't you shoot?" he cried. "And why don't our fellows wait for us?" The trucks continued to roar past as an Arab vehicle stopped at a wide curve farther down the road and began an irregular barrage of mortar fire. At first the shells hit the bank below the road, sending a hail of limestone particles to shower the convoy. Moshe held the Arabs manning the mortar in his sights as they moved the weapon and prepared to fire again. He squeezed off one shot. It hit the ground three feet too short. The hollow sound of the mortar answered, and he ducked as the shell whistled in over their heads. Twenty yards away, a flatbed truck was hit directly. This time, instead of limestone, fragments of matzo bread rained down on them. The truck exploded and rolled, sliding to a halt halfway off the road. A cheer followed from the Arab side of the battle as the last seventy-five Jewish trucks behind the target slowed to a crawl.

The night dissolved into confusion as the familiar shriek of the Jihad filled the air. Moshe fired and fired again, knocking out the men who armed the mortar. He was dimly aware of the voice of Ehud shouting that the wrecked flatbed must be shoved off the road.

"Push it out of the way! Out of the way!"

The tail of the convoy came to a dead halt. *"Death to the Jews!"*

"Get that truck out of the road!" Everywhere, Haganah guards tumbled from the cabs of the trucks and moved toward the rear to hold off the oncoming attackers. They sprinted from truck to truck, firing over one another's heads into the enemy creeping steadily toward them.

"Just ram it! Ram it, I say! Harder!"

Moshe waved his arm and his own men rallied, joining the Haganah guards that wove through the stalled hulks to hold off the Jihad.

"Shoot! Shoot them!" shouted unarmed Philip, nudging Moshe in the back as they ran.

"Seven rounds left," Moshe replied breathlessly. He was grateful that he had not given the weapon to Philip. Surely the ten precious bullets would have been spent in seconds.

The first wave of Arab attackers melted back into the shadows beyond the dump truck at the very end of the procession. The intensity of the fighting slowed as thirty more Haganah guards joined Moshe's troops to form a tight line of defense. Ehud shouted over the sound of bumpers crashing against the disabled truck blocking the road.

"Tonight you will die, Yehudah!" a gravelly voice shouted over the gulf that separated the two forces.

From the corner of his eye, Moshe spotted Emile, now armed with his rifle and a sub-machine gun. He rose up slightly and fired a burst into the shadows. "Then we will see you in hell this night!" he shouted. "And we shall finish this conversation there!" He rattled off another round and a scream replied.

To the right of Emile, just out of his vision, an Arab rose up with a grenade in his hand. Moshe fired three shots and the grenade tumbled from the falling man's hand, exploding far short of its target.

Again and again, Jewish trucks rammed against the shattered chassis of the flatbed. Inch by inch it groaned and moved to the side. Only moments passed, but those seemed like a lifetime as the Haganah held the attackers at bay and the trucks continued to thump against the stubborn hulk. At last, it gave way; squealing like a dying beast, it tumbled off the embankment.

"Withdraw! Pull back! Keep pace with the convoy! Fire as you go!" The Haganah began a difficult withdrawal, running backwards up the long final hill and firing into the now advancing Arabs. One by one, Haganah cursed as their clips emptied; then they raced to jump onto the running board of a truck or dive into the back of a transport as bullets whined around them.

Moshe and Philip ran back along the line, taking a position behind a boulder as the convoy crept past. He had four precious bullets left. The Arab mortar erupted again, and as its crew prepared another shell, Moshe shot again. The stricken Arab fell, spinning the tube of the mortar around and launching the shell squarely into the foremost Jihad vehicle.

"Philip!" Moshe called, as other Haganah men scrambled to escape. "Run for the convoy! I have three cartridges left. I'll cover you!"

There was no answer. Moshe turned to look and Philip lay slumped and bleeding on the ground. His right arm was shattered and rested across his chest. The young man moaned as Moshe touched him. As the hasty retreat continued, Moshe pulled out a handkerchief and tied off a pumping artery.

Two dozen more trucks passed by, not slowing as Moshe's men scrambled to board in the midst of heavy opposition. He glanced up and for the first time felt a sense of panic. There would be no retreat to Kastel. In the time it took him to raise his eyes, he knew that his survival depended on this moment. With a grunt of effort, he threw the full weight of the young man over his shoulder and, staggering beneath the weight, ran back toward the promontory.

Trucks continued to pass as he crawled up the embankment. *Only a half dozen more and they will be gone.* He tried not to listen to the receding sound of the engines at the far front of the procession, or the diminishing rumble as the last of the vehicles slid by one at a time. *Leave the boy and you will live. If they leave you, then both of you will die.*

Moshe refused the thought that urged him to abandon his wounded companion. He slipped and fell; then with a final effort, he topped the bank and stumbled toward the brink of the promontory. *Three trucks.* A huge, cumbersome moving van thumped by, its tires shot away; then a canvas-covered transport moved beneath him. Moshe positioned Philip, ready to throw him onto the tarp. But a moment of hesitation destroyed that chance.

Bullets pinged off the tailgate of the dump truck at the end of the line. There would be no other chance. Clinging tightly to Philip, Moshe watched as the cab of the truck moved beneath him, a full eight feet below where he crouched. Then, his arms beneath Philip's, he hurtled off the promontory toward the hard cases of sardines. He tried to shield the wounded youth from the fall with his own body, and the force of the blow closed over him like the darkness of the night. The sound of Operation Naschon marching that final two miles through the Red Sea was lost to him.

Kadar raised his pistol and fired one last time into the retreating Jewish convoy. He dared not pursue them farther into Jewish territory, lest they descend on him and his men from both sides of the road. "As we were once able to do from Kastel," he murmured, finishing the thought aloud.

Sweating and angry, Yassar Tafara stood at his right hand. "The Jews have Kastel. They are up there. They have taken Kastel."

Kadar laughed bitterly. "Gerhardt's great victory, eh? His *blitzkrieg* against the Jewish attackers and their inferior weapons." He drew his breath, exhaling slowly as he looked up toward the heights of Kastel. "If we attack Jewish convoys here, they will descend upon us and destroy us from behind. Brilliant. How did they know that this night a fool was left in command in Kastel?"

"Gerhardt," spat Yassar.

"Surely the Jews will dedicate a feast to his generosity," Kadar said, still gazing upward toward the cloud-covered peak. "They will sup, while we simply retake our village. While more of our men die because of the blunder of one fool."

"Yes. We shall take Kastel again." Yassar's eyes narrowed. "And perhaps Gerhardt shall die in the effort, as he wished for me to die." In a rush, Yassar told of his fight with Kajuki in the street and Gerhardt's desire that Yassar be killed. "But we will take Kastel and perhaps it will be Gerhardt who perishes."

In the east the sky began to lighten as Kadar pondered the words of Haj Amin's cousin. "It is I who will take Kastel, Yassar. And perhaps we shall, indeed, see the end of Gerhardt. But you must perform another duty for Haj Amin and for Palestine. You shall not stay to fight for Kastel." He fingered the slips of paper that Haj Amin had given him that told of the shipload of armaments. "You will go immediately by airplane to take charge of equipping our army. Yes, I am certain that you can be trusted for this great enterprise. And with what you bring us, Kastel shall never again know the disgrace it bears tonight."

Sarai lay quietly beside her bridegroom. The music of the wedding celebration had long since died, leaving the village of Deir Yassin in silence. With shouts of alarm, the men had run to fight the Jews at Ramle. Deir Yassin, a few miles from the outskirts of Arab Jerusalem, was deemed a target no Jew would care to bother with.

She reached out to gently touch Basil. They had left him behind with shouts and laughter, though he had been willing to go and fight.

"You have done enough!" they cried. "Now stay and guard the women of Deir Yassin! At least guard *one*!"

So he had stayed with her and carried her into his little house on the outskirts of the village. There, he had made her his wife with infinite gentleness. And she loved him fiercely and for a lifetime on that night.

His eyes had been sad when he looked upon her and whispered, "I paid a dear price for you. I surrendered the trust of men I admired. I sacrificed the lives of men who were not my own enemies." Then he had taken her in his arms and said, "But such a love is worth any price."

Now in the predawn light, a distant rumble sounded like thunder over the hills of Bab el Wad. Still, her new husband slept as though the world was at peace and she had always been his wife. She closed her eyes as the rooster crowed. Whispering quietly, she looked fondly at Basil. "Perhaps this very night Allah has made a son within me. A son we shall call Yassar."

Basil turned then and looked at her dreamily. "What is it, my bride?" he asked.

She blushed, and though he could not see the red of her cheeks, her shyness was evident in her voice. "I . . . I was hoping perhaps . . . that we might make a son together."

"If it is the will of Allah, I shall be pleased." He moved toward her.

"And that, if it please you also, we might name him for the one who sealed this happy bargain."

"What is your desire, my wife?"

"That when I give you a son, you call him after my brother."

He did not answer for a moment; then as the rooster crowed again, he took her in his arms. "A son called Yassar. Yes, it is a noble name. A name born of passion and of blood. It is the name of a warrior."

PART 2

The Light

*"There are abandoned corners of
our Exile,
Remote, forgotten cities of Dispersion,
Where still in secret burns our
ancient light,
Where God has saved a remnant
from disaster. . ."*

Bialik

12   Passover Eve

The call of the shofar reverberated through the streets of Jerusalem. Again and again it sounded, crossing the barricades that divided the city; waking Jews and Arabs and Christians alike with its blast. Others joined it until the air seemed alive and defiant.

From the rooftop of Hadassah Hospital, Rachel turned to gaze once again at the bright banner that unfurled and shimmered from the dome of the great Hurva Synagogue in the Old City. She held Moshe's letter to her heart and whispered a prayer for him and then for those she had left behind the walls of the Jewish Quarter. Although the morning sun had pierced the darkness, the long night of her people was far from over.

Gently Rachel touched her stomach. There was not even a bulge to show she carried Moshe's child, and yet she was certain that it was true. "Can you hear me, little one? And can you hear the shofar? Does your little heart beat faster, like mine? Yes. *Yes!* God sees us still, little one. Even after everything that has happened, still Yeshua sees and loves us. That I carry you in my womb is proof enough of His love. Your papa told me that God's love is stronger than time or even death . . ." The echo of the horn resounded and grew to a crescendo as she spoke. ". . . and look at us! Listen to the shofar, little one! It sounds for *you!*"

The blare of automobile horns joined the morning symphony as in the west, a low rumble permeated the atmosphere like the steady roll of a tympani. The sky was crisp and blue; the mists melted away toward the sea. *Where, then, is the thunder?* Rachel thought, wondering for a moment if the battle had raged down from the pass and into the outskirts of Jerusalem itself. She frowned and scanned the rooftops toward Jaffa Road. Shadows were still long in the streets, and yet she could make out the tiny forms of men and women spilling from their apartments and running toward Jaffa Road. For an instant she imagined that this was simply the way the people of Jerusalem greeted the Passover morning; then she remembered: *The holy day does not begin until tonight at sunset! The shofar is being blown a day early!*

At that moment, the doors behind her burst open. Panting and breathless, his yarmulke cocked off to one side, Yacov ran onto the rooftop. His young face was flushed with excitement as he ran to stand beside her.

"Look, Sister!" he cried above the increasing din. "*Look!* It's true! The convoy has come!" He wrapped his arms around her waist and laughed with delight.

Rachel did not reply. *Moshe!* she thought, imagining him within the city limits at this instant. She strained her eyes, wishing that she could see beyond the buildings, wishing that she could run through the streets like the others. While they ran in search of food, she would search for his face. Rachel felt only one hunger, and that was in her heart.

"They made it!" she cried at last.

"Come!" Yacov tugged her arm. "The whole hospital is dancing! Even the lame! It is a miracle, Grandfather says! A *miracle!*"

The halls of the hospital were, indeed, filled with people, some laughing, others weeping.

"Mazel Tov!"

"Mazel Tov, Jews!"

"Tonight we will have a real Seder, eh?"

"I hope they brought lots of matzos!"

"You think they remembered the wine, Morris?"

"And a whole truckload of strudel, nu?"

Doctors and nurses mingled freely among wheelchairs in the crowded halls. Rachel and Yacov moved slowly through the throngs of sick and healthy. "L'Chaim! To life! To Jerusalem! L'Chaim! Mazel Tov!"

Yacov's eyes were wide with wonder. "Did you hear that, Rachel? A whole truckload of strudel!"

Rachel passed the doctor who had told her that she was carrying a child. "Ah, Mrs. Sachar!" he cried. "So now maybe you will have a little nourishment!"

Rachel winked and put her finger to her lips, indicating that the news was still a secret. "Yes?" she asked.

"Of course!" The doctor was jubilant. "That is for you to tell. Just promise me you will eat, eh?"

The celebration in Tikvah's room was a quiet one. Grandfather stood over the tiny baby, his hands outstretched in blessing. Ellie's Uncle Howard leaned against the windowsill, smiling down at the commotion that spilled out the hospital entrance and onto the grounds below. Yehudit sat quietly near the foot of the bed. Her eyes were serene and filled with light.

"Such a day!" declared Grandfather in a soft voice. "Oy! Such a day! That I should live to see such a day!"

"How is Tikvah?" Rachel whispered, touching the child's forehead lightly. A wave of relief washed over her. The baby's temperature had dropped and tiny beads of perspiration stood out on her brow. She slept peacefully, her long dark lashes fluttering and her mouth curving in a smile of contentment. "So *much* better!"

"While you were gone, the doctor came," Yehudit said. "Yes. She is better. Oh, Rachel, I'm so glad we came out of the Old City! He said if we hadn't—"

Grandfather turned his gaze to Yehudit. "The King of Heaven will reward you, Yehudit," the old man said in a voice raspy with emotion. "I know, perhaps, a little bit what courage it took for you to help Rachel and the baby against your father's wishes. You are a brave girl. Very brave. The Torah says if you save one life, you have saved the universe, nu? God will bless you, child."

Rachel embraced Yehudit and stroked her hair gently. "You are much braver than I ever was." Her words were sincere and full of admiration. Of everyone in the room, Rachel understood best what it meant for Yehudit to risk everything for the sake of Tikvah. "Thank you."

Yacov hung back a moment, then approached Yehudit shyly. "I was afraid of you and your Papa Rabbi Akiva. He did not like Shaul, my dog," he sniffed. "But I see you are a *mensch*. A real human."

Yehudit laughed out loud, the first true laughter Rachel had ever heard from her. "And so are you." She straightened the boy's yarmulke. "And do you still have that dog, Shaul? We became friends, you know."

"Yes. He is at the professor's house. He shares my rations and steals from the Arabs. He shares with us also."

Howard did not look away from the window. "Maybe now there will be more to share." He smiled at the circle of dancers who sang and clapped on the sidewalk. "A miracle. A hard-fought miracle, but nonetheless miraculous." His face was thinner now than when Rachel had first seen him, and she guessed that he also had been sharing his rations.

"I was on the roof," Rachel began. "I heard the horns and thought that it was because of Passover."

"No," Grandfather growled. "That will be *tomorrow*, girl. After we have eaten!"

Howard replied, "They say Ben-Gurion flew in about an hour ago. He was on the radio. Our fellows have taken Kastel from the Arabs. The road is open—for now, at least. And the whole city has gone wild with joy."

Yacov stood beside him. "All the city, Professor Moniger?"

Howard followed the boy's gaze to the Arab Quarter of Sheik Jarra just below the hospital. Its streets were an ominous contrast to the noise and bustle of the Jewish Quarter beyond. Empty and silent, the Arab streets and houses received the news with a sullen foreboding that caused Howard to shudder involuntarily. "No, Yacov. Not all. But we will not let their anger color our celebration tonight."

Rachel's heart felt a sudden twinge of fear. "Did he say on the radio how many were killed?" she asked in a rush. Feeling suddenly weak, she sat down and grasped the rail of the bed.

"No. They have no numbers. Light casualties, they said."

"Could Moshe be coming here? To Jerusalem?" Color climbed to her cheeks.

"Now, now, child," Grandfather began gently. "He is still wanted by the English. He could not come here without great risk. True? Of course true."

"But there may be someone with the convoy who has news." She looked with pitiful longing at Howard. "Professor? Professor, could you . . ." Her voice faltered and she looked at the sleeping child.

"You can't ask the professor," Grandfather said. "The convoy will be mobbed by people."

"Of course she can. She can ask me and I will say that I will be happy to go."

"And I will go as well," Yacov volunteered.

"Who knows, we might pick up a little something for supper tonight."

"For Passover?" Yacov said loudly. "You see, Grandfather, I must go along with him or he may buy us food fit only for a

Gentile. I've seen the sorts of things these goyim eat," he teased with a mock shudder.

Yehudit turned to Rachel with concern. "Rachel, you should also go. Let me stay here with Tikvah. She is much better. Go then and look for Moshe. Ask after him. Hear with your own ears what has happened."

For a moment, Rachel hesitated, glancing nervously out the window and then back to the baby. She felt torn between the desire to search for Moshe and the fear of leaving Tikvah. "Thank you. But I can't leave her. Not yet." She looked to Howard. "But if you will go for me and make inquiry after my Moshe. And you as well, Yacov. Grandfather, you and Yehudit should go home and get ready for Passover. I can't leave Tikvah now. She will wake soon and be frightened if I am not here."

For all her longing to see Moshe, for all her desire to hear the news, a terrible fear rooted Rachel stubbornly by the bedside of Tikvah. *Perhaps no one will have seen him at all. Or else they will tell me that he was shot and left wounded to the Arabs. Or that he is never coming back to me. Oh, please, God! Don't let there be such news!*

Yehudit put her arm gently around Rachel. "But you must go yourself. It is plain to see on your face. To wait here for word would drive you mad." Her voice was quiet and soothing. "Our little Tikvah will sleep now, and I will stay right at her side. I will not leave for even a moment."

Rachel searched her face, trying to imagine what it would be like if Moshe were there and she did not go to him. If he were wounded and dying with the convoy and she did not come to comfort him and tell him, *We are going to have a child, my dearest Moshe. Our love has made a baby!* "Yes," she answered. "Yes. You are right. I must go. I must try to find him."

Howard cleared his throat. "I'm afraid your grandfather is right. It would be dangerous for Moshe to stay with the convoy. The best we can hope for now is a bit of news."

"Yes," she said distractedly. "News."

Grandfather patted her on the arm as he shuffled out the door. "So, Rachel," he whispered, "even if there is no word, you think God doesn't know where he is? He brought *you* home, didn't He?"

She nodded and clutched Moshe's letter in her pocket.

As the sounds of the shofar faded, in a dark courtyard of the Old City, Rabbi Akiva struck a match and set fire to a small heap of bread crumbs gathered in a wooden spoon. As commanded by the law, he had searched for leaven in the house on the eve of Passover, and now burned it to usher in the Feast of Unleavened Bread. Over the high walls that surrounded him, he glanced up toward the dome of the Hurva and the newly unfurled flag that sparkled there. Then, as smoke rose before him, he reached into his pocket to remove the hastily scrawled note Yehudit had left for him.

My Father, the note read, *Although I love you, I cannot agree with what you do. The child of Rachel and Moshe Sachar will die without my help. This is an innocent child, yet you refuse to aid in the saving of her life. If I do what my heart tells me is right, then you will beat me and surely cast me out from your house. So I am leaving of my own will with Rachel Sachar in hopes that the child may live. There is no other choice for me but to go against you when your will is against the Eternal's commands. Your daughter, Yehudit.*

Twice more Akiva read the note: then, as his hands trembled with rage, he folded it carefully in half and tore it. He knelt before the smoldering fire and dipped an edge of the paper into its flame. It caught, and he held it up by a corner and watched as the word *Father* blackened and dissolved.

"She has not yet felt my rage," he muttered. "So she has left this righteous home to be at the side of the whore Rachel Lubetkin. She has disgraced me before the community. *By all that is holy*, she has not felt the burning heat of my anger before now!"

He dropped the note into the fire, then turned and strode into the large, empty house to call the British Captain Stewart for the assistance he would need to return Yehudit to the Old City and his control.

In a somber line, the old men, women, and children of Kastel filed past their Jewish captors. Women wailed and carried babies and bundles of belongings in their arms. It was, they knew, perhaps the last time they would see their homes. Already the Jewish attackers had secured positions in the strongest of the stone houses, and explosives were being set around the village to repel any counterattack by the Jihad Moquades. They had lost their homes, but they felt lucky to escape with their lives. Propaganda spread far and wide by agents of the Mufti had proclaimed that the Jews were bent on murder and massacre wherever they would fight. This morning, in the village of Kastel, those words were proved false.

Both Arab and Jewish vehicles were still smoking in the gorge from the predawn battle, but there was no sign of the soldiers of either side. Even the dead and wounded, it seemed, had been whisked away by some silent hand until the battle site seemed devoid of any trace of human involvement.

Children cried for their morning meal, and here and there among the group of two hundred and fifty, a woman moaned. They were like a black-robed herd, shuffling down the cold road of Bab el Wad in search of the Arab defenders who had deserted them last night to fight in Ramle.

By midmorning, they had trudged through the pass and come upon a small encampment of Irregulars stopped along the road for a meal and tea. A string of battered Arab trucks were parked haphazardly beside the road. The men talked among themselves, not noticing the refugees until they were within fifty yards.

A frantic cry rippled through the camp of soldiers. "The people of Kastel! Allah be praised! It is the women and the children! Allah is gracious!"

Then the women wept and searched for the faces of their husbands. Children clung to long robes of their mothers in the confusion.

The majestic black-robed Commander Kadar strode through the crowd, parting them like the sea.

"Who can give me news?" he commanded. "Which of you can give me news of the fall of Kastel?"

Silence fell heavy, and heads turned toward the young man who had been captured by Moshe in the stone quarry. He hesitated a moment, then stepped forward. His eyes were filled with shame and he dropped to his knees before Kadar.

"They were hundreds!" he wept. "Perhaps thousands!"

Kadar frowned at the words and gazed down upon him without sympathy. "Get up!" he said. "Dry your eyes! Are you a woman? I want news, not tears!"

With the back of his hand the boy brusquely wiped the dust, mingled with dried blood and tears, from his face. He stood slowly and drew his shoulders back. Afraid to meet the stern gaze of Kadar, he looked beyond him onto the craggy hillside.

"They came quietly upon us, sir," he said, his voice cracking. "My grandfather and I did not hear them come until it was too late."

"Where is your grandfather?"

The boy broke down again. "He perished, great Commander. As our men fought to regain the quarry, one of our own bullets struck him down."

Kadar put a hand on the boy's shoulder. "You were left to an impossible task." His voice was grim. "Many of us will fall before the Jews are driven from the heights, but again you shall dwell in safety in your homes." He raised his voice to the refugees.

The boy continued, "They drove me before them, like a sheep to the sacrifice, up the eastern slope. And they came behind me, shouting like a mighty army. Their leader was a fierce man, as brave as Antar himself in the legends! He faced the machine gun alone and lived; and when it was done, his troops shouted his name a thousand times until I was afraid to lift my head to look upon him."

Kadar stepped nearer, his black eyes smoldering as he searched the face of the boy. "His name. What is the name of my enemy?"

The boy raised his eyes then to meet those of Kadar. A shudder ran through him and he said in a whisper, "They called him *Sachar.*"

Moshe was still clinging tightly to Philip when the sound of the horns penetrated the thick fog of his consciousness. Herbert Gold's frantic mumbling followed. "Kidnapped! Tied up! Attacked by Arabs, and now this! *This!* Forced to ride with two dead men! Oy! God, this is enough!"

Moshe groaned and opened his eyes. "I am not . . . dead," Moshe breathed, struggling to shift the weight of the young man from him. The noise of the horns assaulted the ache in his head, and a wave of nausea swept over him. "Not yet, anyway."

"Not dead! Not dead!" Herbert Gold laughed hysterically. It was the laugh of a madman. "The other one is! He certainly *is* dead! Look how he stares!"

Wet with Philip's blood, Moshe rolled to his side and sat up slowly, touching the painful lump on his head. Philip lay sprawled across the crates, his eyes half open and gazing sightlessly into the cloudless sky. His mouth was curved in a slight smile and his head was twisted awkwardly to the side. "Philip, boy," Moshe said quietly and a crushing sense of loss filled him. Here was a life that had barely begun, now broken and ended. "Dead." His voice was toneless.

"Yes, yes!" Herbert said impatiently. "Dead before you hit the truck. Shot midair. Lucky the bullet didn't hit you."

Moshe reached out to close Philip's eyes, his hand passing over a gaping wound that had punctured the young man's heart. Moshe groaned. "We were so near to safety. So close."

"Safety! Ha! So, you should have ridden back here all night and you would know a little more of the truth! I saw them coming! I saw them first! I could have been killed! Should have been! Smell the sardines! That's how many cans the bullets pierced! Safety?" he raved. His hair stood up in tight little ringlets, and his eyes were wide and wild. "Lucky he's the only one dead in this truck! We should have all been killed! Untie me!" He stretched out his hands and Moshe saw that his wrists were chafed and bloody beneath the frayed cuffs of his coat. "Untie me! Safety! Safety! Ha!"

"Shut up," Moshe said quietly as he painfully stretched Philip out flat on top of the crates. He touched the young man's forehead and watched for a moment as the last color drained from his cheeks.

"So," Gold was insulted. "Is this your brother or something? Some kind of relative?"

Moshe did not answer for a long time. *Yes. My brother. And brother to the man who killed him. As I am brother to the men I killed this morning.*

"Untie me!" Gold waved his bound wrists before Moshe. "They kidnapped me. Stole my truck and tied me up to die as bait for the Arabs! There are laws, and I will prosecute."

Moshe looked from the broken body of Philip to the demanding little man who sat scowling in the morning sunlight. The triumphant call of Jerusalem's shofars competed with the brave sound of the truck horns. There was grief and loss in this victory, and Moshe knew that these were only the first threads in what was to be a tapestry woven of joy and mourning. He wanted to weep—for the dead young man beside him; for those who lay still in Bab el Wad; for himself and for what he must do. But as the trucks snaked up the final hill into the outskirts of the city, the shouts of joy rose up to conceal the grief and the cost of the triumph.

From the small block houses, sleepy men and women ran to the dusty roadside. Children cheered and laughed as the heavy-laden cargos trundled past. They raised their hands to touch the outstretched fingertips of the heroes who had forded the Red Sea, the living bloody barrier of Haj Amin Husseini. Tonight there would be food! Tonight there would be celebration—for most. Moshe turned to Herbert Gold, who was smiling strangely at the spectacle unfolding around them.

"Look! Look!" cried a small boy as he pointed up to the back of the dump truck. "The rear guards of the convoy! Look at the bullet holes!" Other boys joined him, gawking and waving excitedly.

"Untie me!" Gold's voice was now urgent. Small drops of Philip's blood flecked his face.

"Look there! He is wounded!"

"Yet look how brave he sits!"

"Show us your gun! Show us!"

Moshe sighed and reached out to the hands of Herbert Gold. "You seem to be a hero," Moshe untied the knots. "Tell me, do you have a brother?"

Herbert grimaced. "Why, no. A brother? What has that to do with anything? I have no brother."

Moshe did not answer. He tossed the bloody rope over the side of the truck and it was quickly retrieved by the boys who then fought for it. "Yes," Moshe said, climbing over the edge of the truck, "it seems you are a hero." He glanced one last time toward Philip. "His name is Philip Peres. Of Natanya. He was my brother." At that, Moshe bailed off the slow-moving vehicle. He was instantly surrounded by cheering throngs who clapped him on the back and wept and kissed him. Up and down the long line of vehicles, other members of the Haganah jumped to the streets and disappeared into the crowds as ahead, dozens of British armored cars swept toward Zion Square.

13 Flight Over Cyprus

The little Stinson aircraft hummed over the vacant Mediterranean toward Turkey. In the hours since their take-off, Ellie had listened quietly while David explained all the events that had led to Michael's death. He talked slowly and carefully, correcting himself a hundred times on tiny insignificant details. "And then she called us from her room at about ten o'clock. Or maybe it was closer to eleven . . ." He seemed to be replaying each scene over and over in his mind, asking, *Could I have done anything differently? Could I have changed the outcome? If I had only known or been smarter or trusted what I was feeling, would Michael still be alive?*

"You would have thought we could have figured her out after she shot the guy in her room. One of our *own men*, as it turns out." David shook his head in wonder. "But I tell you, Els, this lady was some kind of an actress. She could have won an Oscar. Here she shoots this guy right in the eye with a little pop gun, and neither Michael nor I ever stopped to question the fact that she's such a great shot, you know? To tell the truth, I just wanted to get out of there. We were ready to believe anything she told us. Michael thought this dame was crazy about him. Gonna marry him tomorrow, you know? And she was sending messages to the Mufti all along."

Ellie poured David a cup of steaming coffee. "Nobody knew who it was. How could you be expected to know?"

"Something wasn't right about her from the beginning." He thumped his chest and looked at Ellie with pain in his eyes. "I thought it was because she was a newspaper woman. Then I figured I didn't like her because she was on the make. And then I was ashamed because she helped Martin and Michael round up all those pilots." He stopped mid-thought, suddenly flooded by the realization that an agent of the Mufti had helped to hire the crews of their fledgling air force.

"What is it?" Ellie asked, alarmed by the look on his face.

"We've got to get word to Martin back in Burbank. Before anything else is done to those planes, we've got to warn him to check out every one of the boys on the crew. At least anyone that Angela contacted personally." He drummed his fingers on the controls. "The whole operation might be thick with termites."

"Arabs?" she asked incredulously.

"Mercenaries. Agents from all over the Middle East are prowling the States looking for flyers. They're paying top dollar. That is, the Arabs are paying. I happened to get hooked up with the outfit that works mostly on credit." He shrugged. "I just figured all along that when the British finally leave, we would be right back up there fighting ex-Nazis from the Luftwaffe. But there are plenty of American flyers looking for a buck, too. And it won't matter who pays them—the Mufti or the Jewish Agency."

"But what can they do in Burbank?"

David laughed a short, bitter laugh. "Plenty. Loosen a bolt here and there. Pull a wire or two. We've got a whole flock of dilapidated birds about to fly to a base in Panama, honey, and you'd be amazed what one wrong mechanic can do to foul that up." He was sweating now with the thought, remembering flaming engines and broken landing gear.

"You're talking murder."

"You're surprised?"

She blinked for a moment as his words sank in. "No. I guess I'm not."

"Well, I am," he said angrily. "I'm surprised I could have been so dumb."

"Nobody knew."

"Except the poor guy she bumped off."

"He was too late."

"For everyone."

"What can you do, David? How can you get word to Martin?"

"Set her down. Get to a telegraph office."

"Can't it wait until we get to Turkey?"

David was already tearing at the ragged map, searching for an alternative. "Not if we can do it sooner."

With a gasp, Ellie looked out the window to her right. A large, verdant island was visible in the morning haze. "What's that?" she cried.

David barely glanced up from the map. "Cyprus. It's an armed British camp. Every illegal Jewish refugee caught trying to land in Palestine is down there. Behind barbed wire."

Ellie counted seven large airships prowling the waters. "I don't have to guess what flag they sail under."

"And look there." He pointed up to a group of planes flying in perfect formation off the tip of the island. "Think we ought to paint a British flag on the fuselage?"

Ellie felt herself pale. "Anything, as long as it isn't Jewish. Ehud named his ship *Ave Maria*, and they never boarded her. Moshe said the English are intimidated by anything that sounds Catholic."

David did not reply. His eyes scanned the map in search of any possibility closer than Turkey. "There's no place. Nothing but Cyprus."

"Oh no, David. You're not going to—"

"There's a small landing strip. Commercial craft. No military, right here." He pointed to a small blue line on the north side of the island. If we can avoid the military patrols, land, refuel and send the wire—"

Ellie flared at the suggestion. "Yes! And we'll end up behind a wall—or worse!"

"Think of the story you'd get."

"You're crazy! They'll be looking for us! By now the British in Palestine have sent word that we escaped. David, you can't mean it!"

"Look. There are a lot of guys back there; four or five hours trying to get a cable out of Turkey might mean losing a few lives. In Cyprus people speak English; it's no trick to get a message out. If Angela St. Martain or Montgomery or whatever her name was brought any of her pals into the operation, we could lose everything. *Everything*, Ellie—everything Michael and I worked for back in the States. I've got to let Martin know. Now." He veered the plane toward Cyprus.

David's eyes flashed toward the squadron of RAF fighters. They banked and began to move rapidly toward the Stinson.

"Uh-oh, David," Ellie said when he fell silent. "Are they . . . are they coming toward us?"

"Yes. If I were in a P–51 and they were Germans, I'd say I was in for it. But they're just coming in for a look-see. Probably trying to raise us on the radio we don't have."

At that moment, their captive began to wake from his slumber. He whined pitifully, like an old dog who wanted in from the cold. Then he moaned and said through the gag, "Hoffaw! Nyah! Nyah! Hoffaw!"

Ellie turned and peered into the dark tail of the plane to where the man lay like a mail sack among the luggage.

"Better pipe down, fella," David warned as the man continued his garbled communication.

"Hewif hoffaw hiyot! Hewif! Hoffaw!"

"What should we do?" Ellie asked as the fighters seemed to gobble up the sky. "Won't they see us through the cockpit window? Won't they recognize us?"

"If they know what they're looking for."

"Hoffaw! Hoffaw! Hewif! Nyah!"

David clucked his tongue. "Give me the first-aid kit. Bobby sent along enough morphine to keep this guy happy for a while. You want to shoot him or should I?"

"Shoot him!"

"Hewif! Nyah! Nyah! Hewif hoffaw!"

David rolled his eyes and handed her the coffee mug. Carefully, he set the automatic pilot controls, waiting a moment to see if the little plane remained steady. It wobbled a bit, then straightened as Ellie watched the approaching planes fearfully. David filled the syringe and climbed over the back seat. As the driver thrashed and screamed, David made a wild thrust with the needle. With a shriek and then a final moan, the man sighed and sank back into peaceful slumber.

David began to untie him, ripping the gag from his mouth.

"What are you doing?" Ellie gasped as David tugged his own flight jacket onto the unconscious Englishman.

"How to make a flyer in one easy lesson," David grunted, and shoved the limp body forward, dumping it over the seat. "Come on, Els. Give me a hand."

With sudden understanding, Ellie grasped the man and began to pull him forward into the pilot's seat. "But he's out cold! They'll notice!"

"Not at three hundred miles an hour. We can hope."

Ellie positioned the hands of the man on the controls as David slumped on the floor behind him and covered up with a blanket. He reached up and held the man's lolling head still from behind.

The driver's eyes were half open and he had a grin of utter

contentment on his face. "How's he look?" David asked in a muffled voice.

"Drunk." Ellie replied. "Now, what about me?"

"Well, get out of there! Into the back!"

The fighters had roared to within two miles and were closing fast in what appeared to be a head-on course.

"David!" she screamed as she scrambled to the back. "They're going to hit us!"

From beneath the blanket, she heard him chuckle. "Naw. Never met an RAF pilot yet who'd give his life for a Stinson."

At that, they were engulfed in the overpowering roar of the British planes. The thin metal of the fuselage vibrated and Ellie's scream was lost in the drone of the engines.

"They'll make another pass!" David shouted. "Hold on!"

The fighters banked and returned, this time slower than before. David held up the limp arm of their captive in a wave that must have satisfied the members of the patrol. Within seconds, the drumming roar vanished as they swept back toward Cyprus.

Another thirty seconds passed before David poked his head up and scanned the horizon for the retreating shadows of the patrol. He patted the "pilot" on his shoulder. "That wasn't so bad, now was it? Good flying there, pal. Scared 'em off."

Ellie sat trembling in the dark. "Are they gone? Can we come out now?"

"Sure. Come on up. Poor old Horace here is beat, aren't you, Horace?" David nodded the man's head for him. "He says you're in his bed and he wants to go back to sleep. Isn't that so, Horace?"

The man moaned and said thickly, "Jew-ish."

"That's right, pal. The Jews have got you. Better be a good boy now." David re-gagged him, then lifted him into the back seat.

With Ellie's help, David removed his leather flight jacket and bound the man's wrists tightly again before dumping him roughly into the tail section.

David took the control, adjusting their course slightly and checking the fuel gauge as they skirted the coast of Cyprus. The water gleamed clear turquoise. A massive stone fortress guarded the entrance to a tiny harbor crowded with small fishing vessels and ringed by an open-air marketplace. A seawall of broken rock provided a crooked finger of protection against small lapping waves.

"Oh, David, someday when all this is over, I want to come back. It's beautiful!" she exclaimed.

He brought the Stinson in low over the fortress. "Look on the ramparts." He pointed at tiny brown men who ringed the towers at each corner looking out to sea.

"Soldiers?" she asked.

"Turks or Crusaders built the place, but the British hold it now. I was there right after the war and sent my dad a wire."

"David, this is no sentimental journey," Ellie said indignantly. "We aren't on the same side right now, in case you've forgotten. They'll catch us."

"No, they won't." His voice was confident. "That little place is Kyrenia, not far from Paphos. The Apostle Paul stopped there on his first missionary journey. Pilgrims come through all the time. We'll paint a saint's name on the fuselage, and they won't touch us."

"These people are Greek Orthodox—they'll shoot us down. Or have you forgotten how the Greeks and Catholics get along?"

"Then I'll tell you what." They roared over the fort, and a dozen heads looked up at the belly of the plane. "I'll wear Horace's uniform and you take pictures. We'll look like a swell English couple out for a bit of a tour. Okay?"

"We're less than an hour from Turkey and you intend to go through with this? Right over their heads in broad daylight?"

"People tend to be less suspicious when you're direct. Besides, like I said, the telegraph here is a sure thing. I even have a few English pounds in my pocket. Besides"—he nodded his head toward the fuel gauge—"unless you'd like a quick dip in the Mediterranean, the fuel made this decision for us."

Ellie squinted and leaned forward, reading the fuel gauge. The red needle pointed distinctly to the E at the end of the meter. "Empty. Does that mean *empty?*"

"For about the last thirty miles," he winked. "Didn't want to worry you."

"What are we flying on?" she gasped and looked down at the little town of narrow lanes and crooked streets as they passed over.

The engine coughed twice and began to sputter. "Does that answer your question?"

Seconds passed in silence as the village streets melted into a pastoral countryside of neatly cultivated fields trimmed with long rows of Cyprus trees. "Where is the airport?" Ellie's voice was breathless with fear.

"On the other side of *that*." David held the controls steady as he glanced up at the towering peak of Mount Olympus. If he felt any anxiety, his words did not betray it.

"The mountain? We can't make it over the mountain!"

"That's right," he said calmly as she swallowed hard.

They followed the course of a narrow dirt lane that led toward a farmhouse with a red-tiled roof. The plane coughed again—a series of short, violent hiccups. "David!" Ellie cried, gripping the seat with white-knuckled intensity as they skimmed the tops of the trees.

"This will have to do," he muttered as the engine finally died. "Glide her in. Real easy like." His face was tense as the wind whooshed over the wings. The little plane wavered a bit as it dipped below the level of the trees. Fields and trees rushed by like a picket fence. Two hundred yards away was the farmhouse. Ellie could see the figure of a man staring toward them, then she squeezed her eyes shut tight and prayed. "Doin' great, baby," David whispered confidently; the wheels touched down with a gentle thump on the lane.

They rumbled over the bumps, and Ellie opened her eyes and gave a cry of relief as the house loomed before them. "Oh! Land!"

"Get his clothes!" David held the plane firmly on course.

Ellie scrambled back and tossed the shirt and trousers up to David before the plane had coasted to a complete stop. Fifty yards from the front door of the house, the bumping motion slowed and then stopped completely. Ellie could still hear the rush of her heart in her ears. "Thank you, Lord," she murmured, feeling faint. "Safe."

"For the moment." David looked through the bug-spattered window to where a swarthy, black-haired man sauntered angrily toward them. He wore a red cap, green corduroy trousers and a heavy cable-knit sweater. His mouth was turned down beneath a thick moustache and his black eyes flashed resentment. Behind him, a woman opened the door a crack and peered out timidly.

David climbed from the Stinson and reached up to help Ellie

out as the Greek approached. He stopped, then stood rooted and seething in the center of the road. He did not look at Ellie; instead, his eyes brooded on the British uniform slung over David's arm. "Why da you land you plane—here?" he asked in a surly voice. "You don' belong here."

"Ran out of petrol, old boy." David attempted a hacked-up version of a British accent.

The Greek cursed. "So why you don' crash in da sea den, you English? No British here." He crossed his arms defiantly.

David tapped his fist against his forehead as though he could not believe what he was hearing. He smiled at the angry man before him.

"But we ran out of gas," Ellie tried to explain. The Greek gave her a cursory grunt and looked away.

His wife stepped out of the house then and watched from the front step as a small girl peered from behind the woman's skirts.

"I can't believe our luck," David chuckled.

"What do we do?" Ellie panicked. "David?"

Clearing his throat, David extended his hand. "You are Greek Cypriot. Yes?" he asked in careful English.

The man nodded curtly.

"How do you like living under British rule?"

Dark eyes fell on David's hand; then the Greek spat on the ground. "Crash you plane somewhere else."

Ellie's face filled with delight. "You want the English to go home?"

The eyes narrowed and considered them questioningly from beneath bush brows. "Yessss."

David laughed out loud, tossing the uniform into the air. "Then you are our man!" He clapped the reluctant Greek on his shoulders. "We just flew in from Palestine. Ran out of fuel, see, and I'm afraid the British would love to throw us into one of those detention camps if they knew we were here."

The Greek slapped his head in relief. His features melted into a warmth of greeting. "Jews? You are Jews, yes?"

"Yes!"

With a string of unintelligible words, the Greek called back to his wife. She threw her hands up and scurried toward them. She smiled a broad smile and laughed loudly, revealing an irregular row of missing teeth. Her face shone with welcome and she embraced Ellie and touched her hair.

"My woman," beamed the Greek. "She say come in and *welcome*! For we share da same fight! I am Andreas Tornahos. Cypriot. A free man and a smuggler of Jews myself. Many years!"

The woman patted Ellie's cheeks and continued to rattle on.

"Tell her I am glad to meet her," Ellie laughed.

"And she say you sent to us by angel of God! An angel! Here! We put you plane in da barn, yes? You eat. We find you petrol, an' you will help us. Yes?"

"Yes." David followed Andreas toward the house, leaving the woman to usher Ellie along after. "An angel," David said quietly.

"Yes! Then is all settle. God be praise!"

Shutters thrown open, morning light streamed into the front room of the little house. A worn sofa was against the back wall, and an oil lamp stood on a small round table next to that. Above the sofa hung an aged and yellowing family portrait ornately framed in tarnished copper. Beside that was a crucifix and an icon of some unrecognizable saint. A heavy-legged plain wooden table adorned the center of the room, bearing a basket of freshly cut flowers beside a still-empty vase. The plank floor was cleanly swept and adorned with a large red Persian carpet.

"We have ate this breakfast." Tornahos took off his cap and slapped it against the cushion of the sofa, then indicated that they should sit. "But Mama can make you food, yes?"

The woman stood at the doorway into a small kitchen. She tapped her fingertips together and nodded expectantly.

"Thank you," David replied. "But there isn't time."

"Just maybe some sweets? An' coffee." Tornahos snapped his fingers and said to the woman, "Mama, baklava! Cafe!"

She nodded and disappeared and Tornahos bellowed at the top of his lungs, "Mikhail! Mikhail!" He opened the door to a dark bedroom and quickly rattled off a string of words as the little girl peeked at them around the corner of the kitchen. Ellie had the distinct feeling of being trapped by the hospitality of these people, and the feeling was heightened as David looked at his wristwatch once and then again within a space of seconds.

Moments later, a tall, stoop-shouldered young man emerged from the shadows of the room. Framed in the doorway, he carefully appraised them. He was dressed like Tornahos in clothes that seemed to hang on his body. A broad leather belt cinched up his baggy trousers. His complexion was sallow, as though he had not lived in the sunlight for a long time. The bones of his face were fine, almost delicate, and on top of his head, he wore a blue hand-knit yarmulke. He held a worn copy of a prayer book in his right hand. Tornahos spoke to him in animated Greek and he closed the book and cautiously extended his hand to David.

"Shalom," he said quietly when David rose to shake his hand. He did not smile, and though his face was young, his eyes had the look of one who had lived a very long time.

"You see!" Tornahos slapped David on the back. "Jewish! What I tell you? This Mikhail Gregovsky. Come outta camp."

Mikhail stared for a long moment at the top of David's head. He spoke in a language that David could not recognize, repeating each word slowly.

"I'm sorry," David replied, looking to the cheerful face of his host. "I can't understand him."

"You don' speak Bulgarian? Bulgaria next to Greece. I speak Bulgarian." Tornahos held up his index finger and addressed Mikhail thoughtfully, chewing his words and repeating himself as he spoke.

The young man hitched up his belt and answered him as he eyed David with suspicion.

Tornahos considered his words, translating from Bulgarian to Greek and then finally to broken English. "He say to me, what kinda Jew is dis? You gotta no Kippa . . ."

"Cap? Yarmulke?"

"Das right. No kippa on you head, an' dis Passover."

"Tell him I'm an American."

"Ah yes! Dis explain it!" Tornahos repeated David's words and the face of the young Jew lit up. He smiled a broad and friendly smile, bowing slightly to David and then again toward Ellie.

Relieved, Tornahos clapped his hands together as his wife came into the room with a tray of fresh coffee and Greek pastries. "So eat, *eat!*"

David looked at his watch again. "The time," he said. "It is very important that I send a telegraph from Kyrenia. Unless there is someplace closer."

"No. No place. Nicosia is close. But not so close. Lots of English all over da place."

"And I need gas. Petrol for the plane. There was a little private airfield not far from here a few years ago, I remember. Is it still open?"

Tornahos nodded. "Yes. Thick with British."

"We'll just have to deal with that."

Ellie savored the sweet, honey-laced baklava as David frowned and thought.

"We getta you petrol. Now, you can take Mikhail away from Cyprus?" asked Tornahos. "He will hang if dey catch him. He comes here on a prison boat and blow up a guard tower in da camp. Is too hard to get off Cyprus in a boat. British ships all over da place. You take Mikhail?"

"If we get the gas, he's gone."

14   Contraband

Civilian cars and crowded taxis jammed the streets of Jerusalem by the time Rachel arrived with Howard and Yacov. Pedestrians walked between cars, slowing the clogged traffic further. Horns blared, now with impatience rather than in celebration, as all of Jewish Jerusalem seemed to press toward the convoy. Howard parked on the sidewalk, five blocks from Zion Square and the shattered remains of the *Palestine Post* offices. The car doors would open only a few inches on each side as the three squeezed out into the tide of human flesh that surged down the side street.

Wild speculation about the cargo swept the ranks.

"Such a day! Such a day! Is it true they brought *fresh eggs* up Bab el Wad?"

"True? Of course true! And truckloads of chickens for Passover."

"What about lamb?"

"Lamb? Of course lamb! You think they would forget lamb?"

Howard scrambled over the hood of the car to grasp Rachel and Yacov by their hands. Rachel's palms were damp with excitement; she craned her neck and stood on tiptoe to peer over the sea of heads. They were pushed ahead toward the square where convoy trucks were parked three abreast, circling the park like a wagon train. Heaps of cargo were piled high in the center where workers from the Jerusalem Jewish Agency bustled about with clipboards in hand to sort out the jumble.

Drivers, basking in the glory of the moment, climbed atop their trucks to shout down joyfully to the people who pressed alongside. Bullet holes were touched reverently; even dents that might have been received in Tel Aviv were treated with awe.

The sparse handful of Haganah guards who had remained with the convoy had secreted their weapons among the boxes and crates of goods. Their comrades had melted into the crowd.

"I cannot see Moshe!" Rachel shouted to Howard as they inched forward. "Do you see him, Professor? Is he among those on the trucks?"

Howard scanned the faces and forms of those who proudly posed for photographers and bantered with reporters who milled throughout the crowd. Tomorrow, their notes would become one international headline: *Jerusalem Siege Broken! Daring Assault Saves Holy City!* But among them all, Howard knew that chances were slim that they would find Moshe. "Not on this side!" he replied, shading his eyes against the bright morning light. "If we can get to the front, there by the trucks, we can ask someone!"

Then Rachel heard a booming voice that was unmistakable. "Right! Unload only those ten trucks! *Only those ten!* The others are for the warehouse, you momzer! Can't you see that cargo is for storage?" Like a captain on the bridge of a battleship, Ehud Schiff towered on top of a canvas-covered heap of crates on the back of a bullet-scarred truck. "Only *those* ten, schmuck!"

Rachel recognized him not from his beardless face, but from the lighthearted insults he hurled from his post. "Professor!" she cried, pointing over the shoulders of a heavy matron. "It is Ehud! Oh, thank God!" Her voice quavered. "Look! *Look!* It is Ehud Schiff, dear Ehud! He will know where Moshe is! *Of all men, he will know!*"

The people jostled and crowded closer to the trucks laden with Matzo bread and fresh eggs that were, indeed, remarkably undamaged. There was no path clear through to Ehud. Hands clutched upraised ration cards. *Powdered milk! Fresh oranges! A little sugar, if you please! Matzo meal! Gefilte fish!* The words were uttered from housewife to husband with a sense of awe at the wealth that had battled up the pass. *And chicken? I hear them cackling in that truck over there! Did someone say they brought also cigarettes? American Lucky Strikes! Oy!*

But there was only one treasure Rachel cared about. Only one hunger she felt. "If Ehud is near, Moshe cannot be far away surely! Oh, Professor! Can you see him?"

"I can barely see Ehud!" Howard's voice was all but drowned by the din around them.

"I can get through," Yacov volunteered, straining against Howard's grip.

"We'll never find you again." Howard held on tighter as they were shoved roughly by a large, red-faced woman who puffed and elbowed her way in front of them.

Matzo meal! A little gefilte fish for soup tonight! Powdered milk and powdered eggs! No! The eggs are fresh? Oy vey! The eggs are fresh, yet!

"Just let me go to Ehud!" Yacov's upturned face was urgent and pleading. "I can reach him before you. He will know! He will have news for us of Moshe!"

Howard glanced toward Rachel's desperate face. He nodded reluctantly and said to Yacov, "Nowhere else. We will lose you." Then he let go of the boy, who disappeared between two women like a mouse in a crack. Moments later, he emerged at the front of the mass. Climbing onto the wheel of the truck, he scaled the wooden slats up the side, and in a flash, hoisted himself onto the canvas at Ehud's feet. Tapping the burly captain on the knee, he waved into his face. Ehud frowned and Howard saw Yacov mouth the words *Rachel's brother.* His face breaking into a broad grin of recognition, Ehud lifted the boy onto his shoulder and gave him a playful swat.

Where is your sister?

There! Yacov pointed. *With the Professor.*

Rachel strained on her tiptoes, waving frantically over the heads of those in front of them. Yacov was shouting and pointing at Howard, who had doffed his hat in the midst of the crowd. After a moment of squinting into unfamiliar faces, Ehud spotted Howard's bald head and Rachel beside him.

"Only a goy would be without a hat in this crowd!" Ehud roared. "There is your professor! And there is Rachel!"

A few turned to stare curiously at Howard and Rachel, then,

at Ehud's stern command, a path opened for them and they rushed to the truck. Above her, Ehud's strong arms reached down to gather her in and lift her to his side. Howard climbed awkwardly after.

Weeping unashamedly, Rachel embraced the captain, who flushed with the honor of such a reception. "Little one!" he cried. "Did we not leave you in the Old City?"

"Tikvah was ill." Rachel brushed her tears away. "We came out last night. Yehudit Akiva arranged it and came out with us."

"Yehudit? The daughter of that swine, Rabbi Akiva?"

"She saved Tikvah's life and saved my heart from breaking. But if I don't have news of Moshe—" Her voice caught as she searched his face for unspoken news. "If you have no news for me, then it may still break."

Ehud enfolded her in his arms again. "Last I saw of him, he lived. Last night he was well."

"Did he come with you? Is he here in Jerusalem? Oh, Ehud, where is he? Where is Moshe?"

"In Kastel. Fighting Arabs, unless they've killed him."

Her features flooded with disappointment and she wept openly. "Oh, Ehud. He did not come. He is there. Yacov, he is not here! How can I tell him? How can I tell him if he is not here."

Ehud patted her clumsily and looked to Howard for help. Howard shrugged and said "Oh, dear me!" several times.

"He is alive if the Arabs didn't kill him last night," Ehud said, trying to comfort her, but his words were not a comfort. "Some of the fellows came down. They were to pick up weapons, you see, but we were attacked from the rear and they couldn't get the cargo. All of them fought well. Perhaps saved the convoy."

"Was Moshe with them?" she pleaded.

"Some were shot. Some came away with us. I did not see Moshe. He is still in Kastel, fighting those demons, I tell you. Most of the Haganah jumped ship on the outskirts of the city. We will meet later tonight and decide what to do for the relief of the fellows still up there." His face was grim. "But he was still alive last I saw of him."

"Captain Schiff," Howard interrupted, "can you come home with us? We can offer you a bed to rest in. Clean clothes."

"You are the uncle of the little shiksa, Ellie Warne, nu?"

"Yes."

"Then I will come and be honored. I am nearly done here. The Agency has taken over. There will be food for Passover tonight and enough for another month if the people are thrifty. Yes, I am quite weary now. A bed, you say? I would be happy for a bed to sleep on."

Rachel raised her head from the captain's broad chest. "Yes, Ehud. You must come." Drying her eyes, she gazed across the sea of heads in one last, wistful search for her husband. *How can I tell you, dear Moshe, that you will be a father? You did not come to Jerusalem.* On the far fringes of the crowd, she glimpsed a tall, dark-haired man. *Rolling walk. The tilt of his head!* She studied the slope of the man's broad shoulders as he hurried away in the company of two other men. "Moshe!" she cried "There he is!" She pointed and Ehud and Howard followed her gaze, hopeful for a moment as the man disappeared up a side street.

Yacov clambered to the side of the cargo. "Where? Where is he, sister?"

"I saw him! I am almost certain."

Ehud shook his head slowly from side to side. "No," he said firmly, "he is in Kastel."

"But it looked so like him."

"From behind. Among the thousands, not so unusual. Come now, he is in Kastel, I tell you, Rachel."

"But, Ehud! Please . . ." Rachel begged, but her words were drowned out by a sudden wail that rose from the side streets, rolling down over the crowds into the square itself.

The undulating siren of British military vehicles pierced the murmur of the crowd, and from the far fringes, sounds of joy dissolved into a scream that rose in volume as it swept toward the convoy.

The slap of boots sounded against the pavement as troops pushed down each side street and a voice echoed over a loudspeaker: *There is no need to be alarmed. Step aside. Step aside, please. There is no need to be alarmed. You will make way.*

"The goyim," Ehud spat. His eyes flashed with bitter resentment as the first of the British troops appeared and fanned out among the people. The blue steel of their weapons glinted in the sun. "No need to be alarmed." His words were sarcastic.

By the order of His Majesty, all cargo must be searched for contraband . . . for contraband.

Women and children fled before them, crowding even tighter toward the center of the square.

"Contraband. . . ?" Rachel asked as the boisterous crowd suddenly grew silent.

Ehud raised his chin defiantly. "Weapons, they mean. They will take from us the very tools by which we brought this food to your people." He stood silent and angry for a long moment as more and more armed troops swept inward, pushing the people back.

All cargo must be searched, by order of . . .

"By order of the devil himself and over the dead bones of Ehud Schiff." He looked briefly at Rachel and Howard. "Get down. Get down now or you may be hurt."

. . . any individual apprehended with a weapon . . .

Rachel did not question the words of Ehud. She put her hand to her stomach and remembered the child. Moshe's child. "Yacov!" she called. "Come. Now." And without hesitation she climbed from the truck.

In the name of His Majesty's Mandatory Government, all private citizens are ordered to disperse!

Ehud drew his shoulders back, and with a voice that raged against gales and storms, he thundered back to his people. "It is enough! Stay where you are!"

Heads turned, gathering courage from the booming voice, the granite jaw, and the fiery eyes.

. . . are ordered to disperse! Return immediately to your homes!

"Stay where you are!" Ehud shouted and the people listened, packing tight like a solid wall against the invading forces. "This is your food! Purchased by the blood of your husbands, sons and fathers! They will take it, these goyim! And they will leave us with nothing!"

The cargo will be searched for contraband . . . illegal weapons . . . return immediately to your homes!

"Jews!" Ehud boomed. "Stand fast! They will not search unless it be through our bodies!"

Rachel felt crushed against the wheel well of the truck. She clutched Yacov to her and gazed fearfully up to where Ehud towered. The barrels of British guns marked the line of soldiers that faced off with the obstinate crowd of housewives and unarmed men. Except for the crackle of the loudspeaker, there

148

was no sound but the click of rifle bolts.

"Sister?" Yacov searched her face fearfully.

. . . you are ordered to disperse immediately!

"We will not!" Ehud shouted, and his reply touched every Jewish memory as his voice rang out. *"Never again!"* he boomed. And then, once more the silence was broken: *"Never again! Never again!"*

Rachel picked up the chant, "Never again!"

. . . ordered to leave this place . . .

"Never again! *Never again! NEVER AGAIN!"* The chant grew in volume, rolling back the dark fearfulness that had threatened to crush their hope. Sweat poured from the faces of the British recruits as thousands of fists raised in defiance to the resounding cry: "Never again! *Never Again! NEVER AGAIN!"*

The sound of the bullhorn was completely obliterated, the siren overpowered by the thunder. Perhaps even in Kastel the Arabs heard the cry that exploded from Zion Square that morning, pushing forward, shoving the soldiers back up the side streets to the empty lorries that waited to carry them back to Allenby barracks in defeat. *Never Again! NEVER AGAIN. . . !*

And when the last intruder was gone, an absolute silence fell on the square. Then, one long, unending cheer engulfed the crowd. Windows rattled in their panes from the tumult. *THIS YEAR IN JERUSALEM!*

––––––––

It seemed like a thousand years since Moshe had been in the little bakery on Harav Kook Street not far from Zion Square. But only a few months ago he had come into the shop as a customer, crowding in among the students of Hebrew University for a morning pastry before their bus ride to Mount Scopus. He had enjoyed the familiar banter of his pupils, and often light conversation had evolved into discussions of archeological finds or ancient religions—and finally, politics. The pastry shop of Mrs. Bett had become a forum of ideas for the young men of Jerusalem; and eventually, it served as a center of Haganah activity operating right under the noses of the British government. Long after the Number Nine bus had stopped running to Mount Scopus and the university, the students still gathered at Mrs. Bett's Pastry Shop.

Moshe and six others from the convoy had made their way

to the pastry shop before the trucks had reached Zion Square. Now they sat together in an empty cistern in the courtyard eating dry matzo bread and sipping warm tea.

Mrs. Bett was a plump, jolly woman whose tiny stature concealed the heart of a true Zionist warrior. Members of the Jerusalem Underground drilled in her empty cistern, and what weapons they had were concealed in its walls. Now there were only two sacks of flour left in her storage rooms, but gleefully she looked forward to the arrival of not only flour and butter for her famous pastries but also the arms that would come with the cargo.

"No pastries, fellows!" she said. "Maybe next week, after Passover, eh? Maybe then we'll be rid of the Mufti; may his brains be turned to steam. And then, for you, Professor Sachar, such a cake I will make, nu? Such a cake as you have never tasted!"

Every muscle ached as he leaned back against the stone wall of the cistern. The matzo was tasteless. He smiled faintly, too weary to reply to her exuberance. Each of the others also nibbled in silence.

"Oy!" she exclaimed. "Such a quiet group! This is the quietest group ever in my shop. Tired, nu?" Her voice became full of compassion as she surveyed the exhausted faces of her fugitives. "You came to the right place if you need rest. You'd have gotten no rest if you'd have gone to Sokolow School!"

Moshe looked up at her questioningly. He had nearly gone to the old school building for refuge. It was, he knew, the headquarters of Mishmar Ha'am, the Civil Defense. It was much nearer than Mrs. Bett's, but he had been certain it was being watched. "Did they blow that up also?" he asked, remembering his shock at the rubble of the *Palestine Post* building.

"Such jokes you make, Professor! Oy! Blow it up? No, indeed! But the place is overrun with"—she lowered her voice and glanced over her shoulder even though there was no one in the cistern but her and seven weary men—"*prostitutes!* You'd have gotten no sleep at all!"

A very small, studious-looking lad at the end of the row sniffed and said quietly, "You might be right." A ripple of laughter filtered through the men; the first sign of life since they had stepped into the cistern and slidden down with their backs against the wall.

An indignant look crossed Mrs. Bett's face. She cleared her throat loudly and said irritably, "They are Jewish prostitutes, and they have to report to the building three times a day! Not for immoral reasons, but to report rumors they hear from British soldiers! It's a rabble! Every woman in the neighborhood makes her husband go to Jaffa Road the long way around, by way of Rehov Hanevi'im!"

"Ah yes! The Street of the Prophets," someone mumbled. "A much safer route. The worst that could happen to a fellow there is that he would become converted and live like an Ashkenazi rabbi! Then he would never sleep again for fear of dreaming of the girls!"

The laughter returned, stronger now. Moshe chuckled and rubbed the back of his hand across his eyes. "Sleep," he said. "I think we should all stay away from Sokolow School *and* the rabbis for a few hours."

"Sleep? I have forgotten what that is."

"Give me a second and I will remember."

Mrs. Bett shook her head as their eyes became dull again. The tea was left untouched. "Blankets you need. More than food, nu? Well, if I had my pastries, you would stay awake. Keep your eyes open just a minute more until I get you pillows and blankets. It is damp down here."

She turned on her heel and climbed up the steps, pushing open the hinged trap of the cistern. In the distance, the roar of voices could be distinctly heard . . . *Never Again! Never Again! Never Again!*

Mrs. Bett hesitated a moment, then muttered softly, "What now? Oy gevalt!" Then she slipped out and slammed the door, silencing the commotion outside.

"What was that?" asked the small man.

"A celebration," said another as someone else began snoring loudly. "They are dancing . . ." The words slowed. "Dancing in Zion . . ."

Moshe let his head fall forward. His body was numb with exhaustion and his eyes too heavy to stay open for Mrs. Bett. Blankets and pillows did not matter. Bread and tea made no difference. He was certain that he could sleep anywhere now, even at Sokolow School.

———

Even before the defiant challenge of Zion Square had faded, yet another strange and dissonant wail rose up from beyond the barricades in the Arab Quarters that surrounded the heart of Jewish Jerusalem.

The cry of mourning, the lament for the fallen, racing through the souks of the Old City as Arabs claimed their dead and heard of the disaster of Kastel.

An eerie chill ran suddenly through Rachel's veins as they hurried back toward Howard's car. *Was it like this on the first morning of Passover so long ago when the Egyptians found their firstborn dead and their enemies victorious? Had Israel fled Egypt pursued by such a demonic howl of grief and rage?* She found herself looking over her shoulder as they walked, scanning the rooftops for the snipers who would surely come in search of revenge.

Above the rooftops a chant began that robbed the confidence of every Jew in the square. "Kastel! Kastel! Kastel!"

Rachel wanted only to be at the side of Tikvah again, away from the howling of rival mobs.

"Kastel! Kastel! Kastel!"

Ehud carried Yacov, and Howard held on to Rachel's hand, pulling her along against the tide.

"Kastel! Kastel! Kastel!"

Her heart thumped a steady counterpoint to their cry: *Moshe! Moshe! Moshe!* Although Ehud had told her he was not in the city, still, she felt his nearness and searched each cluster of people for his face.

"Kastel! Kastel! Kastel!" The Arab fury grew louder as men and boys swarmed from their homes and shops to liberate the captured village. They gathered in a mass in the Square of Omar just inside Jaffa Gate. Bristling with weapons, they were ready to take their revenge. In the distance, a frantic voice over a loud-speaker erupted, silencing the chant. The words were unintelligible to Rachel, but each volcanic phrase was followed by a new chant.

"Jihad! Kastel!"

Ehud growled in response to the echoing voice. "Well and good, you devils. We are here with the food, and you are too late!"

"But what of Moshe?" Rachel cried. "If he is there . . ."

"Then he will fight like a man!" Ehud's eyes were riveted on the Old City wall as the frenzied voices continued. "They are too late. We have a taste of victory at last." His eyes narrowed. "Do you not remember Warsaw, little one?" he chided her. "For twenty-eight days our fighters held the Nazis at bay, nu? How many squads of the Wehrmacht died before we gave up? Do you not remember Dov's stories? We Jews held the Nazis nearly a month before the Ghetto fell. And who are these Arabs? Fanatic shopkeepers, compared to the S.S. and the Panzers. We were only a handful then. We are more than that now." He raised his voice and shouted, "Let them rant! The sea will close over them in the end as it did over Pharaoh!" He glanced to a corner by the wall, where Herbert Gold shared his adventures with a group of boys. "Even cowards are heroes."

Ehud's anger silenced Rachel and she lowered her eyes. How could he know her desperation to see Moshe?

Howard squeezed her hand gently and looked back at her pale face. "He is in the Lord's hands," he said in a low voice.

The professor understands what I am feeling, she thought, and tears stung her eyes at his tenderness. *Say nothing more to me, Professor, or I shall weep in public.*

"Kastel. . . !"

"Let them come against us in Kastel!" Ehud blustered. "To-night we will go to relieve the soldiers there. It will do the Mufti's gangsters no good at all. They rage against the wind! And if your Moshe dies, he will be like the heroes of Warsaw who held the Nazis twenty-eight days before they fell, nu?"

Rachel stumbled and Howard reached out to catch her. He saw the tears in her eyes and turned to Ehud. "Captain Schiff!" There was a demand for silence in his voice. "We will believe that Moshe will live to come home a hero, eh? Now, if you please, it is time to stop competing with the Mufti's henchmen. We are the only ones who can hear you anyway, and our nerves are a bit ragged." He patted Rachel, and her tears finally spilled over. "There!" Howard sounded angry. "Now see what you have done?"

"I?" Ehud thumped his chest in remorse. "Is it something I said, little one? I meant only to call you to courage."

Embarrassed by her show of emotion, Rachel wiped away her tears. "It is nothing. I am just tired."

"Kastel! Kastel! Kastel!"

"Then let's get you home and put you to bed," Howard said protectively.

"Please," she begged as they reached the car, "I want to be with Tikvah now. Nothing else."

Ehud bit his lip, clumsy and uncertain how to deal with this fragile female. "Forgive me," he said. "I think everyone has the hide of a sailor."

"I have!" Yacov said brightly. "You may shout at me if you like, Captain Ehud!"

Ehud squeezed Yacov's arms, testing for muscles. "So. You think you will make a seafaring man? Run the blockades with Captain Schiff?" He redirected his bluster to the boy who devoured the attentions of this hero.

"I already have run blockades quite well. Me and my dog, Shaul!"

Rachel sat silently during the winding drive to Hadassah. Occasionally Howard would glance at her and pat her hand as Yacov and Ehud exchanged tales of daring exploits against the British or the Arabs. When she was able, Rachel decided, she would question Ehud about Moshe and their imprisonment together. Had he mentioned her often? Was he well and happy? But not now. She would not ask him now with the heat of battle still coursing through his blood. She could not stand another word about heroic deaths. Only one thought pushed at her heart: *When will I see him again? Will his strong arms ever hold me again in this life? Will I see the light in his eyes when I tell him about our child?*

15 The Message

Gerhardt brooded silently across the table from Kadar. Hourly, Arab peasants poured into Deir Mahsir. Brandishing their weapons and shouting slogans that now sounded meaningless, they gathered in the village square to await word from the great commander, Ram Kadar. Kadar, right hand of the Mufti, had returned to lead them just in time, it seemed. Not in time to save them from the disgrace of last night's defeat, but this was a new day, after all. The only thing that mattered was that Kadar had returned.

"So a few Jews will eat their religious feast tonight," Gerhardt gestured with disdain. "Do you think the arrival of a few trucks of supplies will make any difference in the end? We will easily take Kastel back from them and close the road. They will be hungry again soon enough."

Kadar did not reply as he studied the detailed maps of the terrain around Kastel. True, in the scope of things, this was a small victory for the Jews. It was, in fact, their only victory. But smaller events than this had turned the tide in battles that had been much bigger, Kadar knew; the stupidity of Gerhardt's error made him tremble with silent rage. "You left Kastel in the hands of old women last night." His voice was as hard as steel. "It will not be so simple as that for us to take Kastel back from the hands of the Jews."

"Jews!" Gerhardt scoffed. "What are they! In the days of the Reich they dug their own graves and waited patiently as we filled them with their own bodies! They do not know how to fight like men. They are only suited to die like sheep."

Kadar turned from him and stared out the window into the courtyard. Several hundred Jihad Moquades sat in clusters in the courtyard. Yet another truck arrived and young men shouted and cheered as they joined their comrades. Food venders moved among them selling *popeetes* and fresh oranges. The atmosphere was one of a carnival. Every man there believed, like Gerhardt, that the Jews could not fight. If they had one small victory to their credit, it was only a fluke.

Only Kadar believed differently; never before had he spoken what he knew to be truth. "Perhaps it was so in the war, Gerhardt, that those of you who served the Fuehrer looked on the forms of Jewish men and women and children but only saw animals ready for slaughter and an open pit in which to bury them." He did not face Gerhardt, avoiding the German's mocking countenance. "But I do not believe as you do. They were men as we are, who died. Their wives and children died with them. And those who escaped you the first time will never more dig their own graves. Some survived to tell what they saw and what was done; those will fight—not like sheep, but like lions."

Kadar now faced the disdain in Gerhardt's eyes. "They will

fight because they are desperate men." He jerked his thumb toward the laughing crowds outside. "And we are only men. Not desperate. Not abandoned. Scarcely frightened because we do not yet believe in the manhood of our enemies—"

"Manhood!"

"Was it not a man you battled beneath the Old City? Was it not a man who fought against the bodyguards of Haj Amin in that cavern? A brave man—a powerful, desperate man?"

"He fought for the sake of the whore. I myself killed for her beauty. She is evil, with the power to make a man—" His eyes grew wild at the thought of Rachel.

"The power to make a man desperate, Gerhardt?" Kadar laughed openly now at the rage that contorted Gerhardt's features. "Then I will tell you something that perhaps will help you fight a little harder when we attack Kastel." He crossed his arms and leaned against the windowsill. "While you ran off to Ramle last night to fight the sheep who came against you, there was a *man*, a Jew, who took Kastel from us. An old friend of yours, Gerhardt. An old friend of mine as well."

Gerhardt leaned forward. His eyes narrowed at the memory of Moshe Sachar and the woman. "It was Sachar, then? The British did not hang him? It was the will of Allah that he live until I see him again face to face! It was the will—"

"Yes. They say he is up there still, Gerhardt. Waiting. Ready for you. And he will not die like a sheep."

"Even lions scream when death comes to them."

Kadar prodded further, seeing Gerhardt succumb to maniacal fury as a torrent of thoughts washed over him. "Someone else may reach him first, you know." He smiled sympathetically. "You have many Jihad Moquades who will compete with you for his head."

"No! This Jew is mine! And I will have him with my own hand! I will be first into the streets of Kastel, and I will find him out!"

Good, thought Kadar as Gerhardt brooded before him. *Desperation may make a man fight bravely, but it may also make him foolish. Perhaps the martyrdom of Gerhardt will not be so difficult to achieve.* "So, my friend," Kadar said smoothly, "you, too, know what it means to be desperate. Above all other men who come here to fight, you hate the Jews the most."

"They are vermin—the cause of every woe that has come upon us all!"

"Yes, this is so." Kadar's tone was studied. "And of all Jews there is one whom you hate even more than the others. Yes? Moshe Sachar. The man who holds Kastel. He took the woman from you; now he has taken Kastel, and you are made to seem a fool."

"I will have his blood! I will have his body crucified on the walls of Kastel's mosque!" His voice trembled and he spoke to himself as though Kadar was no longer in the room. "And then I will find the woman and have her in the dust of the street. I will take her to the body of this Jew and show her who is the man! Who is the conqueror! And then after I have had my pleasure with her, I will mingle her blood with his. They are sheep! They are sheep! And the pit is still open for them."

"Be careful that you do not fall into it yourself."

Gerhardt was looking through Kadar now, scarcely hearing his words as he imagined the battle yet to come. "I want the best men with me! We will storm the east slope while you take the quarry. *Moshe Sachar* in Kastel! You see! It is the will of Allah that I destroy my enemy with my own hands! You can see how plain it is meant to be!"

"Do you not fight for the loyalty of the Mufti as well?"

Gerhardt smiled sarcastically. "The Mufti? Of course. Just as the driver of the American Consulate car allowed us to use him to destroy the Jewish Agency. Ah yes. He was loyal as well. Loyal enough to receive 600 pounds to buy his bride. Oh yes! Fredrich Gerhardt is loyal to the Mufti. And loyal to the Fuehrer and the Reich and a United Arab Palestine. All of that gives purpose to what I most desire." He stood and crossed to the window. "Look at them," he said, gesturing toward the exultant troops. "They proclaim loyalty. They cry out for Holy War, but they fight for the same purpose as I—because they *love* it!"

Kadar stared at him with the revulsion of one who has seen a truly evil creature. "You are a madman," he said quietly, laying aside all pretense.

"Yes! Yes, I am a madman. But I am honest, Kadar. I am here because I enjoy the screams of my enemy. The power of life and death is in my hands." He held his hands high in the light and examined them with admiration. "Like God, eh? And this—the Mufti, Adolf Hitler, *war*—gives me the excuse I need to practice

157

the great talents I have been given."

His lip curled slightly as he stared at Kadar. "My highest pleasure will be to kill Sachar and then destroy the whore for whom I suffered."

Gerhardt grabbed Kadar's shoulder. "Don't you see? It will never end. It does not matter who wins. The grave will never be full enough to satisfy our lust. Forever we will need a noble cause, a reason to kill each other."

Kadar pulled away from his touch; a cold shudder passed over him and he stepped back, certain now that he looked into the face of one inhuman. "You are insane," he muttered again. "You reek of death. It is not Allah who brings men like you onto the earth, but the Evil One: Shetan!"

"And you claim to know the difference, most noble Kadar? You claim to see the right and yet you serve the master of Shetan yourself!"

"I fight for a Palestinian homeland!"

"Of course. So do we all. One without Jews in it. Without the vermin. I am judged insane by the world only because I am honest. The rest of you may hide your evil hearts beneath slogans and high ideals, but you are no different than me. Only better liars. And you will see, Kadar—the Jews are evil, too. They are also butchers at heart. They simply have not had the power to demonstrate their skill at the slaughter."

Kadar did not answer. Carefully he folded the maps on the table and straightened a small stack of papers. If Gerhardt did not fall in battle, Kadar reasoned, then he himself would end the life of this evil creature with his own hand. Gerhardt laughed again, as if he had heard Kadar's thoughts. Then he strode out of the room and into the courtyard among the men.

Kadar watched him walking through the eager volunteers. Their faces were filled with respect and admiration for this man who had destroyed Ben Yehudah Street and the Jewish Agency and stopped the convoys through Bab el Wad. *Yes. Gerhardt the madman is a great hero. And may he make a great martyr for our cause.* Kadar put his hand to his head and groaned aloud at the thought. *The cause. Jihad. Holy war. If his words are true, then there is no cause. There is no Paradise. No Allah. Only a living hell that dwells in our hearts compelling us to dig our own graves.*

As others of the Naschon Convoy found their way into the safe haven of Jerusalem homes, Herbert Gold walked quickly toward the massive building that housed the British Police Commissioner. The euphoria of the triumphant arrival had evaporated for Herbert as soon as he found that his truck was one of those destroyed in the passage up Bab el Wad. And as he had stared at the cheering multitudes, a dim recognition had pushed into his consciousness. *The man in the truck with—he had seen him before!* Vague memories of faces on the front page of yesterday's paper came to him . . . *Terrorist Moshe Sachar Escapes!* And was there not something more in the story? Word of a reward? A reward that might, in fact, pay for the loss of his truck? Herbert looked furtively over his shoulder as he bounded up the worn stone steps of the government building.

The clatter of a typewriter was heard from a back room, and a pleasant Arab receptionist sat at the front desk. She looked up as Herbert removed his hat and stood wringing it nervously in his hands.

"How may I help you?" she smiled, displaying a row of glistening white teeth.

"I have information . . ." He paused. Lowering his voice he added, "I need to see the magistrate. Quickly."

The woman's smile remained steady. Curiosity filled her eyes. "What is the nature of your information?" Her hand remained poised on the button of an intercom.

"It is about . . . about the convoy," he whispered.

The smile faded. "There is little we don't know about that. The magistrate is a busy man—"

Herbert leaned close to the desk. His eyes were wide with a fearful excitement. "That is not all."

"Yes?"

"There were men with it. Terrible men." He held out his chafed wrists for her to see. She clucked her tongue in concern.

"That is hardly news enough, however . . ."

"But you do not understand. These are not just ordinary fellows. I read about them in the *Daily*. They are wanted by the government, and I have seen them—both of them. *Yes!* One had me kidnapped and bound; the other jumped into the truck where I was."

Her interest returned. "Who was this?"

"I remembered where I had seen him before; only by then it was too late! He had slipped away into the crowd, else I would have captured him myself."

"The names of the criminals, if you please. . . ."

"The big man who stole my truck is called the captain. And the other—the other is called Sachar. The professor from Hebrew University. Moshe Sachar, who was convicted of bombing Jaffa Gate."

"Moshe Sachar?" Her face seemed almost frantic at the name. "You have seen the man here? In Jerusalem? He is in Jerusalem?"

Gold stood erect, made confident now at the reaction of the receptionist. "Yes." He raised his chin slightly. "He held his gun to my head all the way up Bab el Wad. An evil and dangerous fellow."

The receptionist stared at Gold with awe for a moment; then her fingers fumbled to push the button on the intercom.

Bouncing over the rough, rutted backroads of Cyprus, David could not help but wonder if, indeed, the Wizard's Kansas tornado had not picked them up and dropped them in Oz. Fields of bright red poppies were splashed across yet unplowed fields. New blue lupines clung to the rocky slopes of the mountains. Any minute David expected to spot the Emerald City glistening in the sunlight. Instead, the ancient Crusader Castle of Kyrenia perched beside the bright aqua water of the harbor.

David wore the wrinkled uniform of their captive, while Ellie had donned an oversized dark-blue dress that belonged to Mrs. Tornahos. Her hair was pulled back and completely concealed beneath a drab navy-blue scarf. Mrs. Tornahos smiled and nodded approvingly, certain that no one would think that the young woman was not a native Cypriot.

"Jus' don say nothin'!" instructed Tornahos as choking dust swirled up and around his head. "Maria an' me, we take carea ev'rything!"

Their little girl, a shy, black-eyed child, clung to her mother's arm and smiled coyly at David. She and her parents did not seem to notice or mind the bone-jarring journey into the village.

The battered automobile Tornahos drove was a weird, mechanical marvel of innumerable salvaged car parts. No two fenders were alike. The chassis was that of a prewar Italian-made vehicle, while the hood was unmistakably American. The hood ornament sported the blue and gold Star of David, identifying the outdated logo of Dodge Brothers automobiles.

"What kind of car is this?" Ellie asked.

Tornahos ground the gears and chewed his lip thoughtfully. "All kinda car. What we say, she'sa puppy with lotsa papas, eh?"

David grinned and glanced back at her. "A sort of mutt, honey."

"That'sa right!" Tornahos roared with laughter and thumped the Ford steering wheel. "She'sa mutt!"

Ellie shifted her weight in a futile attempt to find a place on the seat that was not ruptured by a vicious spring. She could not help but think that this mutt was one mean dog.

"As long as she gets us there and back," David said, suddenly serious as two British vehicles passed on the opposite side of the road.

"Oh sure! She run better thana English General car." To make his point, he ran a slalom around a series of ruts from one side of the road to the other; ahead, a sleek official British vehicle laid on the horn and screeched to a halt. Tornahos howled with laughter at the noiseless curses mouthed by the English driver as they zoomed by. A moment later they were among the narrow cobbled streets of Kyrenia, creeping slowly through crowds of British military who roamed the streets in search of souvenirs.

Banners of laundry dripped from lines strung high above them across the street. The sound of bartering filled the air with a low hum. "Next block," Tornahos said quietly to Ellie. "R'member. Don' say nothin'! Don' look atta men ina face. Eyes down ona ground, yes! You too pretty. Ever'body wanna marry you an' ever'body wanna talk Greek to you. An' you don' talk Greek! Stay with Mama an' we meet you by the castle in thirty minute."

Ellie nodded and fingered the slip of paper on which David had printed the message to be sent to Martin. "Be careful," she said to David, suddenly filled with apprehension.

"You too. I'm just going to get gas. You watch out for Greek bachelors prowling the streets," he winked.

"They're nothing compared to Arabs." Tornahos halted at a busy corner and Ellie slipped from the car after Mrs. Tornahos and the little girl. The child quickly grasped Ellie's hand, and

Ellie had the impression that the girl knew precisely what was going on.

The car chugged off down the street, turning a corner and disappearing in an instant. Feeling suddenly alone, Ellie lowered her eyes instantly to the cobbles and followed the hem of Mrs. Tornahos's skirt. She wound through the human tangle toward the harbor market into the sunlight. A pale pink three-story building faced the water. French doors opened onto small balconies that overlooked a tiny port jammed full of small vessels. A chipped blue sign read *Kyrenia Hotel*, first in English, and above that, in Greek. This was the nicest hotel in Cyprus, Ellie knew, though the plaster was chipped and the paint flaked from the plain double doors into the lobby.

Mrs. Tornahos looked at Ellie and nodded toward the hotel as dozens of petty British government officials on vacation strolled past. They chatted amiably about the weather and the boats and the outrageous prices of copper goods on display in the markets. Ellie was careful not to meet the eyes of anyone of them, fearful that her look might betray her understanding of their words.

She hung back as Mrs. Tornahos stepped into the lobby. A young English couple stood at the dark wooden counter buying stamps, but other than that, the lobby seemed deserted.

Ellie kept her eyes on the black and white floor tiles. The photographer in her struggled not to look at everything. But she remained obedient, clutching the little girl's hand and padding after Mrs. Tornahos's worn shoes past the clerk at the desk to a small office down a narrow, dimly lit hallway.

A tiny yellow sign protruded above the door. *Telegraphe*, Ellie read with relief as they slipped into the room. The office was empty except for a long wooden bench along one wall and a high counter across one side of the room. A bell rested on the counter next to a yellow note pad and a clay jar full of pencils. Mrs. Tornahos raised her eyebrows as if to say, *You see? Quite simple.* Then she nudged Ellie forward and sat down beside her daughter on the bench.

Ellie was surprised to see her own hand tremble slightly as she scrawled the simple message on the blank pad in front of her.

MARTIN FEINSTEINEL HOLLYWOOD ROOSEVELT HOTEL

*STOP HOLLYWOOD CALIFORNIA USA STOP ANGELA GONE
BAD STOP WOODS MAY BE INFESTED WITH TERMITES
STOP ANGELA VARIETY STOP INSPECT AND FUMIGATE
STOP TINMAN*

Ellie counted the words and scanned the content of the telegram. Its meaning was unmistakable and ominous. Termites. Eating away at the core of the operation's safety and success. There was no mention of Michael's death, but Ellie had seen the controlled grief on David's face as he had hesitated a moment and then signed, *Tinman*. His eyes had seemed to say, *And what good is Tinman without a Scarecrow to play to? Was it only yesterday? Less than twenty-four hours?* Then his face had clouded and he had looked up at her and said quietly, "Where is Michael? I mean, what did they do with him? I should be there when he is buried."

That was, of course, an impossible request. There was no time now, not even a moment to remember the fallen. There was only an endless parade of all-consuming seconds that ticked by, perhaps calling them to their graves as well.

Mrs. Tornahos coughed nervously when Ellie lingered too long over the message. Ellie swallowed hard and rang the bell, trying not to think any further about Michael.

Only a few seconds passed before a small, bespectacled clerk emerged from the back office. His features were thick and his head appeared too heavy for his frail-looking shoulders. He scarcely glanced up at Ellie and proceeded immediately to count the letters of the message. Its meaning was of no concern to him.

"One pound four," he mumbled, figuring the cost with acute boredom.

Ellie fished in her deep pocket and wordlessly counted out the bills.

The clerk scribbled out a receipt, shoved it across the counter, then took the message and disappeared into the back office without ever looking into her eyes. Moments later Ellie heard the clack of the telegraph begin. She hesitated a moment, stunned by the ease with which her errand had been accomplished. She wanted to laugh out loud and giggle with the joy of it. She wanted to shout that it had been almost too simple to believe, but she turned to Mrs. Tornahos, who was already on her feet and standing impatiently at the door. *Yes. That's all there is to it.*

The happy chatter of the telegraph key followed them into the hallway. *Easy as pie. Nothing to it. By the time we touch down in Turkey, Martin and the others will know about Angela.*

The relief was so profound that it was difficult for Ellie not to hold her head high and smile at every passerby. But instead she watched the shoes of Mrs. Tornahos as they crossed the black and white tiles of the lobby, then shuffled over the stone paving of the docks. Happy voices rang out around them, but Ellie did not look up. The walls of the castle were worn and rough from withstanding centuries of weather. The great stone blocks had the appearance of a child's sand castle eroding on the shore. But Ellie did not stare up to study the shadows or contemplate which angle would create the most scenic view. Gray slabs of slate and cobbles, a loose thread on the hem of Mrs. Tornahos's dress—these would be Ellie's memories of the picturesque port of Kyrenia.

There were still ten minutes before David and Tornahos were to meet them. Ellie leaned her back against the warm stone walls of the castle and listened to snatches of conversation that drifted in from the British soldiers prowling the fortifications.

"Twelve feet thick, these walls . . ."

". . . nobody past them, I'll wager . . ."

Her senses were lulled by the sun and tour-guide details that seemed to roll out of a man with a high, squeaky voice. She caught herself smiling as she remembered the words of Yacov as he had discussed the difference between American and British tourists. *Americans want to know how much. English want to know how old!* Her smile dissolved into a little giggle as she visualized his earnest face. Mrs. Tornahos nudged her to silence as the boots moved toward them. Tornahos had been right. A smile, a giggle from a pretty girl had proved to be an irresistible bait. But not to the local Cypriots; to an English sergeant instead.

Unmoving, Ellie stared at the shiny toes of his spit-polished boots. She scarcely breathed as he stood before her—a faceless shadow that blocked the sun.

"Pardon me, Miss?" He rocked on his toes. "Do you speak English? Parley Englaise?"

Ellie did not respond, but stood like a deaf-mute, not daring to look at his face.

He cleared his throat and began again. "M'gawd, what a beauty! First one of you Cypriot girls I've seen with such fair skin. Reminds me of home a bit." He leaned down to look in her face, and she quickly averted his eyes. "A shy one, eh? I won't hurt you." He reached out boldly to touch her elbow, and instantly Mrs. Tornahos was upon him like a mother hen defending her chick. With a torrid stream of Greek epithets she attacked, stepping between Ellie and the offender. She waved her arms wildly as the man backed away fearfully.

"Are you her *mum*? I meant no harm! I meant no—"

Ellie controlled her urge to laugh at the flight of her English admirer. She stared downward until at last she heard the distinct chug of the mongrel automobile. Only then did she dare look up and smile at the sight of two large drums of gasoline nestled in the back seat and David sitting triumphantly in the front.

David replaced the cap on the fuel tank with a sigh of relief. Inside the cockpit, the British captive moaned softly and tried to roll over.

Tornahos wiped his hands on his trousers and peered in through the window curiously. "Whadda you got in there?" he asked David in surprise.

"British policeman from Palestine." David rolled the fuel drum away from the aircraft. "We had to take him with us—just one of those things."

"Whadda you gonna do? You gonna kill 'im?"

"No. I figure we'll dump him off in Turkey."

"You gonna just throw him outta the plane?"

"Yeah, but we'll make sure we land first."

"That'sa good. I don' like killin' anybody. Not even an English!" He scratched his head thoughtfully. "So what's wrong with 'im? You hit him ona head?"

"Slipped him a mickey." David reached in and pulled out the syringe.

Tornahos winced at the bent needle. "I think I woulda rather get hit ona head!"

David did not notice the silent figure of Mikhail standing in the dim light of the barn. His arms were crossed and he

165

watched every move David made with a serious, studied expression. Tornahos spotted him first and hailed him loudly in Greek.

"I didn't see him there," David said, a bit irritated as he wondered how long the young man had been watching them.

"Oh, you not gonna ever see Mikhail unless he want you to, I think. Quiet, thisa boy. Quiet, ana move like a fox! He blow up Nazis in Bulgaria. An' then the Communistas come, an' he blow up them too. So they are gonna kill him, an' he decides to come to Palestine, but the English catch the boat an' so Mikhail come to Cyprus ana blow upa British concentration camp! He'sa good boy, Mikhail. . . !" He clapped Mikhail on his back.

Mikhail replied in quiet Greek, his eyes never leaving David.

"What's he say?" David asked, not certain he liked the critical look in the strange young man's eye.

"He say you still don' look likea Jew. But even if you some kinda apostate, he don' care as long as you getta him to Palestine."

David stared back at Mikhail, shook his head, and laughed. "Thanks loads, buddy. I think you're swell, too." Then he said to Tornahos. "Well, tell him we've got to go to Yugoslavia first. So it will be a while before we get him to Palestine."

Tornahos frowned and stuck out his lower lip. "You don' wanna go near Bulgaria with this fellow. They catch him, an' it'sa—" Tornahos drew his finger across his throat slowly. "You know what I mean? Communistas everywhere. Maybe they will like to kill American like you an' Ellie too. Don' go to Bulgaria, eh?"

"There are Communists everywhere," David said. "We're going to Yugoslavia, and Tito is as red as anybody."

"No." Tornahos waved his hands wildly. "Tito's onlya little pink compare to Bulgaria. There, everythinga dark red. Red likea blood. It'sa good thing you stoppa here! Idiot American! You woulda fly like a duck into Bulgarian guns. Where you been? You live undera stone? How come you don' know how bad things is in Bulgaria?"

"I thought a Commie was a Commie."

"In some ways this is so. But some Communistas will eat you up. Bulgaria on the border of Greece, yes? Everybody in Greece is scared of Bulgaria. Listen to me now, eh? Don' go nowhere close to Bulgaria."

David did not reply; instead, he pulled his map out and studied it closely. He and Sam had marked several alternate routes. All of them were sprinkled liberally with British outposts on one hand, or Communists on the other. Mikhail was obviously wanted by the Bulgarian regime, and now, with his fuel tank filled and the wire sent, David was obligated to fulfill his promise and take him along. "What if he stayed here?" David tested.

"The English will like very much to hang him."

David shook his head in resignation. "At last I find we have something in common. Is there anyone who doesn't want to hang this guy?"

"Well . . ." Tornahos rubbed his chin. "I don' think he blows up anything in Yugoslavia yet."

"Maybe we can remedy that oversight," David said sarcastically. "Tell him to help us push the plane out, will you?"

With a flurry of words, Tornahos ordered Mikhail to open the barn doors and then lend a shoulder to push the Stinson back into the light of day. Chickens squawked and scrambled clear of the wheels. A milk cow bellowed her relief that the plane was out of the barn, and Ellie emerged from the farmhouse with her arms laden with two baskets of food. Mrs. Tornahos followed with yet another basket, which was topped miraculously with four bottles of Coca-Cola and a jug of fresh coffee.

"Listen," David said, turning to Tornahos, "we—well, we're really thankful for all your help. Without you—"

"Without us, God would find some other crazy man to keep you from gettin' killed, eh? He take carea you and your Ellie. But be careful anyway, eh? Don' be stupid. Don' land in Bulgaria."

David grinned broadly and shook the big Greek's hand. Ellie turned and hugged Mrs. Tornahos awkwardly around the basket she still held. "Thank you for everything," she whispered. "God bless you."

The nose of the plane was pointed down the lane. After loading in the food, the crew scrambled aboard, and the engine was cranked to a reluctant start. Mikhail climbed over the prostrate body of the Englishman and huddled in the far back corner of the small cargo area. David glimpsed a look of white-lipped terror on the young man's face as they taxied away. Then the jarring rumble ceased, and they were in the air once again.

Mikhail scrambled forward to peer in eager silence out the

passenger window near Ellie's shoulder. As they passed over the pleasant fields of Cyprus, he touched her lightly on the shoulder and pointed beyond the fields. "Yehudah," he said quietly.

"Jews?" she asked, following his gaze to row upon row of Quonset huts, tall fences of layered barbed wire, and guard towers at each corner. Small figures holding machine guns were unmistakable. And below them, crammed into the compound, were more human beings than Ellie could even count.

"David! Look!" she said. "The camps down there—camps for Jewish refugees! They are *prisons*! It's 1948, David, and the Jews are still in *prison* camps!"

David nodded but did not reply. Instead, he banked the plane and on an impulse swooped down low, directly over the camp. The eyes of inmates and guards alike turned up toward them. "There are twenty-seven thousand of them down there behind that wire, and all they want is to go home. That's all they ever wanted. The war's been over for three years."

Ellie glanced at Mikhail, whose hand was pressed against the glass in farewell. His jaw was set and his eyes spoke of memories that Ellie could only guess at. He whispered softly in a language she could not comprehend as tiny faces gazed up and wished for freedom. *"Ani ma'amin,"* he said, repeating the words over and over again as they sailed out over the bright-blue Mediterranean toward the shore of Turkey.

16 Firmly, I Believe

Ehud had carried away Passover rations for six. In normal times, such a pitiful amount would have been scorned on the poorest of Seder tables in Jerusalem. But times were not normal, and for many who had known the starvation of the ghettos and the camps, this was a feast incomparable to any other. *The first Passover in Jerusalem!*

Rachel could only think that it was a Passover without Moshe, a night of dark fears and uncertainty for her. She cradled Tikvah in her arms, careful of the IV needle that was taped to the baby's right hand. Tikvah cried and put her little fist to her mouth, trying to find a thumb to suck beneath the white mass of tape. Rachel felt her frustration.

"I told them to put the needle in your left hand, sweet love," she crooned as Tikvah squawked with irritation and discomfort. "I told them you sucked your thumb on your right hand, but they said they could not find a vein. Soon it will be out, the doctor said, and you will have your thumb again."

Yehudit had long since left to prepare the Passover meal; Ehud no doubt snored on Howard's bed. The afternoon shadows were long, and soon Howard would return to pick her up. Rachel sighed, uncertain that she could go home with him to pretend that this was an evening she could celebrate. *But Grandfather is old. For him, this may be the first and last Seder he might share with me. I must not be so selfish. He needs me tonight. He needs his family about him to comfort him as much as I need Moshe.*

Rachel remembered the last Passover she had spent with her family. Yacov had been no bigger than Tikvah. She smiled at the thought of her father's words as he held Yacov in his arms and read from the Haggadah. "One day soon, Yacov, you will be old enough to ask the questions on the holy night. But tonight you must not squawk so like a chicken getting ready for the stew pot, nu?" They had all laughed as the tiny infant had hushed and stared at the candles with wide blinking eyes, as though he understood every word. So many years ago!

Yes, Rachel decided, she would go tonight and celebrate Passover with Yacov and Grandfather. For Papa and Mama and her brothers who had not survived to see this night in Jerusalem, she would go. Though her own heart felt as if it would break with worry, she would light the candles and watch proudly as Yacov recited the same questions that had been asked for three thousand years of Passovers.

"Last year we shared this night with ten thousand others in a Displaced Person camp," she whispered. "You remember, God? Remember how alone I was? How afraid? You saw me then, though I did not see you. And I must believe that you see my Moshe, though I cannot. So tonight I will go and say the prayers and remember that you are still God. Though the world be overrun with Pharaohs, all seeking the blood of your servants, I will remember tonight how you delivered us."

She stroked the soft head of Tikvah. "How you delivered *me* through the life of your own Son." Tikvah drew a ragged breath as Rachel began to sing softly, *Ani ma'amin b'emunah shleimah, beviat hamashiah. . . . For I firmly believe in the coming of the Messiah, and even though the Messiah may tarry, in spite of this, I still believe. . . .* Again and again she sang the words as she rocked Tikvah gently. The child's struggling limbs relaxed, her eyes drooped and then finally closed.

Although Tikvah slept peacefully in her arms at last, Rachel continued to rock her, finding comfort in her own soul at the closeness of the child. "Moshe told me that babies are God's way of being an optimist," she smiled and whispered, inwardly blessing the child in her womb. "Then, God, you are giving me two reasons to hope for the future. *Ani ma'amin!*" She repeated the words that she had learned as a child in her father's arms. "Papa said that when the oceans parted like the Red Sea and we all came home again, that then the Messiah would come." Her mind was filled with memories of Papa wrapped in his prayer shawl; the light of Seder candles shining on the silk and in his eyes.

Perhaps we shall live to see it, children, he had said. *For it is written in the Prophets that we must return to the land and that our Messiah would then come. Remember; Ani ma'amin! No matter what befalls us, we must remember those words. For they are words of hope! Words that speak of our future!*

Rachel smiled sadly as she recalled the light of courage that had passed from his eyes into the eyes of her brothers. *Yes, Messiah will come!* For ten years of loneliness and shame, Rachel had watched and waited until at last her hope had died, dissipating with the smoke that rose from the ovens in the camp. Now once again, through the love of Moshe and Leah, she found hope that she thought was forever lost. "I promised your mama that I would tell you, Tikvah," she said in a quiet voice. "This is your first Passover. Though you may not understand, I remember how Papa spoke to baby Yacov on his first Seder. . . ."

A tender sadness swelled in her breast. "Poor Papa. Poor dear Papa. Though he did not know all the truth, still he said the words, *Ani ma'amin! I believe!* But I want you to know what Leah told me. Life is so uncertain. Who knows that I may have another Passover to tell you?" She paused, remembering that she never suspected that the Passover she shared with Papa and

Mama and her brothers would be the last they would eat together. There was so much they could not have known that night.

"Someday, Tikvah, your lips will whisper *Ani ma'amin*, and you will know that your mama and papa still live. As our Messiah lives." As though reasoning with an adult, Rachel searched carefully for the right words. "Our Messiah came once to Jerusalem a long time ago. He came to show us how God would have us live . . . with lives full of love and caring for others. Like the Prophets said, the Messiah healed the sick and made the blind to see. And wicked men killed Him. Like the men who killed my papa and mama and yours also. There are those who still despise the innocent and hate the just."

Rachel frowned at untold memories and kissed the sleeping child gently. "He was innocent, and they killed Him. On Passover. He said He was the lamb of God. The final sacrifice for all our sins. And I believe this. I believe that from the cross He looked across the years and saw me. Saw my grief and shame and dishonor. I believe He took it all himself and made my soul new again. Alive again. And my heart was born new like a new baby. Innocent and clean before God because the Messiah died for the world on Passover."

Rachel stared quietly at the chipped tiles on the floor. *You knew all about betrayal and being alone, didn't you? They all ran away and left you to die alone. You knew even then what it was like to have the world turn away. You lived the hour of darkness before we even dreamed that the world could give birth to a Hitler. Did you die with us in the gas chambers? Were you standing among us when we dug our own graves? Perhaps you were there, dying again and again and again. You were among us, innocent of any guilt, dying at the whim of evil men as we were— tossed into the furnace of hatred along with us!* A sudden realization filled Rachel's heart. "Oh, Lord!" she cried aloud. "You *were* there! There in the camps, filthy and starving, suffering and dying with us, *and we just didn't recognize you! Ani ma'amin*, my Lord; I *do* believe!"

Minutes passed as countless faces, now gone forever, paraded through Rachel's mind. Forgotten lessons of her childhood returned to her, words of truth from the Torah and the Prophets that had drifted out from Papa's study. "Tikvah," she said at last, "on this, your first Passover, I will tell you. Messiah died for our sins, and He alone was the only truly innocent man who ever lived. Hitler lived even then. Evil has always been here. It killed even the Son of God. But soon, Tikvah, our Messiah will come again to Jerusalem and the world, and then there will be true justice. Those who hate us and seek to take our lives will be finished. Papa said when we are a nation, our Messiah would come and lead us. The prophets said it. Maybe we will live to see him face to face in our lifetime. And suffering will end. And then we will recognize Him. Until then, my little love, I want to teach you . . . *V'af al pi she yitmameah, im kil ani ma'amin.*"

Rachel stood slowly, holding Tikvah to her breast as she crossed to the window. The flag made from Moshe's tallith still waved in the afternoon sunlight.

Just as the rocky coast of Turkey came into view, the British captive opened his eyes, wailed mournfully through his gag, and kicked out against Mikhail. Jumping back from the thrust, Mikhail looked as though he had seen a dead man come to life. Ellie laughed in spite of herself.

"The albatross is awake again," she said cheerfully.

"Yeah. Well, I'd like to pitch him out right here and see if he could fly."

The frantic moans of the Englishman ceased. "Ha he hood! Ha he hood!" he cried, lying still. The gag had loosened and his words were nearly intelligible.

"What's he saying?" David asked.

"Ha he, ha he hood!"

Mikhail looked on with revulsion at the man lying before him like a mail sack. Ellie attempted an interpretation.

"I think he said he would be good."

The captive's head nodded vigorously. "Heh! Ha he hood!"

David cleared his throat. "Well, what's the use of a gag if we can understand him?"

Ellie shrugged. "Who's going to care what he says up here anyway? He could scream bloody murder and no one is going to care."

"Herhe. Herhe," the man moaned.

"What's he saying now?" David asked with irritation.

"I think he is asking for mercy."

"Nyah! Ha he hood! Wah ah!"

"Give him another shot," David instructed.

"Nyah! Ha he hood! Wah ah."

"Can't give him another shot. You bent the needle," Ellie admonished.

"So what's a bent needle? It's still sharp, isn't it?"

"Wahah!"

"I think he wants water, David."

"Heh! Wah ah!"

David frowned. "Well, tell him if we give him a drink, he has to be quiet when we take the gag off, or it's over the side with him."

"He understands perfectly well every word you just said. You just told him."

"Did you hear that, fella? One peep and you're shark meat."

"Ha he hood. Herhe. Wah ah."

"Poor man," Ellie clucked her tongue sympathetically. "Almost seven hours and not a drop to drink."

"Yeah." David looked smug. "I'll bet that's not all that's bothering him. But he's just gonna have to wait until Turkey. Serves him right."

A pitiful peep came from the captive.

Ellie reached back to fumble with the knot on the gag. "Don't try anything funny, now," she warned, pulling the soggy tie loose and letting it fall to the floor.

The man licked his cracked lips and did not speak as Ellie poured a cup of cold water and held it to his mouth. He drank eagerly, gulping the cool liquid and still not daring to speak until he had drunk his fill. Then, in a panting breath, he said hoarsely, "Thank you, Mrs. Meyer, oh, thank you!" His grateful voice sounded near to tears.

"You're welcome," David said gruffly. "Now shut up."

"David," Ellie murmured, "he's just being polite."

"I told him to keep his trap shut or he's out the window." David banked the plane sharply and roared down toward the water.

"*Please*," the man begged. "For God's sake don't! Don't throw me in the water!" He wept openly now as David leveled the plane, then turned to glower menacingly at him.

"Give me one good reason." David winked at Ellie, playing his role of captor to the hilt.

"You're making a mistake! I'm Jewish! *Jewish!*" he shrieked loudly in desperation.

"Right," David spat. "And I'm Russian. Are you ready, Mikhail?" he called to their uncomprehending passenger. "When I give the word, throw this guy out." Mikhail blinked in reply.

"Please! You've got to believe me! My name is Bernie Greene, and I'm with the Mossad!" He shouted at Mikhail, who inched away.

"Jewish Intelligence?" David scoffed. "You bet. I'll believe that when the Old Man tells me in person."

Ellie looked on in sympathy as the man's tears tumbled down his cheeks. "David? Maybe he's telling the truth."

"Jewish! Yeah. He's on our side all right. Like Angela was. Come on, honey. . . ."

"Mrs. Meyer," the captive begged, "you must believe me! Dear God, if he kills me . . ."

"Oh, he's not going to kill you," she assured him. "Not really."

"Ellie! Stay out of this," David demanded. She glared at him, then turned back to the prisoner.

"At least, not unless you try something," she added.

The captive grimaced and took a deep breath to control himself. "For three years I've thought the British would hang me for espionage, and now my own fellows—"

"Can it, buddy. I've been up against the best liar in the world and you're nowhere close!" David snapped. "Give him another shot," he instructed Ellie. "I'm not going to listen to this all the way to Turkey."

"But the needle, David—" she protested.

"Give him a shot or he *is* going out the window, and I am not joking!"

Ellie rummaged for the first-aid kit and the near-empty vial of morphine. "What if he *is* with the Mossad?" she said under her breath.

"Then he will have a nice painless sleep and we will have a little quiet in here. Believe me, *I* wouldn't mind a few hours sleep."

Ellie tried to straighten the bent needle. "Shouldn't we sterilize it or something?" she squeaked.

"There ought to be a little something under your seat. Glenlivit 80 proof, courtesy of Bobby, if you're worried—"

"How can I convince you?" the Englishman cried as Ellie

rummaged under the seat and pulled out a nearly empty bottle of whiskey. "My name is Bernie Greene. I'm with the Mossad!"

"Did Bobby drink this all himself?" Ellie asked over the protests of the captive.

"Mouthwash. Kills the stink of his cigars."

"No wonder he can't fly straight."

"Bernie Greene, I tell you. Mossad! The password! The password! *Mah nish ta'nah!* Are you deaf! I said, *Mah nish ta'nah!*"

David lost his patience at last. "Forget the shot! Mikhail; if he doesn't shut up, throw him out!"

"Bernie Greene! I'm Bernie Greene!"

"I don't care if you're John Brown's body! One more word—"

"Don't you know the password? *Mah nish ta'nah!* It's Passover, for God's sake! Don't throw me out."

As the plane wobbled a bit, Ellie carefully filled the syringe.

"Nobody told us anything about you, pal," David said. "Or about any password."

"How can you be with us if you don't know the password?" The Englishman asked with a fleeting look of horror on his face. "You knock me out, gag me . . . I didn't know who in blazes the fellows were who arrested you. I didn't know but what they were the King's own guard. I couldn't say a word until I was sure, and by then you had knocked me out. I'm Jewish, I tell you!"

Mikhail shook his head slowly from side to side and smiled with amusement at the British sergeant who lay among the baggage in his skivvies. "*Nebbish*," he commented.

"You call me a *nebbish*?" cried the captive indignantly. "A *nothing*! Well, better men than you have called me *Shayner Yid*!"

Mikhail raised his eyebrows. "*Shayner Yid?*" he asked incredulously. Then he shook his head again. "Nicht. Shaygets."

"What is this. . . ?" David asked.

"Shaygets!" the voice of the captive became angry. "Call me a *Gentile*, will you? For years I serve Zionism. Risk my life and it comes to this! I was ordered to pick you up in case anything went wrong tonight—"

Ellie tapped the syringe and air bubbles popped out of the end of the needle. "I can't stick him, David," she said, wrinkling her nose. "You'll have to do it."

David set the automatic pilot with an irritated sigh. "It would be a whole lot simpler to throw him out." He took the syringe and stared through the clear liquid.

"Jewish! Mossad! Three years under cover with the British forces! Dear God! You've got to—"

"Right. You're Jewish for thirty seconds until we get the cuffs off."

"Bernie Greene. Bar Mitzvah in B'nai Jacob Synagogue in London," he repeated, as though reciting name, rank and serial number for an interrogator. "Password . . . *Mah nish ta'nah!*"

Mikhail leaned forward, then thrust the Hebrew prayer book before the frantic eyes of the distraught Englishman. The page was turned to a section written entirely in the Hebrew alphabet. "Shayner Yid?" he questioned.

"Whatever." David held the whiskey bottle aloft, dumping its contents over the needle and the hip of the Englishman at once. "So where do you want it, pal?"

"Don't! Wait! I'll show you! I can read this . . . *Shemah, O Yisroial!*—" His words were interrupted by a shriek as David plunged the needle in.

Mikhail tapped the Englishman lightly and asked him a question in slow and deliberate Hebrew. As the morphine began to take effect, the captive smiled benignly and answered in fluent Hebrew.

"Hold it!" David said. "What are you two talking about?"

"Well, they sure aren't speaking English," Ellie sighed as the Englishman's words slurred a bit. "Maybe we ought to check before we drop this guy off in Turkey."

The captive chuckled and looked at Ellie drunkenly, "I tole you. *Shayner Yid.* I'm a *beautiful Jew.* Ashk Mikhail. He knowsh a Jew when he talksh to one. . . ."

"He probably just picked up the language living in Palestine," David said defensively. "See what happens when you feel sorry for these guys? Take off his gag and give him water, and this is what we get—"

Mikhail continued to speak in quiet Hebrew. A smile played on his lips as the captive chuckled again.

"Mikhail will tell you," said the Englishman. "Lishen—"

"What did he say?" Ellie asked.

Slowly, the words tumbled out of the captive as his eyes blinked and closed and a peaceful grin fixed on his face. "Mikhail shez how come if I'm the evil Englishhh prioshoner an' the pilot ish the Jew. . ." His voice drifted off for a moment. "How come I shpeak Hebrew an' you don . . ." The sentence ended in

176

a contented sigh as a profound sleep overtook him.

Ellie studied him for a long moment, then looked up at Mikhail, who pointed at and then patted the Englishman. "*Shayner Yid,*" Mikhail said confidently. "*Shayner Yid.*"

Ellie grimaced. "David, did you hear what Mikhail said? Shayner Yid."

"Whatever that means," he growled, the effects of hours without rest taking a toll on his temper.

She gazed down at the knobby-kneed captive in his khaki underwear as he dozed peacefully in a lump between two pieces of baggage. His mouth hung open and his dark brown hair was disheveled. Mikhail took a coarse woolen blanket from the rear of the plane and covered him, taking care to tuck him in against the draft and the cold of the altitude.

"I think it means *beautiful Jew*," Ellie said in a wash of pity for the man.

David cleared his throat loudly and shifted uneasily in his seat. "Is he out?" he snapped.

"Like a baby."

"Well then, take his cuffs off. I guess it won't hurt, if he's out cold . . ."

17 Ragusa

The sun was still high when Yassar Tafara stepped off the silver DC–4 airliner in Cavtat, Yugoslavia. He tugged uncomfortably at his new brown, double-breasted suit and patted the pocket containing a Syrian diplomatic passport and his orders concerning the freighter he was to meet in Ragusa twenty miles away.

He felt uneasy with the mission Kadar and the Mufti had entrusted to him. He looked nothing like a diplomatic aide, yet the grim-faced man who stamped his passport at the customs counter asked him no questions. Yassar felt a vague sense of irritation to be so far removed from the action now taking place in Palestine. There was little glory to be gained in playing the role of escort to a shipment of weapons. While Kadar and Gerhardt led the troops of Holy Strugglers, Yassar was certain that he would be miserable and seasick on the decrepit tramp steamer he was to board in Ragusa.

They have sent me here to get me out of the way. That is all, he thought resentfully. *Gerhardt hates me because my skill is now almost equal to his. Kadar and my cousin the Mufti simply do not want me to be the focus of Gerhardt's fury. So I am sent away like a schoolboy.*

He had known for some time that Gerhardt preferred him to be elsewhere—or simply to be dead. So now he was elsewhere—the most remote corner of the world from where the drama of history was being played out. An errand boy, a page, sent to fetch the sword and armor of the knight. Yassar stormed inside. *Could they not have sent a clerk to perform this mission? I am a servant of Haj Amin and Allah, and am meant to do battle against their enemies. Instead, I shall hand a slip of paper to the captain of this rugged ship, and he shall change his course from Damascus to Jaffa while I rot in a wretched cabin.*

Yassar waited half an hour before a taxi was available to take him to Ragusa. He did not see the beauty of the ancient walled city that butted up against the glistening blue of the Adriatic Sea. Red tiled roofs on quaint buildings and cobbled streets were lost to him. He knew nothing of the Renaissance city Ragusa had been, a great maritime power competing with Venice. It did not matter that its cargo-laden argosies had sailed as far as America and India to amass the fortunes that had built and embellished the churches and halls of this seaport. The ships of Ragusa did not come to his mind as he scanned the harbor for the rusted hulk that carried a more deadly treasure concealed within its bowels.

The battered taxi rattled slowly around the winding thoroughfare outside the towers and massive walls that embraced the Renaissance jewel of Ragusa. Yassar cared nothing for the walls of any city but Jerusalem.

"How long until the waterfront?" he asked awkwardly.

The taxi driver held up five fingers and pointed toward a gulf between two towers. Yassar caught sight of a port and a seawall where innumerable boats were moored. Beyond the seawall, which did not permit the entrance of large cargo ships into the harbor, a long anchor chain stretched out to tether the wretched hulk of a freighter in place. Yassar squinted through the dirty windshield and strained his eyes to read the name that was painted on the rusty bow.

"Yes," he said, "that is my ship. The *Trina*. She is there, as they told me. Although I do not know how she still floats."

The driver grinned at him in amusement. "You sail on this ship?"

"Yes. Yes. I will sail tonight."

———

Tiny waves lapped against the side of the *Trina*. White paint cracked and peeled, and the decks themselves were dried and splintered from nearly forty years plying the waters of the Adriatic and the Mediterranean. Coils of rope were carelessly piled around the aged decks where Yassar stood in angry debate with the unshaven master of the ship.

"But we are not due to sail until morning!" The captain studied the credentials Yassar handed him.

"And my orders are that we are to sail when I arrive. So. I have arrived."

The captain wiped his bulbous nose on the back of his hand. His breath reeked of wine, and there was a ragged hole in his filthy shirt. "But you can see"—he waved a hand absently over the ship—"the crew is gone. Gone ashore. Ragusa Dubrovnik is a pretty port. Nice churches. Cafes. And . . . women . . ." He smiled and winked as though letting Yassar in on a great secret. "You stay the night here and you will not forget these women in this port."

Yassar's face remained stony to the invitation. "Get your crew back to the ship," he demanded. "Do you not see the authority with which I am sent? If you wish to be paid, we will be under way before nightfall."

"But there is a storm coming." The captain spread his hands in helplessness. "We might be delayed three . . . maybe four days."

"You lie." Yassar jerked his chin toward the clear blue of the sky. "We will leave within the hour or you will not be paid for your cargo."

The captain's smile faded. He shrugged and said with disregard, "You will not pay me? You will not pay *me*? I am the captain of this ship. I direct her where she sails. If you Arabs do not pay, there are others who will pay me well for such a cargo."

Yassar met his gaze with an icy stare. "No one else will pay you. From this moment I am the master." He reached into his pocket, pulled out a pistol, and jammed it hard into the ribs of the startled captain.

"I was . . . it was only a joke, sir."

"Yes." Yassar appraised him and smiled. He did not put the gun away. "Yes. I thought you were joking."

The captain laughed nervously and backed up a step. "My crew? You say I should fetch my crew? Of course. A blast on the whistle and they will return on the launch. And then we will sail as you demand." He clapped his hands together. "But I tell you the truth. There is indeed a storm approaching. Very large, they say, and—"

"You are an able captain." Yassar pocketed the gun again, satisfied with the results of his action. "Call your crew and we will sail early. Ahead of the storm, if there is indeed one coming."

"Of course, sir." The captain climbed heavily up corroded steps to the bridge of the freighter. "Just a few blasts on the horn. They will hear and come. Even if they are in church. Even with a woman. You will see. They will come on the launch and we will set sail. Tonight with the tide."

Yassar looked up into the sky. "Before the moon rises."

"Yes. Yes. Of course. No one will even know we are gone until we are out to sea."

"One person must know. Have you a radio here?"

"Yes, but alas, it is in disrepair."

"Then I will have to send a wire from shore. You will come with me." He patted the bulge in his pocket where the pistol rested.

"A good idea! Excellent! Then we shall round up any stragglers among the crew, sir." He laughed nervously.

Yassar stared at the harbor through the salt-encrusted window of the bridge. The captain blasted the horn in three short bursts and then blasted it again. "And if they do not come?" Yassar smiled menacingly at the sweating captain.

"Then we shall return in the launch and I shall sail her alone, sir. I shall—" He gulped and glanced at the pocket of Yassar's coat. ". . . alone I shall sail to Jaffa at your command."

It was nearly three years since the war had ended, yet the devastation of Belgrade was evident. David circled the plane slowly over bomb craters that pocked vast sections of the city. The Danube River was joined here by the Sava, and what was left of the city crowded along their banks.

Ellie gazed down to where nearly a third of the city's dwellings lay in ruin. Church spires poked blackened fingers into the sky. Here and there, it was evident that entire city blocks destroyed by Nazi bombers had been cleared and stripped bare for reconstruction.

Mikhail stared out the window behind her. He shook his head slowly from side to side. The devastation of Belgrade was a scene that had been repeated in nearly every major city in Europe.

"Ratno," he said, pointing to the island that split the Danube.

Mikhail had been here before, Ellie guessed—probably before the war. No doubt Ratno Island was the only thing unchanged in Belgrade.

David, too, looked down at the ground in fascination. "They say this was quite a place before the war," he said. "Nazis didn't like the Slavs much more than Jews, from what I hear. Somewhere around here they rounded up seven thousand schoolboys and shot them. In one day. Imagine. Now General Tito has control of the country. He was a Resistance fighter. Quite a guy, I guess."

"He's a Communist, isn't he?" Ellie took out her camera and snapped a series of photographs in quick succession.

"Yeah. But you heard what Tornahos said. He's not as bad as the Bulgarians."

Mikhail looked curiously at him when he mentioned the name of his native country. Ellie wondered what destruction he had seen and what memories this battle-scarred city held for him.

David directed the Stinson to a small, ragged airstrip on the edge of the swamp outside Belgrade. Bernie Greene still slept peacefully as the wheels of the plane touched down. They taxied toward a brown and green camouflage hangar, and before they even coasted to a stop, a fuel truck had arrived.

The familiar face of Avriel smiled out the passenger window

at them. He adjusted his spectacles and waved broadly at David.

"You know him?" Ellie asked, sensing David's relief.

"Yeah!" David said enthusiastically. "Michael and I went with him to Prague in December to buy some ME–109's. He was there last night when we landed. Had the whole cargo ready for us. Gave us the note about the ship, and . . ." David's smile faded. "Only last night." He said heavily. "Me and Michael."

Ellie looked down at her hands, searching for something to say. There were no words. Only twenty-four hours ago Michael had greeted Avriel, who now rushed to the side of the little Stinson.

David opened the hatch to the cockpit, and Avriel extended his hand in a hearty handshake. "Well," said Avriel, "it seems I am not the only one who did not sleep last night! And where is Michael Cohen?" He scanned the passengers. "Back in Palestine sleeping while you do all the work, eh?"

David blinked hard at him, as though trying to absorb the fact that Avriel still had not heard the news. "Michael . . . uh . . . he didn't make it."

Avriel looked stricken; the joy on his face wiped clean in an instant. "Dear God, David. I . . . I . . . we hadn't heard that. I sent the wire to Tel Aviv as soon as we heard that the *Trina* was leaving Ragusa in the morning. They wired back you were coming, but no mention was made of—" His eyes fell on Ellie who sat quietly in the passenger seat. Then he looked at each of the passengers. "You have a full load already, I see." He sounded surprised.

"Sorry. Uh . . . Avriel, this is my wife, Ellie Warne. I mean, Ellie Meyer."

"Ah yes!" He extended his hand across David. "The famous cadaver! How pleasant to meet you! How very nice . . . and who are these fellows?"

"The man who is sleeping says he is one of us. I doubt it, except that he can read Hebrew. And this"—he gestured to Mikhail—"is Mikhail Gregovsky, a Bulgarian Jew we picked up in Cyprus. Long story."

"Mikhail Gregovsky?" Avriel gasped. "He's practically a legend—a one-man bombing squad." He turned toward Mikhail and rattled off a string of Bulgarian sentences that immediately brightened Mikhail and unleashed a torrent of words. Avriel smiled and led them toward the hangar.

Inside the dingy office, David sipped coffee and listened quietly as Avriel explained the situation.

"Yugoslavia is a Communist country. We are here by the skin of our teeth rounding up what war surplus we can. I don't know how much longer we can continue to operate, but it is certain that we can't blow up the ship in the harbor without bringing everything down on our heads. We won't be here for long." He gestured toward a scuffed leather suitcase. "So what you need to do this evening when you get to Ragusa is drive down and get a good look at your target. She sails tomorrow, and she is a leaky tub at best. When she is out of sight of the coast, you just fly over and drop this little item onto her deck."

"What's in there?" Ellie asked, almost afraid to look at the suitcase.

"Enough explosives to get things started. Believe me, with eight million rounds of ammunition on board, a little explosion will be enough."

David almost laughed at the absurdity of the mission. "A homemade bomb? In a suitcase? We are making a bombing run . . . let me get this straight . . . in a Stinson? With a homemade bomb?"

"It will work," Avriel said matter-of-factly. "Ask Mikhail here. This guy blew up more stray Panzers than most of the Allied Army together. Mikhail earned quite a name for himself. He knows a little bit about what we have in the luggage."

David took another slow sip of coffee. "Yeah. So we've got a hero for a hitchhiker. You could have fooled me. So now that I know how I'm supposed to sink the freighter, what am I supposed to do with Mikhail here? And Bernie Greene?"

"Well . . ." Avriel rubbed his forehead. The hours without sleep were evident on his face. "Mikhail is not safe here, I'm afraid. You'll have to take him with you."

"And do what with him?"

"Just bear in mind you are carrying one of the finest demolition experts in the—"

David's voice was sarcastic. "Well, I've already got myself a bomb. What do I need Mikhail for?"

"He can't stay here."

"What about sleeping beauty out there?" David jerked a thumb toward the plane.

"Sorry. That's your mistake." He shook his head and smiled

183

at David. "Bernie Greene is indeed a member in excellent standing of the Mossad."

David's jaw dropped. "But—but—but—" he stammered. "How—I mean, we took him for English, and—"

"The Mossad is everywhere, David. You of all people should know that. But there was no way you could be sure. You did the right thing, keeping him under control."

"*Shayner Yid*," murmured Mikhail with a slight smile.

"OK, yeah, pal, you were right!" snapped David. "But what do we do with him now? You know this joker's going to kill me when he finally wakes up."

"With all the morphine you've pumped into him, he might sleep all the way back to Palestine. Ignore him. Leave him in the plane if you like, but we . . ."

". . . can't keep him here!" David finished, feeling chagrined.

Avriel thought for a long, serious moment. "You might apologize. Or you might simply leave him tied up until you get back to Palestine."

David glanced at the suitcase again. "If we get back."

"A possibility," Avriel concluded.

David turned to Ellie at last. "It's probably a good idea, Babe, if you stay on the ground for this one. Avriel says there are some good hotels in Ragusa; you can—"

"Nothing doing." Ellie crossed her arms determinedly and drew herself up. "I am not losing sight of you for even a minute, David Meyer. We haven't even had a honeymoon!"

Avriel pushed his round spectacles up on the bridge of his nose. "Well, David," he smiled. "It seems the lady has made up her mind."

David threw his head back in hearty laughter, the genuine laughter Ellie was afraid wouldn't be heard from him again after Michael's body had been laid out beside the plane last night.

"When this is over," he said, "I've promised her a honeymoon—if she'll put away her camera, and the Old Man will give us a little time off . . ."

Avriel sighed wearily. "Ben-Gurion? He does not sleep, so none of the rest of us will sleep either, I think. Haven't you noticed, David? Your life belongs to Israel now, and to the Old Man."

David nodded and looked out the window as the fuel truck pulled away from the Stinson. "One of these days, Avriel, I'm going to get even. Someday, if the Old Man ever gets old, I'm going to tie a string to his cane and watch him try to walk away." He grinned.

"Somehow he has made it difficult for any of us to walk away." Avriel chuckled at the image. But there was truth in his reply.

Reaching out to touch Ellie's hand, David said softly, "A little sleep is enough for right now, right, Babe? One night in Ragusa and we can sink a battleship—not to mention a leaky freighter."

18   Underground

It was late in the afternoon before Captain Stewart could answer the call of Rabbi Akiva in the Old City. The rabbi's house seemed darker than usual, almost oppressive in its quietness. It was a quietness like death, and the rabbi's heavy face reflected a black mood as he spoke.

"It was a man's voice that spoke to you then," Akiva demanded. "And you thought that it was I?"

Stewart pressed his fingertips together and gazed across the cluttered desk. "The call was obviously made from here on the direct line to headquarters. There was no other assumption to be made than that it was you." Stewart's voice was cold and unapologetic.

"And you met my daughter. . . ." The word seemed to rankle him, and he swallowed hard before he could force himself to go on. "Yehudit was at the home of the woman, Rachel Sachar."

Stewart nodded in curt agreement. "There were others there. Two men. An old woman and a boy . . . the red-haired boy who came to warn Moshe Sachar the day he was arrested."

"Treachery!" exclaimed Akiva, slamming his fist on the desk. "Did you not know?" he accused.

"The child was ill . . . I assumed even *you* would desire for an infant to have medical—" Stewart's sarcasm was lost on the rabbi.

"My own daughter! A traitor!" Akiva raged. His skin became

red and his eyes glared wildly at the inkwell before him. "And you believed—"

"I am not at fault in this, Mayor Akiva. The call was placed from your house by a man who sounded like you—"

"It was Vultch!" Akiva shouted. "Not me! He came here to ask for my help—"

"Which you denied him."

"For the sake of not imposing on *you*!" Akiva said, gaining control of his emotions.

"Noble," Stewart said dryly. "And now, as it turns out, not only have I escorted your daughter out of the Old City, but I must fetch her back by night, so no one in the quarter knows of your disgrace?"

Akiva did not reply. His lips tightened as he simply returned the hard gaze of Stewart. "So," he said at last. "Speaking of disgrace, has Moshe Sachar been recaptured? And have the English soldiers who aided in his escape been apprehended yet?"

Stewart shrugged, not at all liking this arrogant man who sat across from him. "It is suspected that he was involved with the Jewish offensive against Kastel last night. Rumors are that he was spotted in the New City of Jerusalem. If this is so, he will be arrested. Our patrols are everywhere. He will not be free for long."

"It seems that none of us are free from these irritating little problems, eh, Captain Stewart? Your disgrace is his escape . . . and the aid given to him by disloyal British subjects. My disgrace is similar. My daughter has been disloyal, siding against me with these Zionists, using my own telephone line to headquarters to betray me! You can imagine what this would do to my authority in the community if it is known that she has done this."

Stewart smiled briefly. "Yes. I can imagine."

Akiva leaned forward and scowled across the desk. "You find this amusing? Well, if my standing as leader of the Jewish Quarter is in doubt, then you have lost your only link here with peace and negotiation between us and the Arabs. You will lose what little foothold you have here. And *that*, my good Captain Stewart, would add further difficulty to your duty here."

Stewart's jaw twitched with anger at Akiva's threat. "I see." He tapped his cap against his knee and continued to smile. "Well, then, your daughter Yehudit makes quite an important hostage to your cause, does she not? Then we shall simply have to retrieve her for you, Rabbi. For the sake of the Jewish Quarter—and your public image."

Akiva leaned back in his chair and appraised the captain with an amused eye. "A sensible decision; I shall personally offer prayers for the fellows of your patrols, that they find the traitors who have freed Moshe Sachar. And that Sachar himself is apprehended before he does any more damage to the desires of the Mandatory British Government."

"Kind of you. The Almighty is as anxious as we are, I am sure, to see the demise of the Jewish terrorists."

"Then we are *all* agreed." Akiva smiled, but his smile was devoid of any warmth or humanity. "The sooner the United Nations is convinced the Zionists will fail, the sooner England can get back to the business of governing and we can all enjoy peace once again."

The light reflected on the visor of Stewart's cap. He toyed with it as he listened to Akiva, wondering if the portly rabbi believed the words he spoke. He stood slowly, his face disappearing in the shadows as he towered over the desk. "Frankly, Rabbi, the outcome of this conflict no longer matters to me. As long as it does not concern me personally, I wish only to go home in one piece. But if you believe that there is any corner of the world that you Jews can scratch out an existence and live in peace, then you are a bigger fool than I imagined."

Akiva stared up at him through the shadows. "How dare you!"

Stewart put on his cap. "Shalom, Rabbi." He turned on his heel. "Doesn't that mean *peace*?"

————

Moshe snuggled deeper under the heavy blanket, but still he could not get warm. A bone-cold ache penetrated him, throbbing in his neck and back, probing into him from the cold stone floor he lay upon.

The sound of other men snoring pulled him into a confused semiconsciousness. *I am at Acre Prison, after all! They will hang me in the morning. Kastel; a dream. The convoy? All a dream. Acre Prison. I am in Acre Prison. Rachel? Where is Rachel?* Then he spoke her name aloud, "Rachel?" His voice echoed hollowly in the cistern and returned to him without an answer. He sighed heavily and opened his eyes, blinking at the weak lamp that burned on a wooden crate in the corner. *Acre Prison? Or . . .* He fought to separate reality from dreams.

He sat up with difficulty, his stiff muscles arguing with every move. He squinted in the dim light, counting six men sleeping side by side to his right, and one more wrapped in a blanket and lying near the lamp. Then he saw the plate of leftover matzo bread and scattered cups of cold tea. He winced painfully as he moved his legs, and the leather of his boots rubbed against his chafed ankles. "No," he whispered, "it was not a dream." *The escape from the English. Luke Thomas. The airplane and the weapons. Kastel and the convoy. And I am in Jerusalem in the cistern of Mrs. Bett's Pastry Shop.*

He remembered clearly the six men who slept to his right, but he could not recall the arrival of the seventh man. Shivering with the cold, Moshe wrapped his blanket around his shoulders and leaned back against the wall. The blanket was all but useless. His teeth chattered, and he was certain that the ache in his bones would not be remedied except by a long soak in a hot bath. The cistern reeked of sweat and filth; and Moshe's clothes were stiff with dried perspiration and the blood of the young man who had died in his arms. No, Kastel and the Pass of Bab el Wad were no dream, but a nightmare he had lived—and perhaps, by tonight, would live again.

A hollowness settled beneath his heart as he thought of returning to battle without word of Rachel. He remembered the faces of Grandfather and the tears of Yacov as he prepared to journey into the Old City. *Have they had word of her since my arrest? Perhaps they know if she and the child are well.* He sat brooding silently, computing the distance and the route he would have to take to reach the home of Howard Moniger. *Rehavia District. We must all gather at the high school there at midnight, at any rate. I will wait until after dark, and then I will go to them.*

His lips moved silently as he pronounced her name like a prayer. It seemed that there was no other way to pray. Her name carried all his thoughts and all his love. *Rachel!* Was she safe behind the walls of the Old City? Had she fallen victim to sickness or the quicker end of an Arab sniper's bullet? If she still lived, had any word of his safety reached her, or did she grieve for him and pray for death to take her too? If there was any news to be had, Moshe knew he must have it, even at the risk of capture. *Will the British be standing watch for me at Howard's home? Yes*, he thought with certainty. *Don't be a fool, Moshe. They will not let you escape a second time.* His face was tense with the thought, but his heart was desperate for news. He glanced toward the light, startled to see the sarcastic grin of Emile as he lay propped on his elbow, staring at Moshe.

"Grieving over your Arab brothers, Sachar?" His words were full of poison. "The fellows you killed?"

Moshe did not answer. "Where did you come from?" he shot back.

"I arrived a bit late. You were all sleeping when the good woman let me in." His eyes fell on Moshe's jacket. "Blood, I see. Arab blood, or your own?"

"*Our* own, Emile. Jewish blood."

"Whose?"

"Philip."

Emile raised his eyebrows slightly in disdain. "Yes. He was certain to be killed. Too big and clumsy. We lost fourteen, you know."

"No, I didn't."

"I stayed with the convoy. Rode into Zion Square and stayed to the end. The British came. Threatened to shoot if we didn't give up our weapons."

Moshe leaned forward in alarm. "And?"

"The British are not like the Nazis. The Germans would have shot first and made the survivors bury their own dead. Not the British. They backed away. Ran from us. They are weaklings." His voice was thick with arrogance. It was the voice of one who had learned well the ways of his enemy, whose heart had become the reflection of that which he most despised.

"No," Moshe said, "they are not weaklings. They simply are not Nazis. Whatever needs to be maintained by force is doomed, Emile. That is the lesson we all learned from Hitler."

Emile seemed not to hear him. "Weaklings. But we will not be so soft with the Arabs when it is our turn."

Moshe felt as though he was speaking only to the stones. There was no soft place in Emile for words of reason to take root. The brutality of his enemies had made him brutal. Hatred for the injustice of life had driven from him any thought of what was just or even human. *It is a disease*, Moshe thought as he

189

watched the fire that burned in Emile's eyes and consumed his soul. *And among us now there will be this same disease. A Holocaust of hatred that destroys our souls just as our enemies murdered us without thought or reason.*

Moshe searched for words, feeling a strange pity for the man who brooded before him in the half-light. "We fight for a homeland, Emile. We fight because we have to or there will be no place safe on earth for Jews to live. Dr. Weizmann has said that those Arabs who live here in this land have the same rights to their homes as we have. If this is not so, then someday they may drive us out."

Emile laughed bitterly at Moshe's words. "Very high and lofty-sounding, Professor. But not practical. This world, *Palestine*, is not a home. It is a hospital. It's a place not to live in, but a place to die. The question is, which of us will die first, eh?" He laughed again, then turned over, facing away from Moshe and ending the discussion.

Moshe did not attempt to reply. Mere argument would never chip away the crust of such obstinate bitterness. Emile had become infected with the twisted belief that good and evil was determined by the borders of nations and races. All Germans were evil, all British, and now, certainly, every Arab in Palestine.

Moshe closed his eyes in the memory of a verse he had learned when he had studied at Oxford in England. He whispered the words, but even the whisper was loud:

The world in all doth but two nations bear,
The good, the bad, and these mixed everywhere . . .

After a moment, Emile laughed again. "You are a child and a fool if you believe such rubbish, Professor. Keep it to yourself, if you please." He jerked his blanket closer around himself and snorted with ridicule. "Sleep now, Sachar. Tonight we will have to relieve the Jewish soldiers at Kastel. We will kill Arabs. Or they will kill us. And then we shall see how much good your verse will do us."

Only a few minutes passed in cold silence. Emile fell quickly back to sleep again, while Moshe hugged himself, trying to get warm. The trapdoor swung open and sunlight streamed in as Mrs. Bett tiptoed down into the cistern.

"It is still daylight?" Moshe asked quietly. The crystal of his wristwatch had been smashed and he was surprised that the sun still shone.

"Yes," she whispered. "But if you are to bathe and clean up before tonight's Seder, come along." She waved a hand in front of her nose. "Oy! Such a stink! Not at the table of Althea Bett! Gevalt, such a smell!"

Three of the others moaned a protest to her noisy intrusion. Another sat up reluctantly. "Where am I?"

"You see, such filth can demolish a man's brains! Where is he!" she scoffed.

Emile did not move or acknowledge her, though Moshe was certain that he must have heard. *He will eat tonight, but he will not wish to eat the Passover Seder. He will not like to be reminded that the Hebrews grieved for their enemies. For the fallen firstborn of Egypt.*

"So, Professor Sachar! You are the only one who looks awake. You would like a nice bath maybe?"

He nodded and his teeth chattered noisily as he stood, a bit stooped, and followed her. The light of the courtyard was almost unbearably bright after the hours in the semidarkness of the cistern. He blinked and shielded his eyes. "Did the English come to search?" he asked, still holding the blanket around himself.

"What else? You think they come to buy pastries in the famine?"

Her nonchalant manner startled him and he stared down at the back of her head in surprise. "You mean they did come?"

She waved her hand as though she were brushing away a fly. "So what else is new? They always come! For weeks now they are suspicious because the university is closed and still the young men are in and out of here; and I haven't got enough dough for so much as a strudel, nu?"

"What did you do with our guns?"

"Hid them in the matzo bread dough. Very unappetizing. No yeast. No sugar. They did not so much as ask for a pinch of a taste." She smiled over her shoulder, and Moshe thought that as a young woman, Mrs. Bett must have been quite beautiful. At this moment, her graying hair pulled back in a bun, her warm brown eyes surrounded by a road map of pleasantness, she seemed very beautiful and brave indeed.

"Were they here long?" he asked.

"Long enough. Tramp, tramp, tramp. This way and that, right

past the cistern, mind you! Oy! These fellows know nothing of Jerusalem and all the secrets these stones could tell! So. They left, as always, wishing for cakes to go with their tea, but I told them this morning that all the leaven was taken out and burned for Passover. If they want cakes they should go back to England, eh?" She winked mischievously. "Of course, not that I wouldn't sell to them if I had it. I charge them four times more than the locals, and the extra goes into the box to buy more bullets for the Yishuv, yes?"

"I will not ever complain of high prices in your shop, Mrs. Bett."

"And I will never charge you again. You think I could deny the hero of Bab el Wad a morning pastry and a cup of coffee? When this is finished, God willing, and the bus to the university is running again, every morning you shall have a pastry for nothing!" She opened the door to a small room on the other side of the courtyard. "On the condition you do not smell like such a —Oy!" The thought remained unfinished.

A small round tub sat in the center of the floor. Steam rose from it invitingly. Several different sets of clean clothes were lined up on a wooden bench—garnered, no doubt, from the willing members of the Jerusalem Underground, who were at the command of Mrs. Bett. "Even fresh clothes!"

"So you were expecting maybe dirty clothes? If you think I should wash those . . ." She swept her hand near Moshe's shirt. "What? Are you crazy? If you have some sentimental attachment for these, you will have to wash them yourself and somewhere else, if you please. Now, Professor. Soap I have and towels. What you do with the water is up to you, nu?" She smiled and exited, leaving Moshe to stare in wonder at the gift of soap and clean, steaming water.

He groaned in audible ecstasy as he sank into the little tub and the water lapped at his aching back. His knees stuck up awkwardly, but never had a soak been so welcome. His ankles were bloody from the chafing of his boots, and every toe had a blister. He washed from head to foot, then let the steam drift into his face. It was, quite simply, better than sleep. He began to relax and feel the warmth return to his aching limbs. "If I could only stay like this a week or so, Lord," he muttered. Then his feeling of peace evaporated as instantly as it had come. *Kastel! Fergus is still there. How long will it be before he can have even a moment of real rest? And Rachel! Rationing water in the Old City, one drop at a time.*

He remembered the light on her face as he had washed her hair the day he had been arrested. Her sighs echoed clearly in his mind and in an instant he felt almost driven mad to know how she was. He gripped the sides of the tub and stared at the white wall of the room. A profound loneliness engulfed him and tears stung his eyelids. This was the first moment he had been able to let go of physical pain and discomfort in many days. And in letting go, he found in its place a greater pain. He forgot Fergus and Kastel and let his mind rush to thoughts he longed to share with Rachel. He remembered quiet nights lying together in their little apartment; the way she had laid her head against his chest and replied in sleepy monotones as he had plotted and planned the defense of the Old City. She had shared him so unselfishly with the desperation of their cause. And her love for him had been as uncluttered with sorrow and worry as though they lived in a secluded garden and there was no danger to steal their joy.

"I want to hear her voice, God," he said. "And I want a lifetime of sharing my thoughts and days with her."

Even with the specter of hunger and defeat hovering over them, they had found happiness. They had found their souls in each other's eyes.

A wave of longing swept over him and an agony more intense than any physical wound. His mind followed the graceful curve of her cheek, and it seemed for a moment that he could almost taste the sweetness of her lips—*almost*. "Turn your eyes from me; they overwhelm me!" He whispered the words of Solomon to his bride. Then, he lowered his head in grief and prayed only one prayer: that he would live to look into her eyes again.

————

The Arab troops who had come to join the assault of Kastel had swelled to over two thousand armed men. As the afternoon sun sank lower in the sky, they waited outside the small stone house that served as Kadar's headquarters.

"They will look to you," Kajuki said gruffly to Kadar as they studied the maps of Kastel. "They are waiting for you to speak to them. It is like the rabble in the marketplace. You must speak to them, that they may find their fury."

Kadar nodded, studying the craggy features of the village headman. Kajuki was a man who understood such things. He understood that without heroes, without leaders, the peasant warriors of Haj Amin were lost. They would fight to the death against impossible odds as long as they had a strong leader to follow. But without such a leader, without a powerful man to stir and rally them, they would break and scatter like sheep.

Kadar did not like Kajuki: he doubted the loyalty of this Bedouin throwback whose strength was in his sword alone, but he knew that he was right. Passion and fury were first born of words that stirred hearts to hatred and fearless revenge. And the task of arousing such passion lay solely in the hands of Kadar.

"We have an hour before sunset."

"Yes. It is just time enough for them to find their rage if you speak now. Go to the roof. They will see you and fall silent to hear your words."

Alone, Kadar climbed the steep steps to the roof of the house. He opened the trapdoor and looked up into the clear blue of the sky. White clouds ringed the mountains, and a flock of sparrows swooped and played high above him. It was spring. Beautiful and bright, spring had come to Palestine. Today it seemed a cruel contrast to the reality of war. Kadar inhaled the sweet scent of new grass and wild flowers that floated on the breeze. As he stepped onto the roof, he looked beyond the boundaries of the village to hillsides splashed with color. In the distance a flock of sheep grazed on a rich green slope.

To fight on such a day as this, Kadar thought, searching for words to exhort his men to hatred and battle. *Battles were meant to be fought in driving rain or searing heat when men drive themselves to conquer even the forces of nature. But when the poppies bloom on the rocky slopes and lupines fill the fields with color, it is not the time for men to die. Let the skies be gray; let the sun be merciless on the backs of the warriors. Then men do not mind death so much. Not so much.*

He lifted his face to the warmth of the sun and breathed deeply, never cherishing life so much as this moment when he must send men out to kill, perhaps to die themselves. *But spring makes us want to live.* His eye followed the flight of the sparrows as they glided so high above the turmoil toward their nests. *Their sweet songs as they hatch their young; the tiny lambs among the flocks—these are things of such importance that all else seems small when I think on them. Perhaps nothing else is of any importance at all, and yet I must rouse them to fury now, these men. I must tell them that those who die in the spring are the true heroes, when the cry of death mingles with the sound of the meadowlark . . .*

Kadar tried not to think about it. He stared at the clouds and prayed for a cold drizzle to chill his spirits, a brutal wind that would blow until the hot scirocco winds came to wither the infant grass and parch the bones of stillborn lambs who never nuzzled their mothers or played in flower-strewn fields. He did not want to love life too much this spring. The British were leaving. Fields of red poppies would be watered with blood, and bright lupines would be crushed beneath the bodies of dying men—Jews and Arabs who would rather listen to the song of the meadowlark.

A cry rang out from the men below him. Rifles raised and a mighty cheer echoed from the mountains as the Jihad Moquades caught sight of their great captain, Ram Kadar.

Kadar raised his arms and stepped forward to the edge of the roof.

"Kadar! Kastel! Kadar! Kastel!" the chant began.

Kadar felt suddenly very weary with the certainty of what was coming and the uncertainty of his own future. He hated the Zionists, yes. But there were days when that seemed unimportant. He gazed beyond the upturned, eager faces of his soldiers, and as he spoke he watched a newborn lamb wobble toward its mother on a far distant slope.

"WARRIORS OF THE JIHAD! IT IS THE WILL OF ALLAH THAT WE DRIVE OUR ENEMIES FROM THE SOIL OF PALESTINE. . . ."

19 Passover Greetings

The plane circled low in the dusk over the harbor of Ragusa. Below them, Ellie could see clearly the decrepit hulk of the S.S. *Trina* and a small launch that plowed toward shore through the water.

"Now we'll know what she looks like from the air," said David, shaking his head slowly from side to side. "Looks to me like we could sink her with a few well-placed spit wads."

Ellie glanced apprehensively at the suitcase that carried the explosives. Bernie Greene still slept peacefully, his head resting against it. Mikhail carefully scrutinized the ship that was to be their target on the open seas tomorrow. He tapped David on the shoulder and pointed down at the open cargo hatch near the bow. As if in response, David swooped lower and passed directly over the opening.

"David!" Ellie protested. "Won't they see you?"

"Doesn't make any difference if they do, sweetheart. Just making a little practice bombing run here. Besides, the deck looks deserted." David dipped the wings as if in salute, then banked and soared away over Ragusa toward the airfield of Cavtat.

"I didn't see any lifeboats on the ship," Ellie said, feeling sick. The reality of why they had come suddenly evaporated any traces of excitement.

"I'm sure there are a couple on board," David said nonchalantly, ignoring Ellie's unspoken concern for the sailors of the freighter. Then he looked at her with a steady gaze. "You might want to stick around Ragusa tomorrow." He was certain now that the assignment to sink the *Trina* would be an easy one. "Mikhail knows what he's doing. He can give me a hand. We're not playing games here, Els. People are going to get hurt. *Them*, not us."

Ellie closed her eyes for a moment, conjuring up a mental photograph of the two men in the launch, their faces staring up at the plane. "You're telling me the lifeboats won't make any difference, aren't you? Those men are going to die."

"Most likely."

"Are they Arabs?"

"No. Slavs, I think. Merchant Marines hired by the Arabs." He put a hand on her arm. "I just want to level with you. There's nothing nice or easy about what we're going to do. But we have to do it. Innocent people get hurt sometimes."

She let his words sink in with a crushing weight. "Usually they are the first to be hurt." She thought about Uncle Howard's housekeeper Miriam, killed in last year's bombing of the Semiranis Hotel in Jerusalem. And Michael. "I wish there was some other way to do this. In the harbor—"

"You heard what Avriel said. We sink her in the harbor, every port in Yugoslavia is going to be looking for Jews. You gotta remember, Babe, that old tub is carrying eight million rounds of ammunition to the Arabs. That's over ten bullets for every Jew in Palestine, and it takes only one bullet to kill a man. That ship could win the war for the Mufti if it gets through. It's no accident that the ship's cargo manifest and ports of call fell into our hands. I don't even think it's an accident that we picked up Mikhail here."

He glanced down at Bernie Greene. "I still can't figure Bernie out, but I have stopped believing in coincidence. There must be a plan for all of this, even if I can't see it." Grief lined his face and his words grew quiet. "No matter how bad it hurts, I have to believe that all the details are already worked out."

"Well then, here's a detail for you. I'm going too. You are not getting out of my sight again until we've had some kind of a honeymoon." She smiled and winked at him. "And Mikhail and Bernie can get a separate room and take the bomb with them. Tonight we won't think about anything but each other, David. Or anyone . . . I just want to look into your eyes and forget for a little while."

David let his breath out slowly and raised his eyebrows. "You'd better go easy on this. . . . Until we get on the ground and into a hotel at Ragusa, or I'm going to shove both of these jokers out over the water and put the plane on automatic pilot . . ."

A few minutes later, the Stinson touched down on the airfield at Cavtat. Darkness settled in quickly as David saw to the refueling of the plane for tomorrow's expedition. Ellie hailed a cab and helped Mikhail rouse Bernie, who was unshaven and disheveled to the point of looking terribly ill.

"Where am I?" he asked as Mikhail shoved him into the back seat of the cab. "What happened? Where are you taking me?"

Ellie leaned in through the open window and whispered, "Shhh. We know who you are, Bernie."

The distraught member of the Mossad ran his fingers through his hair. "Thank God!" he cried. "*Mah nish ta'nah!* Thank God!"

Mikhail patted him sympathetically while Ellie scanned the blackness of the field for David. Moments later he emerged, lugging the leather suitcase filled with explosives. It was heavy, and he strained to carry it, careful not to set it down too hard on the pavement. "Scoot over, Brother Greene," he said, hoisting the lethal baggage into the seat beside Bernie. "You're going to be dressed to kill, pal."

Bernie stared back at him angrily. "I am ready for that. Yes. I should say so. And I know who will be my first target."

David grinned. "Naw, you just think you know."

The taxi driver spoke to them in Serbian. Mikhail replied, and then relayed the message to Bernie in Hebrew.

"The taxi driver wants to know where we want to go."

"Tell him the nicest hotel in Ragusa." David put his arm around Ellie as the message was translated from one language to another and the taxi driver nodded his agreement.

"You might actually come in handy after all, Greene," David said as they rattled off toward Ragusa.

———

The red and white flags of the new Yugoslavian nation were evident everywhere in Ragusa. They were draped over the railing of balconies, displayed from the spires of churches, hung as bunting over large, grim photographs of General Tito. The taxi driver spoke nonstop to Mikhail, explaining the new revolution that had taken the country by storm. Pausing only long enough for Mikhail to translate for Bernie, who then translated for David and Ellie, he expressed a tour guide's view of the new political order.

"He's afraid the Italians won't come here to vacation anymore since Yugoslavia is Communist," Bernie explained. "Of course, the Italians are scared of the Communists, since they are having a big election next month and the Communists are on the ballot . . ."

Through the winding, picturesque streets, the political discussion continued. Mikhail responded with enthusiasm, asking questions that made the driver roll his eyes and lift his hands off the steering wheel. "Ne!" he shouted. "Ne!" A full five minutes of discourse followed and Ellie recognized the name of Tito several times.

"He says," Bernie continued after he received the short version, "that all the Italian tourists are afraid that the people of Yugoslavia will send secret soldiers to Italy. Weapons and the like. And that Tito is really a good chap with the hard job of pulling six separate republics into one. He doesn't want to blow up anyone. He did that already with the Germans." Bernie rubbed his head and sniffed, then added his own commentary. "And our fellows can only hope that the Russians don't move in and take over here like they're trying to do everywhere. We're going to have a dreadful time getting planes out of Czechoslovakia and arms out of this country if that happens."

David grinned at the knowledge Bernie Greene displayed about their operations. "You really are a good guy, aren't you?" he quipped.

Bernie scowled at David. "Quite. And I know the password as well."

The taxi screeched to a halt in front of a weathered old hotel. An aging doorman in a coat trimmed with red braid stood as the last remaining vestige of an age of elegance. High above them on the stone exterior was a faded sign announcing RAGUSA PALACE INN; beneath that was a wide banner with the words written in red: *Proleteri Svih Zemalja, Ujedinite Se!* "Proletarians of the World, Unite!" To the right of the hotel entrance was a small street-side cafe where men and women languidly sipped from delicate cups as they chatted.

The cabby stuck out his hand expectantly and grinned broadly as he uttered one more observation, which Mikhail dutifully translated, and Bernie repeated in a bored tone.

"This is the best hotel. A little run-down since the war, but still the best. He says things are not too bad now, but he expects they will get worse. And the ride is forty kopecks, please. Unless you have American dollars, and that is two dollars."

"Ziveli!" exclaimed the cabby when David paid him American and tipped him another fifty cents. *"Long live!"*

"Now ask him where the telegraph office is, Bernie," David

instructed. He lowered his voice and glanced over his shoulder as two men passed behind them. "You ought to let Mama know we've spotted her."

The muscles in Bernie's jaw twitched. "I suppose that duty falls on me for a reason?"

"Well, you've been asleep all the way," David shrugged innocently. "I'm beat, pal. Got a big day tomorrow. I'm going to hit the hay. Besides, you know the password. I'm just driving the bus." He put his arm around Ellie and ushered her into the faded opulence of the hotel lobby. Mikhail struggled along behind with the luggage.

"You are certain you should risk it then, Professor? For just a word of news?" Mrs. Bett's face was a mask of consternation as she handed Moshe a neatly wrapped package of matzo bread.

"It is not so far out of my way." Moshe stared at the white paper. "But if I don't go now, there will not be time. And with the news from Kastel, I don't know when any of us will get back to Jerusalem."

"So. What can an old lady say?" Mrs. Bett patted his arm. "Of course you must have news of your wife if there is any. So go already, but be careful, nu? The Civil Defense fellows are standing watch at the barricades in shifts so each can eat the Seder meal. They will all be trigger-happy because the Arabs are tonight up to mischief."

"Their mischief is being done in Kastel, though."

"Our fellows in Jerusalem are not so sure of that. They are all on strict alert. And don't forget our friends, the British."

"No doubt they are sitting by a fire drinking gin and dreaming of home." He tried to make light of her warnings.

"You are a wanted man, Professor." She placed her hand on his arm and squeezed gently. "*Wanted.* They would hang one more Jew before they go home, and that would be Professor Moshe Sachar. You know this in spite of your fearless jokes, nu?"

He frowned, certain that her words were accurate. "Yes."

"Good. Now we are being honest, eh? Be careful. The Angel of Death passes through the streets of the Holy City tonight just as he passed over Egypt so long ago. If he finds you careless or unaware, then you will fall tonight."

"I will be careful," he promised. "I would hate to die and miss out on the free pastry you promised me."

She did not smile. "Watch as much for our own fellows as you approach the barricades. Remember the password?"

He nodded. "The first question of the Haggadah. *What makes this night different from all the rest?*"

"So go, already. Don't be a *shlepper.* And don't break the matzo bread!" Her voice sounded light, but there was deep worry in her eyes.

Gently she nudged him out the courtyard gate into the shadows of the Street of the Prophets. The heavy wooden door clicked shut behind him and an iron bolt slid into place.

For a moment, Moshe stood on the narrow ledge of the sidewalk and looked to the right and left of the street. Lights glistened from the windows of the homes of the Orthodox, indicating that the Seder had begun. Inside, Moshe knew, small boys stood at the elbows of their papas and asked the question, *Mah nish ta'nah . . . What makes this night different? Why is this night darker than all the other nights of the year?* Moshe blinked back at the faint glow of the lights and answered, in his own soul, the question.

This is the dark night of my uncertainty. The night of my fear. He stepped from the curb and crossed the deserted street. *It is the night when the Angel of Death and I walk the same slim corridor, and I do not wish to meet him.* A pair of headlights rounded the corner of B'nai Brith Street a block away. An automobile slowed and stopped before the large, stone block gatehouse of the Swedish Theological Seminary. Moshe hugged the wall as the lights swept past him and then winked off. The seminary was almost deserted now, but four car doors slammed, and Moshe heard the sound of English voices drift up the street.

To his right, a huge tree hung over the street and a distinct hissing sounded in its branches.

"Psssst! SSSSSST!"

"Who is there?" Moshe stared up into the black tangle.

The voice of a young boy replied. "Mishmar Ha'am! Civil Defense! Do not walk the Street of the Prophets tonight. British patrols every few minutes . . ." It was obvious that the young guard had seen Moshe come from Mrs. Bett's courtyard and had known that he shared a common mission. "They are everywhere! Because of Kastel," he whispered.

"Is there a safe path?" Moshe called.

"Ethiopia Street. They patrol there only once in a half hour, and they have just passed."

Moshe waved and hurried across the Street of the Prophets to the street of Ethiopia. High walls rose up on either side, concealing the garden courtyards of the wealthy. Many had fled Jerusalem, but behind some of the walls the light shimmered, making the darkness seem even colder. The rough stone brushed his arm as he walked beneath the branches of a huge fig tree that protruded over a fence. A breeze rustled its new leaves, carrying just a hint of the flowers that bloomed in the concealed garden.

For thirty years, in the gardens of a dozen houses along Ethiopia Street, the thoughts and dreams of young Zionism had taken root behind these tall, secretive walls. The echoes of history walked with Moshe as his boots slapped in solitary rhythm on the pavement. *Behind the gates of this big house, Chaim Weizmann lived when the Zionist Committee came to Palestine in 1920. He sat beneath the fig tree and argued with the British for a homeland. Had he seen this night in our future? Had he envisioned this last Passover before our statehood or the final destruction?* Across the street was the former house of Ben Yehuda, who resurrected the language of Hebrew from its ancient grave with the hope that one day a nation would live again. And beyond that was the place where hopes took the substance of words in the first Zionist newspaper.

Along this street, hours had melted into one another, becoming years. Each day had seemed the same as any other, marked by only minute changes. But tiny changes had become seeds caught on the breeze.

What makes this night different than all the rest? Moshe asked the ancient question as though it was new. This was the culmination of every dream and every small action of those who had planned for statehood on Ethiopia. *This is the night we come home at last! Only six hundred thousand, a fraction of those who perished. That is all we are, a tiny remnant, but we are home.*

Ahead, the dome of the Ethiopian Church loomed black against the sky. On the lintel of the gate were carved the words: *The Lion of the Tribe of Judah Hath Prevailed!* This, for Moshe, held the promise of fulfillment of every dream that had ever soared from these gardens.

The Mufti could declare the end of all Jews; his declaration would not make it truth. Anti-Zionist Jews like Rabbi Akiva could declare that there could be no nation unless the Messiah came first; his words were still empty. Men like Emile could rage that there was no God, no hope and no life; it made no difference. In the Book and on the heart of Moshe it was written as truth: *The Lion of the Tribe of Judah Hath Prevailed!*

A mere two miles from where he now walked, Moshe knew, the Messiah *had* first come. Self-righteous men like Akiva had not known Him. The Holy One of Israel had died as the final lamb of sacrifice, loving even the men like Emile who denied and cursed God. He had seen *this* night, *this* man, *this* moment. And He had seen the future beyond that to say, *I have prevailed! Jerusalem is mine!*

"First as a lamb you came, Lord." Moshe gazed up at the lintel as he passed. "Next you will come as a lion and there will be no more misunderstanding."

He quickened his pace as the growl of a British patrol car approached the intersection beneath the large tree where the boy sat quietly observing. Moshe glanced over his shoulder, strangely calm in spite of the nearness of danger. True to the child's words, the vehicle slowed, then passed on up the Street of the Prophets in search of any stray members of the Jerusalem Underground.

You are too late! Moshe thought as he smiled inwardly. *The promise is made. We are in every tree, behind every wall, inside every shop and synagogue. God is not finished with the remnant of Israel. The seeds have sprouted and grown strong in our hearts again. And like Pharaoh on the first Passover night, you have no hope!*

Moshe tucked the brittle matzo bread into his pocket as he walked up the steep slope of Hazanovitch Street to where Strauss Street would run back down into Jaffa Road. Although the path had been easily a mile out of his way, he had seen no other living being as he backtracked toward Jaffa Road. He was grateful he had not gone by way of Sokolow School and the Civil Defense Headquarters. Surely a British soldier stood on every

203

corner in that neighborhood, watching and waiting.

At the top of the hill, the first Jewish checkpoint stretched across the road. Black heaps of sandbags barred the way, and Moshe saw dark shapes move at the approach of his footsteps.

"Someone is coming, Manny. . . ."

"Well, ask him who he is."

"What would anyone be doing out on Passover?"

"Don't shoot him, you fool! It might be the Prophet Elijah or someone else important!"

"So ask, already!"

"*Who goes there?*"

Moshe cleared his throat and called the question in Hebrew: "*Mah nish ta'nah . . .*"

A relieved voice replied, "So, you want to know what makes this night different? We should all be inside having a normal Passover, that's what! Now I have a question. What are you doing out on a night like this?" The words were in Yiddish, and Moshe knew he had come across two young members of the Orthodox Community.

He answered in Yiddish, "I am the first of several who will come this way one at a time. Stay calm, nu? If the British patrol passes, you have seen nothing."

"You think we would tell the goyim anything? Ha!" proclaimed a young voice. "God should strike us dead first, blessed be His name!"

Moshe could not see their faces, but they were dressed in their Shabbat finery, standing guard over their neighborhood in shifts. At the sight of them, Moshe could not help but think of those behind the walls of the Old City. What kind of Passover would they have tonight? *Rachel!* He was filled with a fresh urgency to hurry to Rehavia and hear whatever news there might be. "How many more barricades on this street?" Moshe asked, suddenly impatient.

"Only one. At the intersection of Jaffa Road." The words tumbled out as Moshe brushed past the barricade and into the darkness of the street. "Something big is happening in Kastel, yes?" The question pursued Moshe, but he did not stop to answer. "Is it true that American Jews, fellows from the army, have landed in Tel Aviv by the thousands to fight for us?"

"Rumors, meshuggener!"

"Marvin Telmann heard it on the radio! Fifty planeloads of Jewish soldiers . . ."

Moshe did not stop to explain or correct the details of their story. If the Orthodox Jews of Strauss Street believed such details, he thought, the Arabs would be shivering in their shoes.

Stone-front four-story apartments followed the line of the road, and although the street itself was empty, Moshe could see that at least one window in every home was alive with the lights of Seder. It was here, on Strauss Street, that the boundaries of Jerusalem must hold. Unlike the residents of Ethiopia Street, those who lived here in crowded, noisy flats, did not have the money to move away while the war raged. They had left their various Egypts when they had come from Europe. Bringing with them only what they could carry, they had found their way to Jerusalem so that on this holy night of Passover they might say what their fathers had only dreamed of . . . *Tonight in Jerusalem!* And if they were politely asked if they might be more comfortable somewhere else, they would proclaim with one voice, *There is no room for us anywhere in the world but here!*

There was very little room, at that, on Strauss Street. Moshe looked up to the second story of a building where the light shown from three windows like back-lit picture frames. Through lace curtains, Moshe saw clearly a woman in a shawl, standing before the candles. In the next, a small boy in a white shirt listened wide-eyed to the story of Israel's deliverance from Egypt. In the third, a man stood alone, draped in a tallith. Moshe stopped and stared up at him. It was this third picture that spoke of the hopes of every Jew who had ever whispered the name *Jerusalem!*

The prayer shawl that covered the man's head concealed his face from Moshe. Strong brown hands cradled a prayer book. The shawl was bordered by black bands rather than blue, commemorating the terrible destruction of Jerusalem nearly two thousand years before. *This is the tallith of mourning, not joy.*

Only seconds passed as the man stood in profile before the window. The faint light of a single candle glinted on a band on his finger. *He wears a wedding band, yet he is alone.*

His head was bowed in this portrait, and he swayed slightly as he read the psalms of the Great Hallel as Jesus had done the night before His death.

Moshe closed his eyes and, for a moment, joined the lonely worshiper.

Out of the depths I cry to you, O Lord;
O Lord, hear my voice.
Let your ears be attentive
to my cry for mercy.
If you, O Lord, kept a record of sins,
O Lord, who could stand?
But with you, there is forgiveness;
therefore you are feared.
I wait for the Lord, my soul waits,
and in his word I put my hope.
My soul waits for the Lord,
more than the watchmen wait for morning . . .

Before Moshe stood a man who cried out from the darkness, remembering not the firstborn of Egypt, but grieving for the extinction of a whole generation of children who had not lived to see this night. Had the man in the window survived only to find that his own children had perished? Had he had one last embrace before his wife was torn from his arms?

The thought brought Rachel fresh and vivid to Moshe's mind. *"Teach me, learned Rabbi," she said to me as I held her. Oh, God! How many of us survive this night alone? How many mourn for memories of those who were here in our arms and then gone from us forever?*

It was too easy for Moshe to imagine himself as the solitary man in the window. The hollow ache of longing returned to him and he turned away from the poignant image, afraid that he had glimpsed his own reflection in the mirror of the future.

He drew a breath and began to jog down the street, his footsteps resounding against the stone facades of the buildings on Strauss Street.

———

The delicious aromas of simmering beef and Turkish coffee drifted up the street as Bernie followed Mikhail three blocks to the telegraph office of Ragusa.

Light shone from a sparkling clean window with the word *Telegraphe* stenciled across it in a yellow arch. Inside, a Serb behind the counter smiled and gestured to a coarse-featured man in a brown double-breasted suit. Beside him, a rather obese, unkempt man in a fisherman's cap talked with a voice so loud it penetrated the glass of the office.

"Here is the place," Mikhail said in quiet Hebrew.

"Let those fellows finish their business," Bernie replied, patting his pockets and wishing for a cigarette. "We do not need an audience. Especially not with a cable to Palestine."

Mikhail nodded and sighed, gazing off down the brightly lit thoroughfare of crowded cafes. "Would that I were there! Perhaps next Passover, nu?"

Bernie rubbed his aching hip. "We can hope," he said wryly. "I should be there tonight if it were not for our friend the pilot."

"We are tonight strangers in a strange land, as the Holy Book says."

"It says that?" He sniffed with disinterest. "I wish I had a cigarette." His eyes wandered to the yarmulke on Mikhail's head. "You think you ought to take that off?"

The door to the office jingled as the two gruff-looking patrons came out onto the street. The man in the brown double-breasted suit stared openly at Mikhail, his gaze lingering with contempt of the skull cap atop his head. Mikhail met his look with defiance.

"Ah," said the man, his thick lips curling a bit, "I had no idea there were any Jews left in Yugoslavia. I thought they were all in ashes. . . ." He brushed past them, his cynical laugh following as they entered the well-lit telegraph office.

"Why?" Mikhail shrugged. "This country still has many Moslems. Very few of us left, though. It must rankle them to see one left still wearing a kippa on Passover." He smiled. "Perhaps they will think I am the Prophet Elijah roaming the streets."

"As you wish. But I am in no condition to defend you from insults."

"I am used to that as well."

The broad grin of the clerk faded a bit as he surveyed the skull cap still perched obstinately on Mikhail's head. He nodded slightly in a bow. "How may I serve you?" he asked.

"Yes." Mikhail spoke flawlessly in the Serb language. "We wish to send Passover regards to Palestine, if you please. A wire to my mother."

The grin returned, revealing a row of irregular teeth. "So!

Such an interesting night. Two wires in two minutes to be sent to Palestine. . . ."

"Yes?" asked Mikhail, feeling the blood run from his face. "Passover, I suppose."

"Indeed! That gentleman sends greetings to his papa. And you to your mama. I would not have thought him a Jew, though . . ."

"Such a thing is hard to discern sometimes . . ." Mikhail's voice trailed off and he stared at the counter. Then he nudged Bernie and explained to him in Hebrew that the fellow who had insulted them on the street also had family in Palestine.

20   What Makes This Night Different?

Since Moshe had last walked the streets of Jerusalem as a free man, whole blocks had become battlegrounds between Arab and Jewish neighborhoods. Snipers from both factions peered out from the second-story windows of deserted houses and shops.

Moshe neared the barricade that marked the last half mile before Rehavia district. The guards here were gruff and sea-soned-looking. They made no mention of the Holy Day, and if they longed for the warm lights and food of a Passover celebration, it was not evident. The street beyond them seemed completely dark and deserted. From where Moshe now stood, he was only two blocks away from the demolished Jewish Agency building.

What makes this night different. . . ? Moshe asked as the orange glow of a cigarette butt glowed, illuminating a craggy, toughlooking face.

"Going to Rehavia, too?" asked the guard, stepping aside to let Moshe pass.

"There are others coming behind me," Moshe answered.

"A busy night. We have counted seventy-two before you so

208

far. All going to the high school. And none too soon. We just heard that the Arabs have attacked Kastel again in force."

"And what have you heard from our men?"

"If you fellows are going back up there, you'd better hold your Boy Scout meeting and go in a hurry; that is all I can say," growled the voice of an American. "I'd like to go with you if it weren't for this—"

Moshe looked past his shoulder into the blackness of the Shaarei Hessed neighborhood. He had been unprepared for the desolation that engulfed the street. Windows were boarded, and not a light shone from the buildings along the way. Garbage was piled in rotting heaps on the sidewalk where five months before, joyful Jews had sung and danced on the night Partition was signed.

"Where are the people?" Moshe asked.

"When the Arabs bombed the Agency, not a window within eight blocks was left. Then the Irregulars started sniping from the west. A little girl was killed, and that was the end. Everyone cleared out. And we moved in. We're a little four-block-wide corridor here. We lose this, we'll lose Rehavia and southern Jerusalem. Arabs hold the east and the west." He gave a short burst of bitter laughter. "And the British keep running patrols through here to pick up our guys. We can stall them a couple of minutes here at the barricade, but that's it."

"I should hurry, then." Moshe turned to go.

"Hold it, pal," said the American. "Give it about thirty seconds." He held the light of his cigarette to his wristwatch. "You'll see the patrol car pass on the far end down by Ramban; then run like mad. You'll have ninety seconds to make it down there and across Ramban before those jokers turn around. And in two minutes another armored car will be coming up behind you from here. Good training for the Olympics, huh?"

"How about Rehavia? Is it safer in Rehavia?"

"There are lots of hedges to hide in. I wouldn't hang around. . . ." He glanced at his watch again. "Ten seconds. You ready?"

Moshe breathed deeply and nodded.

"Okay. Here they come. . . ." True to his words, the headlights of a patrol car passed through Ramban intersection and slowly continued up the street. The American slapped him on the back. "Go!" he urged, like the starter of a footrace.

209

Broken glass crunched beneath Moshe's feet as he ran, counting off the seconds with every footstep. Ahead, a pack of starving dogs snarled at one another and nosed through the rubbish in search of even one morsel of food that might have been left behind. There was no other sign of life; only the ominous awareness that from each black building, men watched his progress through the shadows. Perhaps some held the precious weapons David had brought the night before. In these small corners of the Holy City, the Angel of Death waited, daring the Arabs to attack. Yet in the end the blood of both Jew and Arab would be spilled. *Forty-five seconds.* Gone was the laughter of families, the glow of the Shabbat candles. *Fifty-eight seconds, and two blocks to go.*

From behind the closed shutters, eyes watched Moshe's progress, cheering for him silently in the darkness. They knew that he was one of them, moving through the black night toward his own destiny, as they all moved toward theirs.

His breath became heavy as he ran up the incline of the road. Cold air burned his lungs and nostrils, and the wounds on his ankles opened up again, bleeding on his clean socks. A searing pain stabbed through his side, a reminder that he had taken the full force of Philip's weight when he had jumped into the truck. He willed his legs to move, groaning as he heard the slap of his boots slow, then stumble.

Thirty-five seconds. The night began to swim around him; a thousand tiny lights flickered before his eyes as the exhaustion of days without real rest or decent food finally overtook him. The ground rose up before him. He would not make it before the patrol came.

"Rachel!" he cried in what seemed to him was a loud voice. It was, in fact, half-sob, half-whisper. The toe of his boots scuffed the pavement, but he pushed himself forward until, a full block from safety, his knees buckled and he collapsed, heaving, onto the street. Crates of garbage clattered on top of him just as the lights of the British patrol car swept around the corner in a slow, watchful arc.

Moshe tried to move, crawling toward the shadowy alcove of a boarded-up business.

"Be *still!*" hissed a voice. "Lay where you are, fool, or you will bring them down upon us all."

Fighting for breath, Moshe laid his head down on the gravel.

The stink of rotting garbage was oppressive. Closing his eyes, he prayed that no part of his body was exposed. The engine whined as the eerie light probed the cracks and chased the shadows away from sealed doorways. Glass crunched beneath the tires as the vehicle rolled past. He held his breath, feeling as though his lungs would burst. The exhaust of the retreating vehicle filled his nostrils when he breathed, choking him into a fit of coughing.

"Shut up!" the voice whispered from behind the boards. "And don't move. Another patrol is . . ."

As the taillights of one car rounded the corner ahead, the headlights of another turned onto the street. Again, the play was reenacted, this time from the opposite direction. This patrol crept by even more slowly than the first, lights parting the darkness like machetes through tall grass. Moshe opened his eyes to see the detailed weave of the fabric on his sleeve revealed in the searchlight. His right trouser leg, though half-covered by litter, was also exposed, and the light seemed stuck fast to the heap where he lay. He squeezed his eyes shut tight again, like a child playing hide-and-seek. His heart pounded with the low rumble of the engine. *Do not so much as flinch a muscle or they will have you.* He tried to steady his breathing to a shallow, even cadence.

"What is it?" asked a voice from the vehicle beside him.

"I don't know. Maybe it's . . ." The beam swept back and forth over the heap, holding steady on the leg of Moshe's trousers.

Bits and pieces of a psalm ran through Moshe's head like a prayer: *In the shadow of thy wings will I make my refuge, until these calamities be overpast. Lord, they see me. My leg, Lord.* The light wavered and probed again, following the line of Moshe's trousers to where his hip was covered with garbage.

"You want to go out and move the rubbish, Wilson?"

I will cry unto God who has performed all things for me. I am a sparrow, God. Caught in their trap. He wanted to run; to stand and bolt up the street like a boy trying not to be tagged. *They have prepared a net for my steps, they have digged a pit for me, and they will fall into—*

"Well, Wilson, is there something there or not? It stinks!"

"Just a rag, I think. Just an old rag." The light turned away, threading its way across the faces of the buildings as the patrol car whined away toward the blockade.

Moshe stirred, sending another cascade of garbage down, and the angry voice called to him, "Not yet, idiot! Wait until they're around the corner at least!" Thirty seconds passed until the red lights disappeared. "Well, what are you waiting for? Run, you fool!" the voice urged loudly.

A vise of pain gripped him as he stood and staggered up the incline. The fire in his lungs was more manageable now, but still, his legs rebelled against the effort.

From dark corners, voices called to him, urging and cursing as he passed.

"Faster! They're coming back!"

"Hurry, friend, you can make it!"

"Don't stop! Only a few more yards."

Just a few more yards, Moshe thought. *Then Rehavia. And Howard. And a moment to rest . . . and word of Rachel and the child!*

He reached the corner of Ramban and leaned against a street lamp whose globes had been shot out. *Across the street . . . Rehavia.*

"Fool!" shouted someone behind him. "Are you waiting for a ride with the English!"

Moshe lurched off the curb and jogged across the street past a roll of barbed wire and a high fence. Trees hung over their garden fences, and a faint scent of flowers drifted on the wind from somewhere. Trenches zigzagged across once-proud lawns; the windows of the houses were mostly dark, but if there was anyone left in Rehavia, Moshe knew it would be his dear and stubborn friend, Professor Howard Moniger.

———

Howard looked out the window of Tikvah's hospital room. What had once been a spectacular nighttime panorama of city lights was now only a black gulf that stretched out below Mount Scopus.

It was already 7:15. In only a few minutes, the last British patrol would escort the remaining Jewish civilians from the hospital and down through the hostile Arab neighborhood of Sheik Jarra. Then Hadassah Hospital would be sealed off until morning. They were taking a risk, staying so late, but when he had arrived after five o'clock that afternoon, Tikvah's fever had soared once again, and she had held out her tiny arms to Rachel.

It would have been cruel, Howard knew, to insist that they leave then, so he watched patiently until the baby's last contented sigh had been breathed and she had slept to the tune of an old Yiddish lullaby. Now, the hour of curfew was nearing. Gangs of Arab youths and Jewish terrorists would be out on the streets, firing at anything that moved in the darkness. It would be impossible to get home if they missed the escort.

Howard watched as Rachel pulled the blanket around the baby's chin and caressed her one more time with her eyes. Hers was a face that had seen too many goodbyes, thought Howard. His heart ached for the young woman, yet he was filled with a sense of amazement for the miracle that had begun in her soul. Only a few months before, she had come to his home. Filled with guilt and self-pity, she had been able to weep for no one but herself. Now tears flowed silently as she touched the forehead of a child who was not her own. In a quiet moment, Ehud had related to Howard the events in the Old City, how Yehudit had betrayed Rachel to Akiva. And yet, Rachel had brought Yehudit out from the Old City with her. She had embraced her and called her *sister.* There was a glow in Rachel's eyes that spoke to Howard. Instinctively he knew that if she could forgive others, then she had finally found the forgiveness she had thought was impossible. The love of God had finally let her forgive herself, and this was the biggest miracle of all.

She stroked the cheek of the sleeping baby and whispered words that Howard could not understand, but he knew that she was praying. ". . . Koham cie, Tikvah," she finished at last, and then looked up at Howard. "We must go, Professor, yes?"

He nodded. "I'm afraid the escort will be leaving in a few minutes. She will be all right. . . ."

"Yes. God will stay with her, though I cannot tonight," she whispered, then glanced down at Tikvah again as though she were seeing her for the last time. She brushed her tears away with the back of her hand. "It is just that I have learned to hate farewells, Professor." She searched his face and her expression spoke of Moshe and Mama and Papa. "It is the night of Passover, you see, and I dream of a day when all of my own will be with me again. Do you understand?"

"Of course. Yes," he said, feeling a compassion larger than

his words. "It is a prayer your grandfather must have prayed many times, Rachel. And this Passover God has answered the prayers of an old man. God has brought you home to him, and for the first time in many years he will have his family around him. It is an important night for him." He took her arm.

She looked up and then around the room, finally letting her gaze linger on Tikvah who slept peacefully now in the dim light. "Stay with her, Lord," she whispered in Polish.

Without looking back, they walked through the hospital corridors, through the strong smell of disinfectant and urine. A nurse hurried past them, headed for the far end of the hallway where a steady moaning drifted out from a large ward room. For an instant, Howard wanted to turn around and stay at the bedside of the child. *Could there by anything more difficult than leaving her in such a place?* he thought. *Stay here with her, Lord. Don't let her wake up alone.* But he knew there was nothing else to be done; every breath that Tikvah breathed must be in God's hands.

He glanced at Rachel as they passed the reception desk. She was obviously exhausted, yet there was a confidence in her eyes that he had not seen before. Outside, British soldiers stood beside their lorries, impatiently smoking cigarettes and glancing at their watches. Four civilian cars were parked on the opposite side of the street. Howard felt instantly revived as they stepped out onto the sidewalk and a chilly wind swept over them. He breathed deeply of the clean fresh air and hailed a portly British corporal who seemed in charge of the escort.

"We'll get the car and be with you in a minute," Howard called.

The soldier's gaze fell on Rachel. He drew an irritated breath, and his eyes narrowed. "You Mrs. Sachar?" he demanded.

"Yes." Howard answered for her. "She is. But what business is it of yours?"

The soldier raised his eyebrows slightly. "We've heard all about her, mate, so don't go gettin' uppity. Just wanted t' know what we was escortin', is all." There was a sneer in his voice.

"Now, see here!" Howard was outraged. Quickly, Rachel put her hand on his arm to silence his protest. She held her chin high, the confidence never leaving her face in spite of the words whispered among the men at the curb.

"Nazi collaborator. . ."

She did not reply, but simply smiled back at the man who looked at her with such disdain. For a full fifteen seconds she gazed at him, her eyes holding his until he squirmed uncomfortably and blushed. His smile faded and he looked down apologetically.

"Is there much danger in this journey after dark?" Rachel asked him in a steady voice.

He had the look of a schoolboy who had been reprimanded. "I . . . uh . . . we . . . No, ma'am. Not as long as you're with the escort."

She swept the group of eight men with her glance. "Then I am grateful to be with you. Aren't you, Professor?"

Howard nodded, stunned by the strength with which she had faced her accusers. He was angry at the soldier's rudeness, but he did not speak again. Her unshaken reply had silenced any further derision. He took her with him to the car and helped her in, aware of the rumble of engines as the escorts and civilians prepared to leave Mount Scopus.

"Just in time." Howard wheeled the car around, the last in the short line of vehicles.

Neither Rachel nor Howard spoke as they wound their way slowly down Mount Scopus into the neighborhood of Sheik Jarra. Rows of stately houses carried with them an ominous air of danger. Once the neighborhood of wealthy Arab intelligentsia, now the houses were taken over by troops of Jihad Moquades who carried with them the warnings and threats of Haj Amin. To travel to Hadassah and the university in daylight was barely possible and certainly foolish without escort. At night, it was suicide.

The air itself seemed to bristle with tension, and Howard felt the muscles in his neck tighten as they passed the walls of the American Compound, a peaceful hostelry that had been taken over by the Holy Strugglers a week before. Those soldiers who had not run off to retake Kastel watched them now as they wound their way through the streets. They would not be attacked, not while the British patrol cars guarded them front and rear. The last thing the Arabs wanted was a direct confrontation with the English. It was only a matter of weeks before they left, however, and then it was almost certain that Mount Scopus and

Hadassah Hospital would be the first isolated point in Jerusalem to be cut off.

As if she read his mind, Rachel asked quietly, "Will we be able to hold out at the hospital? When the English leave, I mean?"

"I think so. The hospital was the first place to lay in extra supplies. But don't worry. The Arab Irregulars won't completely cut off Hadassah until the English are gone."

"But they have done so with the Jewish Quarter in the Old City. Why not here?"

"The Jewish Quarter is a political prize. Cutting it off shows their strength and their ability to destroy our morale. The hospital is a different story. It is the main hospital of Jerusalem. Until the British leave, they have to allow some access, or they will appear inhumane." After a pause he added, "Tikvah will be safe there."

She sighed with relief and looked out the window to where a small group of three Arab men stood on a street corner. They held their weapons openly, defiantly. "It will all explode, though, Professor. Very soon. Even with the convoy breaking through, we stand on the edge of something very terrible." She turned toward him and he felt the certainty of her words. "When I was a girl in Warsaw, I saw it. First it was like this. Barbed wire and men with guns who waited for the law to die. They simply waited—like them." The eyes of the Arabs followed their progress. "Later came the brick walls that fenced us in without food. And then came the carts to bury us and the trucks to carry us away. And there was nothing left of Warsaw in the end."

"Yes, child," Howard said wearily. "Throughout the war we here in Jerusalem were afraid the Germans would come." He nodded to a concrete cone that jutted up from a sidewalk. "We blocked the main roads with those—called them *Rommel's Teeth*—to guard against the tanks of General Rommel." He shook his head at the irony. "The Nazis never came—at least, not to take the city. But still, their spirit came here at last, didn't it? It is here tonight. I've written some important people in America and I've told them, 'The war did not end when we took Berlin.' And, yes, the worst is yet to come."

For a moment, the moon peeked out from behind a mountain of clouds, illuminating the city. "I know this, Professor. I have watched destruction come before, and I see its signs. I was afraid then, when I was a girl. And when I was a woman I only wanted to survive. Now, I am again in the center of a whirlwind, but I am no longer afraid."

"You have changed, Rachel. Indeed you have."

She smiled at him as they rolled toward the barricade that marked the entrance into the Jewish sector of the city. "Yes, Professor. I am not alone anymore." She held her hand out and cupped her palm. "I used to think my life was like water to run through the cracks in God's fingers. You see? But now I have read what Yeshua says, that not even a sparrow falls unless God sees it. And if He holds the sparrow so gently in His hand, does He not also hold me? And Tikvah? And Moshe?"

"Then you have found the answer, Rachel, to every fear."

"Hmmm. Yes. I have found the *answer*, though I will tell you there are many moments when I wish God would tell me the *reason*. Instead, He says that I must trust Him like a child, nu? And this is the hardest thing of all to do." She was silent for a long moment and Howard sensed that she had something else to say. As they passed through the barricade and turned off from the escort, she groped for words. "I do have one fear left, Professor." Her voice was childlike.

"After all you have lived through, child, what can be left?"

"I am afraid . . . of what . . . Grandfather will say when he finds out how I survived . . ."

––––––––––

The moon hung like a spotlight, outlining the clouds that hovered over Rehavia. The house of Howard Moniger was clearly illuminated. Stately and dignified, it seemed remarkably unchanged on the outside. Candlelight shone from behind the curtains, calling Moshe to come home. *Come home for Passover. Be safe and warm. Never fight again. Never say goodbye . . .*

As he huddled behind a low wall, half a block away, he wanted to stand and run to the front door. To knock and throw open the door as he had done a thousand times. *To see Howard. Rachel. Yacov and Rabbi Lebowitz. Ellie and David.* But tonight, for Moshe, there was no going home. He could not walk to the house or see all the old faces, even if they had been there. . . .

The moon passed behind the clouds again and he breathed a sigh of relief. Though he could not see the soldiers any longer, he knew they were there, standing resolutely across the street from Howard's house. *Waiting. Waiting like I am waiting. Do they know I am in Jerusalem? Do they search for me? Or is it someone else they have come for?* Moshe put his hand to his head in frustration. To be so close to news and not be able to hear it was a torture more painful than a physical beating. He searched the housetops for some sign of other watchers, but there were only the four men, standing in a tight knot together as they stared at the house and waited.

Moshe tried to check his watch, forgetting that the face had been smashed. It was just as well: the pitch black of the night obscured every detail now, anyway. Only the warmth of the windows down the block remained. *I should go*, he thought, his heart heavy with longing. *Before the moon comes out again, I should go and join the others at the school. Before the soldiers see me, I should go.* Yet still he stayed, hoping that the patrol would grow weary and leave. He listened hard for any bits of conversation that would drift his way, but the men were silent in their vigil. *Go now! Before they walk this way and find you! Don't be a fool!*

Moshe inched his way back along the wall away from the house and the soldiers. Slipping between two deserted houses, he stood and peered around the corner one last time. Then the lights of an automobile appeared at the far end of the street. He ducked down out of sight and waited for it to pass. The groan of the engine approached, they geared down and slowed, stopping in front of Howard's home. Moshe dropped to his knees and crept back toward the wall. The soldiers had disappeared, hiding themselves in the shadows as the car door opened and Howard Moniger stepped out.

The clouds parted again, sending a firm light onto the street. *Howard! Dear God! So near.* A lump formed in Moshe's throat, and hungrily he watched every move of his friend. *He is opening the door to the passenger side. Is there a woman with him? Not Ellie. Who, then?* He gasped audibly as Rachel stepped from the car. Reaching his hand out toward her, Moshe drank in every movement. He fought the urge to call her name and run to her. *British soldiers. They wait in the shadows. And she is the bait to draw you into their net.* Reality hung suspended for a moment as she tossed her head and pulled her coat tighter around her. *This is only a dream*, he told himself. *Only a dream, Moshe. Call out her name! Say it.* Rachel! *And she will come to you in this sleep. There are no soldiers there waiting for you. Call her name! Rachel!* Howard took her arm and led her toward the house as Moshe counted every step, willing himself not to move. Unlocking the door, Howard held it open and the light silhouetted her profile clearly. Her eyes were wide and she reached her arms out to be enfolded by her grandfather. *She is well. She is safe tonight. Oh, God, though I cannot speak to her, you have given me my news. Rachel is well! Thank you, Lord.* He wept silently in the shadows, his eyes lingering on her back as she stood in the doorway. Then Shaul stepped out on the porch and raised his chin to sniff the air. Yacov stood beside him as if he, too, were aware of some presence on the street.

"Come, Yacov..." *Rachel's sweet voice.* "You will catch cold. Come in now; we are late for Seder...."

She reached out to put her hand around the boy's shoulder; then she brushed her other hand quickly over Shaul's head. *To be touched by her again . . . Rachel! I am here in the shadows!* His heart cried out to her, and for an instant she paused and looked expectantly out into the darkness of the street.

"Come in, sister," Yacov urged, pulling her hand.

For an instant longer she lingered; then she gazed up toward the moon and turned away from Moshe, closing the door behind her.

Tears flowed freely as he stared at the door. His Rachel was there, safe behind that door. Safe with Howard and Yacov and her grandfather. Tikvah must be inside as well, Moshe reasoned, trying to imagine a Passover table set for all of those he loved. A light winked on in an upstairs window, and he knew she was there. *She is safe! If only I could see her. If only . . .* Suddenly he heard the men as they moved from the shadows back to their posts in front of the house. Moshe shrank back from their presence, but his eyes never left the lighted window. He would stay until there was no doubt that he must go to the rendezvous in the basement of Rehavia High School. *Only to be this near to her is enough. To know that she is well.*

21 · The Meal of Remembrance

The sweet aromas of Passover swirled around Rachel as she entered the house. Her last real Passover had been a lifetime before in Poland, and yet the memories that came were as fresh as the moment. The voices of Grandfather and Yacov were joined by others . . . *Mama. Papa. Daniel. Little Aaron and Samuel* . . . Rachel closed her eyes for a moment and the voice of Moshe came to her as well.

"Rachel! Rachèl! I am with you, my love . . ." But he was not among those who crowded around her in the foyer, and though the house seemed full and bright, there was an emptiness in her heart.

". . . so glad our little jewel is doing so well!"

"And Yehudit has made such a feast for us to celebrate tonight."

"A small thing . . . just a little feast, then."

"Better than any other in Jerusalem. Kreplish! I tell you, the girl has made kreplish and gefilte fish!"

"And chicken soup!"

"Only from bouillon. With a few poor matzo balls in it. . . ."

Rachel smiled and nodded at each comment. Laughter came, but her heart still listened to Moshe's voice. And just when she thought that her smiles would dissolve into tears, Howard took her by the arm and rescued her.

"Come along now, Rachel. Plenty of time for this later." He led her to the stairs. "We have all of us had a chance to rest and get cleaned up. Go on now. Your clothes are still in the closet where you left them. . . ."

She lowered her eyes, hopeful that he would not see the emotion that threatened to break out. "Thank you, Professor."

"And certainly we must have hot water somewhere in the house. Eh, Yehudit?"

"Yes. Yes. I will fetch it right away." Yehudit hurried toward the kitchen.

Rachel wearily climbed the stairs to the familiar hallway. Here she had first fallen in love with Moshe, yet had denied herself the hope of love. She touched the banister where his hand had touched a thousand times. *And all the while I told myself it couldn't be, he was falling in love with me.*

She opened the closet door and smiled back at all the brightly colored clothes Ellie had given her. *Moshe had liked this the best.* She took out the soft blue sweater and skirt and held it up to herself. Turning to the mirror, she tried to imagine him looking at her again. Then his voice returned, strong and sure . . .

"Rachel! My love! My wife! Tonight my heart is with you!"

"Moshe!" she said aloud. "May God protect you for me and for your children. . . ."

Yehudit knocked softly on the door. "There is water in the bath for you, Rachel," she whispered. Then Rachel heard her quickly retreat down the stairs.

One by one the light bulbs were burning out around the house and could not be replaced; Rachel washed herself by candlelight. Feeling a sense of wonder at the miracle that grew within her, she gazed at the slight bulge of her abdomen and tried to imagine what Moshe would say when she told him. Perhaps if it was very much longer until they saw one another again, she would not need to tell him. He would see her and know. Then he would gently reach out his hand and feel the child kick.

The wavering light of the candle reflected on the frosted glass of the window. Beyond that the glow of the full moon rose over the land. Did Moshe look at it now and think of her? *You must think only of Grandfather and Yacov tonight, or you will break.*

She dressed quickly and braided her hair, pinning it up. The reflection in the mirror seemed to her like a different person than the one who had left this house so many months before. *Yes. She has gone away, that girl. And I am here instead. Belonging to God and to Moshe. Now I can remember that last Passover with Mama and Papa without shame* . . . She said in a whisper, "Papa and Mama, your Rachel has come home to Jerusalem. Papa, you have a fine and handsome son-in-law. A professor. You can be proud. And, Mama, you are going to be a grandmother—imagine! I came home, Mama. To Grandfather. To Yacov. I am home. . . ."

The blue of the sweater reflected in her eyes. She patted her cheeks for color and exhaled slowly, composing herself.

Downstairs, amid happy babble and chatter, Grandfather led the way down the corridor to the dining room. The table itself was covered with a freshly pressed tablecloth. It shone with china and crystal wine glasses and silver candlesticks that Howard and Yehudit had retrieved from the packing crates in the basement. Seven chairs ringed the table—six for them and one extra for the Prophet Elijah, should he happen to drop in and announce the coming of the Messiah. Yacov sat beside the place of Elijah and studied the wine goblet of the prophet as though it would mysteriously empty before his eyes.

For Rachel, the Seder table was much bigger than the one where she now sat. Perhaps Grandfather sensed it too as he recited the Kaddish and drank the first cup of wine. Empty chairs ringed her heart as all the old, familiar words and rituals returned. For a moment, against her will, she thought of Moshe, but she caught herself before longing filled her face. *For Grandfather there must be nothing but happiness tonight*, she told herself. *His old eyes have waited long to see me and have this night of joy. I must not grieve and ruin even one minute for him.*

Instead, she looked at Yehudit, who seemed almost beautiful tonight. The girl's plain, downcast features sparkled with delight. She was proud of what she had done, and for the first time in her young life had obeyed her heart instead of acting out of fear of her father. Tonight Tikvah was safe, the house was scrubbed clean, the Seder meal prepared, and Yehudit was happy.

Grandfather stood proudly in his tallith. Rachel remembered Papa as he had stood before their family to recite the most beautiful part of the Haggadah. *Ho-Lachmo Anyo* . . .

"I will explain for our friend Howard," he began in a steady voice. "This is one of the oldest sections of the Haggadah. Two thousand years old, at least. I believe that Yeshua, our Prophet and the Jew you call Jesus the Christ, spoke these very words the night before His death. He celebrated the Passover also, you see. You Gentiles call it the Last Supper. For we who are Jews, we call it the Festival of Freedom. Nu?"

He bowed slightly and picked up the plate of unleavened

bread. "We celebrate freedom from slavery." His eyes met Rachel's and held them, and she knew that somehow his heart had seen the bondage she had lived with. "Tonight we celebrate coming home to the land. And the coming home of our hearts to God. In olden days I would have stepped into the street to say Ho-Lachmo. But, one does not know what one may find in the streets these days, nu? If someone accepts our invitation, then they will have the good sense to knock. . . ." Ehud guffawed loudly at the sensible rabbi.

"Omaine!"

"This is an invitation to the poor. Such as the Rabbi of Nazareth might have recited, Howard . . ."

"Yes," Howard nodded. "I am sure He did."

With the plate held high, Grandfather began the ancient call. "This is the bread of our affliction which our fathers ate in the land of Egypt . . ."

I was a slave, Lord. To my sin and shame. . . , Rachel prayed.

". . . Let all who are hungry come and eat. . . ."

The words of Yeshua on that night returned to her mind. She saw Him standing in His tallith calling out the invitation. *Jesus took the bread, and blessed it. . . .*

"Blessed art Thou, O Eternal! Our God, King of the universe, who bringest forth bread from the earth!"

. . . and he broke it and gave it to them saying, This is my body which is given for you; this do in remembrance of me. . . .

"Let all who are in need come and celebrate Pesach with us. Now we are here. Next year this may truly be the Land of Israel. Now we are slaves. Next year we may be free men . . ."

And you, Yeshua. The Lamb of God who was broken for me. You have set my heart free already. And may you also set Israel free. Come soon as King. We saw you once as Passover sacrifice . . .

Grandfather broke the bread and wrapped the larger half separately, setting it aside for dessert. "This," he explained to Howard, "is called the afikoman. It is dessert at the end of the meal. It takes the place of the Pesach lamb, which was eaten last at the Seder. You see?"

"Yes," Howard replied, glancing at Rachel. "Indeed, this is a familiar custom to Christians."

"It is a pity you forgot the rest of Passover, nu?" He said, gently chiding Howard. "This is an eternal ordinance, is it not?

Something to remember forever, nu? And now here is a little something that Yeshua was also familiar with." He nodded toward Yacov. "Yes. You are the youngest male. And you know the question well. In Hebrew *and* English, please."

Yacov straightened his yarmulke and cleared his throat. He smiled broadly at Rachel and she saw again her other brothers grinning back at her. "Why is this night different from all other nights. . . ?"

––––––––

Moshe shivered in the chill of a fresh wind. The lights still burned brightly from the window of Howard's dining room. He tried to picture Rachel, sitting beside Rebbe Lebowitz. He recited the words of the Seder and pretended that he, too, shared in the meal of remembrance.

In the distance thunder rolled down the mountains. Or was it something more ominous than a mere storm? Clouds scudded across the face of the moon, hiding the forms of the watchers from him, and he from them. For a long time they did not move. What were they waiting for? Who had they come to take? If it was Rachel . . . if they had come to take her from the safety of this place, then Moshe had determined that he would die in stopping them.

He was angry. Angry at their presence. Angry that they stopped him from walking across the street and knocking on the door and reaching out to touch her. *Just to touch her.*

Long minutes passed as the men stood and talked in low voices. They seemed faceless—not like men, but creatures of the darkness, like the legends of Golum who roamed the streets of Warsaw.

Moshe was nearly mad at the closeness of Rachel. *To think that she is there and I am here . . . that I could shout and she would hear my voice!*

Suddenly, the moon shone clearly again on the street and the watchers nudged one another and walked slowly from the curb toward the house. Their footsteps were purposeful, shoulders squared with determination. One man glanced back toward Moshe, and his features were clearly illuminated.

"Stewart!" Moshe gasped. He caught himself and shrank back against the wall where he hid. Praying for the moon to be covered, a million thoughts raced through his mind. *Has he come for Rachel? Is she indeed to be hostage until I am reeled in?* For a moment he considered standing up, shouting and drawing them away from her. Moshe dared to raise his eyes enough to see the four men stop on the sidewalk in front of the Moniger home. One walked quickly around the back of the house. Another remained where he stood and the other two walked toward the door.

———

Grandfather patted Yacov on the head. "You see what a bright boy God has given me to lighten my old age!" he said proudly. Then his eyes lingered on the cup of Elijah as he remembered so many others . . .

The craggy face of Ehud also reflected memories. He frowned and stuck out his lower lip. "I also had sons, Rebbe Lebowitz. And they are not here to ask the questions. They cannot ask *why*."

"Yes," said Yacov quietly. "And my brothers. Brothers I have never known and cannot remember. Why did they die, Grandfather, while I still live?"

The old man's face clouded with the difficulty of the final question, the final *why?* He stared at the open copy of the Haggadah, the story of Israel's redemption. Tugging on his beard, he searched for words. "On this night," he said, "we must remember another child. This is a child of the Shoah . . . the Holocaust, who did not survive to ask. And so, we ask for that child—why?" He paused and took a long, thoughtful breath. "And we are like that child, nu? We have no answer. God has commanded that we remember the day of our going out from Egypt, all the days of our life; even in the darkest nights when we have lost *our* firstborn, we must remember the Exodus and God's miracle of deliverance."

Rachel hung her head and remembered her firstborn, the child lost to the horror of the camps. *Yet will I believe . . .*

"We answer that child's question in silence. In silence we remember that dark time. In silence we remember Jews who still believed in God in the struggle for life. In silence we remember Seder nights spent in the forests, the ghettos, and the camps . . ." The aged rabbi faltered for a moment, then cleared his throat and began again.

There can be no telling of it, God, so the world will believe what it was like. . . .

"We remember that Seder night when the Warsaw Ghetto rose in revolt." He lifted the cup of Elijah, which was only half filled, then handed it to Yacov, who poured some of his own cup into it before passing it on.

"In silence, let us pass the cup of Elijah," Grandfather continued. "The cup of the final redemption yet to be."

And Yeshua said, This is my blood, which is shed for you. . . .

"We remember our people's return to the land of Israel, the beginning of that redemption. We will each pour in some of our own wine, with the hope that through our efforts we may bring that redemption close." He stood up and searched each face. "And now we will open our door to invite Elijah, the forerunner of the future that will bring an end to the nights of our people. And we sing as they did of old, *Ani ma'amin . . .*"

Rusty voices joined him in the ancient song, "For firmly I believe in the coming of the Messiah, and even though the Messiah may tarry, in spite of this, I still believe . . ."

Twice more they sang the song, and Rachel studied the faces of those she loved who were gathered around the table. *How can I tell them, Lord? How can I tell them of the One who is our Redeemer?*

When, at last, they fell silent once more, their questions were still unanswered. Howard's expression was peaceful and confident as he raised his glass and spoke. "Each day I pray that your Messiah and mine will come soon, Rabbi. I believe there is none other in whom we can hope. For peace in Israel and also peace within our own hearts—"

"Then we are agreed." Grandfather sipped his wine, then walked toward the door with Yacov on his heels.

A sharp rapping sounded from the outside and Grandfather froze in his tracks in the foyer.

"It is Elijah!" Yacov shouted, rushing past him.

"Yacov! No!" The old man tried to catch him as he threw back the bolt and flung the door wide open.

Arms crossed and eyes narrow, Captain Stewart stood on the step beside a tough-looking sergeant. "Good evening," he said dryly. "Are you expecting someone?" He looked past Grandfather's shoulder.

The old man sniffed and said in a loud voice, "We were hoping for a visit from Elijah, not the British government." He hoped his voice carried to the dining room where Ehud sat with the others.

"What are you doing here?" Yacov demanded. "It is Passover. Why are you here?"

"We have come for a little visit with one of your guests." Stewart shouldered his way into the house past the rabbi.

"Now, see here!" Howard emerged from the dining room. "This is an outrage! An outrage!"

"You are right," Stewart said, unholstering his pistol. "And I am certain that Rabbi Akiva in the Old City agrees with you. Outrage. You are harboring his runaway daughter. What kind of a Passover do you think he is having tonight, Professor? No one to cook for him . . . eh? Missing his dear daughter. Here in the house of a Gentile. Leaving with a woman who was a Nazi collaborator. An S.S. prostitute . . ."

"It isn't true!" Yacov shouted, throwing himself against the captain. "You are a liar!" Yacov struck at him, and the captain simply grabbed his wrists and held him firmly.

"You cannot have the sanction of your government to storm into a private residence and insult my guests!" Howard wrapped his arms around Yacov and wrested him from the captain.

"He's a liar! Grandfather! Did you hear what he called Rachel! *Grandfather!*"

The old man did not reply. His shoulders sagged beneath the weight of a suspicion that had suddenly become knowledge.

"You have no authority!" Howard spat.

Stewart produced a piece of paper with an official seal across it. "Yes. Authority. The girl is underage. Left under false pretenses. You will fetch her, please. Or I will simply search the house. More unpleasantness, I'm afraid."

"That will not be necessary." Yehudit stepped from behind Howard.

Rachel followed, throwing herself between Stewart and the girl. "You can't take her! Don't you know what he will do to her?"

"That is of little concern to me. I might lay a lash to her myself if she were my daughter. A little Judas, this one is."

"I forbid this!" Howard insisted.

"Then you will spend some time in jail, Professor Moniger. Kidnapping, they call it."

"Please!" Yehudit shouted. "Let me go with him! Let me go!

No more trouble, Rachel! There has been enough."

"But, Yehudit—I cannot let you . . ." Rachel was crying now. She embraced the girl, holding her close, and Yehudit's tears stained her sweater.

"You have been a friend to me. Now let me go. There has been enough grief because of me."

"No! You saved the baby!"

"Then it is enough."

Stewart stepped forward and took Yehudit by the arm. "All this personal rot has nothing to do with it. Your father wants you home. You're going." He sneered at Howard. "Go ahead, call headquarters, Professor. Your reputation as a Zionist is quite well known now. No doubt they will hang up on you."

Yehudit did not look back as he escorted her roughly down the steps and across the street to a waiting car. Rachel stood and watched, weeping in the doorway until Stewart glanced up and waved triumphantly.

Howard tugged her gently inside the house and shut the door, bolting it securely. "It was just as well she surrendered herself to them," he said quietly as Rachel sobbed into his coat. "They would have searched the house, and Ehud would have been—"

"Arrested!" she cried in sudden realization. "Where is he? Is he—"

"Under the table," Howard said calmly. "Akiva will not hurt Yehudit. Not his own daughter . . ."

"He is a very self-righteous man," Grandfather replied in a broken voice. "Very easily angered in the best of times."

His eyes did not meet Rachel's.

"Where has Yacov gone?" she asked, brushing away the tears and suddenly remembering his reaction to the brutal words of Stewart.

"He . . . he . . . uh went upstairs to be with Shaul, the poor beast. He has been locked up while we enjoy Seder."

Rachel knew that the boy had gone for other reasons. She bit her lip and searched the face of Grandfather. "It was not as the Englishman said," she whispered hoarsely.

"No. Of course not, child. We will talk. Yacov and I. He must know; it is time he understand that not always is life kind and fair. Sometimes we are forced to live in a way that is not as we would choose."

Howard left them standing alone in the foyer. Rachel spoke slowly, trying to find words that would explain to her Grandfather. "I did not fight in the forests. Or survive in the camps. I . . . I simply survived. The only way they would let me survive."

"Please." He held up his hand and looked at her with eyes filled with grief. "Say no more to this old man. It is enough for me . . . enough that you have returned from the dead. You have come home from the dark night. From the grave." He reached out to her and she laid her head against his chest and cried like a little girl. He stroked her hair and kissed the top of her head. "*You* are enough. God has brought you home now, and all of that is over, nu? We will say no more about it."

"*Yacov!*" she said heavily.

"Yacov has not known what it is to suffer, child. He is young. He cannot know what it was like."

"Too many children . . . too many *have* known! Oh, Grandfather! And they are all gone! All of them! All but a few. . ."

"Hush now," he soothed. "Hush, Rachel . . . Yes. Yes. We have lost our firstborn and there is no calling them back. And if ever there was innocence and any hope in the goodness of mankind, that too is gone. But God has not changed. We wait for Him still, and that is all we have left."

———

Moshe pressed his cheek against the cold stone wall as Stewart roughly led Yehudit Akiva toward the car. Moshe groaned inwardly and clenched his teeth as Rachel stood framed in the doorway and wept for Yehudit, wept for the girl who had betrayed her. *Rachel!*

Unbearable seconds passed as Stewart shoved Yehudit into the car and Rachel turned her face away. Howard put his arm around her and closed the door. Like a light flashing in the darkness, the image of her tearful face was etched on Moshe's mind. He stared at the doorway where Rachel had stood as though she were standing there still.

The British vehicle roared to a start and Moshe drew back when the headlights blinked on. Too slowly it drew away from the curb, stopping to pick up the last of the soldiers who emerged from beside the house. Frantically, Moshe strained to see into the shadows of the street. Were there any more soldiers waiting there? Any more watchers left behind to bar his way to Rachel?

Five minutes more he waited in the lonely street for any sign of movement. *Let them show themselves now, please God. If this is a trap set for me . . . if walking across the street will end my life. . .* His heart pounded in his ears. He stood and brushed himself off, still wary of the darkness. *Then if it is to be, I will die looking into her face.* He stepped from the curb. The echo of his own footsteps followed him, walking slowly at first and then faster until he ran up the steps and pounded his fists against the door. Inside, Shaul barked fiercely.

"Who is there?"

"Moshe! It is Moshe, Howard! Open the—"

Howard flung the door open, at the same time reaching out to pull him in off the street. "Moshe!" he cried. "But how—"

"Where is she?" Moshe panted, looking past him for Rachel. "Where has she gone?"

His complexion was flushed with excitement.

"Upstairs. With Yacov and Rebbe Lebowitz—"

Moshe shoved past him and took the stairs two at a time. Whining and wagging his tailless behind, Shaul bounded ahead of him, leading the way to where a light glowed from beneath a door. As Shaul yapped and scratched, Moshe hesitated, then turned the knob and pushed the door open.

Rachel sat on the bed with her arm around Yacov. The boy leaned heavily against her, and Grandfather sat on a wooden chair across from them. He held Rachel's hand in his. Moshe did not move as the flow of the candle caught his face. Startled with the intrusion, Rachel looked up and caught sight of him. She did not speak, but her face grew soft and her eyes touched him before she stood. There was suddenly no one else in the room, in the house, in the world. As if in slow motion they moved toward each other, reaching out, touching each other's faces, then melting into an embrace. He smelled the sweet fragrance of her hair, then kissed her gently again and again. She held him tightly, unwilling to let go even long enough to look at him again. *Oh yes! Yes, it is Moshe. Yes, he holds me. This is not a dream!*

At last she said his name aloud and looked into his face. Tears streamed freely down his cheeks, and as she brushed them away he laughed and kissed her fingers. Then he cried again and held her to him and there were no words. No words for this moment.

Grandfather patted him on the back. Yacov called Shaul out to the hallway and the door clicked shut, leaving them alone in their joy.

22   Meetings

Ellie sighed with contentment and snuggled deeper under the soft satin comforter. David's breathing was even and peaceful. His arm was draped across her and his fingertips rested on her cheek. She opened her eyes and smiled back at their reflection in the ornate Roccoco mirror suspended above them by little gold cherubs at each corner. The honeymoon suite at the Ragusa Palace Inn was truly something to write home about.

"Nothing but the best for my wife and me," David had whispered to the innkeeper. "*Honeymoon.*" He had explained. Then, he had jerked his thumb to where Mikhail stood beside Bernie. "You can put these guys in the basement if you want. But I want the best you've got." Then Bernie and Mikhail had gone off in search of the telegraph.

The innkeeper had smiled and winked and ushered them up three flights of stairs to a suite adorned with delicate velvet chairs and Louis XIV tables, gilded lamps with crystal prisms suspended from the globes, and long, white, tapered candles everywhere.

While two bellboys hustled around the room lighting the candles, David had pulled her onto the settee and surveyed the room with satisfaction.

"Can we afford this, David?"

"This one is on the Old Man. Overtime pay, Babe. Overdue overtime pay, and I'm going to collect." Then he had kissed her long and slow as the bellboys gazed awkwardly up at the ceiling and waited for their tips.

That had been three hours ago. Now the candles that flanked Mrs. Tornahos's picnic basket burned low, and long shadows played against the walls of the suite. Ellie's stomach rumbled. They had not eaten since that morning at the Torna-hos's home in Cyprus, and it was well past dinner time.

Ellie turned her head and kissed David's fingertips, then gently moved his arm and slipped out from under the blankets onto the thin Persian carpet beside the tall bed. Wrapping her-self in David's shirt, she padded across the floor to the basket and opened it. Mrs. Tornahos had even provided silverware and plates. Various cheeses and salami were wrapped carefully, but the delicious aroma drifted up and her mouth began to water.

"What are you doing, Babe?" David asked dreamily.

"Fixing supper." She set the table and cut the salami and bread.

"Not cooking, I hope," he laughed.

She thumbed her nose at him and sliced some cheese. "She even made a salad," Ellie said in a hushed voice.

"Why are you whispering?"

"Because everything seems almost holy." She looked at him and smiled wistfully. "This place. The candles. You and I . . ."

David propped his head up on his pillow and pulled the cov-ers back a bit. "A little nicer than the basement at the Jewish Agency, you mean?"

"Hmmm. You could say so. This is our first night together, you know. Without interruptions, I mean."

He patted the bed, "Come back to bed, Els. We can eat bread and cheese anytime."

Her eyes met his and warmth spread through her to her fin-gertips. Tears of happiness welled up. "This place . . . this night is every dream . . ." Weeks of a nightmare of worry and won-dering and grief had suddenly vanished. "I only wish we could stay . . . David . . ." She swallowed hard, savoring the look in his eyes.

He smiled gently and held out his hand to her. "Come on, then. We can eat on the plane tomorrow." He chuckled softly. "Put down the knife and come back to bed."

"I love you, David," she said, letting the shirt fall from her onto the floor.

His grin faded and a soft wonder filled his eyes as she moved toward him. Enfolding her in his arms he whispered her name again and again as his lips found hers. "Every dream . . . my only dream."

"I know that you must leave again, Moshe." Rachel reached up to touch his mouth with her fingertip. "You do not need to say more. I will not . . . ask you to stay."

He gazed into the clear blue of her eyes; then he kissed her hand and held it to his cheek. "If I could stay, my love—"

"Tonight the Lord heard my prayer. I prayed only that I would see you. That I could look into your face and tell you—" She hesitated, uncertain now if she should tell him about their baby. Would it not give him one more thing to worry about, to think of when he must think only of the battle ahead?

"What is it, Rachel?" He had caught something in her eyes that spoke to him before words. "What is it you must tell me?"

She bit her lip, afraid now that she could not speak of the miracle she carried within her without weeping and begging him never to leave her. "I . . . I . . ."

"What?" His smile questioned her gently.

"I wanted to tell you that I . . . we . . . need you to be very careful. Please." She looked down at her lap.

"I promise. I promise I will." He pulled her against him and cradled her gently in his arms. "And together we will remember that God sees even the sparrow, nu? You will remember that for me?"

She nodded once, feeling the rough wool of his jacket against her cheek. "Yes," she said softly, emotion swelling in her throat. "Yes, Moshe, I will remember."

He held her in silence for what seemed like a long time and then said, "And I must remember that as well. If you said one word to me I would not go. I would stay here forever beside you. There would be no promise to my nation, no men to command, no outpost to fight for—only you. Only you, Rachel!" He was torn into a thousand pieces, certain now that it would have been easier to fight and die if he had not seen her this night.

Tears came silently to her eyes. She let her breath out slowly, knowing that she could not and would not command his heart to stay. "We have had this time, our weeks together, these few hours tonight. Some live a lifetime and never know the love we have shared. You have given me a lifetime of happiness . . ." She gasped, trying to control her voice.

"And we shall have a full lifetime together. In Israel. You and I and Tikvah . . ."

"And . . ." Her voice faltered again.

"There is something more you want to tell me before I go, isn't there?" He lifted her chin and caressed her soul with a look. "Tell me then, love. What is it?"

She wiped her tears away and took his strong hand in both of hers. She guided it until it rested over her womb. Then she looked at him and smiled wistfully. "Moshe," she began, "there is another also to live for. . ."

He did not speak. His eyes filled with wonder as he pressed his hand firmly against her, and he smiled a funny smile. "Do you mean. . . ?"

She nodded quickly and they laughed together. He hugged her again, then drew back to touch again where their child grew. "He will be here, waiting for his father. *Here*, growing big until he sleeps just beneath my heart."

"Oh. Oh, God! How I am blessed! How I am—Rachel, my *love*! Can this *be*?"

"Yes. The doctor at Hadassah . . . when I fainted . . ."

His expression became instantly worried. "You *fainted*?"

Words came in a rush to her then. "Yes, but I am all right. I was just very tired. Very tired because Tikvah has been so ill, and I had not slept at all, and—"

She was interrupted by a sharp rapping on the door and Ehud's gruff voice. "Moshe! It is time to leave or we will be late for the meeting! Moshe!"

Moshe grimaced at the intrusion and jumped up to open the door slightly. "Just a few minutes more, Ehud. I cannot leave her now. Not now. She—"

Ehud glanced at his watch and held it up for Moshe to see. "It's nearly midnight, my friend. What with the British patrols, we will have difficulty getting there on time as it is—"

"Listen. You go ahead. We should not travel together anyway. Ehud . . . I need more time with her. Just a few minutes. I will come along after you."

Ehud shrugged uncomfortably. "As you wish. Be careful, friend."

"Shalom. I will be along shortly." Moshe shut the door and turned again to embrace Rachel and soak in the wonder of her miracle.

Ehud stood against the back wall of the basement at Rehavia High School. The room was crowded with faces he recognized and with many he had never seen before.

News from Kastel was grim. Several thousand Jihad Moquades had gathered to attack, and the hourly plea from Fergus Dugan was for reinforcements and supplies.

Bobby Milkin stood before a large topographical map that bore the logo *British Foreign Service Cartography Dept.* It had been stolen from the British Foreign Office by some enterprising young clerk, and now, Bobby marked where the concentrations of enemy forces had gathered.

". . . and by air, near as I can make out, these villages surrounding Kastel are about deserted—"

Emile Dumas stepped forward. "Then would it not be to our advantage to occupy additional villages?"

Ehud growled at the suggestion of Emile. Here was a fellow, Ehud knew, who had dark connections with the terrorists of the Irgun and the Stern Gang.

"We barely have enough here to sneak into Kastel the back way!" Bobby replied. "You don't know what you're up against."

"There are others in Jerusalem. Others who may be more Zionist than even those gathered here. They will follow with us if we furnish them with weapons," Emile answered.

"You speak of the Irgun!" Ehud shouted. "We will have nothing to do with them!"

"And that is why we may yet fail!" Emile returned fiercely. "Our forces are divided while the enemy is *united*! We must be *one*!"

A loud murmur of approval rippled through the room.

Ehud strode forward, parting the men with his hands. "We cannot be one with cutthroats and murderers! Or we have become the enemy!" He faced Emile, towering over him and glowering down.

"These are men who are not afraid to fight! And who are you?" Emile's lip curled in disdain. "You are nothing but the captain of a fishing boat! Commander of sardines! Spokesman for Moshe Sachar! And he is nothing . . . nothing but a professor."

Agreement again echoed in the room. "Emile Dumas is a

fighter from the Resistance! A brave man who killed the Nazis by the score! Killed them while they slept or while they supped. Emile! We should listen to Emile!"

Ehud wished that Moshe would come. He prayed for the arrival of this man of reason. "We cannot split these troops!" Ehud insisted. "Listen to Bobby Milkin! We do not know how many we will come against! To split our troops to take a few small villages—"

"Then go! I am not suggesting that we divide those who are here! The Haganah and the Palmach should go to Kastel! I do not advocate division! No! I am for uniting! For the taking of enemy territory by JEWS! By our brothers!"

"They are not brothers of mine!" Ehud boomed.

Emile ignored Ehud and appealed to the men assembled. "I say we unite. There are men willing to fight with us . . ."

"And with our weapons . . ."

"The weapons of Zionism! These brave soldiers will double our strength against the thousands of the Mufti! And we could also double the territory we take! What better time to strike against Arab villages than when their men have gathered to fight us in Kastel?"

"Where is Moshe Sachar?" Bobby raised his voice above the din of argument between Haganah officers. "Has anybody seen Sachar?"

"He left before me," said Emile. "If he were coming, he would be here—"

"He is coming!" Ehud raised his hands for silence, but there was no silence. "We should wait to hear what he says! I say he will be here!" he shouted.

"Where is Moshe Sachar?"

"It was he who led the forty to the convoy. Why is he not here?"

"I have not seen him since morning."

"Has he been picked up by a patrol?"

"It is he who knows Kastel best! Where is Sachar?"

"On his way here, I tell you!" Ehud cried. "We must wait!"

Emile stepped in front of the map. "There is no time to wait!" He slapped his hand against the hill marked *Kastel* and then against the cluster of houses that marked Deir Yassin. "The Irgun could easily take this village and then join us in Kastel—"

"You trust the Irgun to take our weapons and use them to

help us?" Ehud exclaimed, calling on the mistrust and rivalry between the two Zionist factions. "They will take our guns and fight wherever they choose, and we will be left to defend Kastel on our own and with one hundred fewer rifles!"

Agreement moved through the men as they pondered the past deeds of the Irgun.

"If we are to supply them weapons and bullets . . ."

"If the Irgun is to share with us, then they should fight at our sides!"

"Of course they could take an empty village! So what is the difficulty of that? We could take an empty village with sticks and rocks! If they want to share our arms, then they should bear arms with us . . ."

"They cannot be trusted unless—"

"Unless one of our own goes with them!"

"Emile! Emile Dumas is the one!"

"Emile knows their leaders! If Emile will lead them—"

Ehud shouted loudly, "Do you think this will make a difference, eh? It was the Irgun who blew up the Semiramis Hotel and Jaffa Gate! So you think they will suddenly fall in line if Emile Dumas is with them? They are terrorists!"

"We can use them! They are fighting men!"

"We can use every man!"

Emile nodded and raised his hands. Clearly he had captured the attention of his audience. "It is only sensible that we include such fighters. One of their captains served with me in the Resistance. He alone is worth ten men for his brave heart! Yes! Yes! I can say with certainty, if we share our arms with them, they will be shoulder-to-shoulder with us at Kastel."

A shout of assent replied to his words and Ehud rolled his eyes. He had been beaten. He stepped back beside Bobby Milkin, who removed his cigar and spat on the floor. "If only Moshe had been here!" Ehud said. "No one would have listened to this meshuggener."

"Where *is* he?" Bobby whispered, as Emile called out ten men from the ranks and took four crates of rifles away to meet with the leaders of the Irgun and the Stern Gang.

———

By the time Moshe reached the basement meeting room, small groups of armed men were already stealing off through the darkness to rendezvous just beyond the train station.

He shoved his way down the stairs past a group of grim-faced fellows with rifles slung over their shoulders.

Ehud stood near Bobby Milkin between an open crate of weapons and another of ammunition. He looked up and scowled at Moshe as he made his way through the Haganah men waiting in line.

"I am sorry I was delayed," Moshe said as he reached Ehud and Bobby.

"Sorry will do us no good now!" Ehud spat angrily. "Where were you? You cannot make love after we have made a nation, eh?"

Moshe's brow furrowed. "What has happened?" he said, feeling a sense of foreboding.

"That Frenchman," Bobby replied. "Emile Dumas. That Resistance fighter—"

Moshe stared hard at Bobby, hardly daring to ask for an explanation. "Emile. Yes. I know him," he said, not adding that he did not like what he knew.

"Yes. The meshuggener, Emile. A very nice fellow," Ehud spat out sarcastically. "And he has very fine fellows as friends, also. Now suddenly we are all going to be friends . . . He talked our men into joining up with—"

"Out with it quickly, Ehud," Moshe demanded impatiently.

"Well, then, I will! They didn't want to listen to me. I am only a . . . a . . . commander of the sardines! No! But they would have listened to you if you had not been dallying. So now we are stuck with it, and there is nothing else to do."

"Bobby, what is he trying to say?"

"Emile has connections with the Irgun and the Stern Gang. Yeah. You heard me. Real sweet guys. So now we're all gonna be one big happy family. Take Kastel together and never mind that if ever anybody in Palestine deserved to get hung, it's them guys."

"They are going with us to Kastel?" Moshe repeated in disbelief.

"That's the plan, pal."

Ehud stuck out his lower lip. "Because you were not here to argue the matter. No! You had to have another few minutes in her arms—"

"Shut up, Ehud," Moshe snapped, running his fingers

through his hair. He tried to think if there was anything to be done.

"You were a fine and brave fellow," Ehud said accusingly. "A man on time for any battle! Now you've become a—"

"Shut up!" Bobby admonished. "This ain't gonna do nobody any good, Ehud. You're just ticked because they don't listen to you!"

"Ticked? Ticked?"

"Yeah. Mad. Teed off. Blow your top. Explode."

"Angry!" Ehud said loudly. "Well, and what if I am? He could have come. What difference would it have made, eh? So Moshe had his mind on other things, and now see what we have come to! Cutthroats! Murderers!"

Moshe frowned. "We can use more soldiers. They will fight, won't they? Well, won't they?" he demanded.

"Only if they fight against women!" Ehud raised his voice to a shout, and the others in the room fell silent.

"It is cast, and there is no changing it," Moshe returned his anger, wishing that he had not come at all. *The Irgun!* "They will fight with us. We don't have to like them. But they can shoot as well as we—"

"Think of what you say! To stand with the Irgun—" Ehud cried, eying him with disgust. "You've left your brain in the bedroom!" He turned on his heel and stalked off.

"They have weapons?" Moshe quietly asked Bobby.

"*Ours.*" Bobby's eyes followed Ehud as he strode from the basement room. "Emile took them. Four crates, I think. Left with a few of our guys who were in favor of the plan. Said it would take him a while to round up these guys, but that he'd be there. Be in Kastel with the rest of you." He paused. "Maybe it will work out for the best. You know. Bury the hatchet. They're Jews, too."

Moshe's jaw twitched with anger. He was angry at himself for not thinking more clearly, for thinking a few minutes would not matter. "We can hope for that. Hope for the best. The Irgun is skilled only in homemade bombs and molotov cocktails. This will be the first time they carry real weapons into battle. But we can hope."

Bobby chewed his cigar and grimaced. "So," he said. "You seen your wife, huh? She okay?"

Moshe nodded, a sense of guilt washing over him. He had

believed for a moment the lie that his leadership did not matter. "Yes. She is well," he answered quietly. "She is safe . . ."

———

"Wake up!" Bernie Greene hissed through the heavy carved door. "Meyer! You son of an apikorsim! Get out of bed!"

A blanket wrapped around him, David cracked the door slightly and peeked out into the dark corridor where Bernie and Mikhail stood.

"What's the problem?" he growled.

Mikhail wrung his hands and Bernie pushed at the door, trying to get in. "I'll tell you what the problem is—" He lowered his voice and looked over his shoulder. "I'll tell you—the ship!"

"What about it?" David demanded as Ellie called sleepily from behind him.

"What's wrong, David?"

"Let me in!" Bernie said with an edge of desperation in his voice. "It won't do to talk out here."

"This had better be good!" He stepped aside and pulled the curtain on the huge canopy bed as the men rushed into the room and then to the window.

Pulling the draperies back, Bernie pointed to where the moon shone down on the harbor. "Well, it *isn't* good. See for yourself."

David hesitated a moment, not sure he wanted to know. Then he padded over and looked out past the small boats that bobbed on the water. The place where the *Trina* had been anchored was vacant. The *Trina* was gone!

David groaned and put a hand to his forehead. "How long ago?" he asked in a solemn voice.

"I don't know." Greene's eyes were fixed on the place where the freighter had been. "I got up a while ago. Couldn't sleep. You've got my nights and days turned around now, you know . . ." he said with disgust. "Anyway, I just looked out the window, and it wasn't there. I saw it quite clearly in the moonlight before we went to bed. Mikhail pointed it out to me and filled me in on everything I missed when you drugged me and left me to rot . . ."

"Okay, pal. You've made your point," David snapped. He stared hard out the window and watched as clouds swept past the moon. "There's a storm coming," he said under his breath.

240

"One heck of a breeze blowing around up there . . . What time is it?"

"Quarter past three."

"One thing is for sure." David rummaged for his clothes. "That old tub isn't going to make very good time. If we can catch her before the moon goes down, we could be back by morning."

Ellie poked her face out from the curtained chamber. "You're not going without me."

"Ellie—" David protested. "I said we'll be back by morning. You stay here—"

"Mr. Greene," she said calmly. "Mikhail. Would you mind leaving the room? We are about to have our first argument."

"Meet you in the lobby in five minutes!" David held up his fingers as they scurried out the door. "*Alone!*" He looked pointedly at Ellie.

Five minutes later, David and Ellie tramped down the stairs. Mikhail had already hailed a taxi and while David settled the bill, the suitcase full of explosives was gingerly lifted onto the seat. Ellie winked into Bernie Greene's disapproving face and marched past him to the cab.

A strong wind whipped her hair and she looked up at the moon and behind to where a dark bank of clouds obscured the stars.

"We're in for it, Mrs. Meyer," Bernie remarked in a clipped British accent. "And I'll have you know I don't believe this is any place for a woman."

"You wouldn't believe the places I've been, Mr. Greene. You just wouldn't believe it."

In the village of Deir Yassin, Sarai Tafara sat beside the window and listened to the sounds of distant battle at Kastel. To the south, a new rattle of gunfire had begun, and a runner from the forces of Ram Kadar had come shouting into the village streets.

"We need more ammunition! English pounds for ammunition! Jewish forces have come from Jerusalem! They counterattack in the south! More ammunition!"

Then her new husband had jumped from his bed and, lugging cartridge belts along, had kissed her goodbye and run to join the Jihad Moquades who fought to regain the slopes of Kastel. That had been a half an hour before. Now she sat weeping, wondering if she was to be a widow before she had been a wife for even two days.

She shuddered with the cold draft that suddenly came from the next room. Wrapping her blanket tighter around her, she wiped away her tears and went to the dark bedroom to close the window.

"If only Mama were here to keep me company! Yassar would not have thought less of my new husband had he forsaken battle to stay here with me. . . ."

She stood in the doorway and squinted into the blackness. A distinct breeze blew through the room, ruffling the curtains. "Did my husband leave the window so before he left?"

Then, as she strained her eyes to see, a cold chill struck her soul. From the slight gap in the curtains, she saw a shadow, a movement; then slowly the blue steel barrel of a rifle probed into the bedroom.

Her own scream erupted at the exact instant fire burst from the gun and scorched the fabric of the draperies. . . .

PART 3

The Dawn

"Each blade of grass has its spot on earth whence it draws its life, its strength; and so is man rooted to the land from which he draws his faith together with his life. . . ."

Joseph Conrad, 1900

23 In the Eye of the Storm

For nearly three hours the little Stinson battled the intense storm that struck over the Adriatic, yet to Ellie it seemed as though they had not moved even one inch forward. Lightning cracked the darkness, revealing strands of rain like guy wires suspending the plane in the center of the clouds. Then the strobe winked off and the aircraft bucked and pitched against the driving headwinds.

They had long since given up hope of finding the *Trina*. Now, their only prayer was that the sun come up and that they find land—*any land*—before the fuel gave out. David had not spoken in a long time. His face was rigid and his mouth set in a grim line as he wrestled to control the plane. Ellie did not ask, but she could guess the seriousness of the situation as the needle of the fuel gauge hovered just above the red *E* on the dial.

Mikhail and Bernie Greene sat terrified in the back. They gripped the seats and sometimes gasped or cursed when ragged seams of lightning tore the air around them and huge swells of the Adriatic seemed to draw them downward.

Finally, Bernie shouted over the din, "How much longer can you fly in this?"

"I'm hoping a little longer than it takes to get where we're going."

"And where is that?"

"Land!" Then the plane slipped sideways and shuddered.

Ellie stopped looking out the window and turned her gaze on David. His hands gripped the control stick with such intensity that his knuckles were white in the darkness. He squinted through splattering drops that obscured all vision.

"And how far is land?" Bernie called.

"That's what they asked Columbus." He tried to joke, but his words fell flat.

Ellie heard Mikhail reciting the *Shema* under his breath and soon Bernie was also staring out the window as his lips moved silently.

"I shouldn't have let you come." David glanced briefly toward her. There was a hollow tone to his voice that sounded as though he, too, had capitulated to the tempest.

"I didn't give you much choice," she replied.

"I wouldn't mind so much if you were safe." The plane groaned again and dropped lower in the sky.

In a series of flashes, Ellie saw the whitecaps breaking on the enormous swells beneath them. White foam slid down mountains of gray water in swirling currents that seemed always the same.

"I don't want to be safe alone. I want to be with you." Thoughts of Jesus walking on the stormy sea of Galilee came to her mind. And men in the little boat with Him as water had surged over the top of the mast. *Save us Lord*, her heart cried, *or we will die! Calm the storm or bring us light and land, or we are finished, Lord. Look at David's face. I've never seen him look like that. He as much as said he was sorry for bringing me along to die with him. I'm scared, Lord! Really scared!*

No voice called out *"peace!"* to the waves and wind. The violence still buffeted them, but within moments, the pitch black began to lighten to a slate gray. The needle on the fuel gauge dipped lower.

"How long till we have to set her down?" Ellie asked, following David's nervous glance at the dial.

He did not answer, his fingers flexed nervously on the controls. "God!" he said, leaning forward to peer out the windshield. "*God!*" His words became urgent then. "Bernie!" His shout was a demand. "Get that suitcase out of here. It'll explode on impact with the water."

Bernie froze, his face a white mask. "You mean—"

"I said *get it out!*" David shouted angrily. "Snap out of it! Ellie!" he barked as they drifted close to the waves. "Help him!"

Without a moment of wavering, Ellie pulled the latch on the side window and heaved it up. A blast of icy rain stung her face and wind drowned out their voices as Bernie and Mikhail worked together to heave the lethal bomb forward and out the opening. The plane seemed to balk at the added resistance of the wind, and the leather straps of the suitcase hung up on the metal lip of the window frame.

"God help us!" Ellie cried, but her voice was obscured by the turmoil of the gale. "Help us!"

Mikhail groaned as he forced his shoulder against the obstinate case. A small triangle of glass shattered as the corner caught and then began to edge slowly out beneath the wing. Bernie joined him in the effort until the case tottered halfway out of the window.

"Get that thing out of here!" David commanded at the top of his lungs. "Or we're done for! Land! There's the beach! I'm going to try to set her down—"

Ellie rose up on her knees and added her weight to the struggle. Inch by inch the leather scraped until with a triumphant cheer the three heaved it out. It tumbled downward a hundred feet and exploded in a huge geyser of water and mud.

Ellie slammed the window down, but still the rain and wind howled in around the bent frame.

"Get your heads down!" David held the controls steady as a narrow strip of beach loomed ahead of them. "Get *down*!" He bellowed at Ellie, who froze with her eyes wide with fear. "Head on your knees!" He was scared, too. There was only a narrow band of sand between the turmoil of the surf and sand dunes that would tear them to pieces. "We're comin' in. Comin' in! Easy now, little girl!" He did not cut the power, certain that the wind would roll them instantly if the engine hesitated even a fraction of a second.

Mikhail and Bernie cried out the *Shema* above the scream of the wind and the engine. David dropped low over the water and strained to see the beach. There were no rocks to tear the landing gear from the little Stinson, and for a moment David held the desperate hope that he could bring her in intact. The beach was crescent-shaped and David came toward it over the water, then turned slightly. Airspeed was slow. "Seventy-five," David called to himself as the waves and the beach merged ahead. Then, when they were still over the water, the engine suddenly coughed and lost power. In a split second, David punched the throttle, trying to force the engine back to life. He worked to keep the nose up as they nearly cleared the surf. Then the plane sagged and the landing gear caught the top of a wave.

Ellie's scream was drowned out by the deafening groan of the flimsy metal shell of the aircraft as it tumbled and crunched in the surf. And then a strange, peaceful silence surrounded them.

The voice of Moshe Sachar crackled over Bobby Milkin's radio as he circled high above the battle, "Can you see Emile's reinforcements? Over."

Bobby held the field glasses to his eyes and focused down on the rocky terrain below. Moshe's Haganah troops held a fan-shaped wedge that pointed up the southern face of the slope of Kastel. Arab concentrations fired sporadically at the left front of the wedge as other Haganah men fought their way slowly up toward the remains of the castle and the village. Weary forces, the original troops who had taken Kastel, still held the strategic points within the village itself and the rock quarry. The dead from both sides lay sprawled on the hillside or draped over ledges where they had fallen. A Haganah mine exploded beneath a group of five Jihad Moquades who sneaked up a deep ravine toward the fortification. The troops Emile had promised were nowhere to be seen.

"Ah, negative. No sign of them. Over."

From the air, Bobby could see the dilemma. Once the wedge of men had retreated to the safety of the Kastel fortifications, it would be difficult for Emile and his men to break through the circle of Arabs that would certainly close in. And yet, the troops could not hold the southern face of the slope without difficulty. Although they had dug shallow trenches, they were still vulnerable to a slight rise two hundred yards to their left. Although their position gave them a distinct advantage over the Arabs who charged up the exposed hillside in fits of religious frenzy, the most advantageous shelter was in the stone houses of Kastel itself where Fergus's few men held an entire army of Irregulars at bay.

Bobby banked the plane and turned back along the route that had brought the first wave of reinforcements to Kastel from Jerusalem. There was still no trace of Emile's men. They had not been ambushed and butchered by Arabs. They simply had not arrived.

While Arabs cowered in the rocks in the bottom of the gorge, Fergus Dugan and his men held them off and prayed for ammunition to replenish their dwindling supply.

"I'm going down a little closer," Bobby said, "for a little look-see. Find out where those guys have gone."

"Invite them to join us if you see them," Moshe quipped sarcastically over the receiver as rifle fire popped in the background. "Over."

"Watch your right flank, Mama," Bobby warned as he quickly flew over the land it had taken several hours to cross on foot the night before.

On a distant hill, he saw the tiny white stone houses of Deir Yassin and beyond that, Jerusalem. One tiny human ant scrambled down a ravine that twisted downward toward Bab el Wad. Bobby watched the figure stumble and fall, then pick himself up again. Curious as to whose side of the war this panicked traveler was on, Bobby lifted the field glasses again and traced the craggy wash.

"That ain't a man!" he said, taking a second look.

The filthy form of a woman staggered over a rocky path. Her clothes were torn and bloody. Her hair seemed to be shorn, and she was only half clothed. He leaned forward, struck by the sight of this pitiful creature; her face was contorted as though she were in pain. Her feet were bare . . . and, he noted, she was an Arab. Her course lead from the village of Deir Yassin.

He banked the plane in a slight turn and headed toward the collection of tiny white houses. Within moments he circled over the square in the village.

Far below him was a scene of indescribable horror. Little rage dolls of bloody flesh lay everywhere. Lines of women and children lay side by side where they had been executed. The old and the young alike were piled in tumbled heaps. In disbelief, Bobby swept low over the village. "Dear God in heaven!" he groaned as he absorbed the grisly nightmare of Deir Yassin. And the worst nightmare of all was the sight of the troops of Emile Dumas looting the houses, dragging the last of the survivors from their hiding places and shooting them in the streets.

As Bobby passed overhead, a soldier of the Irgun turned his eyes upward toward the plane and waved broadly with a brand-new Haganah rifle.

————

Sarai Tafara stumbled upon the men of Fredrich Gerhardt's company first. Among the burned vehicles at the bottom of the gorge, she raised her hand and cried out; then collapsed as the men ran toward her.

"This is the sister of Yassar Tafara, is it not?" The men clustered around her in a circle as she lay in the dust and sobbed hysterically.

"She was a bride only two night ago."

"Where is her husband?"

"Dead. Killed this morning just short of Kastel wall."

At that, the girl wailed loudly and laid her face against the hard gravel of the road.

"Where has she come from?"

"What has happened, woman?" The soldiers stared at her hair, chopped off in chunks nearly to her scalp. Her breasts were exposed and her clothing torn. A soldier quickly took off his outer cloak and draped it over her.

"Who has done this thing to you?"

She sobbed even harder and did not raise her head to answer. Behind the circle of men, a strong, ominous voice said loudly, "Who do you think has done this thing?" It was the voice of Fredrich Gerhardt. He shoved his men to one side and strode forward to the young woman. He towered over her, his eyes coldly surveying the ravaged sister of Yassar Tafara. "I shall tell you who has done this thing, although you know." They stared back at him in horror. The abused body of the once-beautiful bride told them every detail. "Not even your wives are safe from the vermin. If we allow the Jews to live, they will rape our women and murder our children!" he shrieked.

"Kill me!" sobbed Sarai. "Do not let me live with this disgrace! I beg of you! End my life!" She repeated the words that she had cried to the men of the Irgun as they had abused her.

Gerhardt tore the robe from her, revealing her again to his soldiers. "Look upon her! Then cry for the Jihad! Look what they have done to this daughter of the Prophet!"

A clamor arose among the men. Rifles fired into the air as others heard the fearful cries of those who had left family in Deir Yassin.

"What of the others?"

"What has become of my children?"

"My wife! My father! Have they killed them all?"

Positions along the front were abandoned now and by the hundreds, Jihad Moquades swarmed back to where the young woman was on display. She hid her face as Gerhardt pointed and shouted and worked the crowds of men into hysteria.

"The Jews! It is the Jews who have done this thing! She says they have butchered everyone in the village! Old men and women! Even children raped! The wife of Iman Tallan was murdered, then her child was ripped from her womb by a Jewish woman soldier!"

Men dropped to their knees and wept at the news. Others raised their fists to curse the beasts who had come to steal the land of Palestine.

At last Ram Kadar came, dirty and exhausted from a night of battle that had not yielded even one yard of Kastel to him and his Irregulars.

"Kadar! Allah be praised! Ram Kadar has come! He will know what is to be done!"

Kadar's teeth were clenched as he laid eyes on the sister of Yassar Tafara. He grabbed the robe from Gerhardt's hand and again laid it over her as she wept and heaved in the road. Then, he turned and struck Gerhardt hard in the face with the back of his hand. Silence fell on the soldiers as Gerhardt was hurled backward and fell on the ground.

"How dare you?" Kadar shouted. Then he turned to two men who flanked him. "Take her to my car. She is not an animal to be displayed thus! She is a cousin to the Mufti, a woman of Islam, and her disgrace becomes our own."

Gerhardt did not attempt to rise. For a long moment he rubbed his chin thoughtfully and stared up at Kadar. At last he smiled as the girl was led away and Kadar stood panting with rage. "Did I not tell you, Kadar?"

Kadar turned on him with fury in his eyes. "You are an animal, Gerhardt—an animal who takes pleasure in this, for it proves that others are as evil as you are."

Hard steel glinted in Gerhardt's eyes. "No, Kadar. If I am evil, then you are a fool. For this action will condemn the Jews before the eyes of the world. Six million died unjustly?" He stood slowly and faced Kadar. "Will the outrage be any less over one small village? Over the rape of one Arab woman?" His smile returned. "They have proved what they will do to Palestine if there is statehood. No, Kadar. We must show this girl to everyone. We must cry out with rage that she alone has survived, beaten and raped by the beasts we seek to drive from our homeland. And when the world has seen her bruised body, they will rally to us and we shall have yet one more purpose—revenge!"

By the hundreds, Arab warriors withdrew from their positions around Kastel and retreated up the road toward Jerusalem. Moshe's men raised their rifles and shouted victoriously at the sight of their enemies' backs. At the top of the hill, from bullet-pocked outcroppings, the soldiers who had remained behind with Fergus stood slowly in wonder as the Arabs drifted away.

Unshaven and exhausted, Fergus Dugan staggered from the shelter of the old castle wall itself. He waved his arms wearily to where Moshe perched behind a rugged boulder on the hillside. Even after a full night of fighting, this was the first contact the two men had had.

Moshe waved back with less enthusiasm. He clutched the microphone of the radio with apprehension and listened to the final words of Bobby Milkin's grim report. "Yeah, the Arabs is leavin', but don't count on 'em to stay away. Not when they get a load of what's happening at Deir Yassin. They ain't leavin', pal. They're just takin' a little time off to go to a wake. They'll come to your funeral later. Over."

Moshe's mouth felt dry, but it was not for lack of water. He licked his lips. "Raven, did you catch a glimpse of Emile? Over."

"Not personally. But when I do, I'm gonna ram this control stick down his throat!" Milkin cursed loudly then. "You ain't gonna believe what that creep and them Irgun slime done down there, Staff! You ain't gonna believe it!" Another string of curses crackled over the receiver. "Hey, Staff. Gotta go. A couple of Limey planes headin' this way. Headin' over Deir Yassin. And when they see the mess, they're likely to shoot me down for the heck of it! Raven out!"

Moshe exhaled loudly and set down the receiver. Fergus was walking down the steep slope toward him as the two forces met and embraced and laughed with the joy of their reunion. Everywhere, stories of the attack on the convoy were repeated by Moshe's men and those who had served as convoy guards. From fifty yards away, the towering form of Ehud emerged from a ravine. His face was grim as he strode toward Moshe, reaching him at the same moment as Fergus.

"You're a sight fer sore eyes, lad!" Fergus cried, clapping Moshe on the back. "We thought y' had deserted us!"

"Got caught in the Arab pursuit up Bab el Wad. There wasn't time to get supplies from the trucks. Crossfire. The only choice was to join the convoy. . ."

"Or die!" Ehud finished.

"Well, I'm glad t' see y' make it. There's no problem with food. The Arabs eat well enough. But we're down to five rounds a man."

"Five!" Moshe exclaimed.

"Aye! They kept at us all day yesterday. An, y' know what it was like here last night! If they hadn't withdrawn, you'd have been fightin' alone, an that's the truth of it!"

"How many have we lost?" Moshe asked.

"Three dead. Enough. And seventeen wounded. We'll have t' get them out somehow. My lads are needin' a rest. It's not let up at all."

Moshe stared at the distant cloud of dust stirred by the retreat of the Irregulars. "You'd better get out now. They'll be back. That is certain. Twice as strong as before."

"Where is Emile?" Ehud growled. His eyes narrowed as he caught an ominous tone in Moshe's voice. "Where is that—"

"I don't think he's coming. He . . . he made another conquest on the way to Kastel."

"Why, that—!" Ehud spat on the ground. "May God turn him to salt! May he be cast into the Dead Sea and sink!" He lowered his chin like a bull ready to charge. "Where has he gone?" he demanded in a voice so loud that the happy greetings on the hillside dropped to silence. All eyes turned to the trio. Somewhere a meadowlark sang and the wind sent a hushed whisper over the new grass.

Moshe opened his mouth as if to speak, but the breeze carried on it a name that echoed back from the warriors of Ram Kadar.

"Deir Yassin! Deir Yassin! Deir Yassin!"

24 Dragon on Mount Scopus

Rachel's dreams of Moshe were so vivid and real that she found herself resenting the first light of morning as it filtered through the window. The smell of coffee drifted up the stairs, but still she did not open her eyes. Instead, she imagined that he was still there beside her as he had been last night; that she had only to reach out her hand to touch his head on the pillow. And so she clung to her dreams in the drowsy warmth of the blankets, and resisted any movement that would bring her to the reality of yet another day without him.

But at last dread and disappointment came in a sickening wave that screamed to her senses, *He is gone! No arms to hold you. No Moshe to smile into your eyes or whisper sweet words against your cheek! He is gone. Gone to battle and Kastel!* She opened her eyes to the emptiness of the bed and the room. There was no sign that he had even been there last night. She reached her hand out and laid it on the pillow. *Perhaps I have dreamed this also. Was he here? And did I tell him of our child?*

With difficulty, she attempted to reconstruct the torrent of events of the last few days and hours. Again her mind replayed the kindness of Yehudit Akiva, the arrival of Captain Stewart to take her back to the prison of her father's house in the Old City, the accusations of Stewart, and the broken heart of little Yacov when he had realized what survival had meant for her. *How he wept for me! And for us all. Grandfather, too. And now there are no secrets left to fear. They know everything and will not turn away from me as Rabbi Akiva and the members of the council did.*

She sat up and clasped her hands around her knees as she looked at the door. Again she saw the tall, lean figure of Moshe as he flung the door open and stretched out his arms to her. *It was not a dream.* She smiled as his image returned clear. It was as though every movement and word had been etched in her mind. Words and whispers; a touch to never be forgotten or erased; the sensation of his hand against her skin. More real than any other memory. Crowding out all other thoughts. *It was not a dream! He came to me last night. He was here with me, and he touched our child.*

She felt weak at the thought of him. How she longed to lay her head against his chest! He was right: those few hours had not been enough. For an instant she wondered if she should have begged him to stay with her, never to leave again, to let others fight and die. *Kastel! Oh God, watch over him. Watch over him, please. When I was very young I believed that good men would not be cut down with the wicked. I cannot believe that anymore. And so I can only ask you, God. Watch over him. Bring him home to me!*

Then another image pressed against her—the image of other men standing in fields green with spring and sprinkled with flowers. Each man wore the yellow Star of David sewn on his coat. *Like a flower in their lapels. The Star over their hearts. And before them were the trenches. The graves. Filled high with those who had gone before. And the birds had sung even as the guns fired and the Stars fell into the pits. Oh, God! Don't let Kastel be like Poland!*

The face of Moshe was suddenly clear before her, standing among those who faced the Nazi machine guns on the other side of the mass graves. She shuddered and shook her head to force the image from her mind. Resolutely resisting the horrors of her memory, she climbed from bed and began to dress.

"That is why Moshe has gone to fight at Kastel," she whispered as she filled a basin of water. "So there will never again be good men who stand at the edge of the pit. You know this better than I do, Lord. And though I know that good men often fall to the strength of the wicked, still, I ask that you will bring him back to me safely."

———

Rachel heard the soft, insistent words of the radio newscaster before she even stepped into the kitchen. Howard sat at the table with a cup of coffee in his hands. He did not look up as she entered.

Shortly after midnight, troops of the Jewish Haganah attempted to break through Arab forces positioned around the perimeter of the village of Kastel. There has been no word of casualties; however, the Arab High Committee confidently says that they expect Kastel to be back in Arab control by nightfall. Mean-

while, volunteers to the effort of Arab Palestinians are flocking to the aid of the Irregulars now attacking in the Pass of Bab el Wad. . . .

Furrowing his brow, Howard reached forward to tune in yet another broadcast. Startled by Rachel's quiet presence, he switched the radio off instead.

"I didn't see you there," he said solemnly.

"I have only just come down." She tried to smile, glancing at the sink piled high with dishes. "I smelled the coffee. I see I have some cleaning up to do."

"Forget it," Howard said. "It will give Yacov and me something to do later while you're at Hadassah with the baby. The others aren't up yet. There's another clean cup there. Pour yourself some coffee."

Rachel ignored him and filled the kettle to heat water for washing. She needed to keep busy this morning. Her mind fought to return to the grassy field in Poland. "So what is the word from Kastel?" she asked, not looking at Howard.

"Oh, you know. Propaganda. The Arabs are already claiming a great victory. The British are staying totally out of this one. The BBC will report the news on both sides, and I don't think our side has had much to say about the action. Kastel is holding so far; I think there is a good chance—"

"Please, Professor, I would also like news. Do not turn it off because I have come into the room."

Reluctantly, he turned on the radio again, then grabbed a towel to dry the dishes.

The several thousand Jewish infantry men who attacked Ramle two nights ago—

"Ha! Several thousand! That's good. Let them think that!" Howard cheered as though he were listening to a football game.

British authorities have managed to arrest a small number of those who participated in the diversionary attack; however, government sources say that the majority of the army has—

"Melted into the woodwork! That's what!" he said with satisfaction. "They even reported that American Jewish paratroopers had landed outside of Ramle, and that's why the Arab Irregulars had such a time. No word on Luke Thomas or his fellows, though. Ehud told me that the captain had done a marvelous job in Ramle. He thinks probably that Luke will hide out in Galilee. They are training fellows on a kibbutz up there."

"That is good," Rachel replied, her heart feeling lighter with Howard's optimistic chatter.

"They'll need good leaders up there. The Syrians are as mad as hornets, and I heard yesterday that Haj Amin Husseini is planning on making the village of Safed his capital until Jerusalem is taken from the Jews."

Jerusalem itself was quiet last night with only a few minor disturbances interrupting the Jewish celebration of Passover. It was estimated that the food brought from Tel Aviv in the daring push up Bab el Wad will feed Jewish Jerusalem for...

"They make no mention of the weapons David Meyer brought from America." Rachel carefully washed a fine china plate and handed it to Howard.

"That is yesterday's news. The photo of the wrecked cargo plane was in international newspapers yesterday. David Meyer is being sought for questioning; I wouldn't want to be in that young fella's shoes right now. Although I would imagine that Ellie has him tucked safely away right now out of harm's way."

Rachel smiled wistfully. "Yes. I think from what Moshe told me last night that she will not leave David's side for a long time. I can understand such devotion." She gazed out the window to a bright blue patch of morning sky. She wondered if Moshe was seeing it as she did now, if his thoughts flew toward her as hers were directed toward him.

Howard cleared his throat self-consciously and did not reply to her words. "Well," he said, stacking the plates, "I suppose you will want to be first up Mount Scopus and through the doors of Hadassah."

"Of course. But I do not wish to impose if you have other plans this morning."

"No, I rather fancy a drive through Sheik Jarra with the British convoy." He glanced at the clock above the table. "First convoy will leave at eight o'clock. I will be happy to drive you. We were the last to leave last night, and if we hurry we can be the first to arrive this morning."

Relieved, Rachel finished the dishes with a new enthusiasm. She knew that Tikvah had most likely been awake for a full two hours. Her arms ached to hold her; her heart yearned for the sweet comfort of the child's cheek against her own. Somehow, the thought of Tikvah pushed all her doubts and anxiety into the background.

The Jewish Agency reports that rationing coupons will be available in the following locations . . .

"There," Howard said in a matter-of-fact tone. "I can drop you off and do the shopping. Had I known what an enjoyable pastime it was to run a house, I might have retired from the school years ago and simply—"

We interrupt this program to bring a special bulletin. The serious tone of the newscaster brought Howard's lighthearted banter to an end. A sense of dread filled Rachel. Her hand poised above the warm water; she listened to news of yet another flower-strewn field where cries of mercy had gone unheeded. *It is not known the extent of the atrocities committed by Jewish terrorists in the village. A young survivor, reported to be a cousin of the Mufti, has said that rape and mutilation were widespread . . .*

"My God!" Howard backed into a chair and sat down slowly. "How can this be? There must be some mistake!"

There has been definite confirmation of the reports of the massacre. British officials have indicated that the incident will be thoroughly investigated, and perpetrators will be apprehended . . .

Rachel did not move from the sink, but fixed her eyes on the tiny patch of blue sky where a pair of sparrows darted and soared above the earth. "Jews could not do such a thing," she whispered. "It is not possible. Not possible. It must be Arabs who have done this. We could not do this to another. Not knowing ourselves what it means . . ." Again, long lines of people wearing the Star stepped to the edge of the pit. Only now, as she closed her eyes, she saw the faces of women and children. Across from them stood men in black uniforms. Bolts of lightning glistened on their collars. *The S.S.! Even women they killed without second thought. Women holding babies. Babies like Tikvah! But they were Nazi S.S., not Jews! Jews could not—would not!*

Howard moaned as the report continued. *British reconnaissance planes passing directly over the area have reported a large number of Arab civilian bodies lying in the streets. At this time, British military forces have been called to disband the groups of Jewish terrorists who have taken possession of the houses in the village. Resistance is expected to be fierce. . . .*

"We are Jews!" Rachel cried, putting her hands to her face to shut out the picture that taunted her. *Men in black. Smiling and laughing as they shot the children before their mothers. Men in black with guns of their own. And the Star of David stitched to their uniforms. . . .*

———

Ellie felt no pain. She opened her eyes to the worried, dripping face of David as he knelt over her on the beach. Someone was moaning, and the sound of the waves crashing on the shore reminded her instantly of where they were. She tried to sit up, but David held her gently on the sand.

"Give yourself a minute," he said as she coughed. "You swallowed half the Adriatic, I think."

Indeed, the sky spun around her and she closed her eyes. "The others. . . ?" she asked, coughing again.

"Bernie's okay. Good thing he was along—" A low moan sounded again. "Mikhail's pretty busted up; broke both arms—bad. But we're alive, Els." He touched her on the forehead and exhaled with relief. "Do you hurt anywhere, hon?"

She opened one eye and gave him a half smile. "Not yet. It's always worse the second day, they tell me."

"Well, the Stinson has had it." He looked to the half-submerged wreckage that undulated with the swells fifty yards out from shore. "We're lucky . . . more than luck, I'd say."

"Where are we?" she asked, turning her head slightly to see Mikhail lying on his back with both arms across his chest. His hands were frozen in claws of agony. Bernie Greene leaned over him, concealing his face.

"I don't know exactly," David frowned. "Somewhere on the coast of Italy."

"What about Mikhail?" She swallowed hard and took David's hand to pull herself tentatively into a sitting position.

"Easy—" He supported her. "Since you're okay, I'm going to hike over the dunes and see if I can find a road, find out where we are. Get some help."

"Mikhail looks bad." Ellie rested her head on her knees and waited until the spinning slowed and stopped.

"Yeah." Then David called to Bernie, "Cover him up with dry sand, Bernie. Keep him warm, or he'll go into shock."

Bernie looked grim as he scooped sand over Mikhail like a blanket. "He is already in shock, I'm afraid. You'd better fetch help . . ." He glanced at Ellie. "Glad to see you awake. Had us

259

worried a bit." Then he added, "Bad luck about the plane." His condolences were sincere; surviving the ordeal had seemed to help dissolve the hostility between him and David.

"Yeah." David looked down and muttered. "The *Trina* must be halfway to the Mufti by now."

Ellie touched him lightly on the arm. "David, you did your best."

"Wasn't quite enough this time, was it?" he smiled sadly. "This was supposed to be easy. Now we got no bomb, no plane, no ship. My best wasn't enough."

"Look on the bright side . . ." She wanted him to be grateful that they were alive and still had each other.

"The bright side, huh?" He stood and brushed himself off. "Yeah. Two Haganah planes wrecked within a couple days. Maybe the Old Man will fire me, and we won't have to worry about this mess anymore." He forced a grin.

"I guess it's possible," she replied. "Then we could go home; I'll set up a photography studio and you—"

"I could always sell life insurance. God knows I'm convinced we all need it." David was grateful for Ellie's attempt at humor. It was a much needed counterpoint to his misery. He bent to kiss her. "I'll get back as soon as I can. Don't go anywhere."

"I promise."

The rain began again, almost as soon as David's head disappeared over the first sand dune. The deluge pummeled them with cold drops that seemed to pierce their already drenched clothes. Ellie's teeth chattered as she stumbled across the beach to where Bernie waited with Mikhail. A hard wind blew in from the sea and the tail of the Stinson bobbed and waved a final farewell as it sank out of sight.

"Maybe we should move behind the dunes!" Ellie shouted to Bernie above the din. "At least we would be out of the wind."

Bernie nodded and carefully explained to Mikhail, who cried out as they brushed away the sand and helped him to his feet. They could not support him by holding his arms, so Ellie slipped an arm around his waist and held tightly to his belt while Bernie did the same on his other side.

Every step across the sand was agony for Mikhail. He raised his face and shouted into the rain; then his eyes rolled back and he collapsed in a heap just short of their goal.

"Out cold," said Bernie, surveying him with pity. "Merciful. You think you can help me carry him?"

Ellie nodded, wordlessly straightening Mikhail's long legs. "Please," she said, looking at the swollen arms. "I can manage this end if you'll carry him by the shoulders. If I drop something, I'd rather it not be one of the broken parts."

They hoisted him up and staggered up the face of the dune, then slipped carefully down the other side. Immediately the howling wind was blocked and they sat down in weary silence to wait. The roaring surf sounded distant, almost peaceful.

Ellie held her hand over Mikhail's face to protect him from the pelting rain as Bernie covered him with sand that was somewhat drier and warmer than that on the beach.

Above them, two sea gulls circled and swooped in the air currents. The wind caught them, and held them almost still in the sky. Ellie lay back on the sand and closed her eyes for a moment, feeling relief from the roar of the biting wind, and then almost miraculously, she slept.

A perverse expression of satisfaction marked the face of Fredrich Gerhardt as he sat in the battered jeep behind Ram Kadar. The young sister of Yassar Tafara crouched trembling on the floorboard of the vehicle as thousands of voices echoed the chant: *Death to Jews!*

For now, this moment, the assault on the Jews that held Kastel had been abandoned. Many more Arabs would soon swell the ranks and return to defeat the butcher Jews: of that, Gerhardt was certain. Meanwhile, the jeep crept slowly up the road, hindered by the raging human tide that surrounded it. Ahead was the Jerusalem suburb of Sheik Jarra where grief-stricken citizens already swarmed in the streets.

Gerhardt tapped Kadar on the shoulder, and Kadar responded with a cursory glance. He did not look at the young woman who lay sobbing and trembling behind him. "You see," Gerhardt smiled, "did I not tell you what vermin we battle? Did I not tell you there is no such thing as a good Jew?"

Kadar did not reply. His eyes were riveted on the heights of Mount Scopus where the huge likeness of a seven-branched candlestick perched on Hadassah Hospital. He felt a wave of anger tighten in his belly. "It is as you have said," he responded at last. "We fight against wolves who would tear children from the wombs of their mothers and devour them. Yes, it is as you have said, Gerhardt."

Weapons were raised in open defiance. Men and women alike ran from their houses and the outcry grew.

"We shall turn this to our advantage," Gerhardt said, feeling as pleased as if he had arranged the demonstration himself. "No Jew will be left standing on the soil of Palestine."

"That has always been our goal," Kadar said.

Gerhardt gazed up at the commanding hill of Mount Scopus. The Romans themselves had recognized the importance of the mount. They had taken it, and then taken the city. Gerhardt would do the same. "Tonight we will recapture Kastel," he said with confidence. "Tomorrow we will take Hadassah. We will cut it off from the Jews as we cut off the head of an enemy! They think they have destroyed a village. But they have fed a dragon who will devour them without mercy."

———————

Great black clouds of smoke billowed up to bruise the skies above Jerusalem. Waves of grief and passion racked the city, and by midmorning the wails and shrieks had merged into one defiant cry—*Deir Yassin!* Riots exploded in every quarter, and sniping erupted from nearly every Arab rooftop. The British, reminded of their own losses at the hands of Jewish terrorists, sat back complacently and watched, unwilling to stem the tide of destruction and rage.

Even before Howard and Rachel reached the last Jewish barricade before the departure of the escort to Hadassah Hospital, Rachel was certain that passage was hopeless. "Tikvah!" she said wearily.

Howard did not reply: instead, his eyes fell on the nearly deserted streets of the Jewish district. Sensible Jews remained indoors today and listened with shocked disbelief to the reports that came from the demolished village of Deir Yassin. As they approached the barricade where Jewish guards crouched behind sandbags, Howard rolled down his window. "We are trying to get to Hadassah Hospital!" he shouted to a young man who did not rise up to come to the car.

"You and every other doctor in Jerusalem!" returned the young man as a companion pointed to yet anther spiral of smoke that rose to the north of the city. "No one is going to Hadassah today! No one! Not even someone who is sick! Not unless they want to die in Sheik Jarra! The British are even afraid to go up there in their armored cars!"

"But Tikvah! She will not do well if I am not there," Rachel said quietly.

"This woman has a child at Hadassah," Howard called. "Are you sure the British are not offering an escort?"

"Ha!" the man laughed sarcastically. "The English will offer a Jew an escort to the edge of a cliff today. Nothing else!"

Rachel felt ill. "Professor, will the Arabs attack the hospital itself? Will Tikvah be safe up there?"

Howard tapped his fingers nervously on the steering wheel. The thought had occurred to him as well. Mount Scopus and Hadassah Hospital were totally surrounded by Arab districts. This was high ground that was certainly coveted by the Arab High Committee and the Jihad Moquades who claimed that they would soon take all of the city in the name of Arab Palestine. Howard shook his head from side to side. "Honestly, Rachel, I cannot answer that question." He looked up at the pillars of smoke. "I don't know what defenses we have up there."

"Please!" Her voice sounded like that of a frightened little girl as her thoughts swirled around the helpless child at Hadassah. Jews had not spared the children of Deir Yassin, and now she was certain that the Arabs would not spare Jewish children. "Please, will you ask this fellow if we have soldiers at the hospital who will defend?"

Howard nodded curtly. "What kind of defense do we have on Scopus?" he asked the guard who still stared with rapt attention at the spreading black haze that darkened the sun.

"Not enough, I can tell you!" The man's tone was grim. "Not enough anywhere."

The man's eyes flickered resentment. "If you want to try it, go ahead. Be my guest. Otherwise, unless you want to be shot to pieces, *go home*! Try again tomorrow. That's all I can say." He lowered his voice as a distant cry seemed to swell out of the earth itself.

Deir Yassin! Deir Yassin!

"Tomorrow," Howard sighed, disgusted. He reached out and put a hand on Rachel's arm. She was trembling all over.

Death to Jews! Deir Yassin! Death to Jews! Deir Yassin!

263

"My baby!" Rachel laid her head back against the seat. "My baby!" She squeezed her eyes shut, trying to close out the darkness that swept over the Holy City with the wind.

25 Sanctuary

With an aged Italian farmer in tow, David returned to the beach as the pelting rain slowed to a drizzle.

"Near as I can make out, we're about five kilometers from a little town called Bari," David informed the trio. "This guy doesn't speak English, but he's got a truck and he understands American money." David patted his flight jacket. "Thank goodness for map pockets. The stuff is soggy, but it still spends."

Now conscious, Mikhail gasped with pain as he staggered to his feet and began to stumble back toward the road. David supported him as Ellie had, and Mikhail grimaced and bit his lip to keep from crying out. He muttered something to Bernie, who translated.

"He says he thinks his arms are broken."

"Hmmm," David agreed, looking at Mikhail's grotesquely swollen limbs. "Yeah. I'd say he won't be untying his shoes for a while."

"Pity you did not save a bit of that morphine you pumped into me," Bernie muttered. "While he was unconscious I had a bit of a look at his arms. The left forearm is worst. Bone is nearly pushed through the skin. We will have to be quite careful with him on the way to the hospital."

Ellie paled at the revelation of Mikhail's injury as she looked at his ashen face. He walked with his eyes shut, as though darkness would shut out the pain. He made no sound as they reached an ancient flatbed farm truck loaded over the top of the cab with chickens crammed in wooden crates. There was no glass in the windows of the vehicle, and the door on the passenger side was missing.

The men helped Mikhail slide in. He laid his head back against the torn upholstery. His teeth were clenched and his arms lay bent and helpless on his lap.

"Ellie," David instructed, "you ride up front with him. Bernie and I will ride back here with the chickens." As the farmer protested loudly, David and Bernie unloaded enough crates to give themselves room on the flatbed. David waved another bill beneath the nose of the farmer and instantly his squawking ceased.

"Gracia! Multi gracia!" The exultant farmer jumped into the cab of his decrepit truck and it lurched and fumed down the one-lane road toward Bari Harbor. The farmer seemed oblivious to Mikhail's agony; he smiled as he sang an aria from *The Barber of Seville*.

Ellie kept a hand gently on Mikhail's shoulder. She winced with him whenever they hit a particularly jarring bump. Feathers flew; the constant clucking of the chickens, along with the warbling tenor of their host, set her nerves on edge. She tried not to look at Mikhail's claw-like hands or the pained expression on his face. Feeling impatient and irritable, she reached across and tapped the farmer on his arm. He looked startled and somewhat offended when she put a finger to her lips as a request for silence. Somehow, it seemed inhumane for anyone to sing so joyfully when another was in such pain. Occasionally she glanced back, but she could not see David in the cloud of swirling feathers. She did, however, have a clear view of the coastline, and mile after mile told herself how truly fortunate they had been to find even a fragment of beach where they were not beaten to death by mammoth waves pounding against the rocks and shore.

As they neared Bari, the gale seemed to find new fury. It howled into the cab and drenched chickens and passengers alike. The old truck crept through the narrow lanes of the port town. Evidence of bombing was seen here, too. Ragged children peered out from pitiful hovels constructed of cargo crates and pieces of metal from burned-out vehicles. As in Yugoslavia, dripping political banners swayed in the wind. Here and there an occasional pedestrian scurried along the street, but Bari seemed to have gone into its shell as the storm raged anew.

The chicken farmer shook his head from side to side in disgust, then shook his fist at the unrelenting sky. He cursed loudly in Italian as the rain beat harder in response. If the man had intended to sell his chickens at the market today, he was certainly bound to be disappointed.

"Hospital!" Ellie said loudly. Then she repeated the word several more times. "Hospital pronto."

"Si! Si!" The farmer guided the truck past a weathered stone cathedral, then turned up a side street so narrow that Ellie could reach out and touch the stone faces of the buildings. After what seemed an interminable drive through stinking alleys, past tenements and shacks, at last they pulled into the rear loading dock of a large stone building. The farmer jumped out of the truck and ran to the heavy wooden door. He knocked hard; then the door opened slightly and a round-faced man peeked out. Two skinny young boys in white aprons hurried out to begin unloading the crates of chickens. Angry at the delay, Ellie watched as David jumped onto the dock and grabbed the farmer by his shirt front.

"You were supposed to take us to the hospital first!" he shouted as the man quaked and his toes barely touched the dock. "The *hospital*! Can't you see you've got an injured man in there?"

Arms laden with crates, one of the boys looked up at David with wide brown eyes. "You American?" he asked in clear but accented English.

David let the farmer down easy. "Yeah. You speak English?"

"Okay. Hot dog! Wow!" The boy displayed his vocabulary. "Si. Yes. I speaka some English."

"Then tell this guy he was paid to take us to the hospital."

"Si. Okay." The boy rattled off David's instructions and the angry farmer flared and straightened his coat in the rain as he replied.

"What did he say?"

"He say . . . you stupid idiot American. He bringa you to the hospital an' you standa here ina da rain and shout . . ."

David wiped the water from his face and peered at the boy. "Where are we?" he asked.

The boy laughed. "You know any place else need so much chicken soup? He bring you to *Our Lady of Mercy*. He tell Mario to bringa da Sisters out to help you friend. They be here ina minute . . . Why you stan' here all wet ina rain? Go ina da hospital!"

Chagrined, David fished in his map pocket for another soggy American dollar, which brought a new smile onto the face of the old Italian farmer. At that instant, two black-clad nuns swooped out of the back door of Our Lady of Mercy Hospital. With tender sympathy they herded Mikhail through a kitchen filled with huge steaming kettles. With barely a pause, he was handed over to the merciful care of a tiny Italian doctor who set his bones, then gave him to a two-hundred-pound nun. With all the care of a Yiddish mama, she crooned and spoon-fed him hot chicken soup until he belched happily and lay back against clean white sheets to sleep.

Lured by the musty scent of David's damp dollar bills, the boy on the loading dock led David, Ellie, and Bernie back through the filthy streets of Bari Harbor to an aging hotel that seemed to list slightly to starboard. It overlooked the harbor, crowded with freighters waiting out the storm. The Bari Harbor Hotel teemed with sailors seeking both refuge from their crowded berths and the company of the women who used the hotel as their place of business.

By now, the deluge had nearly washed David and Ellie and Bernie clean of the salt and sand they had picked up at the beach. The storm showed no signs of calming. It was, the boy said, the worst storm of the season. And he informed them how lucky they were to have found a guide to the only hotel available near the hospital.

"I've seen worse." David stepped first into the seedy lobby, reeking of old furniture and cheap perfume.

As Ellie's eyes adjusted to the dim light, she spotted a half-dozen young women sprawled around the room. "Where have you seen worse?" There was no amusement in her voice.

Bernie blinked innocently. "Any old port in a storm, as they say, eh?"

"*Who* says that?" Ellie replied, noting a heavily made-up woman sitting on the lap of an old sailor in a dark corner of the room. "David," she whispered. "I don't think I want to stay here . . ."

"No place else, lady," their guide informed her. "Not close to da hospital. Maybe ona other sidea town, but not here. Okay?"

"Maybe we should call a taxi." David rubbed his nose and grimaced.

"You don' gonna find no taxi now. Streets all under water. You lucky to find dis place." His brown waif-like eyes gazed up at them in sincerity. "Maybe tomorrow da rain she stoppa. You crazy you go outta here now."

Grit chafed in Ellie's underwear. Her head and neck had begun to ache and the rain pounded harder against the window of the lobby as if to accent the boy's point. "Are you sure there's nowhere else close?" she asked the boy.

"Not so nice asa dis place, lady," he replied earnestly.

Ellie glanced at David. Both of them were exhausted, dirty, and resigned. Bernie was scanning a small group of five bored-looking women who sat against the far wall. One of them winked at Bernie while another crossed her legs and blew a long cloud of cigarette smoke toward David.

Ellie lifted her nose defensively; when she took David's arm, a disgruntled murmur rippled through the group of ladies of the Bari Harbor Hotel. "I didn't think women like that were out of bed before noon," Ellie muttered.

The boy replied loudly. "Naw. These ladies ain't beena to bed yet. Stilla few customers come in froma da ship."

"That does it!" Ellie snapped. "I am not staying here, David. If we have to sleep on a park bench—"

"Ina da rain, lady?" asked the boy.

"Yes. In the rain." Ellie turned her back on the laughter of the ladies in the lobby. "I mean it."

David shrugged and said to Bernie. "Sorry, pal. You're on your own."

Bernie rubbed his chin thoughtfully. "Not if *they* can help it . . . Well, boy," he looked at their guide. "How much for a single room with a bath?"

"Hey, Mama!" the boy shouted to a fat lady behind the counter. "I gotta one customer!"

Ellie led the way back out onto the narrow lane. Water overflowed the low curbs as it whooshed over the rubbish-strewn cobblestones toward the harbor. She breathed deeply and cleared her senses of the smell of the heavy perfume. David appeared moments later. He lifted his face to the pelting rain and the gray sky. "Where to?" he asked with a grin.

She drew herself up and glared. "*Where* have you seen worse?" she demanded.

"I was just trying to be polite to the kid." He raised his hands in surrender. "I didn't know his mama ran the joint. That's the worst I've *ever* seen—honest, Babe." He bent down and looked right into her outraged face. "That lobby had the biggest roaches I ever saw in my life." He grinned. "Poor old Bernie doesn't know what he's in for."

"All I want is a hot bath and a clean bed," she said firmly, walking upstream against the flow of water. "And maybe dry clothes, someday. And a night of uninterrupted sleep."

"You're talking about heaven, Els. That won't happen here on earth. I've given up on it. I'll settle for a roof to keep the rain off . . . and maybe some breakfast."

"I'd be afraid to eat in this neighborhood," Ellie said indignantly.

They rounded a corner and found themselves in a large, deserted square where every other street seemed to converge. An enormous cathedral took up an entire block facing the harbor, its spire almost obscured by the gray rain. Saints gazed down at them, and the massive door was ajar.

David took Ellie's hand. "Come on, Babe," he said quietly. "I know a place where the door is always open."

The huge nave of the church was totally deserted. Thick stone walls loomed up into shadowed vaults above them. The only light was that of dozens of red votive candles that flickered in niches before the statues of various saints stationed around the room. Shadows danced on a large crucifix on the wall behind the altar. The face of the Christ looked sadly down to row upon row of candles that blazed on a tiered table below the cross.

Where once stained-glass windows had graced high arches in the walls, now solid planks boarded up the opening, allowing only thin lines of persistent light to penetrate. The wind whistled loudly through imperceptible cracks. Water dripped noisily into several pans placed strategically around the room. Ellie wondered who was left in this vast, faded place who cared enough about leaking roofs and candles to take care of such details. She shuddered, as though they had stumbled into a graveyard crypt instead of a church. Her eyes riveted on the broken drying figure of Jesus. *Crown of thorns. Nails through hands bent like Mikhail's. Ribs protruding. Knees bent and feet rigid, supporting the weight of the body on spikes that impaled the flesh.* The shadows of the candles flickered on the body like bruises from the lash.

"David," she said after a moment. The strength of her own voice startled her. It jumped back from the vaults and she lowered her volume to a slight whisper. "David, let's go. I don't like it here." Indeed, the faded glory of the place gave her an eerie feeling—empty, as empty as the great hall itself.

"Go where?" he returned. "Listen to that." He jerked his thumb to where the wind shrieked through boarded-up windows. "There's no place to go unless you fancy communing with Our Ladies of the Bari Harbor Hotel. Quite a sisterhood in this neighborhood."

"It's so . . . cold . . . in here."

David put his arm around her and led her toward the cluster of candles. He held her hands over the warmth of their flames. "Your hands are cold; you're cold all over."

She pulled her hands away. "These candles aren't for warming hands. They're for prayers; people lit them to show they're praying for something."

David took her hands firmly in his and held them to the warmth again. "Somewhere, somebody must be praying for you right now that you are safe and warm. God heard the prayers already. I think He'd like us to get some practical use out of these candles. We've had a terrible night, after all."

She leaned her head against him. "I'll bet the windows in this church were really something," David said finally, his tone hushed as if he had glimpsed a brief vision of a long-vanished glory. His eyes met Ellie's. "At least it is still standing. And there are still people to come and fix it up. I heard—Michael told me—there's not one synagogue left as it was in Europe. And nobody left at all to come back and rebuild them." The momentary wonder left his eyes. "That's what Michael said . . ."

"He was wrong, David." Ellie put her warm hands on his cheeks. "They are going to be rebuilt—where they are meant to be, in Palestine—in Israel."

"Not unless we do something about that ship." He furrowed his brow. "I gotta get another plane somehow."

"What? In this weather? David, you have done everything you can do."

"Then we've got to get word. Bobby Milkin can fly out from Tel Aviv and maybe intercept—"

"Look, if we got caught in the storm, so did the ship."

"They left way before we did. Probably they hugged the coast of Yugoslavia all the way. Ducked into some little port if it got rough. We're in Italy now because this is the way the wind

270

was blowing. We didn't have a choice. They did. I'm afraid I fouled this one up good, Els."

"What could you have done differently?"

"For one thing, I should have never taken my eyes off that freighter. Not for a minute. I should have sat out on the balcony all night with binoculars in my hand."

"There were guns on the ship, David. Not pretty girls," Ellie teased, sitting down on the step. "And I needed you . . . to look at me." She felt suddenly exhausted. "David . . . I need you to look at me now. Just for a little bit. We haven't even had a proper honeymoon yet. Not to mention breakfast. And I need you to stop thinking . . . just for a while. I need you not to think about anything but us. Can we think about good things for a few minutes? I'm so tired." She laid her head down on her arms and said wistfully, "Last night in Ragusa was so beautiful. How could you want to look at a ship instead of me?"

Instantly remorseful, David sat down beside her and took her in his arms. "Just stupid, I guess. Stupid for even saying it. How were we supposed to know the *Trina* would sail twelve hours before it was scheduled . . . they sure weren't about to let us in on the secret." He held her close against him. "It's just that . . . I keep seeing Michael. Smiling and okay one minute and then . . . I just wish you weren't involved in this. I just wish . . ."

"We can't change that. Not any of it. I wish we could but we can't bring Michael back. Or the *Trina*. And the truth of it is, David, I don't want to change last night. That was you and me and for a while anyway I forgot about all this other stuff." She touched his cheek, guiding his lips to hers. "Make me forget . . . again."

He kissed her long and slow, silencing her complaint and his worry as they embraced in the soft glow of the candles by the altar. Gently, he pulled her back and they lay together, wordlessly gazing up into the darkened vaults of the ceiling. Slowly, gloomy shapes and shadows took the form of painted frescos above them.

"Look," David whispered.

"You see them too . . ." Ellie said after a long time of silence, "I'll bet they wished they were somewhere else too."

On the cracking plaster of the ceiling, a small fishing boat sailed through the stormy waters of Galilee. Ancient men raised their hands and voices in terror as a wave crashed across the bow. And all the while, Jesus slept . . .

"Look at their faces," David said. "Real men. Scared."

"Look at *His* face." Ellie pointed to the second panel where Jesus stretched His hands out and cried, "*Shalom! Peace!*" and the waves grew still. This mural, painted centuries before by some forgotten artist, spoke quietly of help in times of need, peace in times of fear.

"A little lesson of who's in charge, huh?" murmured David. He pulled Ellie to him, and she rested her head in the crook of his arm.

Outside the storm raged, while the sound of rain dripping into pots and kettles thumped out a pleasant melody of different notes and rhythms. Ellie smiled and closed her eyes to rest. Even the wind seemed to sing in tune. *Waves over the mast now. But we're asleep in the boat with Him.*

David's breathing became deep and regular as they slept, leaning together in the pew beneath the faded frescos. They did not hear the quiet footsteps of the man who had watched them from the alcove of Saint John. They did not see his eyes as he studied them and listened to their words.

———

The wounded Jews who had defended Kastel were loaded onto makeshift stretchers of blankets slung between antique rifles. Of the seventeen, nine were seriously injured. One young woman had been shot in the stomach, and Moshe doubted that she would survive the arduous trek back to Jerusalem.

Of all those haggard defenders, Sergeant Hamilton alone declined to leave. He crossed his arms across his massive chest and said firmly, "Your lads will need someone with a little experience to stick by. I've lived without sleep before, and I can do it again."

"Aye," agreed Fergus, extending his hand in farewell. "That's all a sergeant-major is good for. Any private will tell y' they never sleep."

The two men shook hands in silent understanding. "Another day and I'll be looking for a place to lay my head. An' don't you forget it."

Fergus directed his gaze at Moshe. His eyes were glazed with the exhaustion of the last days and hours. "We'll be back. Keep the rear door open for us, if y' will. Tomorrow morning, me an' the lads will be back."

Moshe nodded curtly. "They haven't left defeated, Fergus. And when they return, it will be with a firmer purpose. If the Arabs take this place again, I doubt they will be content to take prisoners alive."

Fergus cocked an eyebrow and replied, "Then y' must not let 'em take it. Aye, they'll be back. But you've a few hours now that we didn't have. Form a defense perimeter an' blow up the rest of the village. Your strongest points are the quarry an' the house of the muhqtar . . ."

"We're pretty firm in the quarry. I've taken the liberty of assigning a relief squad to the buildings."

The wounded were lifted by their weary comrades and one by one carried past where the three men stood. "They'll not try for the quarry." Fergus rubbed his hand over the back of his neck. "Concentrate your lads there"—he swept his hand toward the row of houses in the front of the village—"and a squad each on either side to the right and left flank. They'll come tonight, wailin' like banshees and all decked out in their head gear. The fools—they'll not take off their white sheets even when it makes 'em easy targets." His brow furrowed in thought. "The ones to beware of are the English deserters."

"Like us," grinned Ham.

"Aye." Fergus did not smile. "An' the Arabs have their share of them. They know what they're about. They're paid well to fight, and that is their chosen profession—to fight well. When they come up that slope after dark, you'll not spot them so easy as the Bedouins." Then he added, "Hold fast, lads. We'll be back. Good luck."

Fergus saluted smartly and turned about-face to march off at the head of his men. Ehud emerged from the house of the muhqtar at that moment and hailed Moshe from the doorway.

"I'd best get back to the boys in the quarry," Ham said, his voice betraying the same raw edge as that of his sleepless companions.

"Ham," Moshe offered as he strode away, "I'm glad you are staying. The fellows will gather courage from you."

The hefty sergeant did not reply. Moshe gazed at his retreating form and silently wondered what had driven such a man to sacrifice everything for a cause that was certainly not his own.

It was not money, like his countrymen who had been lured to the side of the Mufti with promise of great reward. Ham had served as a sergeant with Captain Luke Thomas throughout the war, and Moshe knew that it was not Luke's way to keep silent about his convictions. Perhaps Sergeant Hamilton also believed the promises. But was it reasonable for a man to give up his career and his nation for ancient promises made to a handful of Jews? *Only if the promise is fulfilled,* Moshe mused. *And that, as David Meyer would say, is what makes a horse race, eh, God? Again we are staking our lives on the belief that you can help us run faster than the chariots of Pharaoh. Or that you will open the Red Sea for us.*

"Moshe!" Ehud shouted from the street. "Come here!" His tone was impatient, even angry.

Moshe shook himself free from his thoughts and strode toward Ehud. The interior of the muhqtar's home was decorated simply with a few pieces of furniture and intricate oriental rugs on the floors. Two electric lamps glowed on a dark wooden sideboard, and as the only generator in the village rattled noisily in the background, a battered radio shrieked the gruesome news in Arabic. Moshe and Ehud understood each word distinctly as the Arab newscaster wept openly and raged as he read the brutal reports before him. His shrill voice no doubt echoed throughout the far corners and the poorest villages in Palestine, and each atrocity was reported in grisly and precise detail. *Infants smashed against a stone wall . . . ears severed . . . torture before death . . .*

Ehud looked pale. For the first time since Moshe had known him, he was sickened and revolted until he groped for a place to sit down. "These are not *Jews* who have done this thing, they are the Nazis reborn; they are not *men*; they are animals!"

Moshe put his hand over his mouth and squeezed his eyes tightly shut as the death of a pregnant Arab woman was described. Rachel loomed in his mind. *That could have been Rachel!* He fought not to believe what he was hearing. "Perhaps—" he faltered. "Propaganda."

Ehud's head snapped up and he glared at Moshe in fury. "If it is even *half* true, if only a tiny fraction—one child, one old woman, one rape, then we stand accused before the world! And justly! They have wiped the slate clean against everything they ever did to us. *To my wife!*" His booming voice cracked. "*To my children!* Emile and his beasts have made our cries for justice meaningless."

He is right. Oh, God! Moshe thought as the broadcast continued. *One woman. One child. Rachel!*

Ehud's words turned against Moshe in one final burst of anger. "If you had been there! If you had come with me when you should have, this would not have happened! They would have listened to you! They would not have let Emile go alone with his murdering friends! If you had been there. But no! You must stay with your woman one hour more, and so a whole village is massacred!"

"Shut up!" Moshe shouted, hurling the radio to the floor. It smashed in a shower of sparks, leaving a silence broken only by the chugging of the generator engine. "How could I have stopped it?"

"The men looked for you!" Ehud stood to his full height. "They looked to you for advice, and you stayed to—"

A fury rose up in Moshe. He stepped forward and for a moment clenched his fist and fought to restrain himself from striking Ehud. "I am one man! I cannot stop a Holocaust—Arab *or* Jewish! I am only one man! As you are."

"A learned man. And what am I? When I spoke, he mocked me. Commander of Sardines, he said! They would have listened to you! What am I?" He held out his scarred and calloused hands.

Moshe felt drained. He stared at Ehud. "You are a man—*still*, and he is an animal."

"And do we fight to make a home for such demons as this?" There were tears of doubt and disappointment in his eyes. His hands trembled. "What is the use? If we are no better than the worst, what is the use?"

The same aching question filled Moshe, and he backed away, leaning against a cold stone wall. He thought of the *Ave Maria* thumping through the waves toward the shores of forbidden Palestine, her decks and hold crammed with Jewish women and children, Captain Ehud Schiff at the helm. "How many children we brought to Palestine, Ehud? You and me and the *Ave Maria*, nu? We ran the blockades and outran the storms while they puked in buckets below. And now how many of those children—*our* children—are in Jerusalem?"

Ehud raised his eyes to meet his gaze. "Yes." His voice was

quiet. "Your own wife among them."

"And my child," Moshe answered.

"Little Tikvah." Ehud almost smiled.

"And there is another, Ehud." Moshe's words were gentle. "Rachel carries my child within her."

Astonishment filled Ehud's face. Without a smile he muttered, "I did not suspect."

"Nor did I."

"Mazel Tov, my friend . . . *Mazel Tov!*" There was concern on Ehud's face.

"If you can remember no other face from the deck of the *Ave Maria*, remember hers, Ehud. Do you know what the Arabs will do now? Since Deir Yassin? Do you realize what will be done to our women? Our children? To Rachel, if—" His words nearly choked him as he spoke.

"Enough!" Ehud shouted, grasping Moshe by the arm. "We must stop! It must stop! We must make a place where this cannot happen ever again—to anyone, *ever!*" His fingers dug into Moshe's flesh. "There is work to do now! We shall start here to end this brutal contest! *Here!*" With that, he turned away and walked into the bright sunlight of Kastel to shout orders to the men who remained to hold the rocky hillside for the sake of Jerusalem. For Rachel.

26   Confrontation

The storm outside raged even more fiercely, but there was something else that pulled David from his sleep. He felt the presence of someone long before he heard the rustle of the thick musty velvet of a curtain.

David did not open his eyes or move as Ellie snuggled closer against him. Soft and furtive, a footstep sounded against the stone floor. It moved quickly toward them; then a shadow crossed them as a man stepped between them and the candles.

"Well, I have seen a few gulls blown in on a day like this, but this is a first," said a deep American-accented voice. "*Americans!*"

Ellie woke with a start and cried out as she sat up. David opened his eyes and blinked up at the round, friendly face of a priest who grinned down at them.

"Oh!" Ellie looked around in embarrassed confusion. "I'm sorry; we didn't mean to—"

David sat up and ran a hand across his unshaven cheek. "Sorry, Padre. I thought you were someone else," he said with relief.

"Who else would I be?" he asked.

"Hey!" Ellie said. "You speak English!"

"I also speak Italian and Latin if you like . . ." He cleared his throat. "Whichever you prefer. *Fiat voluntas Tua* . . . or as our Protestant brethren say, Thy will be done, eh?"

Suddenly weary, David stood, towering over the tiny, rotund priest, who seemed to be not more than five foot two inches in height. "How'd you know we're Americans?" David asked, helping Ellie to her feet.

"A lucky guess. Your flight jacket, friend. *Fons et origo* . . . Look to the origin . . . that *is* American, is it not?"

"Well, yes . . ."

"Of course. I suppose I have seen ten thousand of those same jackets," continued the priest. "I was a chaplain with the Fifteenth Air Force during the war. Yes. Right down south of here in Foggia."

A sense of relief filled David. "Yeah? You don't say? You were with that mob, huh?"

"Mob? *Fronti nulla fides* . . . never judge a book by its cover." The priest smiled slightly and his eyes narrowed as he looked closely at David. For a moment he seemed as though he wanted to say more, but he did not and there was a pause of awkward silence as David looked away self-consciously from his gaze.

It suddenly occurred to both David and Ellie that this American priest might have connections that would not be helpful to them now. "The Fifteenth . . ." David stumbled for small talk. "Rough flying over the Alps into Germany."

"*Fortuna favet fortibus,*" he replied with a smile.

Ellie found his habit of speaking Latin somewhat irritating. She nodded without comprehension as David searched his memory for the translation. "That is uh . . . fortune . . . *favet* . . . favors uh *forti* . . ."

"Fortune favors the brave." The priest nodded with satisfaction. "Very good. Yes. The fellows of the Fifteenth were very brave . . . a mob, perhaps, but very brave." He extended his hand to David. "I am Father John Antonell," he nodded curtly. "And you are?"

"Uh, David . . . Miller. And my wife Ellie. Ellie Miller."

"Very pleased to meet other Americans so far from home. Very pleased, indeed." His eyes twinkled with delight as he observed their matted hair and damp, sandy clothing. "Your friend at Our Lady of Mercy is doing quite well, the Sisters tell me. I was curious where you might show up." He looked around the auditorium. "Wasn't there another in your company? An Englishman?"

David was taken aback by the knowledge Father John seemed to have about them. "We left him at the hotel; some kid took us to a hotel—well, not a hotel exactly—"

"A home for wayward girls? Who happen to be still wayward?" Father John stuck out his chin and nodded knowingly. "You were wise not to stay. The least you can catch there is fleas. Quite a hotel. Several of the single working mothers of my parish frequent it. It is no place to go if you need a good meal and a night's sleep."

Ellie blushed and David laughed out loud, his laughter bouncing irreverently from the roof of the church. He liked this priest. He might speak Latin, but he translated like a Fifteenth Airforce Captain. "And where might we find a meal and a clean bed, Padre?"

"Only last night I was praying for a bit of American conversation. My own home is quite roomy; I have several extra beds. And my cook is *nulli secundus*. I would be honored to entertain you, since you have chosen our poor parish as a place to land, however unwillingly." He searched Ellie's face again and his smile faded. "What did you say your first name is?"

"Ellie," she replied, looking briefly at David. He shifted his weight nervously as the priest frowned an instant, then looked curiously at David again.

"The Sisters say your plane wrecked just off the coast."

"We were blown off course."

"And where were you going?" He had forgotten his invitation now as his curiosity sparked and blazed.

"We were in Ragusa. Dubrovnik, they call it now. On our honeymoon."

Father John nodded. "A lovely place, Yugoslavia."

He pressed his lips tightly together in thought, then rubbed his hands together briskly. "*Amantes sunt amentes*," he muttered, not bothering to explain that he had just quoted Shakespeare's observation that *Lovers are lunatics.* "With that in mind, perhaps I should feed you two, eh?"

He crossed himself and led the way out the side door and through an ancient cemetery that bordered the rectory on the north.

The wind whipped at his black cassock, and strands of hair, carefully combed over his balding pate, stood on end. Ellie shuddered with a fresh chill as they passed through a tall wooden gate in a high, thick wall.

The garden of the rectory was overgrown with weeds and thick, tangled vines. Only one small corner was cleaned and cultivated. A pile of dead leaves was blown across the broken bricks of a patio. The walls of the house itself were marred with the tracks of ivy vines that had been pulled from their anchors.

Father Antonell tugged at the swollen door and stepped aside to let his guests pass into a bright, freshly painted foyer stacked high with shipping crates.

"You must excuse the mess." The little priest looked flushed from the cold as he slammed the door against the torrential downpour. He stamped his feet on the red tiled floor. "The rectory fell into sad disrepair, I'm afraid, during the war. I decided to start repairs on the inside. Fresh paint. A little plaster. A lot of soap." He paused and gestured toward the crates. "These boxes have just come from back home. Clothing for the children."

"Children?"

"Yes, from the orphanage . . . no doubt there will be men's clothes and women's as well in there. They may be a bit out-of-date, but no one will object if the castaways borrow a few castoffs." His bright blue eyes twinkled in the light and he spread his hands in gracious invitation. "You are welcome to whatever you can find." He reached into a scarred umbrella stand and handed a crowbar to David. "And you, young lady." He directed his gaze to Ellie. "You look as though you could use a good soak in a hot tub."

Ellie nodded mutely as David pried up the lid of a large wooden crate. It was packed with a jumble of trousers and smelled of mothballs. Yet the thought of dry clothes seemed next to heaven to Ellie. "Everything went down with the ship," she said, searching through the box for something close to her size.

"Usually the stuff we get deserves that fate," said Father Antonell. "But the Sisters are miracle workers with the material. We can wash your own clothing for you in the meantime." He frowned and pursed his lips as he examined David's flight jacket. "Your jacket will not be quite so soft when it dries out."

"That's okay." David triumphantly pulled out a pair of blue wool trousers, nineteen-thirties vintage. "I've had a couple of dunks in the Channel before. A little saddle soap and it'll be fine."

Ellie held a pair of boy's trousers up to her waist. They were brown tweed and looked as though they might iron out to a decent pair of slacks.

"I'll have Sophia draw your bath and press those for you," the priest said. He tapped the lid of a second crate. "This one is labeled shirts and sweaters. Help yourself."

With the enthusiasm of a shopper during a sale at Macy's, Ellie rummaged through the crates as Father Antonell slipped away to arrange for a hot breakfast and a room with a view.

———————

The upstairs bedroom was comfortably furnished in dark burled walnut that contrasted sharply with the stark white walls. The only adornment was a crucifix over the head of the bed. French doors opened onto a small, weathered balcony that overlooked the neglected garden. Beyond that, David had a clear view of the harbor.

As Ellie bathed in a small metal tub of steaming water, David gazed out at the ships. Even in the safety of Bari Harbor they bobbed as great swells crashed in lacy lines of spray against the seawall.

"We can hope the *Trina* has gone down without our help," he said softly. "But I need to get word to the Mossad in Rome somehow. They can relay the message of what happened to us."

"Maybe the priest—Father Antonell—can help."

David shook his head. "We don't dare tell him what we're doing here. The guy's an American. One word to the American Embassy or anyone in the military—and I'm going to end up in

280

jail. I just landed an illegal cargo of weapons in Palestine, remember? The British have passed the word along to the Americans. I'm a wanted man, Ellie. Wanted even by my own government."

"But he's a priest—priests are supposed to be trustworthy. Besides, they're sworn to maintain secrecy about things they are told."

"You mean the privacy of the confessional? Maybe, Els, but it doesn't work that way for us. We're just going to have to figure out what to do on our own. If the storm lets up, maybe I can hitch a ride to Rome tonight. If I can make it to Mossad headquarters—"

"You know where that is?"

"Sure. Michael and I were there a few months ago, before we bought the fighters in Prague. We met Avriel there . . ." He frowned at the thought of Avriel. "That guy. What I wouldn't give to talk to him right now. He's in the middle of everything . . . knows everything and everybody who can be trusted. Me? What am I but an airplane jockey? And I've lost my plane, to boot."

"David, if you're going to Rome, I want to come too."

He turned to face her. "You can't. And this time I mean no, Els."

"But David—"

"Listen to me. You've got to stay here; tell the Father that I'm sick or something. If he wakes up tomorrow morning and we're both gone, he's going to get real curious and start nosing around. You want to end up in an Italian prison? Maybe jeopardize the whole operation here in Italy too?"

"He's going to get suspicious if you don't come down and I don't let anyone see you. He's a bright man. Did you see the way he looked at us? It's not that he *knows* anything. It's more like he *feels* it."

"Yeah. He's sharp, all right." David ran his fingers through his hair. "I don't know. You're just going to have to stall. I can leave tonight. Maybe get back tomorrow night. You need to stall him. One day is all, and I'll get word to someone who can do something about this mess."

The smell of cooking food drifted up the stairs and into their bedroom. "David, I don't know if I can do this alone."

"Just one minute at a time, Babe," he said. "Remember the disciples in Jesus' boat. Remember who's in charge."

The brown tweed slacks pressed out nicely and seemed almost stylish with the dark brown sweater Ellie had found at the bottom of the second crate. Although she smelled of mothballs, she was comfortable and satisfied for the first time in hours. She wore men's boxer shorts and her socks needed darning, but David had discovered a nearly new pair of boys' Wellingtons that miraculously fit her feet perfectly. David was wearing the blue wool trousers and a black turtleneck with a small hole in the elbow. Father Antonell had managed to find a jacket that nearly fit him. There were no shoes large enough, however, and so he sat at the table in Father Antonell's dining room in his stocking feet.

Fresh black coffee steamed in their cups and heaps of rolls overflowed the basket. David had devoured a huge plate of eggs and sausage and was beginning on his second as Father Antonell looked happily out the window toward the stormy harbor and talked.

". . . and so after the war I had a look around. It is incredible how these people have suffered under the hand of tyrants. The world has been turned upside down. So I went home like everyone else, and I was offered a little parish in central California not too far from my family. But I have family here in Italy, too. My father was born not far from here. Anyway, I couldn't forget this place. Americans have it easy. I couldn't forget the children. So I came back. The language is no problem. I grew up with Italian at home and English spoken in school. The parish here in the heart of Bari's worst slum district was left without a shepherd after Father Guimarra died. Within a few weeks my application was accepted, and . . . here I am . . . *stillicidi casus lapidem cavat*, as they say, *dripping water hollows out a stone*, eh. A little bit at a time we are making progress."

He directed a steady gaze at Ellie. "And that is how this expatriate came to be here. You still have not explained your choice of Yugoslavia for a honeymoon. You are from California, aren't you?"

Astonished at Father Antonell's ability to guess, Ellie chose her words very carefully. "I was with an archeological dig, as a photographer. David and I had known each other in the States."

The priest smiled. "And you decided to follow her, eh, Mr. Miller?"

282

His mouth full of sausage, David nodded. "Hmmm."

Father Antonell frowned. "What were you doing with passengers, you being on your honeymoon?"

"We . . . uh . . . thought we might be going to Rome. A few extra dollars, you know," David said. Then he snapped his fingers. "I'd like to let Bernie Greene know we're here. Have you got a phone, Padre?"

"All the lines are down, I'm afraid. Telegraph as well, in case you had someone you might wish to contact out of the region. I can send one of the boys down to the hotel after lunch, if you like. Most of them have mothers who work there. More than half of the lads are products of our American forces here."

"That's what I was saying about that Fifteenth Air Force," David teased, but Father Antonell did not laugh.

The priest wiped his mouth and folded his napkin. Questions still filled his eyes. "As for Mikhail, the fellow at the hospital—" he returned to his original probing—"he is Bulgarian?" He looked straight into David's eyes with the skill of a man who could read truth between the lines.

"I suppose he is."

"Not a Catholic, however."

"No," David replied, sipping his steaming coffee, "I guess he's not."

Ellie buttered her toast and did not look up at the thoughtful face of their host. "Good," she said, lamely attempting to change the subject. "Very good food."

Father Antonell dismissed her small talk and forged ahead. "Yes. One of our Sisters escaped from Bulgaria. She had a very nice chat with Mikhail. And where did you pick him up?" His tone dared them to lie.

"Cyprus. Near Kyrenia," David replied evenly, meeting the challenge.

"Also on your honeymoon?"

David lifted his chin slightly. "Yes. I was with the Ninth Air Force. First in England, then North Africa—"

Recognition sparked in Father Antonell's eyes. "The Ninth. In Bengasi, wasn't it?"

"I managed to hit all the high spots when I was there. I wanted Ellie to get a look at where I was when I was writing home. Lots to see." Father Antonell considered his explanation in silence.

"And how did you like Bengasi, Mrs. Miller?" he asked with a smile.

"Well, I—"

"We haven't made it that far. We were going to circle around and touch down on the way back." David interrupted. "A hitch-hiker or two along the way were going to help pay expenses. I don't know . . . now that we've lost the plane."

Father Antonell sat back and patted his stomach with a sigh. "Well, you are welcome here. Most welcome. I cannot tell you what a pleasure it is to hear an American voice again. This poor country is in such turmoil. Next month are the elections, and everyone is terrified the Communists will win. Or that if they don't win at the polls, they will simply take the country by force. Like in Bulgaria, Czechoslovakia and—"

"Even in the States, Padre," David interjected, relieved to be off the topic of their travel itinerary. "The hearings in Washington have everyone in an uproar."

Father Antonell's face became serious again. "And what do you think about the Communists, Mr. Miller?"

"Call me David, please, Padre. Here we are staying at your house. Call me David, huh?"

"All right then, David. Communists seem to be taking control all over. What do you think about it?"

"I'm with Patton. I think we should have chased them out of Berlin and clear back to Moscow, but I guess everyone was just too tired to finish. Have you heard about the hearings in Washington? The blacklists in Hollywood?"

The little priest nodded. He had not stated his own views on the topic. "Occasionally a stray newspaper or magazine comes with the charity crates from the States. I have read bits and pieces . . ." He trailed off and stared hard at David. "It is hard anymore to know who is telling the truth, is it not? *Vox et prae-terea nihil* . . . a voice and nothing more. Empty words from everyone. There is no truth at all in words, I think. Only in actions. I say, *ecce signum* . . . look at the proof. In Bulgaria and Rumania they have turned the churches into stables. The clergy is in prison. They say Stalin has killed millions more than Hitler in his purges. *Ecce signum* man's great plans for equality have failed. So what is left?" He scratched his cheek and looked at David as though he expected an answer.

"I guess everyone has to follow his conscience."

The little priest slammed his hand down suddenly on the table, rattling the dishes. "No! You are wrong!" His pleasant exterior dissolved. "The conscience of man is flawed and twisted. The conscience of man is tuned only to his own wishes and desires, not to that of others. It may be appeased and soothed with the most inane acts of kindness! That too is a voice and nothing more . . . it may even be the greatest liar of all." He looked at them both fiercely. His cheeks were red and his eyes seemed to see through them. A long silence followed until at last Ellie cleared her throat and spoke.

"You're right, Father." She glanced nervously at David, who seemed embarrassed by the outburst.

"I didn't mean—" David began. "I meant . . . people know what's right, and they ought to do it."

"Ah yes." The priest raised his finger. "But you see, *what's right* means something different to everyone, doesn't it? In the mountains, the rancher prays for rain so he will have grass for his cattle. While in the valley, the farmer prays it will not rain until his cotton is harvested. If it rains too late, the rancher curses God. If it rains too early, the farmer curses God." He smiled. "The farmer would sacrifice the rancher for what is right for him, you see? And in the end, sooner or later, everyone blames God. A better example might be what happened in Palestine last night." He looked from one face to the other. "Of course you haven't heard the news. I only just heard it myself."

Ellie leaned forward against the table. "What? What has happened?"

"We all know about the millions who died unjustly. We know the Jews of Europe who are left deserve a homeland. That seems right to the conscience of the United Nations. But not right to the Arabs who live there. And now, last night, it seems the Jews have butchered a whole village of women and children just outside of Jerusalem. Murdered them and raped the women, just as Jewish women and children have been butchered."

Ellie felt ill. She put her hand to her forehead. "Terrible," she whispered.

"The conscience of men," said Father Antonell simply. "It justifies what a man does by what has been done to him, you see? What are a few Arab children, more or less, when a million Jewish children have been killed?"

"How could they do it?" David asked. "Are you sure?"

"All I know is what I heard on the news." He reached around to a dark walnut sideboard behind him and opened a drawer. Pulling out a worn copy of *Life* magazine, he laid it on the table beside the plate of toast. He flipped the pages until he came to a double-page spread featuring a sorrowful photograph of David standing beside a sealed coffin bound for the United States. A mug shot of Ellie was beneath it. "Perhaps you would like to begin again, eh? Perhaps there is some other reason you chose Yugoslavia as a spot for your honeymoon?" He paused as both of them sat rigidly at the table.

"It seems that the rain is falling on Jews and Arabs alike in this, and in the end, God will be praised by one people and cursed by the other. That is inevitable. But I am curious, since the Jews themselves are now proving what they are capable of, what is your role in this drama?" He smiled at their uneasiness. "The name is *Meyer*, isn't it? Captain David Meyer. War ace of the Ninth?"

David nodded, "Yes."

"Thank you." He addressed Ellie. "And you are Ellie Warne. Of *Life* magazine. A favorite of mine. I had not heard that you were alive, and I must admit, it took me longer to place you. Captain Meyer was more simple. I was hoping you would be honest with me."

"What are you going to do?" David asked grimly.

"I guess that depends on you." Father Antonell folded his hands before him. "Certainly there is nothing at all to do until the storm is past. Telephone lines are down. I could lock you in your room. Or you could overpower me and lock me in mine. Neither alternative sounds pleasant. Perhaps we should talk, then. Perhaps you should explain what you, American citizens, are doing in the company of men who would murder innocent civilians."

27 When the Sparrow Falls

A pile of dispatches lay on the desk of Haj Amin Husseini. Each relayed to Damascus the horrifying details of the massacre of Deir Yassin. Haj Amin fingered the latest news from Ram Kadar. The sister of Yassar Tafara had survived but was driven mad by the ordeal. Two hundred and fifty others had perished. By afternoon, the Jews had been driven from the village by a thousand Irregulars. Only Kastel remained in the hands of the Zionists, and Jerusalem was rocked with the fury of the Arab populace.

He threw the message onto the stack and sat back in his chair. Pressing his fingers together, he stared at the telegram that had come from Yassar in Ragusa.

ARRIVED AS PLANNED STOP SHIP SAILING AHEAD OF SCHEDULE BEARING WITHIN THE GLORY OF ARAB PALESTINE STOP INCH ALLAH! YOUR SERVANT AND THAT OF THE PROPHET STOP YASSAR TAFARA.

"The Jews have not known the meaning of vengeance," muttered the Mufti. "The act has only ignited the torch that will set ablaze their pyre."

The *Trina* held within her womb the instruments of final destruction for the enemies of a free Arab Palestine. It did not matter now that the United Nations joined in mourning for the people of Deir Yassin. It did not matter that their great halls were now filled with regret that Partition had even been an issue. For Haj Amin, the question of a Jewish homeland was settled. With the cargo from the *Trina* and thousands of Arab soldiers armed with modern weapons, Haj Amin would offer the Jews a homeland of graves along the shores of the Mediterranean.

"Yes. The Jews will know peace in Palestine—the same peace as the people of Deir Yassin!"

———

Throughout the afternoon, news of the massacre of Deir Yassin and the riots in Jerusalem faded in and out of the static-ridden broadcast on Father Antonell's ancient radio.

Ellie sat with her head forlornly against David's arm as the priest looked at them with a mixture of suspicion and curiosity.

From riot-torn Jerusalem, David Ben-Gurion proclaimed that the actions of the Jewish terrorists were an abomination, detestable. Meanwhile, a furious outcry has arisen in the United Nations General Assembly. Once again, the feasibility of Jewish independent rule is seriously in question. Said members of the American Delegation, "If it is to be Jewish policy to butcher peaceful residents of Palestine in their beds—"

Father Antonell switched off the radio. He gazed at the downcast faces of David and Ellie across from him. "*Ecce signum* . . . look at the proof, eh? So much for justice in Zionism."

"You heard what David Ben-Gurion said!" David frowned at the statement of the priest.

"Empty words, Captain Meyer, all empty, I'm afraid. And Palestine is full of Catholic Arabs. Will they be exempt from this sort of action?" He rose wearily. Glancing out the window, he said to no one in particular, "Will it never end?" Ellie knew he was not speaking of the storm.

"You know it will not end," Ellie said quietly. "Not until everything is fulfilled as it is written. Israel *will* be a nation, Father Antonell. It is promised. And there will be wars right up until the minute Jesus comes again to stop it. But only He will make it end."

He raised his eyebrows in surprise and amusement at her words. "A theologian," he said.

"No," Ellie answered with irritation, "but I can read. And that's what it says in the Book. Whether you're a Jew or a Catholic or a Baptist, we all have the same book, and on that point we all agree. The Messiah will come when Israel is a nation again. And no matter what evil men do—both sides, Father— Israel *will* be a nation."

"But the question is, Ellie Meyer. . ." He lowered his chin and looked at her down the bridge of his nose. "The question is timing—*timing*. Did you know that in the third century Justinian sent Jews back to Jerusalem to rebuild the temple? And when they began to dig the foundations, gas and fire erupted and consumed several hundred workmen in an explosion—a fact of history. You see, God has His own timetable, not to be rushed by men with guns or shovels. I believe the Scriptures. It is the rushing, pushing timetable of men that I doubt. If in fact Israel is to be a nation in my lifetime, then every day I will look up and expect to see Christ's return to this earth. But until that happens, I will expect the bloody soil of Palestine to open up and consume men who seek to hurry the will of God!" He looked at David. "I suppose it was the weapons brought to Palestine that killed the people of Deir Yassin . . ."

"I have prayed that isn't so, Father." David looked at his hands.

"Yes. I'm sure you have." He winced. "Watch what ground you tread on, young man, lest it open up beneath you. Christ has said His eye is even on the smallest sparrow. Those people were worth much more than a sparrow, and they are dead."

"Those were not our men," David repeated for the hundredth time.

"So you have said." Father Antonell looked out at the darkening harbor. "I will have supper in my quarters; I have much to pray about tonight. And I would not advise you to leave. I doubt that you would get far."

"Have you forgotten the six million Jewish sparrows, Padre?" David asked angrily. "Do you think the Mufti won't finish the job if that arms ship gets through?"

"God alone knows those details, David," the little priest said wearily. "He sees the sparrow. I am just a man, looking at the deeds of other men. You are wanted for criminal activity by several governments; now I must decide what I am to do since you have sought shelter here." He turned away. "Do not attempt to leave, Captain Meyer." His voice was stern as he left the room.

David leaned forward, staring at the floor. "He's right in a way, you know. Somebody gets crazy and kills a bunch of kids, and it makes you wonder, Els. I mean, I have to wonder what we're doing here." He looked at her; deep circles were beneath his eyes. "They blow us up, we blow them up. They kill a kid, we kill ten. Then twenty. Then two hundred and fifty—"

Ellie did not answer. The shock of the atrocity hung heavy on her heart. She thought of Miriam and the old woman's family. Arabs. Innocents. And dead. "I don't know," she said. "But God knows, David. Every detail. We really are more important than sparrows. If we fail, or fall, then He's going to be there to take over when there's nothing left for us to do."

"Like now," David groaned and sat back. "Like now."

In the headquarters of the Arab High Committee, Ram Kadar offered his grim report on the events in Damascus. A dozen muhqtars stared back at him as he repeated the words of the Mufti, "We of Palestine have been betrayed by our brothers. They would carve up Palestine among themselves, just as the Jews have carved up the people of Deir Yassin. They withhold our rightful weapons from us, but our leader has outsmarted them! A shipment will come to us directly within a matter of days—enough to equip our entire population with a weapon for each Jihad Moquade! And then we will drive the Jews into the sea!"

"May Allah grant it to be so!" spat an aged, jowly chief of the Bedouins. "And we shall slay their wives and children as they have butchered ours!"

"Today the Jews still hold Kastel as the people of Palestine grieve for their dead," said another. "And in this they have a victory!"

From a solitary corner of the room, Fredrich Gerhardt stood and spoke in a clear voice. His thick jaw tight with rage. "Then let it not be so. I have made a vow that I myself will take Kastel! I beg your consent that tonight I may take the choicest of the thousands and end our disgrace! And end the life of one Jew who holds that village! For the sake of my vow, I ask that I alone command the assault of Kastel!"

There was a murmur among the committee at the words of Gerhardt. Was it not he who had left Kastel unguarded?

A faint smile played on Kadar's lips and he answered in a thoughtful and deliberate voice. "Commander Gerhardt has proven himself a thousand times—"

"And what did he prove yesterday when our siege against the Jews was broken? Last night they laughed at us as they feasted," came the angry response from a withered Sheik.

"One mistake," Kadar defended, to Gerhardt's amazement. "He was deluded as all of us were. But he is an able soldier of the Jihad." He did not add his thought that the fanatical Gerhardt might easily be killed in such an assault, and the Jews would certainly be worn down in both stamina and ammunition during the night. Then he, Ram Kadar, would finish what had been begun by another. He would finish it with all the fury he felt in his soul. As much as Gerhardt desired the blood of Moshe Sachar, Kadar also desired to face the Jew once again—to prove who was the stronger between them.

"You do not wish to participate in this attack, Commander Kadar?" Curiosity filled the voice of a muhqtar as he narrowed his eyes and appraised Kadar.

"Retaking Kastel should be a minor skirmish," Kadar answered, noting Gerhardt's swelling irritation at the remark. "The Jews took it with a few men, after all. Commander Gerhardt will have a thousand? Two thousand? Of course, if he has difficulty—"

"Ha!" Gerhardt scoffed. "Difficulty? What are they? Are they more than inept scum, scraped from the remains of their dead kindred? No! There will be no difficulty."

"The people respect Commander Gerhardt. He is a great hero of the Jihad. They will follow him, and because of his courage they will find their purpose. I believe this," offered another member of the committee.

A few moments of murmured discussion preceded the consent of the leaders who had been chosen by Haj Amin to rule the various villages and districts of Arab Palestine.

"Yes!" Gerhardt answered triumphantly; then he turned to face Kadar. "I have made a vow," he menaced. "The head of Moshe Sachar shall be born into Jerusalem on the point of my bayonet! And then perhaps I shall share with you all my plans for the capture of one more hill—"

"We all know well your ability to go where others would not dare," said one of the muhqtars. "Inch Allah! May it be his will that you succeed. And now, brother, tell us what has come to your mind? What plans do you conceive?"

"Tonight we take Kastel!" Gerhardt raised his chin proudly and looked at each face. "And tomorrow, I vow to you that we shall take Mount Scopus and the Jewish stronghold of Hadassah Hospital!"

Kadar raised his eyebrows along with the others in the room. "You may take Kastel without my help." The tight-lipped smile returned. "But Hadassah will not fall so easily."

"You do not know the mind of Fredrich Gerhardt, my friend." He held his hands up to the light of the smoking oil lamps. "Has not Allah made these hands for his purpose? For his vengeance? And also for mine. You shall see, Kadar. All of you shall see, tomorrow, when I have drunk the blood of my enemies at Kastel. *Tomorrow!*"

It was nearly sunset when the little plane of Bobby Milkin rattled over Kastel. His voice was clear over the radio. "Staff, this is Raven. Trouble comin' down the road, Staff."

Moshe pushed the button and answered Bobby. "Right, Raven. Can you give us an idea of numbers?"

A confused voice replied. "Well, that's just it, Staff. From the look of it most of them guys is still at the wake. Or hung over or something."

"Muslims do not drink, Raven. So what are we up against?"

"Don't look to me like more'n eight or nine hundred. Less than a thousand. Gimme a mustang and I'd strafe 'em good. Send 'em packin' back to their tents." His voice crackled as he flew away toward Jerusalem. "Deir Yassin is full of British and Arabs. Looks like there ain't one dead Jew down there. Emile just cut an' run!"

Moshe clenched his teeth in fresh anger at the mention of Emile Dumas. Indeed, the Irgun had taken their rifles and then had simply run away. There had been no effort to even contact Kastel. Moshe regretted the loss of the weapons and ammunition. "Only eight or nine hundred?" he asked again. "You sure of that, Raven?" Moshe was surprised that the force was not greater.

Bobby's voice began to fade. "Sure, unless them guys got someone in their robes with 'em. This . . . watch . . . front . . . village . . ."

"I am losing you, Raven . . . come in, Raven . . ." There was no reply as the plane disappeared on the horizon. Bobby was finished for the day. Without daylight, he could be of little use to them anyway.

Moshe put down the receiver and turned to Ham and Ehud. "Well, there you have it. Less than a thousand Arabs."

Ham scratched his head in wonder, and looked at the darkening sky. "If that is all that come, I won't be disappointed."

"And our fellows have seven thousand rounds of ammunition between them. That is one hundred bullets per man and seven bullets to kill each Arab." Ehud sounded confident.

Ham did not tell them that during World War II, it had taken three thousand bullets to stop each enemy. Instead, he nodded. "One hundred rounds of ammunition is not so much as you think. We'll have to caution the lads to only shoot at certain targets, not just shadows in the night."

"Each squad has a flare gun"—Moshe made a mental checklist—"and one barrel bomb to each ten men."

Ham rubbed his chin. "Those should be used only in the case of a direct assault. No use wastin' . . ."

Moshe was grateful that the large, ruddy-cheeked sergeant had stayed. He was an expert in weapons and ammunition. And at his suggestion, explosives had been packed into oil drums, and a short fuse had been attached for use as an improvised bomb. The houses of Kastel had not been blown up, but rather a network of trenches had been dug linking them together. Perhaps the most enterprising idea had been to attach fuses to oil drums that were empty. A few loose stones had been tossed in for the sake of noise, but other than that, the drums were harmless. It was the hope of Sergeant Hamilton, however, that the seven barrel bombs that were authentic would not only do damage physically to the enemy, but also instill a healthy respect of tumbling oil drums.

"Mazel Tov." Ehud stuck out his big paw to the sergeant. "Good luck."

Ham nodded. "Hold the rear door open for Fergus an' the fellows. That is most important. Nothing will mean a thing if they can't get in tomorrow morning with more ammunition."

"Yes," Ehud growled and narrowed his eyes. "And we shall hope they take a few bullets from that Emile and his Irgun swine, eh?"

"Right now I would take bullets from the devil himself," Ham remarked. "Me an' the lads can hold the quarry all right."

"And I will remain here at the muhqtar's house. Ehud there." He pointed across the courtyard. Heads of the Haganah men were visible in the trenches between the houses. Each window facing the hillside was held by a soldier equipped with the precious one hundred bullets, and every other man had a hand grenade. The men of the Mufti were in for a stiff fight.

As Ehud and Ham hurried to take their positions with the men, Moshe checked and rechecked his rifle. His bullets were tied into a sock dangling from his belt. He sat at the window that looked down the tumbling, terraced slope that led to the road. *He who holds Kastel controls the road to Jerusalem.* Midway between Kastel and Tel Aviv, the Arabs held the fortress of Latrun, but that could be bypassed. Here at Kastel the feeding of the Holy City would be settled. To hold Kastel meant that the siege was broken indefinitely.

The Arabs came silently in the darkness to the slope of Kastel. They had left others to their chants in Jerusalem. These few handpicked warriors were the exception to the average peasant warrior. Gerhardt had chosen them for their loyalty and their experience. In one capacity or another, he knew each of the officers who now served under his authority. Most had held Kastel with him and were skilled in the techniques of silent ambush.

It was their participation over the months that had stopped every Jewish convoy that had rumbled up the pass—until the last. They knew every rock and outcropping, every ragged bush and tree. They had spent weeks living among the villagers of Kastel. They had slept in the houses and drunk from the wells and prayed in the shabby mosque. Yes, Gerhardt was confident that they would retake the village easily. The handful of Jews were merely trespassers on the familiar territory of these hardened warriors of Kastel and Bab el Wad.

Stealthily, they divided and found the ravines and rocks that concealed them effectively from their Jewish enemies. In small packs they crept up the slope. Although the cry of *Deir Yassin* was in their hearts, they did not speak it. They did not chant or shout. Only the muffled rattle of their weapons striking against the rocks was heard. Like the clacking of a crab, they clattered closer and closer to the perimeter of their enemies. The houses loomed before them in the darkness only one hundred yards away. There was no sign of life in the village; their silence was answered by silence.

The presence of Fredrich Gerhardt strengthened their hearts. He had given but two orders. The first had been to retake the village. The second had offered great reward to the man who brought the Jewish commander, Moshe Sachar, to him alive. With the promise of gold, he had instilled in each of the eight hundred his own desire.

Above them was the house of the muhqtar. Strong thick

walls protected it, and windows gazed down like empty eyes. To take the house of the muhqtar would give them the strongest central point of the village.

Gerhardt crept from group to group, whispering his command. "The house of the muhqtar. The first row of houses on the perimeter. When you hear me shout, then attack! And attack! And attack!"

Closer and closer they moved until it seemed as though they might steal into the village itself. And then, from the top of the mosque, a loud crack was heard and a flare streaked high into the air. It trailed a white tail of smoke, then exploded in a burst of light.

Gerhardt raised his gun above his head and shouted, "*Allah Akbar!*" And with the courage and daring of a man insane with passion, he led them up the hillside toward the houses.

Bullets ricocheted off the worn, rocky soil. Their screams were answered with the screams of Jews who fell wounded at their posts. The light of the flare faded and still the men of Gerhardt pushed on in waves, searching the darkness for the telltale sign of fire leaping from the barrels of Jewish guns. In the darkness they aimed for the flame, and still more Jews toppled before them.

The first assault came to within fifty yards of the houses, and then a terrible rumble sounded as a barrel lurched over the edge of a barricade to cascade down the slope toward a group of ten warriors crouched in a ravine. The barrel crashed against stone walls and bounced high into the air to crash down again against another terrace. It careened wildly off a huge boulder, turning in the air above the heads of the ten, and then exploded into a million deadly, white-hot shards of metal. In the light of the explosion, ten died before the eyes of their comrades. Half a dozen more screamed in agony as shrapnel tore into their flesh and left them helplessly wounded where they fell.

All along the front line, men shuddered at the sight and searched the gloom ahead for signs of another barrel that might blow them to pieces. Still Gerhardt shouted and cursed, slapping the hesitant men back into action. "Are you a woman? Attack! Death to the Jews! Attack! They shall not stand against us! They shall not!"

Fearful of his fury, they followed him. Wave upon wave they charged up the hill, only to be thrown back by the furious defense of their enemies. Two more of the deadly bombs rolled down upon them, ripping the life and breath from yet another dozen Jihad Moquades. They fell back once again until, shamed by the words of Gerhardt, they found their courage and moved up the hill once more. This time they were careful to avoid the ravines and gulleys that served as traps for the rolling bombs. They fired from behind the boulders and tumbled fences that gave them some protection.

They grew cautious and calculating in their aim, firing only when they spotted the flash of a Jewish gun. Many times a dreadful scream of agony rewarded their patience. The battle became less furious; inch by inch, they began to make real progress as whole spaces along the Jewish perimeter began to crumble.

"Victory is ours!" cried the hoarse voice of Gerhardt as he spearheaded yet another assault. "*Nashamdi*, brothers! They grow faint!"

─────────

Rachel slept fitfully, a dozen times waking to the cry of a baby who was not there to comfort. How many times in the night had she reached out for Moshe, only to find that he, too, was gone? For the first time since Tikvah had come into her care months before, she found herself totally alone.

After midnight, she rose and slipped quietly to the window. Pulling back the shades, she stared hard at the black void toward Kastel. As she watched, a distant flare rose up to arch across the sky, then burst into a thousand tiny fragments and sprinkled the earth. She could not hear the now-familiar pop of gunfire. The city seemed filled with an ominous silence, a foreboding heaviness that had not drifted away with the smoke of the riots.

She squinted to see through a slight haze. One single bright star shone above her. It was unchanging and familiar—the star she had wished upon when she was a small child in Poland; the star she had wept beneath as a young woman in the camps. And now it appeared still when all the others seemed to have faded away.

"You go on shining," she murmured. "When all the world seems caught in a whirlpool, you do not change, little star." She bowed her head and thought of Moshe, then of the baby. "Lord," she prayed softly, "you are still there. Above those I love. I cannot see them or touch them. Will you touch them for me? Tonight will you hold them as I cannot? My heart reaches up to touch you, and if your arms are also around Moshe"—her voice caught with the ache of wanting him near—"and around my Tikvah, then you hold us all together and we are not alone, nu?"

Yet another flare slashed the darkness over Kastel, and as its light faded, Rachel still looked at the one certain pinpoint of light. *You are still there, God. More certain and unchanging than the stars. And though my heart might break tonight, I will trust you. Though I ache to my soul, I will believe that you see us all and love us. Though the earth itself break away and fall into the sea, I will believe—because there is nothing left to do.*

28 The Miracle

The Arab attack was unrelenting. It seemed to Moshe that the Arab soldiers had an inexhaustible supply of ammunition. For every precious bullet fired by Moshe and his men, they were answered by a hundred Arab bullets in return. The walls of the houses were pitted and scarred. Deadly aim left four of the Haganah defenders lifeless in the mud of the trenches, and eight more were seriously wounded. Again and again they attacked, their cries striking terror in the hearts of those who held the defense of Kastel. Again and again the attacks were repulsed by the daring of Moshe's troops.

Six of the barrel bombs had been used, exacting a toll on the enemy that was evident by the sound of their cries. By three in the morning, only one barrel remained, perched on the roof of the muhqtar's house where Moshe and two others held off yet another attacking wave of Jihad Moquades.

Up and down the Jewish line, the Haganah solders cowered down against the hail of bullets. On his belly, Ehud Schiff crawled into the house.

"Moshe!" he called. "My fellows are almost out of ammunition!" There was genuine fear in his voice. And Moshe knew that the others had not been as sparing with their bullets as he had. "Moshe! Are you alive?"

"Here!" Moshe called from a bedroom, as a bullet whistled in over his head.

"Well, you are the only one, then! Your two companions are both dead." He inched toward Moshe. "Come on! We can retreat to the quarry! The line is crumbling all around. Come before you are killed!"

From the hillside below, a terrible voice echoed from the darkness, a voice that had haunted Moshe since that terrible night in the tunnels below the Old City. "Jews! Sachar! You thought that you killed me, but I have come for you! I have come as I said I would!"

"What the. . . ?" Ehud growled.

"Filthy Jew! You think you will succeed, but you will only die here in the dust of Kastel! Tell Sachar that Fredrich Gerhardt has come! Tell him I have come for his head!"

"Who is this?" Ehud whispered hoarsely as another volley pounded the house.

"The Nazi who came for Rachel," Moshe said dully, feeling suddenly very weary. "The beast from the tunnel."

Ehud tugged his sleeve. "Come on. I have ordered my fellows to pull back. We can hold the quarry until Fergus comes—"

"Wait!" Moshe snapped, pulling away from Ehud's grasp. "On the roof! We have one more little package! Stay here." He handed Ehud his gun and ran toward the steps that led to the roof.

Below him, the cruel voice of Gerhardt echoed up from the slope. "There are no more bombs for you! Your guns grow silent! Run, Jews! For I have come to take this village! To take your lives! I will have the head of Sachar, for it is the will of Allah! The will of Gerhardt!"

Moshe crouched low and crept toward the barrel that lay by the ledge of the roof. He felt in the darkness for the fuse, then patted his pocket for matches. He opened the matchbook, revealing only three. He struck the first into a tiny, feeble flame. It flared and was snuffed out by the breeze that blew from the west. *Dear God!* he prayed, striking the second. It, too, flickered as he shielded it, then died. *God!*

"Commander Gerhardt!" came a shrill cry in Arabic. "There!

on the roof! I see someone on the roof!"

A barrage of bullets slammed against the ledge and whistled above Moshe's head. He leaned closer to the bomb and prayed silently as he held the matchbook against the fuse and lit the last match. It sputtered and flared, catching the paper of the matchbook, and then the fuse hissed to life. With a grunt of effort, Moshe hoisted the barrel over the edge of the roof; then he threw himself flat as it crashed and banged down toward the voice of Fredrich Gerhardt.

Even as the explosion lit the night, Moshe had hurled himself down the steps and back into the house. "Come on!" he cried to Ehud. "Come on! Run for it!" And together they sprinted back to the rear line of defense among the quarry buildings.

The barrel bomb that tumbled from the roof of the muhqtar's house rumbled ominously as it bounced from one terrace to another. The men surrounding Gerhardt shrieked and threw themselves against the ground in terror as it smashed against the stump of a tree and flew high into the air above them.

With a sickening roar, the barrel erupted in a cloud of light and fire. Two among them died instantly and fell twitching to the ground. A flaming, jagged piece of metal twisted through the air and slashed through Gerhardt's leg before it slammed into the face of yet another of his men.

Gerhardt fell to the ground as the white-hot pain of his wound tore his breath away. He lay in the grass beside the body of a fallen soldier and cursed the Jews. He reached down to touch his leg and pulled back a bloody hand. From hip to knee, his flesh was ripped open to the bone. "Help me!" he cried feebly as he felt his blood pumping from the open wound.

A man crawled quickly toward him as the battle raged on. For an instant, Gerhardt was filled with terror at the sight of the white-robed figure moving toward him. *Was this death?*

"Help me!" he cried again. "I am wounded."

Deft hands reached out toward him, pulling him away from the bodies of the fallen and into the shelter of a stone wall. Quickly a cord was tied around his leg and the gush of blood was stopped.

"Stop them!" Gerhardt muttered. "Gold for the capture of Sachar." He slipped into a delirium as word of his wound was passed from one weary Jihad Moquade to another along the front line of battle. "Kill the Jewish whore!" Gerhardt raved as his men bore him down the slope to the road. And then he passed out.

———

One candle burned on the night table, casting long shadows against the white walls of the room. Again and again through the night Ellie replayed the words of Father Antonell. Had they not told him the miracles they had seen the last few months? But still he doubted. At this moment, shadows of doubt fell over Ellie as well. It was one thing to fight for what was just and right. It was quite another when mass murder tarnished the bright image of a cause.

David slept a profound and deep sleep; Ellie lay awake beside him, her hand on his head, her fingers tangled in his hair. He had sacrificed everything for Israel, for a nation that was now to be born and bathed in the blood of those who had lived there for centuries before.

She thought of Howard's housekeeper Miriam and her family. How many generations had lived in Jerusalem? *I remember her telling about Sunday picnics on the Mount of Olives, how they used to look up and hope that they would see Him coming. And now they are all dead. How many more will die without reason? What are we doing here, God? Are we finished? Have you brought us here to stop us from sinking the Trina? Have you finally put an end to the madness? Here we are against the wall with no way out. We're done, and nothing short of a miracle will get us out of this.*

Ellie remembered the words of Father Antonell—perhaps the timing was wrong. Perhaps they had been misinterpreting the signs, making everything fit their own script. And now men would justify their own brutality by what cruelties they had endured themselves. She thought of Rachel. Of Moshe and Ehud. This was their battle—not the fight of David and Ellie Meyer. *What are we doing here, Lord? What have we done?*

She slept little through the long night as the storm battered the house unmercifully. Wind shrieked around the corner of the building and howled Ellie's doubts out loud. The voices of ten thousand dying children accused her; were they Jews or Arabs? She fought to see their faces through the fog of her dreams. Voices cried out for peace and justice; were they Jews or Arabs? And in the end she saw that they were simply children without

300

race or nationality, all crying for home.

When at last the dim light of morning filtered into the room, Ellie awoke exhausted, still wondering why they had been brought to Bari Harbor, why they had lost their plane, their bomb, and their purpose. She opened her eyes and found her first thoughts directed toward the people of Deir Yassin. The storm had not relented. Still it raged and pounded. She remembered the children; their questions echoed in her ears even as a soft tapping sounded on their door.

For the first time in nearly nine hours, David opened his eyes and blinked hard, trying to get his bearings. "Yeah?" he called drowsily. "Who's there?"

"Father Antonell," came the muffled reply. "May I see you?"

David glanced at Ellie. "Morning," he said, sounding slightly confused. "You mind if he comes in?"

"Come in," Ellie called, almost anxious to hear the result of the little priest's night of thought and prayer.

The door cracked and then opened slowly. Father Antonell entered carrying a tray with a coffeepot and three mismatched cups. He closed the door with his heel, then set the tray on the night table beside the candle stub. There were dark circles under his eyes also, and Ellie wondered if he had seen the same children in his dreams.

"I am sorry to disturb you so early," he said, pouring the coffee. "I will have to be gone today, and I wanted to speak with you both." His tone of voice was serious and vaguely uneasy. "I have spent the night in prayer." He waited as they sat up; then he handed them their cups.

"I see the storm hasn't let up." David cleared his throat and took a careful sip of the steaming brew.

"No. No. I'm afraid it hasn't . . ." Father Antonell paused and tapped his saucer. "Captain Meyer," he plunged ahead. "I have given our conversation much thought. Last night you spoke of events you consider to be miracles. The scrolls of Isaiah coming to light on the very night of Partition. The fact they are the scrolls that mention the return of Israel as a nation. Quite impressive—"

"And more than coincidence," said Ellie.

He did not reply to her comment. "You spoke of President Truman, that he was somehow swayed by these ancient texts. I cannot doubt that. But I do not believe he foresaw, as the outcome, atrocities committed by the very people he hoped to help."

"None of us could see that," David answered, feeling a sense of foreboding in the priest's words.

"No. And I am certain that the United Nations could not see the utter disaster the Partition has become. That is why they are reconsidering. That is why we who are simple men must abide by their decision. We must not attempt to change history—or move the hand of God unless He is willing that it be moved."

"What are you saying?" David asked.

"*Ecce signum*, Captain. Look at the proof. Yes, certainly you have gotten the cargo manifest of this Arab ship. You found out when she was sailing and where she was bound. Would it not have been more sensible to turn the information over to the authorities?"

"I explained that," David said quietly. "The Arab states may legally purchase and transport arms because they are independent sovereign nations. The Jews of Palestine will not be a nation until May fourteenth—"

"If at all," Father Antonell sighed. "Be that as it may, Captain, don't you see? What you believe is miraculous may in fact only be cruel coincidence. Certainly you had the right information, but look what happened with it. Instead of sinking your ship, you lost it. You almost lost yourself in this storm. Your plane is wrecked, your friend badly injured. And now, David"—the priest looked steadily into David's eyes—"Now you have come here, to my parish, into the home of a man who recognizes you and your wife, into the home of a man who can stop you from any further action in this hopeless cause."

David set down his cup. Ellie felt tears come to her eyes.

"Stop us?" David's words sounded hollow. Suddenly the wind ceased and a hush fell upon the room and the world.

"What you saw as a miracle was only a delusion. You are a brave man, David. But you have been fooled into a wrong course of action."

"You believe that."

"With my whole heart. I also believe that your continued association with this madness will lead to other men being led astray. Other pilots—men who served in one war and survived. It is time," he said slowly, "that someone says, *enough*."

"What will you do?"

"I will go to the American Embassy in Rome. See if I can help you get home without any penalty. What you have done is enough to lose your citizenship, maybe land you in a federal prison. You know that—"

David's eyes did not look away. "I have known all that from the beginning." There was an edge to his voice.

"I can help you. If I explain that you were misled, that it was simply an error in judgment . . ."

"David," Ellie said. "Maybe we should listen to him . . ."

"You see, Captain Meyer, the true miracle in all this is simply that you are here in Bari. That you have come to a man who can help you get home. You believe in miracles—that God sees the sparrow when it falls. Well, yesterday you fell out of the sky, and here you are. There is no other reason for you to be here. *None.* Except that God cares enough to extricate you from this dreadful fiasco in Palestine."

David did not answer. He closed his eyes tight and listened to the utter silence that engulfed them. No wind. No rain dripping from the eaves—nothing but the words of this American priest. This man who could maybe get them home again. There was no ship, no reason to stay. The whole world was going crazy after Deir Yassin . . .

"What could you do?" Ellie sounded almost eager.

"I know people at the Embassy," the priest continued. "David Meyer is an American hero, after all. No one will hang him for an error in judgment." He smiled apologetically. "Why else would God have directed you both here?"

David rubbed his hand through his hair. All of it seemed to make sense. Suddenly it was as though the hand of God had reached down to set them back on a path that would lead them from turmoil to a life of peace and quiet back home. "The storm," David said. "It's over."

They sat in silence for a long time. "Yes, David," said the priest, "it's finished."

As he spoke, the silence was broken by a loud thud against the windows of the French doors on the balcony. It sounded like something had been hurled against the glass, but the window did not break.

"What was that?" Ellie cried, wrapping her borrowed housecoat around her as Father Antonell rushed to the doors and pulled open the heavy draperies. She and David watched as the little priest stood dumbfounded at the door. "What is it?" Ellie asked again as he opened the door and stepped onto the balcony. She climbed from the warmth of the bed and followed him. He knelt on the balcony and cupped his hands, then stood slowly in the utter silence of the morning and opened his hands to David and Ellie. In them was the tiny stunned body of a sparrow. "You see," said Father Antonell in an awed whisper, "it is a sign. Why else would He direct you to Bari Harbor and my parish?"

David reached out a finger to touch the feathered creature. Then he raised his eyes beyond the shoulder of Father Antonell to where a team of tugboats guided the listing hulk of a freighter through the channel and into the harbor. He blinked hard and raised a trembling hand to point to the bow of the ship. "There! *There,* Padre!" he cried. "*There* is the reason!"

The priest whirled around and, still cradling the bird in one hand, gasped and crossed himself at the sight before his eyes. "Holy Mother of God," he whispered. "It is not *possible!*"

Ellie laughed out loud as her doubts dissipated. Battered by the storm, the wounded ship being towed into Bari Harbor bore the faded name of *Trina!*

29   Star of Yeshua

Grandfather stirred a few precious grains of sugar into his weak tea as Rachel silently busied herself about the kitchen with her morning tasks. A dozen times he had attempted conversation with her, but she had answered in monosyllables, and any further discussion had fallen flat. The radio, set to the Jewish station, played Yiddish folk songs nonstop. There was very little news to either encourage or discourage the Jewish citizens, and the very lack of information was itself frightening to Rachel. Yacov came into the room and flopped heavily into the chair across the table from Grandfather. He did not speak either, but simply put his chin in his hand and stared out the window. Only Shaul sidled up to the old man to be patted on the head.

"So!" declared Grandfather. "You are the only one with any *sachel*, nu? With any good sense. Everyone else is unhappy when as yet we have nothing to be unhappy about." He scratched the big dog behind the ears and Shaul replied with a happy moan.

"What is there to be glad about?" Yacov replied glumly. "Mush again for breakfast?"

The old rabbi raised an eyebrow. "Sit up!" he demanded. "Elbow off the table. You think I am raising here a *proster Jew*? You want to grow up to be a man of *yiches*; then you will start by showing a little respect for breakfast, nu?"

Properly shamed by Grandfather's reprimand, Yacov sat erect and folded his hands in his lap. He lowered his eyes and murmured, "Yes, Rebbe Grandfather. I am sorry."

"And so you should be. With a handful of nothing to cook, your sister has managed to make each a pletsl."

Yacov brightened. All the news in Palestine could not have been so welcome as the thin, crisp roll garnished with poppy seeds. "For this I can be thankful!"

Rachel did not reply. Her mind was far away, divided between the barren slopes of Kastel and a tiny crib that for now seemed just as unattainable. Grandfather spoke loudly again. "You would be thankful for mush if that was all we had!" he proclaimed. "There will be none beneath my protection who grumble like the Hebrews in the wilderness when God gave them manna to eat. And then what did God do?"

"He gave them quail to eat instead."

"And quail! And quail! Morning, noon and night until they begged for the sweet manna again!"

"To me pletsl is like manna," Yacov said. "Better than mush for breakfast. Did you make one for each of us?"

"Yes," Rachel replied quietly. "Did you hear the professor? Is he awake yet?"

"He's not here," Yacov said. "He left an hour before we got up. Shaul whined to be let out and I saw the auto of the professor as it turned the corner two blocks away. I thought perhaps he had gone for rations while the city was still quiet."

"Many will be lining up early after yesterday's riots," Rachel agreed.

"He is a good man." The old rabbi sipped his tea. "Scarcely a Gentile, like the people of Holland during the war, Yacov—"

He directed his gaze to Rachel. "I heard a story from a shop-keeper in the Old City, a Dutch Jew who came here during the war. He told us how when the Nazis demanded that Jews wear the Star for identification, then all the people of Holland wore the Star as well. Everyone came into the streets wearing the Star of David."

Rachel smiled curiously at the story. She had not heard of such a thing before. "And were they all arrested?"

"The Nazis did not know whom to arrest. So they chose one hundred and executed them."

"And that stopped the demonstration?" Rachel asked.

Grandfather shrugged. "What else? But for a day at least, everyone wore the Star. For one day we were all alike. Jews and Gentiles together against the evil ones, nu?"

"There are some Jews who should not wear it at all," Rachel remarked bitterly, recalling the massacre of two nights before.

"True," the rabbi said. "And there are many goyim who have such a star carved upon their hearts, as the Holy Scripture has said. We are to be a light to the world, to the goyim, even, that they find God. It is from our people that the Messiah will come. The Star that guides in the night."

Rachel lowered her head and a wave of grief washed over her. *How can I tell him, Lord? How do I say what I know is true? Can I speak now and make him understand?*

"You see, Yacov," the old rabbi gently instructed, "God has given His people the Star as a sign. Many centuries before, David was given this as a symbol of his kingdom." Carefully, he sketched a triangle pointing up, then superimposed another pointing down on top of it. The lines were intertwined until the six-pointed Star of David was formed. "Here is an arrow that points down from heaven to earth, nu?"

Yacov nodded, and Rachel came to stand at Grandfather's shoulder. "Is that God?" Rachel asked, staring hard at the Star.

"A good Yeshiva student you would make, Rachel! You should have been a man! Pay attention to your sister, Yacov. She is bright!" He was pleased with her interest. "So, from heaven God reaches down to man through the Torah and the law of Moses." He tapped the pencil lead lightly to the image. "And what do you suppose this triangle represents, eh? What is the arrow that points up, Yacov?"

"Us, maybe? Reaching up to God?"

"Good! Yes! Very good indeed, Yacov. And so you see the two are intertwined . . . interlocking. And each side of the triangles represents the three sides of God and the three sides of man. We have a mind, a body and a soul, yes?"

"So when you put them both together," Yacov tested cautiously, "both halves of the star are King David?" he asked.

"No," Grandfather shook his head. "But the One who shall come after. The promised Messiah of Israel who shall be completeness and perfection, when man and God are at last perfectly united. Our Messiah shall be the Star of David. God reaching down to man and man reaching up to God."

The old rabbi spoke the truth and spoke with understanding. Rachel felt her words stick in her throat. She wanted to shout the name *Yeshua*; *Salvation* in Hebrew. But had not the Gentiles taken the very cross on which He died and smashed that holy Star of Messiah? Had not those who called themselves Christians made the symbol of the Messiah into a badge of shame and a mark of destruction? The old man had lost all but Yacov and her to such as those. How, then, could Rachel show the old rabbi that the Star had come to earth as a light in the darkness? That He embodied all the love and perfection of God and, in fact, had offered himself to die for all their failures—for all the times they had chosen not to reach up to touch God?

". . . and when our Messiah comes, Yacov, He alone will bring perfection and goodness into the world. We will be a nation, as the Prophets foretold. And through Him each man will find peace and joy."

"Grandfather—" Rachel hesitated. "I . . . have seen this Star of which you speak. I have . . . He has come." She touched her heart. "Here. In my heart."

The old man turned to face her. Amusement twinkled in his eyes. "Oh?"

"His name . . ." She swallowed hard. "He is called Yeshua."

The old man absorbed both her words and the fear with which she spoke. "His name is *Salvation*?" He nodded thoughtfully. "I suppose that is one name. The Book calls Him by many names, Rachel, and all of those names point to the Messiah. I know what courage it takes for you to tell me this," he added.

"I believe as you do that He will come to Israel," she said, gathering courage. "That we will see Him face to face when we are a nation as the Scripture says. But I also believe that He has come once to us, and that in that day His name was called Yeshua . . . Salvation. He was the Lamb of God. He was the sacrifice God sent as a gift to us. This does not make me less a Jew. No! I am more what I am meant to be."

Rachel expected an outpouring of rage from the aged scholar. She thought that he would tear his coat and close his eyes and shout her out of his presence. Instead, he gazed at her with a bemused smile. "You have been speaking to Howard Moniger, I see," he said.

Rachel raised her chin slightly and drew a deep breath. "No. Not at first. First, I heard these things from Leah, the mother of Tikvah. And then . . . from Moshe."

"From *Moshe*!" The old man tugged his beard. "Oy! I see there is a minyon among us . . ."

"Yes. We believe, Grandfather, and we have found such joy that we wish to share with everyone . . . everyone."

Still amused, he put a finger to his lips. "Go gently, daughter. Gently."

Yacov looked almost fearful at the confession of his sister. "Does this mean that you will not keep the Shabbat? That you will go to church with the goyim?" His young voice trembled.

Rachel rushed to him and bent down to embrace him. "Oh no, Yacov! Never will it mean that I am not a Jew. It simply means that Yeshua came first to us, but that He also came for the goyim. And many . . . not all, but *many* Gentiles have also seen our Messiah, and they too wore the Star engraved upon their hearts."

"Did I not say that very thing myself?" Grandfather asked. "There are many who call themselves Jews who are no better than the vilest goyim. We have seen this among us. And there are many goyim who in their hearts are better Jews than a Torah schoolteacher, nu? On Yom Kippur we meditate on our sins, boy, on our unworthiness; in the end it must be only the mercy of God that saves us." His eyes held Rachel's. "Any man, Jew or Christian, who believes otherwise is a fool. When all is said and done, we will look up and know that Salvation, or as we say in the Hebrew, *Yeshua*, alone comes from God . . . nu?"

Rachel nodded eagerly. "Yes. And He answers all who seek Him."

Yacov sat back in shocked dismay. "Grandfather?" he whispered hoarsely. "Are you *one of them*?"

"No, Yacov," he replied conspiratorially. "But some of *them* are one of *us*!"

Moments later, Howard burst into the house and called loudly in search of Rachel. "Rachel! Rachel! Good news!"

Her heart already full, Rachel threw back the kitchen door and welcomed him back with a cup of hot tea. "What is it?" she asked.

"I drove down to the blockade, my dear. The British are planning to escort a rotation of the Hadassah Hospital staff up Mount Scopus at three o'clock this afternoon."

"May I go?" she asked breathlessly.

"You and I are first on a waiting list. There are over one hundred scheduled to go up. Doctors and nurses. Aides and the like. If someone cannot go, then we will be allowed to take their place."

"Will it be safe?" Grandfather asked with concern.

"I have little worry on that score," Howard replied. "There will be armored transports, British Bren-gun carriers, and plenty of British soldiers. The Arabs will think twice before firing on the English. It's the Jews they're angry with now."

"What should we do?" Rachel seemed almost flustered. The thought of seeing the baby again drove everything else from her thoughts.

"We'll be up there a few days. Pack lightly, but take a few clean things to change into. They said if you get to go—and I said *if*—you'll be asked to earn your keep up there. They'll most certainly put you to work."

"And what about you, Professor?" Grandfather tugged his beard.

"I have important business at Hebrew University. Some things Moshe wanted me to take care of for him. Notes that need to be locked away for safekeeping, and a few artifacts he hadn't had a chance to take care of."

"Any word on the battle at Kastel?" Rachel clutched his arm. "Did they have any news?"

"You mean you haven't heard?" Howard exclaimed. He noted the doleful strains of a Yiddish melody wafting over the radio. In one swift movement, he turned the dial until a clear British voice whined into the room.

. . . *Some eight hundred Arab Irregulars turned back from Kastel this morning after their leader was seriously wounded in a bat-*

tle that raged throughout the night. Although there has been no official word from the village of Kastel, it has been confirmed that it is still in the hands of Jewish Haganah members.

———

The huge, once-elegant house in Sheik Jarra was now crowded with weary Arab volunteers and soldiers, all waiting anxiously for word on the condition of Fredrich Gerhardt. He would live, but the jagged, gaping wound would keep him from battle. His voice could be heard above the hum of conversation as he cursed the English doctor who had come to stitch him up.

Ram Kadar, two bandoliers of bullets across his chest, stood talking with six men who had just left Kastel.

"We thought they had run short of ammunition," said one young man, rubbing a hand across the stubble on his face. "There were fewer shots fired, even though we were within fifty yards."

"They concentrate on the front row of houses, you say?" Kadar asked, making mental notes.

"Yes. And the muhqtar's house. The bomb came from there. We thought it was over. Commander Gerhardt was shouting a challenge to this hated Jew, Sachar. All of us wanted the reward for capturing him, but it was the commander himself who wanted him most. He put himself at the front, shouting to chill the blood of the Jewish swine. And then from the darkness came the bomb— crashing and booming down toward us, followed by the terrible explosion."

"The barrel bombs," Kadar repeated thoughtfully. "Of the same sort Moshe Sachar used to blow up Jaffa Gate. How many through the night?"

"So many . . . it seemed a hundred. Some sent down were not armed. Only meant to frighten the men."

Gerhardt's angry curses rose to a crescendo in the next room. Kadar smiled bitterly, not expressing his disappointment that Gerhardt would have served the cause better if he had died a martyr in Kastel. "And after Gerhardt was wounded?"

"We withdrew. Daylight was fast approaching . . . no one wanted to face another hour fighting without the commander," came the simple explanation.

Kadar knew that these troops were of little use unless galvanized by the passion of a powerful leader. Now he would fill that void himself and finish the work on Kastel that Gerhardt had boasted would be so simple. "Gerhardt will not be returning to Kastel. But I must. If my subordinates cannot complete such a task . . ." The sentence was unfinished. "You must go out to the souks now for me; call on every man who is a fighter for the Jihad!" His voice was electric with emotion. "I will lead them myself. Tell them that Ram Kadar, right arm of the Mufti, calls them to destroy the Jews who have shamed us in Kastel!"

"Inch Allah! As you will it, Great Commander. The men of Palestine would follow you to Hell or Paradise if you so request it! It is you they will follow! They long to share in the glory of your courage—"

"Then let it be done. We will depart this very morning for Kastel." Kadar bowed slightly. "Go now and tell them to come quickly."

At that moment, the doctor emerged from the room. His sleeves were rolled up and he had a look of absolute disgust on his face. "You are Ram Kadar?" he snapped.

Kadar inclined his head in acknowledgment. "I am."

"Your friend in there wishes—no, demands—to see you. And there is no need to worry about him. He may be off his feet a while, but one so mean as that is difficult to kill. He will live. And I hope to be out of Palestine before he recovers." He shook his head and pushed through the crowds of men standing in groups in the walnut-paneled drawing room.

"Kadar!" A shout from Gerhardt punctuated the doctor's remarks.

The men stepped aside respectfully as Kadar made his way to the room where Gerhardt lay. Gerhardt was pale. Dark circles ringed his red-rimmed eyes. He seemed to Kadar even more evil as he grimaced in rage against the injury that now left him helpless on the bed. His leg was bandaged, and dark red stains soaked through and stained the sheets. "You are well?" Kadar asked, knowing the question would rankle Gerhardt further.

"Well enough to fight!" Gerhardt shouted. "They brought me here without my consent! I could have reached out my hand to grasp Kastel, and they retreated without my permission."

"You know how our fellows are," Kadar answered in a flat tone. "They will not fight without a commander who gives them the passion to do so. Without a leader they are lost sheep who would tend their gardens and raise their brats happily—"

"Do you say I cannot lead my men?" Gerhardt raged. "Get me a stretcher! I will show you how I lead them!"

Kadar's voice was patronizing. "No. You must rest. Did you not vow that today you would take Mount Scopus?" He mocked Gerhardt, who rose up on his elbow with difficulty.

"And so I will! Where are my men? My warriors?"

"They are going back to Kastel. With me!"

"You cannot do this! The Arab Committee has given Kastel to me to take."

"But you did not take it. You have failed, Gerhardt. *Failed*." He smiled at the contorted face of the man before him. "But never mind that. I shall not fail. The warriors have one leader of the Jihad who will lead them to victorious battle."

"You have planned this thing," Gerhardt said menacingly.

"What? I? Plan your wound? Be reasonable, Gerhardt. Allah himself has made this decision." Kadar drew a satisfied breath. "Had I planned it, the madman Fredrich Gerhardt would lie in state as a cold martyr of the Jihad. *That* would make some use of your pathetic, twisted life. Perhaps then men would fight for your memory, at least." His eyes became hard as flint as he gazed at the sputtering Gerhardt.

"We shall see!" Gerhardt shrieked. "Get me Abou Irkat!" he cried at the top of his voice. "Abou Irkat!" And the walls seemed to echo with his fury as he called for a man who had served with him at Bab el Wad and then again last night. Then he turned on Kadar as Irkat entered the room. "Get out!" he shrieked to Kadar. "You shall have your reward, but the day is not finished yet! I am not finished!"

Kadar laughed out loud and turned on his heels to sweep majestically past the quaking Abou Irkat, who stood timidly inside the doorway.

The village of Kastel was deserted and quiet when Fergus Dugan arrived just after dawn with eighty men and fifteen thousand rounds of ammunition.

Moshe, Ham, and Ehud emerged cautiously from the quarry buildings at the sound of their approach. Rested and clean, Fergus hailed him loudly. Nearly all of Moshe's men slept soundly around the quarry.

"You are a welcome sight, little goy!" Ehud boomed, enfolding the Scotsman in a giant bear hug.

"Aye. An' so are you, Captain!" He looked into the pale morning sky. "I see you've run 'em off."

Moshe scratched his head. "Yes, but I'll never know how or why they left. I thought they had us for certain. We used the last barrel bomb. We've checked ammunition and there is far less than I thought last night. Less than five rounds per man."

"Well," Fergus said, "there's not a sign you've killed even one Arab. The hillside is swept clean. I hate t' be discouragin', but if you're going t' use bullets like that, you'd best be sure what y' aimin' at, lads!"

"They've taken their dead with them," Ham said defensively. "And last night we held Kastel as sure as the 'ighland Light Infantry would have done it. No complaints until we've had a bit of sleep, if you please!"

"I know what you're sayin'." Fergus tipped his hat in apology. "Looks like the sergeant-major needs a bed, after all."

"I don't understand where they've gone," Moshe said in wonder as they walked back into the village. "Indeed, there were no dead Arabs on the slope. Only new grass and wild flowers that waved slightly in the breeze."

Moshe showed the interior of the muhqtar's house to Fergus. The walls were scarred inside and out from the battle of the night before.

Dead Haganah soldiers were removed and laid out by their tearful comrades. Each body was identified, then buried in a shallow grave as the wounded were prepared to be carried back to Jerusalem. This time, Ham would not stay. The exhaustion of three nights without sleep had proved too much for him. He slumped silently in a chair as Moshe rehearsed the Arab tactics of the battle.

"Knowin' those fellas," Fergus said grimly, "they'll not stay away for long. You'd best be on your way now, lad. Get your wounded to the hospital. Bring back a Legion tomorrow, will y'?"

Moshe nodded and shook Fergus's hand as his weary men prepared to leave. Moshe suddenly found his energy renewed. For a few hours, perhaps, he would be able to see Rachel again. This afternoon she would sleep in his arms as others held Kastel.

30 Recovery

The sparrow recovered within moments, but Father John Antonell was changed forever. With the arrival of the *Trina*, his well-conceived theory of miracles was swept aside, and he stood face-to-face with the reality of David and Ellie's mission. His objections dissolved, and he converted to the cause of Zion with all the fervor of a Saul on the road to Damascus. But his anxiety increased as David told him again of the impressive and deadly cargo within her hold.

As David and Ellie hurriedly dressed, the priest sent out a team of boys from the orphanage to spy along the waterfront. A note from David was sent to Bernie Greene by way of yet another child, whose wide brown eyes concealed the clever resolution of a street urchin skilled in survival.

Father Antonell stood anxiously at the window now as they waited for word. His hands were clasped tightly behind his back and he rocked nervously on his toes. "I knew this feeling waiting for the boys to get back from bombing runs over Germany," he said tensely. His eyes never left sight of the listing hulk in the harbor. Pumps had been brought out from the docks, and water spilled from the ship with such force that already the ship had begun to right itself. "They'll have her back right in the water soon," he said with alarm. "Now that the storm has passed, they'll have her under way in no time. Unless we can do something—*something!*"

David finished his coffee in silence as the little priest fretted at the window of the dining room. Ellie felt almost giddy with the affirmation that they were, indeed, where they needed to be. With every breath she thanked God for the arrival of the freighter. And she prayed silently for details yet unseen that would have to fall into place.

"The lines to Rome are still down?" David asked.

"They expect them to be down for days," said Father Antonell. "I heard it on the news . . ." He glanced impatiently at his watch. "Where is that boy? He should be here with your Mr. Greene by now. It is not that far." Then he abruptly changed the subject. "I could drive you to Rome, I suppose. To your fellows there. Perhaps they would know what to do—"

"How long would that take?"

"Depending on the roads, several hours at best, I'm afraid."

The bow of the *Trina* rose higher in the water each minute. "That might be too late." David tapped the rim of his cup nervously.

"Yes." Antonell furrowed his brow. "Eight million rounds of ammunition, you say—eight million? And this is being *legally* transported by the Arabs? By the friends of the Mufti?" He tapped his fist against his palm. "Somehow we must stop it. Somehow. Even without your associates in Rome, eh? Somehow. . ."

―――――――――

As the morning sun dried the streets of Bari Harbor, the small boy ran frantically toward the Bari Harbor Hotel. Hand in his pocket, he clutched the note entrusted to him by Father Antonell. *For no one but the Englishman. His name is Greene. Tell Madame Hortencia that Father Antonell has sent you to find him. You must find the Englishman.*

Panting with the exertion, the boy slammed through the door of the hotel and ran to the desk where the fat woman sat reading the newspaper in the dim light.

"Madame Hortencia!" he said in an urgent whisper. "The Father has sent me here!"

The woman raised an eyebrow and gave the boy a quizzical smile. "The Father?"

"Yes. Yes! He has sent me to find an English named Greene who is staying here."

"And what does the Father wish to do with this English? Save his soul?" She laughed, then lit a cigarette.

"No. I must deliver a message." He lowered his voice and looked furtively around the room to where a few women dozed in ragged chairs.

The madame eyed him dubiously. "And what is the message?"

"It is here." He patted his pocket.

She stuck out her sausage fingers, snapping them to demand the sacred slip of paper. "I will see he gets it."

The boy frowned and drew himself up. "No. The Father says I must give it to him myself—"

"You! I cannot have you disturbing the customers when they are busy. Give the message to me."

"The Father says if you give me trouble, I am to tell you he will see you at confession and you will not have communion." The boy was confident of his threat.

Madame Hortencia pulled her shoulders back in indignation. "So. The Father says *that*, does he?"

"Yes." He almost smiled at the look on her face.

She hesitated stubbornly for a moment, angry, then doubtful. Finally she snatched her keys from a tarnished hook. She stood and raised her hand as if to strike the boy. "And not a word of this to anyone. Do you hear me?"

He dodged her meaty hand and circled warily behind her as she led the way to the groaning lift in the lobby.

"This one!" she muttered when they reached the room. She pounded heavily on the thin wood, then inserted the key and threw the door open. Alone in the room, Bernie Greene sat wide awake and alert in an overstuffed chair by the window, his eyes riveted on the listing ship in the harbor. He scarcely glanced up.

"What do you want?" His voice was gruff and excited.

The fat woman cleared her throat loudly. "A note for you, Englishman. From the parish priest, eh?" She was amused. "Perhaps he knows you, yes?"

Bernie turned, his eyes intense as the boy stepped forward and handed him the note. He tore it from its envelope and devoured its content with his eyes. "The *priest!*" he said under his breath. "They are with the priest!"

Not more than five minutes passed before Bernie stepped onto the lift with the messenger. "How long to the church, boy?" he demanded.

The boy answered in broken English. "Only moment, sir . . ." The cable moaned as the lift dropped slowly to the lobby and the metal cage opened.

Before them stood a man that Bernie Greene recognized clearly. Clutching a rumpled newspaper with headlines that screamed *Deir Yassin* was the same man who had been in the

316

telegraph office at Ragusa two nights before. He was unshaven, and his bloodshot eyes seemed almost wild with rage. He looked past Bernie—*through* him—unaware that another human being stood before him. Bernie looked down quickly and put his hand to his forehead as he stepped past him, out into the lobby.

One glance at the newspaper the man held told Bernie that his hunch had been right in Ragusa. *Yes. This fellow has family in Palestine. And he is indeed with the* Trina!

————

Bernie Greene glanced at the crucifix on the wall and then at the black cassock and white collar of the Catholic priest who stood fretfully by the window. He scratched his head in some confusion. David Meyer was odd enough as a member of the Haganah; this priest seemed ludicrous!

Bernie looked from David to the priest, then back again. "Uh, David, may I speak to you privately?"

"He's okay, Bernie," Ellie volunteered. "Father Antonell, this is Bernie Greene."

Bernie eyed the priest with suspicion. "David—"

"He really is okay, Bernie. He knows everything—"

Blinking with astonishment, Bernie demanded, *"Everything?"*

"Enough to know he'd like to help us stop that ship."

"But you're a priest, aren't you?"

Father Antonell nodded. "Of course. Of course. I heard the name of the *Trina* mentioned yesterday morning in the church; I put two and two together and thought perhaps I should help Captain Meyer come to his senses. Then the sparrow hit the window, and the *Trina* came into the port, and—" David laid a restraining hand on the priest's arm. Bernie obviously was not following this line of reasoning.

"You're American, too?" Bernie's eyes grew wide.

"And he's okay," David said firmly. "Did you see what blew in this morning?" He gripped Bernie by the shoulder and pointed to the hulk at dockside.

The thought of the ship agitated Bernie again. "I saw it come in this morning. Watched them tow it around the point. I kept hoping it would just sink."

"A splendid thought," agreed the priest.

"Quite." Bernie took a cup of coffee from Ellie. "Now it looks as if it is back in our hands again, and our suitcase has already blown up a little stretch of Italian coastal water. I have been racking my brains; I assume the lines are still down to Rome?"

The three nodded in unison. "We've been over that a dozen times. It comes down to those of us in this room."

"What about Mikhail?" Ellie said.

"His arms are broken."

"But his mind is not!" Bernie snapped his fingers. "The chap is an expert with explosives."

"If we *had* explosives . . ."

Father Antonell furrowed his brow. "You'll not find anything here that would help you, I'm afraid. What with the political elections, the Communists—everyone in Italy is frightened of what they might do. A farmer may not even blow out a tree stump without a list of signatures from the officials . . ."

"I can only think of the black market in Rome," Bernie frowned. "It is still possible to purchase some war surplus. It is dangerous, of course—risky."

The priest sighed. "Even the black market has dried up, and with good reason—threats from the Reds. Terrorist groups. The government has cracked down completely."

"Probably the only people who have what we need are Communists, Padre," David said unhappily. "They got it all already." He raised his eyes quizzically. "You wouldn't happen to know any personally? Anybody confess lately they've made a bomb out of illegal TNT?"

Father Antonell shook his head. "I'm afraid not. Those kinds have little association with the church or the clergy. *Cave quid dicis* . . . beware what you say to whom." He turned and stared at the ship, wishing, as did all of them, that it would simply slip beneath the surface of the water. Instead, the bow rose another several inches even as they watched.

A sharp rap sounded on the door, and a small, breathless boy stumbled in with his hat in his hand. He addressed the priest in a stream of excited Italian. His cheeks were flushed and he pointed toward the ship. Father Antonell questioned him carefully for several minutes as the others looked on. Then he led the boy to the door and positioned him outside like a miniature guard.

"As I was saying, beware what you say . . . Little Pieter says the sailors of the *Trina* expect to be under way before nightfall. There was no damage to the ship. Only water in the hold." He gestured toward the pumps. "And as you can see, that will soon be remedied. The fellow in charge came aboard in Ragusa."

"I have seen him," Bernie interjected. "He's at the hotel now, no doubt trying to recover from the twenty-foot swells."

"Could we capture him?" Ellie ventured. "Hold him here? They wouldn't leave without him, certainly."

No one answered as each played out the possibilities in his own mind. At last a light appeared on Father Antonell's face. "No, young lady, we cannot hold him," he whispered. "But perhaps the government officials of the Port Authority of Bari might—"

"He's an Arab," said Bernie gloomily. "I saw him send a wire to Palestine when he was in Ragusa—"

Father Antonell raised his chin. "Do the Port Authorities know this for certain? We must buy time. *Cessante causa cessat et effectus . . .* when the cause is removed the effect disappears."

Bernie scratched his head and looked at David in confusion. "Do you know what this chap is saying?"

"I do!" Ellie said loudly. "How is anyone to know that this guy that Bernie saw isn't just *pretending* to be bound for the Middle East with a legal cargo. He's a long way off course, after all!"

"The storm!"

"That's just an excuse." Ellie carried her plotline further. "He's no Arab!"

"Els—"

"Listen!" demanded the priest, his excitement mounting. "Suppose the man is in actuality a Communist. Perhaps the entire crew are Communists who have come here with eight million rounds of ammunition and many thousands of rifles to take over Italy. Don't you *see*?" he exclaimed. "One word, even the tiniest *hint*, that this might be so will set the government upside down with panic. That crew will not be on the street for more than ten minutes after such a story leaks . . ."

"And who will leak such a story?" asked Bernie, leaning forward in his chair. "Who would the Italian authorities believe?"

Father Antonell stood and drew himself up, and he suddenly seemed quite tall to Ellie. "There may be one among us who could pass the word that these fellows might be Communists."

319

He held up a finger. "I said *might*. When they examine the cargo, let the officials draw their own conclusions."

David glanced out at the workers manning the pumps on the deck of the freighter. "I am certain they don't know yet what her cargo is."

"Imagine the alarm of the government when the *Trina* is inspected and they discover that the rumor is true—eight million rounds! Thousands of weapons!" Then, for an instant, Father Antonell looked stricken. "You are certain of your information, aren't you?"

David patted the pocket with the cargo manifest. "This is all we have to go on, Padre, but I don't think I was sent out here to sink a ship full of melons."

Father Antonell stuck out his lower lip and rocked back on his heels. "Well, then, I suppose that this could save lives." He tugged uncomfortably on his collar. "If we are wrong—"

"We aren't wrong, Padre."

"Well, *if* the cargo is not what we have been led to believe, where's the harm? Then I shall simply say that it was a rumor and that I felt it my duty to . . ." The thought that men could die in this game filled his mind. Doubt flickered in his eyes for the first time.

"You're doing the right thing," David said quietly to the priest. "You may never know *how* right!"

Father Antonell smiled wistfully at David. "Funny. All the young flyers I prayed with and sent off to drop bombs in Germany—I must have told them the same thing a thousand times. One may know in one's mind, but still not always be *sure*, eh? I hope my words were more comfort to those men of the Fifteenth than yours are to me. If this plan succeeds, perhaps I am helping to speed someone's entry into eternity."

David lowered his voice and said with certainty, "And if we fail, Padre, a whole lot more will die. And there is no question about that." Then he repeated, "You're doing the right thing to help us."

"I have never been the least bit Zionist." The priest shrugged as though amazed by his own commitment. "At least I wasn't yesterday."

Bernie cleared his throat. "Time. You're just buying us time now. They won't hold the crew indefinitely. Once the legality of the arms sale is established, the ship will be free to sail. Mean-

320

while, you're buying us precious time."

"And if it doesn't sail," Ellie added, "remember the sparrow, Father."

"I can do no less than this," agreed the priest. "The rest must be up to you—and to God." He took his coat from the hook on the back of the door. "I hope you aren't offended that I wish I weren't involved. I would rather you and the *Trina* were elsewhere."

"We'll need to get in touch with Mikhail." David studied the sensitive priest with compassion. He hoped the doubts would disappear again as suddenly as they had come upon him.

"Of course," said Father Antonell. "I'll send the lad along with a note to the Sisters at the hospital." He brushed lint from his long black coat. "And as for me, I will do what seems right and pray that God will control the rest. So *Mox nox in vem* . . . or as they said in the Fifteenth, let's get this show on the road."

———

Moshe and his men had not traveled half a mile before they heard the tramp of the thousands who followed Ram Kadar back toward Kastel. With one swelling voice they sang songs of victory as they approached.

The faces of the Haganah soldiers paled at the sound. Moshe held up his hand to halt his men, who slumped gratefully to the hard ground while Moshe crept forward to peer over the next rise.

What he saw turned his blood cold. The road back to Jerusalem was clogged with a living tide of Arabs who moved *en masse* toward one goal. They blocked the way back to Jerusalem for Moshe and his exhausted soldiers. *Another fifteen minutes and they'll overtake us*, Moshe thought, looking back toward his men. *There is no hope of reaching Jerusalem.* He looked through the field glasses and gasped as his eyes fell on the majestic figure of Ram Kadar. A silver crescent medallion glistened on his chest. *"Kadar!"* Moshe scrambled back, not daring to shout, lest he be heard by an Arab soldier. "We've got to go back!" he commanded urgently. "Several thousand Arabs are on a dead straight course for us. We've got to get back to Kastel!"

"How many?" someone asked in disbelief as the sound of Arab voices echoed in the hills.

"Thousands," Moshe replied truthfully. And his answer stimulated his men with a rush of fear-inspired energy. With the speed of men refreshed by a full night's sleep, the battle-weary troops hurried back across the now-familiar terrain to where Fergus prepared to battle a much smaller force than the army that now flowed toward them like water from a broken dam.

––––––––

Only one hundred men of Gerhardt's original troops remained behind at the summons of Abou Irkat. While the others merged with the thousands of volunteers from the Jerusalem souks, these few well-armed men remained loyal to their wounded commander.

Now, as clouds gathered in the west, they hid along the route that led from Sheik Jarra to Mount Scopus and Hadassah. Gerhardt was borne on a stretcher to a ditch along the roadside at the foot of Scopus. Here, at this deserted bend in the road, he instructed his men as they quickly planted a land mine just below a small rise where the lane narrowed and turned. The wires were fed to a plunger that Gerhardt himself held in his hands. The buildings of the American Colony became a fortress for these men, so skilled in stopping the convoys of Bab el Wad. They had learned their craft well in the gorge, and there was no reason why the same devices could not be used on other roads—even within the city of Jerusalem itself.

––––––––

Unlike Gerhardt, Ram Kadar was a patient man. He spent the afternoon in conversation with his officers, planning the strategy that would win him the victory he was confident was to come.

As thousands camped around the hillsides in full view of the pitiful Jewish contingent of Kastel, Kadar laid a small stack of gold coins on the table before him. He smiled as the eyes of four British deserters lit up.

"The four of you will man the mortars. Two directly facing the front houses of the villages, and one each on the flanks. The Jews have little more than bullets, perhaps a few hand grenades and possibly homemade mines. No match for the mortars."

"You're right on that account, Cap'n!" proclaimed one

scruffy deserter who still had not taken his eyes from the glistening pile of coins.

"There will be eight hours from the time we fire our first shot until sunrise. If the village falls within the first hour, each of you will have eight gold coins as a bonus. For each hour we lose, you lose one of these from your pocket." He smiled a tight-lipped smile at the look of calculation that played on their faces.

"That's a lot 'o gold there!" One man licked his lips and another wrung his hands.

"An' we're your men, Guv!"

"Good," Kadar said quietly. "We will bombard the Jews in a crossfire. They will have very little chance of withstanding that. I would like this completed with as few dead as possible—*Arab* dead, I mean." He poured the coins back into their leather pouch and tied it firmly to his belt.

"And *English* dead, I trust, sir?" added another man, smiling a gap-toothed smile.

"Of course. How else could you collect your bonus? We will begin shortly after nightfall, then. Say, three hours from now?"

The bedraggled expatriates snapped a crisp salute to their new commander, then turned and marched out of the tent.

Kadar stood in the doorway and watched as they slapped each other on their backs and guffawed at the good fortune that had befallen them. He shook his head in wonder at the small payment a man would offer to die for. *Of course, they do not expect to die, do they?* he mused. *Does any man here expect that he will not outlive the grass on these hills? Or that he may not see the sunrise tomorrow? No. Only Jews have learned well about death. Only they have learned to expect that it will come to them because they are Jews. We taught them well that they will die for simply being Jewish. And now they are teaching us that we may die for being Arab.* "How black are the hearts of men," he said quietly. "How rocky and barren are we. How without any hope at all, except to escape the last assassin so that we may outlive the flowers of this terrible spring."

From the safe distance of the rectory dining room, David watched through binoculars as the Italian police swarmed aboard the *Trina* like angry ants. The fat, disheveled captain of the vessel stepped out onto the deck as three Italians rushed toward him with their guns drawn. The captain's eyes grew wide; he raised his hands high, then stepped back against the side of the hulk as though he wished to become invisible. David chuckled as two dozen more policemen clambered down the steps into the hold of the ship.

"Now we're gonna see some fireworks," he said softly.

"Let me see." Ellie tried to take the field glasses, but David held a tight grip on them until, moments later, triumphant Italians emerged onto the deck again. Czech rifles were in their hands and loops of ammunition dangled around their necks.

David gave a low whistle at the first glimpse of the cargo. "The tip of the iceberg." He handed the glasses to Bernie.

"And I don't even have a camera!" Ellie fumed in frustration.

"This is one story you're going to get scooped on, Babe." David put his arm around her. "At least, I hope so."

"Quite," Bernie replied as the crew members of the *Trina* were punched and shoved down the gangplank into four waiting vans. "We should be content that we are the ones *making* the story." He smiled smugly and passed the binoculars to her.

Someone switched off the power to the pumps as Ellie watched handcuffed men climb awkwardly into the vans. She could see clearly the angry scowls of the Italians as their mouths opened to shout orders to their confused prisoners.

Bewildered and terrified, the captain was the last to leave his ship. His great belly drooped over his belt, and his neck and head were rigid between his upraised arms. Only his eyes darted wildly from side to side as though he expected to be shot at any moment. Hauling handfuls of the weapons along as evidence, the Italians followed after. A dozen policemen remained stationed at various points around the deck. As the vans drove off, they relaxed and lit cigarettes and chatted back and forth about the amazing find on board the *Trina*.

"What about that guy Bernie saw in Ragusa? And then again this morning at the Hotel?" Ellie asked.

"The Padre will take care of him too, I'll bet." David poured himself a cup of coffee. "Some little guy, that priest," David added admiringly.

Mikhail arrived a full thirty minutes before Father Antonell returned, breathless and excited. As Bernie translated for Mikhail, the priest recounted the sequence of events. "It was a simple matter of reporting a rumor, you see—the rumor being that the Communists were planning a complete takeover of Italy, starting with the Vatican! The Pope in chains! One does not contemplate such a deed lightly if one is an Italian Catholic!" He grinned, and Ellie could see that he was quite satisfied after all. No one had been injured and the deadly cargo was impounded.

David lowered his chin and stared seriously at the little priest. "Father!" he said, addressing him properly for the first time.

"Yes? What is it? What? Is something wrong?"

"That will be one hundred Hail Marys, if you please," David chided playfully.

Only Mikhail did not seem impressed by the events. He sat glumly with his arms raised at half-mast and firmly set in the plaster casts. As the others discussed the events excitedly, he cleared his throat and interrupted in a monotone of quiet Hebrew. Bernie listened; his smile faded and he blinked and frowned, his face displaying Mikhail's concerns.

"Well?" asked David. "What does the grim Partisan have to say?"

"He wants to know what will happen to the ship and the cargo once its legality is established?" Bernie's reply was greeted by silence. Mikhail spoke again and all eyes turned to him as Bernie interpreted. "He says that the weapons might be taken off the ship soon."

"That is true," agreed Father Antonell. "They will be stored."

"But as soon as it is verified that these weapons are the legal property of a sovereign state—"

"They'll go back on the *Trina*," David finished. He put his hand to his head. "He's right, and then the *Trina* will sail."

Mikhail nodded as their enthusiasm paled in the cold light of reason. He spoke again, and his words reflected his years as a fighter in the Resistance against the Nazis. "He thinks we should do what we set out to do," Ernie said. "We should send her to the bottom."

"With what?" David asked, holding out his empty hands.

Mikhail shrugged as if to say this was not a problem. "Everything we need is on the boat," Bernie replied; then he spoke for himself. "He's right, of course. The boat is a tinder box."

"Right," David agreed sarcastically. "Are you going to blow up with her? Even if we could get on board—and I said *if*—how are we gonna set the stuff off without getting caught in the explosion?"

Bernie pondered David's words, then repeated them to Mikhail. He smiled and wriggled three fingers that protruded from his cast. "He says that's simple. In the Resistance he taught ten-year-old boys how to do the same. We will need three things! A cigarette, twine, and matches. He says it's good that you brought him with you. Very good."

Mikhail nodded eagerly at their confused expressions. "Okay," David nodded grudgingly. "Supposing he can show us some magic trick to make the boat disappear in the water. That's one thing. Get us on the boat, and I guess we could come up with a way to blow her up, and maybe we can get clear. But none of that answers the question of how we're gonna get on the ship."

Father Antonell rose and slowly went to the window to stare at the dock. He rocked on his toes as the others considered the challenge. "There might be a way." He did not look at their faces. "Perhaps I can help you with that." He cleared his throat as though his own thoughts embarrassed him. He quickly crossed himself and looked briefly upward. Then he leveled his gaze on Ellie. "If you are willing, young lady, I am certain there is a way."

Relieved and grateful that she was to be part of the plan, Ellie leaned forward across the table. "What can I do, Father? How can I help?"

He nodded and smoothed the strands of hair across his balding head. "*Mundus vult decipi*—there's a sucker born every minute." He narrowed his eyes and looked her over critically. "Yes. Definitely. I would say that you are equipped to make a sucker out of anyone. A little makeup, the proper clothing—and a little help from Our Ladies of Bari Harbor."

31 The Road to Hadassah

Not far from Mrs. Bett's Pastry shop, on the Street of the Prophet Samuel, a large group of men and women stood beside two armored buses. Among the people waiting for the short two-and-a-half-mile journey to Hadassah Hospital were the elite of Jewish doctors and scientists. They had come from the four corners of Europe to escape the Nazis, and had brought with them little more than their own minds and skill. With that they had built the ultra-modern Hadassah and had staffed Hebrew University with scholars that rivaled any in the world.

Two armor-plated ambulances, marked with the Star of David, were also part of the convoy. One armored car was at the front, while another brought up the rear for protection.

Howard chatted amiably with those who had gathered for the journey through Sheik Jarra. He knew most of the hospital staff members by name and introduced Rachel as the wife of their colleague Moshe Sachar. A dozen expressed concern for him, and in the midst of such familiarity, Rachel felt welcome and strangely at home. These bright and intelligent people had known Moshe long before she had, after all, and she found herself listening with pleasure to their stories of his work at the university.

She, in turn, responded to their questions without hesitation, explaining about Tikvah and her time in the Old City. Two of the doctors promised to look in on Tikvah's progress personally.

It was nearly three o'clock before the lead armored car pulled away from the barricade to check the road through Sheik Jarra. In it was a British officer and an officer of the Jerusalem Haganah. There were only two other British soldiers in the area, and they eyed the prestigious group with a detached interest.

"I thought this was to be a British escorted convoy?" Howard asked Dr. Chaim Liebermann, who stood beside his wife near the first ambulance.

He shrugged. "Insofar as they have promised to keep a sharp lookout on our behalf," he said. "They'll check the road. Look for signs of trouble. Personally, I think everyone is weary of trouble today. Besides, what would the Arabs want with a collection of doctors and professors?"

"Let's face it," Howard grinned. "Most of the Arab doctors and professors have left the country. They may be a little short on intellectuals."

"Perhaps we should have the intelligence to leave as well," joked the doctor.

As their names were read from a list, passengers boarded the gloomy buses. It was well after departure time when the armored scout car returned and the British officer climbed out.

"The road is clear!" he said with a broad wave. "Clear to pass."

A young man with a clipboard stood beside the open door of the first ambulance. Only Rachel and Howard remained standing on the narrow sidewalk. "Sorry," he said grimly. "No room for you two."

Rachel's spirits plummeted. "Please, there must be a place!" She blinked hard as tears threatened to fill her eyes.

"No, I'm sorry. Everyone on the list is here, and there just isn't any more room. We have orders to carry only those who are vital to the—"

The voice of Dr. Liebermann called out to the young man. "We can easily squeeze together. This woman is the wife of one of the university's most notorious professors." A ripple of laughter followed his words. Moshe had indeed become notorious.

The young man looked down at the list again as Dr. Liebermann climbed out of the back of the ambulance and turned to help Rachel inside. "Well, if Dr. Liebermann orders it—"

"Yes," replied the doctor. "We need Mrs. Sachar in Pediatrics . . . As for you, Howard," he winked, "we can put you to work cleaning pots, eh?"

Rachel felt like embracing the distinguished-looking gentleman who had come to their aid. Instead, she tossed her bundle into the back doors of the ambulance and grasped the hands that reached out to help her in. Howard followed and they crammed in together, feeling a sense of adventure and camaraderie.

Mrs. Liebermann sat across from her. Next to the doctor's wife was a portly man who wiped his brow repeatedly, and did not chat with the other six passengers as the ambulance lurched forward. The back of the vehicle was almost totally dark except for two slit windows, and Rachel could not see the faces of the men who shared the space with them.

As Howard talked and joked with their companions, Rachel simply closed her eyes in relief and laid her head back against the cool metal wall of the lumbering ambulance as it wound its way through the crooked streets. *Only a few minutes more and I will hold Tikvah.* Rachel smiled in the darkness. There was no sense of danger for her in this short journey, only an awareness of her destination. The torture of wondering about the baby's well-being would soon be over. Only for a moment did she feel the shaking rush of foreboding. But it did not come from the streets of Sheik Jarra, only from uncertainty. Perhaps Tikvah had not improved, perhaps in Rachel's absence the child's condition had worsened. This alone made the ride seem interminably long and frightening.

———

"They are coming! They are coming up the road!" came the hoarse whisper. The rumble of the vehicles bound for Hadassah preceded even these excited words.

Gerhardt was ready. He flexed his fingers on the plunger of the detonator. His entire body ached. His leg was on fire, yet his mind was clear and dedicated to a single purpose.

The first of the vehicles lumbered into sight, an armored car creeping over the rise like an enormous black bug. It was followed by a Jewish ambulance, then two buses, yet another ambulance, a supply truck, and finally another armored car.

"What we have done in Bab el Wad, we can do here. As we have starved Jerusalem, we shall starve Hadassah," he repeated to Abou Irkat, who crouched beside him in the ditch.

"They will not forget this day!" Irkat's face was flushed with excitement as the vehicles crawled nearer and nearer.

"Get down!" Gerhardt hissed. "If they see you, they may yet escape, you fool!"

Irkat ducked obediently and pressed himself against the dirt bank to listen to the moan of the engines. Hadassah was within sight above them. Only a few more yards would mean safety for the hospital convoy. When they reached this turn, they would be celebrating safe arrival. But Gerhardt had another ending in mind for them.

"You must tell me when the lead car is over the mine," Gerhardt demanded.

"Only a few moments. Yes, the lead car is speeding up. He thinks the end is in sight."

Gerhardt laughed cruelly. "And so it is." His fingers played impatiently on the plunger. The engine's roar drowned out his words.

"Nearer! Only a few yards! Ready . . . ready. . ." The armored car came even with them; Gerhardt could see the treads of the tires. *"NOW!"* shouted his assistant.

At that moment, a deafening roar shook the ditch as a geyser of dirt and rocks rose into the air inches in front of the armored car. Gerhardt had depressed the detonator a fraction of a second too soon. He cursed loudly and tossed the box away. The brakes of the vehicles squealed, but it was too late. It slid to the brink of the giant crater in the road and with a sickening moan, rolled into the pit.

"We have caught the beast!" shouted Irkat, as the wheels of the toppled vehicle spun uselessly in the air.

At that signal, a barrage of rifle fire slammed into the other vehicles as they stopped dead behind their disabled lead car. Gerhardt threw his head back in delighted laughter as the rear car and the supply truck fought to turn around on the narrow road. Bullets clanged against their metal shells; engines revved as panicked drivers jockeyed their reluctant vehicles, turning the wheels back and forth in their effort to escape. Jihad Moquades, frustrated with defeat the night before, now cheered with frenzied passion at the fate of their clumsy prisoners.

The instant before the explosion, Mrs. Liebermann had opened a thermos of hot tea to celebrate their passage. Now the tea had spilled onto the floor and the portly man beside her slumped down as a bullet found its mark through the narrow window slit.

"He is dead!" cried another of the male passengers. "Dead!"

The whoops of the Arab attackers accompanied the sound of bullets slamming against the metal sides of the ambulance. Rachel crouched low and cried out as the frightened driver cursed loudly and tried to turn the vehicle in the narrow space between the fallen lead car and the ditch where Arabs shrieked out with gruesome delight at their predicament.

"Today you will die, Jews!"

"Today you die like those of Deir Yassin!"

"Allah Akbar! God is Great!"

"Revenge for the Jihad martyrs of Deir Yassin!"

Rachel could see the ashen face of Mrs. Liebermann in the dim light. "My God!" Mrs. Liebermann exclaimed in sudden realization. "We are going to die. They are going to kill us here!"

"Turn us around!" echoed the clamor from the other passengers. "Turn us around!"

A hundred bullets, ricocheting off the side of the ambulance, all but drowned out their fearful cries. Howard reached out to grasp Rachel's cold hands. He pulled her to him, shielding her with his own body. "Are you hurt?" There was real terror in his voice.

"Will I ever see my child?" she wept. "Will I ever again see Moshe?" She hid her face against him.

"Deir Yassin!"

"You die for the martyrs of Jihad!"

"Remember the children of Deir Yassin!"

Rachel could think only of Tikvah and Moshe and the child she carried within her. Strangely, as the tumult without grew more fierce, her heart grew more calm. The certainty of her own death left her with only one regret—that the child she carried would die with her.

A loud thump sounded near the front of the ambulance. "They've blown a tire!" cried Dr. Liebermann.

"If only we could get around!" he cried, trying to see through the smoke that obscured his vision out the slit window. The ambulance was turned halfway around in the road. Courageously, Dr. Liebermann peered out the slit window back along the only route of escape.

"Forget it!" he shouted to the driver up front. "The truck and the rear car have escaped. But the others are worse off than we are. The bus behind us has blocked us in."

The shrieks of those passengers were plainly heard and he slammed the door tight as bullets took aim on the open crack.

The driver did not give up. "Maybe I can ram the bus and get by that way." There was certainly no escape past the pit and the ruined armored car in front of them. Two more loud thumps sounded; the ambulance was running only on its rims.

Mrs. Liebermann covered her face with her hands and wept as the assault increased in intensity and the crash of bullets against the steel plate became almost maddening.

"We should make a run for it!" shouted the man nearest the door.

Howard reached out a hand to steady him. "You'll be cut down in seconds! Stay where you are! The British will come. They'll stop this! Just give it a little time. Stay clear of the window slits and give it a little time!"

"They'll blow us up! We'll be trapped in here and burned to death!" sobbed the terrified passenger.

Dr. Liebermann's soothing voice called back. "Calm down! The English must know by now. Listen to the professor! We'll be rescued. We must believe!"

The ominous chant replied to his words as hundreds of Arabs swarmed from the souks to join in the destruction of the Jewish convoy . . . *"Deir Yassin! Deir Yassin! Deir Yassin!"*

Captain Stewart had only just come on watch when the harried voice of the British officer on the Street of the Prophet called in the news of the plight of the Hadassah convoy. "Right, sir. I called for a cease fire. To no avail. Arabs are all along the route and more arriving every minute. I am requesting half a troop of armored cars and an observation officer to arrange for shelling of Arab positions."

Stewart felt irritated at the bother of such news. He pursed his lips angrily and considered the requests. "Negative on the shelling of Arab positions, Chandler. We're bound to neutrality." His explanation sounded flat.

"But, sir, there's no stopping them! We're not dealing with a military situation here. We're talking about a massacre of the doctors and scientists from Hadassah Hospital!" His voice was urgent, pleading.

"And what do the Jews expect?" Stewart snapped. "After Deir Yassin?"

A long silence was the only reply; then the gruff voice of the soldier called back, "Then the armored cars at least. To get these people out of here. An ambulance and a supply truck managed to escape, but we've got two busloads of civilians trapped. And more in another ambulance. I think those in the armored car are okay. They're firing through the slits, holding the Arabs off."

"What do they need the help of the British for?" Stewart replied bitterly. The rancor in his heart for the Jews swelled with the words of the soldier. Had not the Jews murdered Stewart's own brother? And now they had killed an entire village. "What do they expect?" he asked again, as though the issue of the fate of the convoy was already settled. Stewart had long ago decided that only one eye for an eye was not enough. Not one more English life would be lost for the sake of the Jews who had torn Palestine to pieces.

The soldier tried once again. "Requesting permission to use three-inch mortars, sir. Against the Arab attackers." The sound of gunfire crashed in the background clear over the radio receiver.

Stewart set his jaw. "Permission denied, Chandler. Or are you deaf? Our orders are *no interference!*"

A loud explosion sounded. "For the love of God, Captain Stewart! Contact the high command! You don't understand!"

"I'll send along the armored cars as soon as possible. Make the best of it, meanwhile."

A full hour passed before Stewart contacted the drivers of the armored cars. It was almost dusk before they were given orders to move.

32 The Shadow of a Certain Death

There was no need for Bobby Milkin's reconnaissance report. Moshe and the others knew already what they were up against. Arab women from the villages had flocked into the Arab encampment to feed their hungry men before the battle of Kastel. The enemy soldiers were relaxed. They had reason to be.

"I figure three thousand, Staff," Bobby said grimly. "And a few more busloads moving down the road now from Jerusalem. There would be more, but there's a little action in the city itself right now."

Moshe did not press him for information about Jerusalem, but simply assumed that more riots had broken out within the city. Mercifully, Bobby did not mention the name *Hadassah* as he flew high overhead. Moshe answered on their feeble radio. "Raven, *B* group was unable to get back to the city. We have a number of dead and wounded. Tell Tel Aviv we need more men. As many as they can spare, and quickly—"

Bobby's voice was humorless. "Yeah, Staff, I was thinkin' the same thing exactly. I'll pass the word along. And we'll try not to mention the Alamo in the next report."

Ehud squinted at the incomprehensible words of the American. "I can never understand that meshuggener. Half-goy. What is an Alamo?"

"You do not want t' know, Ehud," Fergus answered. "Rather like the Campbell Massacre."

Ehud stuck out his lower lip distastefully. "Massacre, you say? Oy. We know enough about that."

Moshe looked out to where the little Piper hummed above the gorge. A distant echo of Arab gunfire sounded as the Jihad Moquades took aim on Bobby. "It ain't a fit night out for man nor beast," Bobby quipped in one final pass. "They think it's duck huntin' season down there. Headin' back to roost, Staff. I'll relay the word. This is Raven. Out."

The receiver crackled with static and Bobby dipped his wings in salute. Moshe lowered the microphone, feeling suddenly very cut off from the rest of the world. "God go with you," he muttered as the plane vanished in the deepening hues of dusk.

———

Furious with the inaction of the officer on duty, Corporal Chandler paced beside the Haganah officer who had examined the road with him before the convoy had left. As night approached, there was still no sign of any British intervention on behalf of the Jews.

"Where is the Haganah?" Chandler shouted as the attack increased in intensity.

"On the way. Three cars." The answer was curt and angry. "If you Englishmen will allow us to rescue our people without shooting our men down, that is." Chandler stared at the man who had been friendly to him only a little while before the event had begun. The Haganah guard held the list of passengers in his hand.

"I'll try British High Command again. May I borrow your list?" Chandler asked quietly.

The Haganah man handed the list of precious human cargo to the Englishman. He rushed to his radio and once again called in the urgency of the situation. This time he read the list of names to a shocked colonel who sputtered and granted immediate permission for Chandler to assist the Haganah with the use of his mortars. Then, as Chandler left the meager defense to the young Jews who manned the barricade, he hurried off to Saint Paul's Hospice to find vehicles for his own rescue attempt. Moments later, three armored Haganah cars roared up the Street of the Prophet, bristling with Bren guns and rifles. The Jews who had stood by in helplessness now cheered as though the cavalry had arrived to chase off the attacking Indians. Bystanders shouted encouragement, and hearts again held a moment of hope for the fate of those who had come to Palestine to heal, not to kill.

———

The inside of the ambulance was stifling from the heat of the occupants' own bodies. Rachel ached for fresh air; it was a luxury which she knew she might not ever experience again. Outside, it began to grow dark. Only a few rifle shots seemed to hold back the flood of Arabs who had come to sharpen their marksmanship on the bodies of the Jewish doctors in the convoy.

"The fellows in the lead car in the ditch," said Dr. Liebermann. "They are firing. They are still alive."

"That is more than the rest of us will be," spat the bitter, frightened man who sat beside the doors. "Where are our own fellows? *Where?*"

Moments later, his question was answered by three armored cars, clearly marked with the Star of David. The roar of their engines competed with the sound of Arab rifles. Cautiously, Dr. Liebermann peered out the slit and reported the rescue operation.

"They are firing back as they drive toward us . . ."

Rachel wanted to look, but she still hoped for her life and

that of her child, so she stayed low. "They are Haganah?" she begged hopefully.

"Yes!" Dr. Liebermann cried. "You shall see! Soon they will have us out of here!" Then a loud explosion was heard and the doctor groaned. "They've been hit! My God! Up on its wheels and now—" The first Haganah vehicle righted itself and, with smoke pouring from its engine, swerved past the trapped buses and the ambulance, onto a bank and then finally up the road to the relative safety of Hadassah Hospital to deposit its wounded.

The second and third cars were not so lucky. Each of them took direct hits, exploding into fountains of flame and smoke as the passengers of the ambulance wept for their own fate and for those who had died trying to save them.

"What are they doing?" cried Mrs. Liebermann. "Why do they not just finish it? Why do they not simply charge us and be done with this terrible game?"

Howard held Rachel close to him, feeling a great pity for the young woman who had lived through so much. He grieved for Moshe, and ached that there was not some way that he could protect Rachel's life. "They have a plan in this," Howard said calmly, seeing the picture clearly. "They want to show the world that the power is theirs to do as they want. That the British will not help, that our own people cannot help. They take their time, and all of Jerusalem watches—just as the world will watch when the British leave next month."

A low moan came from one of the men in the back. "Doesn't anyone see? Doesn't anyone see us?"

Among these acquaintances, Howard knew that he would meet his death. He answered softly in a voice meant to comfort, "God sees us, my friend." Only moments passed in the suffocating heat of the ambulance as Howard talked about his faith and his hope. *Where can I go from thy Spirit? Where can I flee from thy presence? If I ascend into heaven, thou art there: if I make my bed in hell, behold, thou art there . . .*

And his comrades, who sat entombed with him in the shadow of a certain death, listened to his words.

As the crew of the *Trina* languished moodily in the dank and dripping cells of the Bari Harbor Jail, Yassar sat in the office of the Chief of Police and answered his questions through an interpreter.

"You should admit the truth," the magistrate said with a patronizing smile on his face. "We already know the truth, so it would save you and me both much time if you would simply admit to the charges."

Yassar's thick lips curled in disdain as he listened to the paunchy, graying incompetent who sat across a cluttered desk from him. "You have my passport. I am a diplomatic envoy on special assignment from Syria. What you do here today is illegal. To detain the cargo for a sovereign nation is illegal, and your head will roll for it."

The magistrate's smile faded as the words were repeated. He eyed Yassar coldly. "Passports can be forged. These days in Europe, it seems everyone has a false passport. Everyone who ever raised his hand to salute the Fuerhrer now has a different identity. It seems that no one living ever raised a fist to fight against the Americans or the British. If Nazis can become expert craftsmen in the art of passports, then we can assume that Communists can also forge new passports for their own purposes, no? Purposes such as attacking the Vatican itself? Such as capturing the Pope as hostage until after the elections?" His eyes narrowed as he searched Yassar's face for reaction to his words.

Yassar laughed bitterly. "Absurd! I am Yassar Tafara, messenger of Haj Amin Husseini, who now resides in Damascus."

"And who is this Husseini? A Marxist? A protege of Stalin?"

Again Yassar laughed. "No! A man who resists the Communists as they vote in the Security Council of the United Nations. Have you not read a newspaper and seen that it is the Russians who vote for Palestine to be divided up between Jews and Arabs? Was not Karl Marx himself a Jew? I am no Communist! I and the nations I represent fight against the Jews!"

The magistrate listened to Yassar's explanation with new interest. "So you claim that you are taking these weapons to fight the Jews?" He studied Yassar intently for a long moment. "Have you read the news this morning, then?" he asked.

Yassar's face contorted with anger as the memory of last night's atrocity was mentioned. "Why do you hold me here?" he cried, losing control. "Do you not see that we have lost precious time already? I am a representative sent from Damascus!"

"That would be easy to check; but alas, all the wires are

blown down. We here in Bari will decide. And I cannot take any chances." He tapped Yassar's passport. "You seem to have some passion on the subject of Palestine. But perhaps that passion is also a forgery. Communists are very tricky fellows. We have been warned."

"I am no Communist, *fool*! Cannot you see plainly that I am Arab! I have not one concern for you or Italy or the Pope in Rome! May you all perish in your stupidity!"

The magistrate crossed himself at the outburst and held up the leather folder bearing Yassar's identification. "As I have said. Your identity is easy enough to check, once we can communicate with the outside world again. But it will not be written in the history of Italy that I was a fool and let the weapons go that killed the Holy Father and destroyed the nation! You shall have our most comfortable cell—just in case you speak the truth. You will find the accommodations to your liking." He lit a cigarette and inhaled deeply, indicating that the interview was at an end.

The blackness of the night was profound. Stars glistened like crystal, and a faint breeze carried the scent of Arab fires to the men of Kastel.

Each man waited in trenches or behind stone walls for the attack that would inevitably come from the thousands under Ram Kadar. Somehow the waiting seemed worse than the actual fighting. Nervous hands played on gunstocks and tapped lightly against triggers.

From his post in the house of the muhqtar, Moshe thought that he could see some movement near the foot of the hill. He held his breath and listened, hearing for the first time the quiet thumping of men moving stealthily toward them.

Like last night. Only so many more. Main group attacking the front of the village. Two groups on the flanks. Each of his men was better armed tonight—an additional fifty bullets to each rifle. *But there are so many more Arabs. Maybe we can hold them until morning—if reinforcements arrive.*

His thoughts had come too soon, for even as he had whispered the hope of holding out until morning, the first of the Arab mortar shells thumped from its base and whistled in with deadly accuracy toward the front-line perimeter of Jewish defense.

"*Coming in!*" came the terrified shout from someone in the trenches. Jewish rifles clattered to the ground as Haganah men ducked for cover. The shell exploded in a flash of light as it careened through the roof of a small house. Instantly two more shells followed and then another from the opposite side. The screams of the Jews had not died before yet another barrage honed in with deadly accuracy. And, as yet, not one Jewish bullet had been fired.

"No wonder they were not in a hurry!" one of the men stationed beside Moshe cried. "They'll kill us all and never get within range!"

Again and again the shells boomed against the perimeter, shattering houses and bodies. In reply Moshe fired a flare gun, illuminating the hillside and the white keffiyehs of the Jihad Moquades as they inched through the darkness toward the Jewish positions. In the eerie glow of the flare, they seemed like a vast flock of sheep. "Fire!" Fergus shouted to the men on the right flank. "Fire, lads!"

At that, volley after volley was fired and the Arabs fell as bullets found their marks. The explosions of the mortars were punctuated now by Arab screams as others along the perimeter aimed at the bobbing white headgear that rolled like moving stones up toward Kastel.

For nearly an hour, the crossfire of mortar shells rained down on the Jewish troops, and they replied with a hail of lead so thick that the Arab advance fell back into the ravines and boulders below. Three barrel bombs, newly rigged since the night before, were aimed in the general direction of the mortars and shoved away, tumbling down over the cowering bodies of the enemy. The explosions took a toll on the Arab courage, and the attack was further slowed. But nothing seemed to stop the barrage of mortar fire crashing down against the houses. The dead and wounded were everywhere, and still the Haganah held fast to the line. The wounded were carried back to a house near the quarry, even as a fresh round of mortars slammed in to reap another harvest.

The house of the muhqtar was as yet still basically undamaged. Its position just to the back of the left flank had placed it out of range of the four mortars. Still, the Arabs crawled up the terraces just below Moshe's position. He could hear their voices and occasionally see them as they ran from one cover to another. A dozen times robed figures reared up like ghosts in the darkness as a Haganah bullet stopped the progress of an Arab. Yet still they came; wave after untiring wave they swarmed on.

The deck of the *Trina* was well lit. Its lights glistened on the water of the harbor.

Ellie felt a pang of anxiety as she walked in the midst of six young women from the Bari Harbor Hotel. At the request of Father Antonell, they had been handpicked by Madame Hortencia. With incomprehensible giggles and comments in Italian, the girls and the Madame had dressed Ellie to fit the company she now walked in.

She felt ridiculous in the low-cut, flimsy dress she wore, and the chilly wind that blew in from the Adriatic raised a host of goose bumps on her exposed skin. Behind thick, dark-red lipstick, her teeth chattered uncontrollably. Rouge and heavy eye shadow made her feel conspicuous; the powerful perfume they had drenched her with made her want to sneeze, but she dared not do it for fear of blowing all her makeup into Bari Harbor. Each of her companions also had red hair.

"Nobody gonna be lookin' ata you face anyhow!" Madame Hortencia had said to her. "If alla da girls have red hair, da fellas not gonna remember whatta you face looka like!" This seemed to Ellie like uncommonly good sense. Madame Hortencia had been told that she was a reporter on a secret assignment to get information about the Communist arms ship. She agreed easily to help Ellie get on board, and a fair bribe exchanged hands. Then the Madame had turned to Ellie, decked out in her full regalia. "Hey, you don' looka half bad!" she said. "If you job don' work out, you come back an' see Madame Hortencia, no?" She had pinched Ellie's cheek, removing a fair amount of rouge.

The half-dozen guards who now stood on the deck of the freighter instantly came awake at the sound of female giggles and sight of such a group strolling along the wharf. A stream of enthusiastic whistles and invitations followed.

Ellie tried to act like the rest of the girls, laughing and waving at the men who leaned over the rail of the ship shouting in Italian. Ellie was relieved that she did not have an understanding of the language, and wondered if David and Bernie were watching the performance. She threw her head back in a wild laugh as one of the men singled her out and called something to her. He seemed pleased that she found him so witty, and moved from his post as they neared the gangplank of the freighter.

One hefty, big-bosomed woman, who seemed to be the leader of the party, stepped onto the gangplank and blew a kiss to the guard nearest to her. His eyes grew wide with interest as she spoke to him in tones that were unmistakable in any language. Ellie felt her face flush with embarrassment beneath the rouge. *Okay, Lord,* she prayed silently as they all moved unhindered up the walkway to the deck. *When Caleb and Joshua and the other guys went to scout out the Promised Land, you used the prostitute Rahab in a mighty way. Bless these women, and please remember, Lord, I'm just a journalist and I don't want to work for Madame Hortencia.*

Her heart thumped wildly as all the guards converged to greet them, arguing who would escort the group down below decks to view the wonder of the smuggled Communist arsenal that they so courageously guarded. Ellie fought to remain in the very center of her companions, and as though they sensed her fear, four of them ringed around her and playfully shoved away any eager young males who reached out to touch her. She simply smiled until her cheeks ached, laughed when the others laughed, and thanked God for the protective spirit these women seemed to have for her.

In her hand, Ellie clutched a small handbag. In it was a small roll of twine, a pack of Camel cigarettes, and a book of matches, as Mikhail had instructed. She also carried a piece of blue chalk borrowed from the orphanage school just for this purpose.

The steps into the hold of the ship were steep and narrow. With one guard at the head and another at the rear, the ladies squealed with excitement as they carefully stepped down the steps. The first fellow extended his hand to each of them, helping them from the bottom step onto the slick metal deck below. Each woman made some flattering comment to him in Italian. Panicked, Ellie simply batted her eyelashes, which pleased him sufficiently. He winked back, then gestured broadly as he showed them the cramped galley where the Communist conspirators had undoubtedly taken their meals on the journey to Italy to blow up the Pope. He guided them through the narrow

341

passageways to yet another steep set of steps that led almost straight down.

One by one, Ellie's game companions took the rails and climbed downward into the deep, cold hold of the ship. The guide's voice echoed against the metal sides of the hulk. The stench of stagnant water was in the air, and the metal floor was wet and slippery. Rusty bolts and beams spoke of the age of the *Trina*, and Ellie marveled that it had stayed afloat in the midst of the storm. *It would have been a whole lot easier, Lord—* She did not finish the thought as their guide opened a heavy metal door with the flourish of a magician. He switched on a dim light, revealing hundreds of crates, all marked alike: *Damascus.* Below the word on each crate was another phrase Ellie did not recognize.

Truly curious by now, one of the bolder women coaxed him to open a crate. He complied with a shrug and smile and pried the top from a large wooden box. Ellie joined in the cries of wonder as they all crowded forward to see the deadly cargo that would have snuffed out the life of the Holy Father and ended hope of a democratic Italy.

Hand grenades! He has opened a box of hand grenades! Ellie thought excitedly. Row upon row of the deadly orbs rested in the box like eggs in a basket. And each of the crates in this particular storage compartment bore the same lettering. The entire room was loaded to capacity with hand grenades. Ellie backed against the metal wall and opened her handbag to pull out the chalk. Still showing the proper amount of awe for the revelation, she carefully drew an *X* behind her.

As if on cue, the largest redhead looked her in the eye as if to ask, *Have you seen enough?* Ellie smiled and mouthed *Gracia*, the only Italian word she knew. Then, with exclamations of wonder, the large woman took the guard by the arm and escorted him out of the room. Two others likewise fastened themselves onto the second man, flattering and teasing him as they made their way back toward the steps.

Ellie followed, pressing the chalk discreetly against the side of the hull. A faint blue line traced their path from deck to deck and finally back up the steps to the top deck.

Here Ellie slipped away from the others. When they turned right toward the gangplank, she turned left to emerge on the back side of the *Trina* facing away from the dock. Still tracing a line along her path, she walked rapidly to where a coil of rope lay near the cabins. A knot of fear formed in her stomach as she scraped the blue line directly to the rope. Looking over her shoulder, she found the end of the coil and tied it firmly to the rail of the freighter. Breathless with the effort, she heaved the heavy coil over the edge and listened as the end slapped against the water. Then in final fulfillment of the plan, she propped the handbag against the side of the cabin just opposite where the rope dangled.

The voices of the women were loud and raucous. They had kept the men on board the ship busy and amused. Ellie felt near to tears with gratitude and relief as she found them all standing beside the gangplank. Two of her protectors spotted her and hailed her as if to ask where she had been. Ellie feigned embarrassment and shrugged, pretending to be lost, and they all laughed and teased her in words she could only guess at. One woman on each elbow, they surrounded her again, according to the express orders of Madame Hortencia. Quickly they led her past the leering members of the guard and down the gangplank to the solid safety of the wharf.

Catcalls and whistles followed them from the dock, and the jovial laughter of the men could still be heard echoing up the dark street as they returned to the Bari Harbor Hotel.

———————

Twenty minutes later, Ellie explained to David the exact position of the rope, the handbag, and the faint blue line of chalk.

"You mean the whole room was filled with grenades?" David asked in wonder.

"Crates and crates of them," she answered.

"Did you see anything else? Guns? Ammunition?"

"Only the grenades. Isn't that what Mikhail said would be best? Grenades?"

"Yes," David answered, excitement filling his voice. "But a whole room of them! And right in the bow."

Bernie Greene poked his head into the room. His face was smeared with grease, as was David's. "You ready?" Bernie asked.

David nodded, then kissed Ellie's smeared lips. He looked at her a moment, and the realization of what he was about to do fell heavy on both of them.

"David?" Ellie's voice was shaken, almost pleading. "Be careful, will you? It's a long way from the cargo hold to the deck. Don't take too long, okay?"

He nodded and grasped her by the shoulders. "You're really somethin', Babe," he said softly. "Really you are." He kissed her briefly. "See ya . . ."

"Yeah, see ya," she said. As the door closed behind him, she added in a whisper, "I love you, David."

33   Fire and Water

Gerhardt had been moved onto the hill directly above the site of the ambush. Now, he sat with his leg stretched out, taking careful aim with a rifle. His target was the narrow slit window on the first ambulance.

Below him lay the smoking hulks of the would-be rescue cars; the stench of burned flesh filled the air of the street. From his perch, he had directed every action of his men, relishing the slow agony with which the convoy carrying the Jewish elite had perished. He had been confident that the British would not interfere with his attack. The Jewish deeds at Deir Yassin had been a license for him to do whatever he wished. Before, he had done his work in the darkness of Jerusalem back alleys. Now, he was at liberty to attack in the open anyone he chose for a target. And this was only the beginning.

It had grown dark in the street. The wails of the dying Jews had become more faint. He turned to Irkat and spoke calmly, like a man ordering coffee at a restaurant.

"It would be nice to have a fire to light the night, I think. A very large fire. Molotov cocktails should do it." He smiled. "Tell the men to finish the game."

Irkat nodded and quickly left the room as Gerhardt again raised the gun to his shoulder and took aim on the crippled ambulance.

A frantic pounding sounded against the back of the ambulance. "Get out!" cried a voice. "You will all be burned alive!" Then the voice shrieked and died.

At that moment, Howard rose up to peer out the slit into the street. A sheet of orange flame was moving toward them. The bus directly behind had already caught fire, and as its passengers jumped out and ran, they were shot down by snipers.

Dr. Liebermann also peered out his opening. He turned to his wife after a silent moment pierced by screams from outside. "It is finished," he said sadly. "They have won." Then a single bullet found its mark through the narrow window, and he slumped over, dead in her arms.

She cried out, and the ambulance driver shouted, "There are better ways to die than burning!" He opened the door and rolled out onto the road. The man in the far rear followed suit, plunging out into the night as the fire moved nearer.

"Professor!" Rachel cried as the other passengers followed, sprinting toward a dark ditch. For the first time Rachel saw the faces of the men who had shared this coffin with them.

"Come on!" Howard shouted, urging her to the open doors even as a man fell dead a few paces from them. "Keep low! Stay beside me!"

Together, they leaped out of the van. Howard pulled her low to the ground and shielded her with his body as they ran for the cover of the ditch. Behind them the flames followed the trail of gasoline, spreading and licking the tires of the ambulance. Moments later it exploded in a ball of light and flame.

Howard pushed Rachel hard into the ditch, then rolled in beside her. The dead ambulance driver lay four yards away.

She covered her head with her hands as the bright flash of the fire illuminated a living hell at the foot of Mount Scopus. Rachel was sure that the people at Hadassah now watched the fires that devoured the lives of their colleagues. "God!" she cried from the depth of her soul as machine gun bullets tore the bank in front of them. "Be merciful, God!"

A choking smoke rose up, concealing them in a thick haze. From the midst of the darkness Rachel could hear the sound of an engine.

"Stay down!" Howard shouted, covering her with his arm.

"Someone is coming!" she sobbed, a glimmer of hope rising in her heart as the engine came nearer.

Someone else toppled into the ditch, still and crumpled where he had fallen. Figures darted through the fire and smoke, searching for safety, but ultimately tumbling into the inferno. Rachel could feel the heat of the flames as they rose high in the air. Still the rumble of an engine crept nearer. "Keep down!" Howard held her tightly. "It could be Arabs!"

But the headlights of an armored vehicle moved just out of reach of the burning bus. The hatch opened, and the British corporal who had inspected the road poked his head out. "Come on!" he shouted to a wounded woman in the road. "Come on!" He waved her on as she crawled toward him. An uninjured man darted from the shadows and helped her up, scrambling into the vehicle.

"We can make it!" Howard yelled. "We can make it to the transport!" He yanked hard on her arm and they crawled along the ditch on their bellies until they were even with the armored vehicle. Again, the Englishman called to a survivor.

"You can make it! Run for it!" A man ran, limping to the hatch, and was swallowed up in its safety.

"We're coming!" Howard called. "Don't leave yet!"

"Hurry!" replied the Englishman, spotting them where they crouched. "Run for it, old chap! My gunner's just been hit!" The soldier ducked back in, but left the door ajar as he revved the engine.

Howard sprinted from the ditch, dragging Rachel after him. A barrage of bullets tore the ground just behind them. He flung the hatch wide and shoved her in. Then, at the moment he leaned into the crowded interior, he was hit in the back by a bullet. It sounded like a slap. He groaned once and tried to climb in, but lost his footing. The British soldier cursed and stretched out his long arm to grasp Howard and pull him into the car.

"Professor!" Rachel cried. "Dear God! Please . . . please!" The metal door clanked shut, and as Rachel held Howard tightly, the British corporal slipped the transport into gear and worked the wheel wildly as he tried to maneuver around wreckage and flame to safety.

As the metal skin of the vehicle was pelted with a fresh barrage of bullets, a Jewish passenger moved the dying gunner and scrambled to take his place at the machine gun.

Rachel closed her eyes and prayed; the car rocked violently

as it careened around corners and over debris and wreckage in the road.

Howard's breathing was labored. Rachel stroked his hair and spoke to him through her tears. "Please, Professor. Not you . . . don't—"

"We're almost to Hadassah!" shouted the winded British corporal. "Hold on. If you're wounded there will be medical attention! Just another minute or two!"

The sound of crashing bullets faded. Now the only sounds were sobs and the groans of the wounded. The headlights of the car shone on the sidewalk of the hospital, crowded with men and women with tear-stained faces. Deftly, they assisted in unloading the injured passengers from the vehicle.

"This one is dead," said a grim-faced doctor, closing the eyes of the gunner.

The English Corporal Chandler hung his head and said softly, "I'm so sorry. So, so sorry." Then he sat down on the curb and wept as the fires glowed brightly at the foot of the hill.

———

Full of apologies, the Magistrate of Bari Harbor hurried through the dank, rat-infested jail toward the cell of Yassar Tafara. He carried in his hand the prisoner's passport, along with a furious telegram from the Syrian Embassy in Rome.

Legal cargo . . . unlawful seizure . . . immediate release . . .

The magistrate feared for his position and cursed as the guard fumbled with the key in the rusty steel door. He laughed nervously as Yassar shielded his eyes from the light and sat up on the straw pallet. "What do you want now?" Yassar demanded.

"A thousand pardons, sir. A silly mistake. Of course you are a diplomatic envoy! And so important!" He waved the passport. "Damascus! Yes. You go to fight the Communist Jews, no? Well, one cannot ever be too sure. We have only had a few hours' delay!"

Yassar stood and snatched the passport and the telegram from the babbling Italian as his jumbled words were translated. "A silly mistake. Yes! You fool! And you have cost me even more hours! Where is the crew of the freighter?"

"Why, I have sent men to fetch them. There are vans waiting outside now to return you to the *Trina* in haste. You may certainly sail with the tide, just as you would have had this not happened!" The official's voice was trembling. He would speak to Father Antonell and track down this terrible rumor which might well cost his job. "And rest assured that we will find the men responsible for your delay. Perhaps they are Communists themselves?"

Yassar studied him with contempt, then pushed past him into the stinking corridor. The rattle of other keys told him that, indeed, the crew of the *Trina* was being released.

———

The chill of the harbor water made David and Bernie ache to their bones. A thin film of oil on the top of the water clung to their hair as they swam quietly toward the *Trina*.

David was already tired when they reached the coarse rope that dangled from the rail thirty feet above where they treaded water.

Drawing a deep breath, David grasped the rope to hoist himself up. Oily hands and his own weight seemed to hold him down, and he hung there, unable to move for a moment until Bernie hissed impatiently, "Hurry it up, Yank!"

With that, David pulled himself upward hand over hand in a slow, slippery climb to the deck of the freighter. At last he grasped the rail with a slick hand. Shivering with the cold, he hoisted himself under the railing and rolled over toward the wall of the cabin. *Just like she said! Good girl, Ellie!* He silently cheered her as his hand touched the little handbag propped against the metal wall of the ship. As Bernie inched his way upward, David scanned the dark metal for the faint blue chalk line. Barely visible in the dim light, it pointed back toward an open hatch.

David looked furtively from side to side, ready to dive back into the harbor if they were spotted. There seemed to be no one patrolling this side of the ship, and as Bernie arrived, dripping and breathless, David pulled him along Ellie's trail.

The echo of voices could be heard as they neared the hatch. David plastered himself against the dark metal and waited, listening for footsteps. There were none. He tapped Bernie lightly and moved to the steps that led downward. Their bare feet made no noise against the metal, but water from their bodies left a clear trail as they crept through the belly of the ship and traced the chalk line down narrow corridors through a series of hatches to yet another set of steps. The sound of boot heels clanked on the deck above them, but there was no one below deck to interfere with their mission.

David held Ellie's handbag tightly as they hurried down the last set of steps into the cargo hold. Here, the line nearly faded out completely, but her instructions had been so thorough that David knew the way to the forbidden cargo as though he had been with her on her journey.

"Here," he whispered, alarmed by the sound of his own voice. He turned the latch on the door and shoved it open. Bernie followed him in and shut the door behind, leaving them momentarily in total darkness. David groped for the light switch and the dim bulb winked on, displaying a remarkable collection of precious crates.

"Incredible!" said Bernie in a hushed voice as they raised the lid on a nest of hand grenades. "Astonishing!" He lifted one deadly orb to the light and examined it as David opened the handbag and emptied its contents onto the lid of another crate.

"Cigarettes, twine, and matches. Combine with one grenade, and we've got a bomb," David muttered, rehearsing Mikhail's instructions. "And now for the hard part—"

"This little fellow looks as good as any," Bernie said with a trembling voice. He laid the grenade beside the other ingredients. "After you."

David glanced around the room at the crates that contained thousands of grenades. He gulped hard and unwound the twine as Bernie tore a dozen matches from the matchbook and pulled a cigarette from the pack. "Our fuse," he whispered.

"Mikhail says this will give us about ten minutes. Plenty of time to get out of here." David looked him in the eye and picked up the grenade. "You want to hold it, or should I?"

"Go ahead," Bernie nodded his head. "My hands are shaking."

"So are mine." David swallowed hard and depressed the firing mechanism on the grenade.

"Don't release that, Yank, or it's all over."

While David held the lever, Bernie positioned the cigarette against the grenade and began to wrap the twine carefully around it until the twine held the lever down and the cigarette in place beside it. Then he wove the matches into the twine near the base of the cigarette. "Let's get this straight, shall we?" he muttered.

"Mikhail says it will take the cigarette ten minutes to burn down to the matches. When they ignite, they burn through the twine. When the twine burns away, the lever on the firing mechanism releases, and kablooey! Right?"

"That is what I understand. Ingeniously simple—if it works."

David still held the lever down, afraid to release it even though it appeared to be securely tied with the twine. The pin remained in the grenade, however, so he slowly released his grip to find that the lever was tightly pressed in place. The end of the cigarette protruded beyond the top of the orb. "You light 'er." David handed the grenade to Bernie, who took a deep breath and struck a match. He held the wavering flame to the tobacco, which began to glow as he drew in his breath.

"All right, Yank. Ten minutes and counting. Pull the pin and let's get out of here!"

David closed his eyes and prayed silently as he jerked the metal loop away from the grenade. There was no going back. The bomb was armed and deadly now as the cigarette burned down toward the matches. With infinite care, David placed it on top of the nest of grenades. Then, as though they were being pursued, the two men pushed open the thick door and tumbled from the room. Without looking back, they ran for the steps in the heart of the freighter.

David and Bernie had climbed only to the top of the first set of steps when the police vans rolled to the dock. David froze for an instant as the boots of the guards clanked noisily on the decks above them.

"Something's up," David whispered.

Bernie nodded in agreement, then tapped his wrist to indicate that time was rapidly passing. He nudged David to say there was no time to worry about anything now but getting off the *Trina*.

Outside, Yassar Tafara stepped out of the van and strode angrily up the gangway. Shouting and cursing the Italian guards, he ordered them from the ship as the magistrate stood on the wharf wringing his hands and affirming Yassar's orders to his men.

The somewhat bewildered captain and crew of the *Trina* emerged from the police vans more slowly. The Italians hastily took their places inside the vans for the short trip back to the station. Yassar stormed from one side of the deck to the other, shoving Italian guards toward the gangplank and answering their obscene gestures in kind.

David's heart was thumping with terror as they scrambled through the narrow corridors toward the exit. The blue line of chalk seemed to pull them along, but in his fearful mind, David reasoned that the line would also point to them if it was discovered. They had reached the tiny galley, twenty paces from the final stairway, when a raging voice called down in Arabic.

Bernie understood the words, and his eyes grew wide with the knowledge that they were about to come face-to-face with the Arab from Ragusa, the same man who had been at the hotel this morning. "What is this?" the Arab stormed. "The deck is wet! Someone is aboard!"

Bernie drew David back behind a drab brown curtain into the cook's quarters. He held a finger to his lips as the voice again shouted down the stairwell. "If anyone is down there, you have ten seconds to come up! Then I, Yassar Tafara, will throw your dead body from this ship!"

David looked to Bernie in hopes of an explanation, but Bernie shook his head violently and again held his finger to his lips as Yassar counted down the ten seconds.

Tapping his wrist, David felt a rush of panic. He envisioned the smoking cigarette, its orange glow eating its way through tobacco and paper toward the ring of matches that would burn through the twine. *About ten minutes, Mikhail said. About. Maybe more, maybe less.* The terror of time passing and the man blocking their escape took David's breath from him. He jabbed Bernie hard, tapping his wrist and motioned frantically with his thumb toward the steps.

"I am coming down!" menaced the voice of Yassar.

Bernie grasped David firmly by his arm and pulled him farther back into the tiny alcove. This time David tapped his wrist and pointed down to where the bomb was set two decks below. Foremost in both of their minds was the chain reaction of explosions that would undoubtedly rip the bottom out of the ship. They would have to be far from it, or they, too, would be certain casualties.

Sweat poured from David as the sound of boots clacked against the cold steel of the steps. "I can hear your breath," Yassar said as he paused a moment. "There is someone down here. I hear your fear as you breathe."

Bernie closed his eyes and tried not to breathe so rapidly. A low chuckle came from Yassar as he stepped into the corridor, now firmly blocking their path of escape.

An inch and a half of tobacco ash fell onto the grenade. Only a fraction remained until the heat of the flame reached the first of the matchheads woven into the twine.

"I see your mark here along the corridor." Yassar's words were oily and confident. "I see the water here along the floor. You are not a guard. Not Italian." He laughed again. "I know you are here. I hear your breath. I smell your sweat. You are a *Jew*! You had me arrested; it almost worked—almost." His footsteps came slowly toward where they hid.

Bernie froze in terror, trapped between the rapidly diminishing fuse and the man in the corridor. David shook himself loose from Bernie's grip. He was certain now that there was no more time to spare. With a shout, he jumped from behind the curtain, striking the Arab full in the face with his elbow.

A shot resounded from a small pistol that clattered to the floor. Yassar fell backwards, slamming down hard against the cold steel as David and Bernie struggled to clamber over him.

Yassar's flailing arms pummeled at them. He caught Bernie by the foot and held him back as David raced to the steps.

"He's caught me!" Bernie cried, struggling to free himself from the iron grip of the Arab.

David whirled around and ran back; Bernie fell to the floor as Yassar turned over and held him more firmly. There was no time to fight fairly. With the careful aim of a punter on the fourth down, David drew his bare foot back and kicked Yassar full in the face with his heel. He flew away from Bernie and slammed against the galley table.

Above them, men ran toward the sound of the commotion as David half-dragged Bernie to the steps that led to the deck— and ultimately, to the water and freedom.

"Stop them!" Yassar shouted, his face bloodied and his eyes wild with rage. "Stop the Jews!" he shrieked as David emerged from the hatch. Half a dozen Slavic sailors spotted him at once and rushed to where he pulled Bernie onto the deck. In seconds the rough crew was upon them. David scrambled over the wall of men in one final burst of energy.

"Bernie! Jump for it!" David shouted as a pair of arms reached out to grasp his oil-slick waist in a vise-like grip. He struggled toward the rail, kicking out against the faceless hulk who held him back.

"Catch them!" Yassar shrieked, staggering from the hold of the freighter.

With a cry, Bernie tumbled into the water. David grasped the rail and dragged himself close to it. Mustering a final surge of energy, David kicked at the man who held him, catching him in the groin. With an agonized cry, the man fell away and David leaped from the deck into the murky water below.

Angry shouts from the deck of the *Trina* resounded in the harbor. Within moments, searchlights clicked on and squads of harbor police ran up and down the wharf, shining lights onto the pilings as they searched for two oil-smeared Jews.

Two minutes later, Bernie and David hauled themselves into a small dinghy moored beside a fishing trawler. They lay panting and breathless in the bottom of the little boat. Ten minutes and more had gone by, and the *Trina* was still tied peacefully intact to the dock.

"It didn't work!" David gasped, holding the ache in his side.

"So much for Mikhail's secret weapon," Bernie groaned.

"All this for nothing—"

At that instant a terrible roar sounded in the belly of the *Trina* as a searing light split her aged seams and lifted the bow out of the water. Windows for two blocks shattered under the force of the blast; even the Bari Harbor Hotel listed a little farther on its foundation.

David covered his head as debris splashed around them. "It worked!" they both cried in unison, laughing loudly as great swells rocked the tiny boat where they hid.

34 Dawn in Zion

Ram Kadar was pleased. With only four mortars and an ill-equipped army of volunteers, Kastel was falling before him. It had taken longer than he had anticipated to wear them down, but the Jews were giving up the village by inches and yards, and with very few Arab casualties. This night, Allah had smiled on them. Kadar had taken a mindless rabble and pulled them together into a fighting force that would follow him anywhere.

Gazing up into the predawn sky, Kadar breathed a sigh of satisfaction. "Four mortars," he said aloud. "Only four small mortars! How the Jews will quake when the shipment of *real* weapons comes to this shore."

An excited young man ran toward Kadar and bowed low. "We have routed them!" he cried. "Everywhere along the line they pull back. The Jews flee in terror to the quarry. That will fall by dawn. Victory is ours, Commander Kadar."

"So it is finished," said the commander, suddenly hungry. "We will raise the flag at sunrise and eat our breakfast in the house of the muhqtar."

"The men wait for you! They call for you!"

He paused as a distant chant rolled down from the slopes. *Kadar! Kadar! Kadar!*

The Jewish defense of Kastel had crumbled beneath the heated attack of Ram Kadar and his followers. Moshe ran from house to house now, shouting to his men, helping the wounded as they pulled back to the final line of defense, leaving the demolished houses to triumphant Jihad Moquades.

In the deep shadows behind a wall, he and Fergus quickly conferred.

"If we can at least hold the quarry until reinforcements come . . ." Moshe began. "Another hour till dawn . . ."

"We could hold the quarry if we had ammunition, lad," Fergus warned. "But they've not let up! They've not given us a minute's peace all the night through! Y' must get your men out any way y' can, in my opinion . . . or there will be another Campbell's Massacre—another Alamo—right here."

Even as he spoke, a shell whistled overhead, exploding in the courtyard. "Don't be a fool, man." Fergus grasped him firmly.

"The quarry!" Moshe insisted. "We can hold until dawn, until reinforcements—"

"An' what if the reinforcements don't come?" Fergus insisted in dismay as the shouts of *Jihad* came nearer.

"Look, Fergus," Moshe said quietly, "we are going to have a miracle here. Either God is going to assist us, as He has in the past, or there will be a real miracle, and the army will break through."

Fergus wiped grime from his face. "Ah, you're all madmen, you Jews! And I'm a madman for joinin' ye," he sighed. "All right. The quarry it is!"

Suddenly cries for help emanated from the open door of the muhqtar's house, where Moshe had just given orders to pull back. Fergus nudged him, and the two of them zigzagged back to the house. It seemed deserted; then a feeble cry for help came from a bedroom that faced out over a high ledge of limestone with steps carved into its face.

On the floor, a young Haganah boy of eighteen lay bleeding from a bullet in his right shoulder. "Help me," he begged. "I can't walk . . ." Moshe touched his wound. The flow of blood was heavy. "They're all around down there!" the boy whispered hoarsely. "I can hear them."

"It's all right. We'll be out of here in a—" He stopped and listened as the sound of footsteps moved up the stone stairs.

"Who's there?" Moshe called in English.

The reply returned in Arabic, "It's us, men." The voice was confident that the victory had been won. Obviously, the men on the steps did not expect any members of the Haganah to still be this far forward.

Moshe slung the boy over his shoulder as Fergus aimed a sten gun out the window and sprayed the hillside below them. Then, goaded by a healthy respect for the Jihad troops that swarmed toward them, Moshe and Fergus bolted across the village square toward the rock quarry, still firmly in Jewish hands. There they would wait until the dawn brought either the miracle of reinforcements or the last battle of Kastel.

Sirens wailed as antiquated fire engines roared to the wharf of Bari Harbor. The bow of the freighter protruded from the water and flames leaped up, threatening the dock itself.

As Bernie rowed the little boat toward the far side of the harbor, David craned his neck back to see in the distance little men running about, but making very little headway in extinguishing the inferno on the *Trina*. As the glow reflected in the water, he could make out the bobbing figures of the crew who had been knocked into the water by the explosion. Now they clung to pieces of debris as other members of the crew tossed them ropes and hauled them up like fish on the end of a line.

"Bet they're mad at us," David said.

"We've given them reason enough. Blew the bottom clear out of her," Bernie replied. "I'd say there'd be little damage to anything but the boat, if those idiots would learn how to handle a fire hose."

David laughed as he watched the force of water in a hose knock a team of men into the harbor beside the drenched crew. "Reminds me of a fraternity party, complete with a bonfire, and ending with shoving everyone in the pool." He grinned and looked at Bernie, whose hair hung down in oily strands on his forehead. "You don't look so good yourself. I'm trying to figure out how we're going to get back without getting caught—two wet guys in oily underwear. Somebody might get suspicious."

"At this point I can tell you, my friend, no one is even thinking about us, with the possible exception of your wife—and perhaps our Arab friend back there."

"Yeah. I hope he doesn't know how to swim." David peered over the edge of the boat into the murky water.

"That is exactly what the Mufti said, you know."

"Yeah? When did he say that?"

"He told the United Nations he would drive us Jews into the sea—"

"Hey," David grinned as they bumped up against a ladder on the deserted south dock of the harbor. "Jews don't *need* to know how to swim, pal. It's Passover, remember? A pillar of fire behind to hold off the Arabs and *poof* the Jews cross over on dry ground. Isn't that the story?"

"You still believe in miracles like that for us?" Bernie asked, genuinely curious.

"Yeah, pal." David grasped the ladder. "That's what we're all doing here in Bari."

———————

Only thirty-seven men of the Haganah forces were still able to fight. Bullets were consolidated and distributed to the positions that held the rock quarry. The approaching Jihad Moquades had first overrun the village and now sought to scrape the Jews from their final foothold on the mountain.

Moshe ran through the darkness to a small building where Fergus and Ehud defended twenty-seven wounded young fighters; their bodies were jammed together side by side from one wall to the other. Fergus ducked low beneath one window, while Ehud fired a sten gun through the other.

"When is help coming?" cried one of the wounded.

"How long can we hold out here?"

Moshe ignored their questions. He had no answers for them, only hope for a miracle. "Fergus!" He tossed the little Scot a small pouch of bullets. "That ought to hold you a while."

Fergus hefted the pouch, not impressed by its meager contents. The expression in his eyes said, *I told you so.* But he did not speak the words. They might have gotten out a half hour ago; now, as dawn approached and the Arabs surrounded the quarry, it was impossible. His jaw set grimly, Fergus said simply, "Alamo." Moshe understood the meaning.

Moshe replied, "Keep hoping. The men in Tel Aviv know our situation. Dawn is coming. They'll be here by sunup."

"They'd better be!" Ehud cried, firing another round at a pair of Arabs who sneaked cautiously toward them. "With the village under an Arab flag, our reinforcements will have difficulty doing anything more than rescuing us."

A call for ammunition sounded from a second building, which also housed wounded Haganah soldiers. Moshe glanced around the room at the faces who looked to him for leadership. He had failed them. *Alamo!*

A young man held up a bayonet and said hoarsely as the blood soaked through his bandages, "I will take a few with me." A murmur of agreement rippled among the men, some of whom could not even lift their heads.

"It is still the week of Passover," Moshe replied as the cry for ammunition again echoed across the quarry. "Remember the miracles, boys. Think of the Red Sea, and pray."

"Aye," said Fergus without a hint of humor. "Aye, I'm prayin', man. An' it'll take more than reinforcements to save our skins." He raised the rifle to his shoulder. "From the looks of it, God is not handin' out any miracles for Jews—or Scots, either." He fired, and a scream answered the report of the rifle. "But there's one we'll not have t' worry about . . ."

"There is no miracle like a dead aim," Ehud said. "Not in the Jewish army, anyway."

Fergus cracked a smile for the first time, and Moshe ducked outside to pick the safest approach to the stone house opposite him. He crouched low and dodged from stone block to stone block. "It's Moshe here!" he shouted before he dared to push open the door.

"Ammunition, for God's sake!" shouted a harried man at a window that looked down on a hundred Arabs stealing up toward the house.

Moshe gave him what there was—forty-two rounds, and as the soldier cursed, Moshe prayed and waited for a miracle; waited for men from Tel Aviv, and hoped that *if* they came, they could break through the wall of Jihad Moquades who pressed in around them.

"Your last dawn, Jews!" a fierce voice echoed against the stone walls of the quarry and filled it with an ominous foreboding. "Look to the east! See your last morning!"

"Jihad!" shouted another.

"Remember our fallen!"

The ring of bullets ricocheting off the stones increased as the sky grew lighter and the hope of the Haganah grew dimmer. And as Moshe shouldered his gun at the final line of defense, his thoughts flew toward Rachel. To Tikvah. To the baby. *Even if this is the end, it is not*, Moshe thought. And though he wanted nothing more than to spend a lifetime with them, he knew that if a lifetime was not possible, eternity would still be their hope. *Comfort her heart, if I am gone*, he prayed as the gravel from Arab bullets sprayed his face.

"Death to the infidels!" came a cry from behind a stone.

"How brave they are in their thousands!" whispered a wounded soldier.

"Your graves are dug, Jews!"

Moshe heard Ehud's booming voice reply, "And you will fall into them!" He punctuated his remark with another round that hit the edge of a stone and sprayed a Jihad's face with fragments. The Arab fell to the ground, clutching his eyes, but even as he fell, two more moved up to take his place.

The sky lightened and one bright morning star shone down on the handful holding off the hordes. Still there was no miracle to turn them away.

Dressed in clean, borrowed clothes, Rachel stood against the wall of Howard's hospital room and watched as he drew one ragged breath after another. He was ashen, his skin waxy and pale. He seemed to blend into the sheets that covered him.

She wanted to run back to Tikvah's room and stare in wonder at the only spot of beauty and innocence left for her in the world, but she could not go. Howard Moniger had called for her repeatedly, and now they said he lay dying—*dying!* It seemed impossible, and yet, long ago Rachel had learned to see the impossible as inevitable. *So many goodbyes—too many.* She thought of Moshe with a renewed fear. Were there no miracles left for God to spare? Would he, too, fall in the battle of Kastel before the fires of the convoy to Hadassah had abated?

She held her hand over her womb and closed her eyes to hold back tears. *What kind of a world will I bring you into, my little one? Where is there hope on this earth for peace?* The answer came clearly to her as she watched the life fade slowly from the dear man who had cared for her and taken her family in as his own. *There can be no peace unless it is found in a man's heart. And that cannot be unless he first knows God and then comes to love himself and others with a love like Yeshua. Like Howard Moniger.* She smiled as she remembered the words of Grandfather, *Some of them are one of us*—God himself had carved the Star of David on Howard's heart. "Bless this kind man, O Eternal," she whispered, the words catching in her throat.

At the sound of her voice, Howard's eyes fluttered open. He muttered her name and turned his hand palm up on the bed. She brushed tears stubbornly from her cheeks and knelt at his side.

"Yes, dear Professor. I am here. It is Rachel . . ."

"You . . . are all right?" he asked weakly.

"Yes." She fought to control her emotions, knowing that she owed her life to this man. "If it had not been for you, Howard—" She used his given name for the first time, and he smiled when he heard it.

"Tell Moshe . . ." He faltered. "Asked me before he left . . . wanted me to look out for you . . . and the . . . baby. Bungled it, I guess."

She squeezed his hand. "You saved both me and the baby. Both of us."

"Tikvah?" he asked, confused.

She realized that he did not know she carried Moshe's child. "Not Tikvah, Howard. I mean the child I carry. Moshe's baby. . ."

"Hmmm," he replied drowsily. "One more reason to hope. Spring. Lambs . . . and new grass. Shadows. Shadows of what it will be . . . beautiful shadows . . ." His words drifted off, and she knew that he was saying goodbye to all the things that were.

"Yes, Howard, new babies. Lambs and flowers. Hope that keeps coming back in spite of us. Now *sleep* and get well. Get well and hope again, Howard." The facade of her control cracked and she laid her cheek against his hand and wept. "Please get well. There is so much to do still . . ."

"It will get done anyway. . ."

"Think about new grass and the wild flowers in Moab and—"

"Shadows. They don't know where Zion is . . . They don't . . . see." He gasped and Rachel clung tightly to his hand.

"No, Howard. No. No one knows."

He raised his hand and laid it on his chest. "I am planted in . . . another place. Jerusalem. Where He lives now . . . Tell little Ellie—" His words became tense and urgent.

"Yes, Howard." Rachel's heart beat rapidly as his breath became short and shallow. "What do you want me to tell her?"

He licked his lips. "Not to hate . . . any man . . ."

"I will tell this to her, Howard. I will tell her."

"I am . . . thirsty."

Rachel stood and turned to pour him water, but even as she poured, he exhaled with a low rattle in his throat, and in that instant glimpsed the One he had lived for.

Rachel covered her face with her hands and quietly spoke

the words of the Shema: "Hear, O Israel, the Lord thy God . . ." She hesitated a moment as all the words of the passage played before her. She looked then on the peaceful face of Howard and finished the command: ". . . *and thou shalt love thy neighbor as thyself.*" She stood over him and smiled as she finally understood that this righteous Gentile had himself lived the words of the Shema in all their fullness. She repeated softly what he had whispered, "Not to hate any man." She nodded and reached across to touch the light to the nurses station.

"I will tell her, Howard. And I will remember, too."

Rachel made her way back down the dark, solemn corridor to Tikvah's room. She entered quietly and shut the door behind her. Leaning against the doorjamb, she closed her eyes and listened to the soft, steady breathing of the one who had brought such joy and light into her existence.

Tikvah was sleeping. Rachel tiptoed to her crib and gently lifted the child into her arms. She put her cheek against the baby's soft hair, and for the first time since the long night had begun, Rachel inhaled hope. Tikvah nuzzled her and squeaked a little protest. She was not ready to wake up. How could she know what despair this night had brought to the yet unborn nation of Israel? Seventy-five of the dearest and the best were lost in those dark hours, yet still the world crept on, waiting for the dawn, praying for miracles.

Tikvah shook her fists and bleated unhappily in soggy diapers. Tears streaming down her cheeks, Rachel washed and changed her, grateful for this small and loving task to take her mind off a sunrise so slow in coming. Then Rachel rocked her and sang softly as the baby gulped the warm liquid of her bottle and closed her eyes again in contentment. Rachel held her to her heart, finding some comfort in the nearness of one who had no knowledge of doubt or fear. *She is content here in my arms. While the world crashes down and the dawn is slow in coming, she is still content.*

Rachel cried again, salty tears falling on Tikvah's blanket. "If only I could trust half so well," she whispered. "If only I could trust you, Lord, like this child. If I could lay my heart in your arms and remember that you know when even one sparrow falls." She rocked harder as all her ongoing fear surfaced. "Can you love us more than that sparrow? Do you care that we fall?" For an instant she was angry all over again at the silent God who had not moved to stop the nightmare on the road to Hadassah. "How many more will not see morning? And you claim to love them? *How can this be so?* When will you say *enough*, and make an end to our sorrows?"

She found no answer. Gazing down the hill to where the burned-out buses were concealed by darkness, she prayed for Moshe and then for Ellie, who would not know of Howard's death for many days. She prayed for the unborn child in her womb, and for this yet unborn nation that caused the world to cry out in the agony of such brutal birth pangs.

Looking out on the shattered city below her, Rachel heard the words of Howard once again: *Hate no man!* Wiping her own tears, she remembered that Yeshua himself had wept for Jerusalem. He had looked down the long corridor of time and had wept for this very night. He had seen every baby in its mother's arms and had known who would choose the way of evil and who the way of peace. Two thousand years had passed, and still Messiah wept with pity for them all because He saw their end. Each flower withered and died as its season passed. Still, men lived with the illusion that their season would never end. They planted their lives in the barren soil of this world as though there was no other dawn to hope for.

At last, Rachel prayed for herself, for a small miracle in her own heart that would let her lie in the arms of a loving God and trust that He wept with her.

The sky began to lighten and the stars dimmed. Then Rachel understood the tears of Yeshua when He had cried out, *Jerusalem! Jerusalem! How often I would have gathered you under my wings . . .* He was there waiting still with His arms outstretched; it was man himself who chose to walk away.

"All of us are as fragile as the grass, Tikvah," Rachel said quietly, feeling her bitterness dissipate. "The good and the evil alike. Some plant their hope in this world only, and they will vanish. But there are others, like the professor, who plant their hearts in God alone. And they will bloom forever in Zion, little one. Baby lambs. Flowers in spring. They are only glimpses of what it will be." *Shadows. Reasons to hope.* "And so we must look at them, we must look at Jerusalem and see *what it will be!* Even when there is nothing else to hope for on this earth."

She placed Tikvah gently in her crib and leaned against the top rail to watch the baby sleeping. For a long time she prayed for Moshe and for those who fought and died beside him. And she wept for them. Then her heart turned to those who fought against him. *"God help me!"* She bit her lip and forced herself to remember the tears of Yeshua as He wept for Jerusalem. *Help me! Give me tears to shed for our enemies. For they, too, are only grass on the hillside that will fade and die in the sun.*

The final Jewish bullet in the quarry was spent. Moshe held the last grenade tightly in his fist and gazed around the dark room of the stone hut at the wounded and dying men under his command.

"Surrender, Jews!" shouted an Arab from the cover of a boulder fifty feet away.

Moshe glanced at Fergus. "It will not take them long to figure out that we have no more ammunition."

"They'll not be wantin' to take prisoners," Fergus whispered. "Not after Yassin."

A young soldier at their feet moaned quietly, "Do not let them take us. You know what they will do if they take us alive. Use the grenade!" he said urgently.

A feeble chorus of assent rose from the others in the room.

Moshe licked his lips and stared down at the grenade in his open hand. "I . . . I cannot." His mind swam with thoughts of Rachel and the child with thoughts of those who were now to perish with him.

"Throw down your weapons, Jews!" shouted the Arab. "Kastel is ours! It is only a matter of time, and we will take the quarry! Surrender to us!"

"They will torture us, surely," someone said in a voice racked with pain. "End it! Do not let them have the victory over us."

Moshe passed the deadly orb to Fergus. "I cannot." He leaned heavily against the wall as another volley of Arab fire slammed against the building.

Fergus slipped down beside him and stared at the door where soon the Jihad Moquades would break through. "When they come, we will at least take some with us. It isn't yet dawn. I fancy one more sunrise, m'self."

"Yes," Moshe said hollowly as he closed his eyes. "They will come at dawn."

One of the wounded called for water as the threats of the

Jihad Moquades assaulted them again and again.

Fergus cradled the grenade and muttered quietly, "Aye. This is one time I'd have rather not said I told y' so."

"You are English," Moshe replied. "Perhaps they would not kill you. Perhaps . . ."

"I'll not be the first t' venture out now with a white flag." He sighed heavily and rubbed his hand through his hair in exhaustion.

"Come out, Jews! Come out! Why do you not fire back? Are you dead? Have you finished your bullets?" The voice came nearer and was joined by other voices. They shouted back and forth, each conversation gaining confidence.

"They are finished!"

"Come out, Jews, and you may find mercy!"

"Mercy! Ha!" Fergus screamed a reply. He crawled to the window. "Come in after us, lads! Give 'er a try!" He raised his voice defiantly. "We're ready for you!"

"You bluff, Jew!"

"They think we're joking, lads!" Fergus yelled. "Let's give 'em a taste of wha' we're made of!"

Moshe took a deep breath and cleared his throat. In a rich baritone he began to sing Hatikvah, *The Hope*. Feebly at first, and then with the strength of men about to die, the others joined him in the song and somehow found a fragment of courage in the words. But hope itself was dead.

"Very pretty, Jews!" replied the Arab. "But that will not keep us from you!" The clatter of boots sounded outside as they moved nearer.

"Well, maybe this will!" Fergus raised up and pulled the pin on the grenade. With all his strength he hurled the missile toward the approaching Arabs. They shrieked in terror, and a second later an explosion silenced them. Yet another round of rifle fire pelted the stone walls and Fergus plastered himself against the floor. "There's more where that came from!" the little Scot threatened. "Come in for it, if you've a mind."

There was no response from the Arabs as they stared at the bodies of their foolhardy comrades. *So the Jews are not finished yet!*

"We can wait!" called a voice in English. "It is just a matter of time! We've called up the mortars!"

"Aye!" Fergus gritted his teeth at the sound of one of his own countrymen among the Arabs. "Give it your best, laddie! You've not seen ours!"

"We can wait!"

Moshe smiled with amusement and said hoarsely to Fergus. "And so can we, eh, my friend?" Now that the final grenade was spent, there was no question that they had simply delayed their execution.

In the distance, the faint roar of an airplane was heard, and Moshe scrambled over the prostrate bodies of his men to where the radio was propped in the corner. If they were to die, then at least the world would hear their last words as they relayed them to Bobby Milkin. At least the truth of their end would be known. Moshe cranked the generator, then spoke with a quiet urgency into the receiver. "Raven, this is Staff. Come in, Raven."

———

Ram Kadar lay still and silent in the new grass of the hillside. The young warrior who had come to fetch him to the celebration of victory stared sightlessly into the sky, a bullet hole in his chest. Between the two men a small bunch of blue flowers bloomed in the pastel light of pre-dawn. Kadar blinked at them, aware that the flowers would live longer than he.

Strangely, he felt no pain—only regret. He could not move or call out for help from his men as they moved forward to take the demolished village. The bullet that had pierced his neck had severed his spinal cord, leaving him helpless as his life's blood drained away into the uncaring soil of Palestine.

"Where is Commander Kadar?" a gruff voice called from inside the captured house of the muhqtar. "They say the quarry will fall within the hour . . ."

"I sent that little fool Ibrahim to fetch him an hour ago! We should not raise the flag without Kadar. What would victory be without his presence?"

Kadar wanted to shout that they were traitors for uttering such words, but he knew it would not matter. When they found his body all would be for nothing . . . for nothing. As they had done so many times before, the Jihad troops would turn back and disperse without a leader to unify them. Even this close to victory, they would scatter like sheep.

He shifted his eyes upward to the limestone outcropping below the house of the muhqtar. In the east, his last sunrise began as a silver line broke over the Mountains of Moab. Its bright, unchanging rays shone upon a faint outline carved on the face of the rock. *My men will forsake Kastel in their grief*, he thought bitterly. *I am dead even as I lie here, and still some ancient Jew mocks me from his grave.*

He traced the carving with his eyes. Probably it was only visible from here when the sun rose at dawn. Two triangles hewn to interlock as one star—the Star of David loomed above him on the face of the stone! It seemed to shout that his victory was meaningless, his life lost for nothing.

In the distance, a meadowlark called a new day into existence, and for an instant Kadar tried to rage against his death. But the issue was not his to decide. His eyes wide, Kadar surrendered his life in a final ragged breath.

Others were sent to find their leader as the crescent flag was raised over Kastel. Moments later a cry of grief rang out that hushed the sound of the lark.

"He is fallen! The great commander! Allah Akbar! All is lost!"

Hundreds, and then thousands, swarmed from their newly taken positions to gather around the body of their fallen hero. They tore their robes and smashed their faces against the butts of their rifles as an expression of anguish at the sight of their dead leader.

———

From the broken rocks of the quarry, those Haganah men who remained alive looked up at the arrival of Bobby Milkin's little observation plane. They listened with curiosity to the outpouring that echoed from the hills around them, and they cheered with joy at the news of the approach of five hundred Haganah soldiers on their way to Kastel.

Moshe raised his voice in a song, and Ehud joined the others as again they sang *The Hope*. The terrible wails of their enemies seemed a strange counterpoint. And then, miraculously, the cries of the Jihad Moquades turned away from Kastel and the quarry.

As the army of Ram Kadar gently carried his body down the mountain to be mourned by all of Arab Jerusalem, only the crescent flag remained behind to wave in empty victory over the deserted village.

Epilogue

With Fergus and Ehud at his side, Moshe walked between the rows of bodies laid out in the street before the mosque of Kastel. Jews and Arabs lay side by side in death. Moshe pointed to each Jewish soldier harvested from the hillsides and trenches by Haganah reinforcements. In the bright, crisp light of the morning, features of the men who had died in the night became vivid and clear.

Sergeant Hamilton lay beside a young Arab who looked to be no more than twenty years old.

"Hamilton," Moshe said in a choked voice. "An Englishman. But one of us."

The clean-shaven Jewish officer who walked slightly behind them made a notation on his clipboard. "A Gentile?"

Moshe nodded. "Yes. A good man. A Christian."

"Well then, we should contact his own people for burial," said the officer matter-of-factly.

Moshe blinked at him without comprehension. "What?"

"Well, if he is a Christian, his people may want him buried in the Christian cemetery. Or shipped back to England, or—"

Moshe dropped his rifle, and it fell with a clatter against the hard ground. He put his hand to his head. Finally, raising his eyes to the long rows of men in the street, he moaned. "Not even in death, it seems, not even *then* can we be at peace!"

The Jewish officer frowned. "Jews must be properly buried in the Jewish cemetery. Moslems in the Moslem. Christians in the—you see, Professor Sachar?"

Moshe did not reply. He simply stared at the faces of Ham and the young Arab. He felt terribly weary.

Ehud took him by the arm. "He is right, Moshe. That is the way the world is made, nu?"

Moshe winced and shook his head slowly. "No, Ehud. That is the way *we* have made the world." He knelt in the dust and reached out to touch the curly hair of the young Arab and then

367

the pale cheek of Ham. "*This* is what men have made of the world."

The men who stood around him did not understand his words, but it did not matter to Moshe. He let his tears fall on the dusty face of the young Arab as well as the English sergeant who had fallen among Jewish troops in a battle that was not his own. At last Moshe spoke again. "And in the end, this is what the world makes of us." He rose slowly and turned away to find a transport to carry him back to Jerusalem.

———

*If you would like to contact the authors,
you may write to them at the following address:*

Bodie and Brock Thoene
P.O. Box 542
Glenbrook, NV 89413